JOSHUA KAPUSINSKI

The Awakening

First edition

ISBN: 978-0-578-29651-7

This book was professionally typeset on Reedsy.
Find out more at reedsy.com

Acknowledgement

To my agent, Crosland Stuart, who took a chance on a freshman in high school. This novel would not be half the story it is today without your guidance and instruction.

To D.J Goodwiler, who inspired me to write novels. In teaching me the great books, you showed me that writing is something worth pursuing.

To Quinton McCurine, who taught me what writing really is. There are few people in this world who can match the clarity of your criticism. You have the uncanny ability to see both the big picture and the small details. Thank you for making me a better writer and a better man.

To Mom and Dad, whose belief in me overshadowed my self-doubt. Writing is a lonely job, but your belief in me makes me feel like it's all worth it. Some days, that's all I need to keep me going.

To Jim Hamilton, who helped me create new words for the jargon in this world. The creation of many of these terms is indebted to your passion for etymology and your charity to help me construct the right words.

To Alejandro Jamett, the illustrator for this novel. Your cover design exceeded my wildest expectations. Thank you for bringing this world to life through your art.

To Haley Hom, who has read more of my work than perhaps anyone else. At this point, you've read maybe three versions of this story and continually offered advice on things to change and affirmations of what you love. I hope I got it right this time.

To my early readers: Jordan Fredette, Aaron Briggs, Haider Ghiasuddin, Jim Hamilton, Emma Kim, Clark Mummau, Luke Eldridge, Stuart Rozendal, Andrew Lee, Natalie Kim, Mom, Grandma, Quinton McCurine, and Haley Hom. Some of you only read parts of this book. Others read the whole thing. All of you, however, played a role in turning this novel from ideas in my head to a story that others can enjoy, and for that, you have my thanks.

Prologue

Perhaps the most puzzling part about the Republic is people's obsession with paintings. The age-old art was dying in the stifling confines of Vrin's New World Order, but soon experienced an unprecedented revival in what art historians are now calling the "Interstellar Renaissance," chiefly because the art forms that had been lost on Earth did not experience their return again until mankind inhabited other worlds. In the New Pantheon, the casual observer will find a host of dazzling frescoes of the Republic's modern leaders, cast as gods, colored in shades of lapis lazuli blue and rich gold. The most famous portion of this masterpiece, painted by Jan Van Iktinos, depicts the legendary Boris Gerumandian in glorious splendor. The bald, burly general stands defiantly on top of a dying Waion, capturing the moment he fires the beast's own blaster into his screaming, blood-burst face. Boris, draped in splotched green, stained with blood and mud, holds the Republic flag in his other hand, raising it high above a war-torn, smoky battlefield of Gerumandian soldiers. One can almost hear the cries of joy from the common troops who see their leader rise victorious, the high flag signaling that the planet of Leshkodine, commonly known now as "New Earth," has now fallen under the Republic Imperium. To the casual observer, this is the message of the painting: *victory*. To the trained eye, the painting speaks more discreetly: *victory at great cost*.

Beneath the shade of a red and blue hovercraft, one can see a shadowy figure, draped in brown, monastic robes, standing among a squadron of armored troops. The detail is so small it often is missed by those touring the New Pantheon, but to those who spend a great time before Iktinos' work, the figure comes to represent a stain on the Republic's optimism. The gray-bearded man gazes solemnly at the display around him with a syringe in one hand and a sphere in the other. Unmistakably, this is the "great doctor" Robert Dain: the creator of the Advancement of Life treatment (commonly known as AOL), the founder of the Republic, and the man who died by Vrin's hand. The inclusion of Robert Dain, given Iktinos' personal beliefs, is not a cause for further celebration but is a cause for lament. The same problems that plagued earth (rampant overpopulation, AOL as a means of power, finite resources, and pernicious greed) travel with Dain because they travel with AOL. Without death, humanity evolves into a kind of sinister beast, because as long as human civilization has existed, death has functioned like gravity. It is the great equalizer, the combatant to entropy, the combatant to chaos. Iktinos shows us that in as much as AOL travels with humanity, its problems travel with us too. The only question that remains for the modern peace the Republic has experienced since the great victory of 2095 is how long until a new Vrin, a new dictator, rises up with perilous greed and slides the world back into the tyranny that sealed our civilization away from the stars?

Midday Madness

A faint, almost undetectable jolt of electricity awoke Dakari Minathi from a night of restless sleep. In the darkness of his bedroom, his hazy eyes opened to the sight of his sleeping wife, Desta, lying peacefully beside him. The electromagnetic alarm caused his body to twitch a second time. He shifted beneath the sheets and raised his left arm above his head, his eyes squinting from the light of the convex screen surgically installed into his dark-skinned forearm. He slid his finger across the screen to dim the brightness of his datapad, shut off the alarm, then faced his wife and gently stroked the side of her hair. A rotating fan hummed in the background. The irony of Dakari's peaceful mornings never escaped him. If this was the only snapshot someone would ever see of his life, they would never assume he spent the rest of his waking hours arresting bewildered children in the city of Dain.

They're not just children, he thought. *They're psychics.*

This was always enough to get Dakari out of bed in the morning, but it was never enough to console him at night. Dakari was a state arbitrator for the Republic at the prestigious Central Dain Arbitrator Department (or CDAD for short). With years of experience in the field, the green-as-grass graduate from the Gerumandian Academy had risen up the ranks to the position of Captain, where he now spent his days organizing field operations and overseeing most psychic arrests. Psychics were AOL humans gone wrong. They were the most dangerous beings in the Republic. They were also the least understood.

"I'll go make the coffee," Dakari said, slinging his navy blue coat over his broad shoulders.

Desta shifted in bed and mumbled something that sounded like "Thanks."

In the Republic, approximately 99% of the population were AOL standard: recipients of a drug that stopped aging around someone's mid-thirties and prevented death from natural causes. In other words, in the 2100s, people didn't age and people didn't die. Of course, the inevitable tendency of human error brought some casualties. The AOL drug couldn't save your life from a blaster beam to the face or being flung off a five-thousand-foot building, but barring those things, most humans would live long lives. The Cephei Institute of Modern Science presumed that theoretically, the anti-aging properties of the AOL drug could grant its recipients unending lives.

Dakari was not one of those recipients. He was what the Republic called an *impurity*: someone who willingly refused AOL treatment. This meant that not only could Dakari age, but like his wife and son, he could die. To say that he questioned his convictions was an understatement. Each night, as he laid his head to rest and stared at the dull ceiling, he thought about how each day marched him closer towards death, causing him to wonder if he had done the right thing in rejecting the drug.

Like most impurities (or standard, traditional humans to avoid the derogatory term), Dakari's convictions were passed down from his parents. Some impurities were merely skeptics of modern science, choosing to take their convictions to the graves in the grassy, hidden hillsides of the city of Dain. Others, like the Minathis, always believed that life was best lived when one's days were numbered. Death, Dakari's father had always told him, was the great equalizer that gave a man a measure for well-lived days. *A man lives better when his days are numbered.* Dakari's religious convictions told him too that a better world waited beyond this one. That had been easy enough to believe as a child. It was harder to believe when his grandparents passed away when he was ten to terminal cancer, when his mother died from heart disease in her mid-fifties, and when his father followed her to the grave only two years later from a sudden stroke. The feeling of being the oldest in the Minathi line left him with a kind of existential uncertainty.

All of them would still be alive if they had taken AOL, he thought. *They would probably be living well, too.* The seed of doubt that continually arose in Dakari's mind as he prepped his morning coffee was the simple thought that the AOL drug and well-lived lives were not mutually exclusive. The birth of Zane, his only son and child, had caused that seed of doubt to grow into a blooming flower of regret. The thought of missing his future, the chance of dying before his graduation at the Gerumandian Academy, or passing before his marriage and kids, terrified him.

It is a terrible thing to die. Why should I not resist it?

Because his parents and religious mentors told him not to? That seemed like a decision he needed to make for himself. Yet for some reason he had never brought himself to get treatment. The opportunity had presented itself before him numerous times and would continue to remain an option as long as he was alive. AOL treatment was efficacious for any age. Dakari was thirty-five, with only hints of gray spotted along his thin black facial hair and trimmed head. He sipped his coffee quietly at the kitchen table as Desta strolled into the kitchen in arbitrator regalia. She waved to her husband, who waved back and scrolled down his datapad, entertaining his mind with bits of morning news.

Desta, dressed in her navy blue uniform, her cropped back hair hanging neatly above both shoulders, brought a smile to Dakari as she poured herself a cup of coffee.

"Zane called yesterday," Desta said.

"Really?" Dakari asked. "How'd he do at the debate tournament?"

"They lost in quarterfinals. Zane's partner had a meltdown."

"Mirabelle's not one to lose her composure."

"That's what Zane said too. Apparently one of their opponents said something to her before their crossfire. Then she lost it and punched him in the face."

"What'd he say to her?"

"I don't know. Zane said she wouldn't tell him."

"Couldn't have been anything good." Dakari's gaze drifted towards the window. Their view from the 30th floor of their apartment complex afforded them a narrow sprawl of towering, several-thousand-foot spires. The ceaseless air traffic of hovercrafts and wind-piercers soared in aerospace lanes between buildings. "What's your day looking like?"

Desta sipped and smiled, her brown eyes piercing through the swirling steam that rose from her mug. "Got a rogue A.I. Chief Weston wants me to look at, says it's been infiltrating user interfaces and finding neural pathways to create voices in people's heads."

"Sounds interesting."

"Unfortunately my role will be paperwork, not interrogation."

"A pity. You always were pretty persuasive." Dakari dumped his mug off in the sink and gave his wife a kiss before leaving. "Have fun."

"Oh, I will. It may not be catching psychics, but it's a close second."

"I'll try to take that as a compliment."

Desta smiled.

"The Middletons might come over after work today."

"Samuel too?" Dakari asked, inching towards the door. "That stick in the mud never does anything fun."

"I hear he has the day off."

"Then let's do it. Lasagna for dinner?"

"It is a famous Minathi recipe."

"Then I'll see you at dinner." Dakari opened the door. "See ya."

"Bye."

The door closed.

* * *

Raindrops raced down the glass of Dakari's armored wind-piercer: the standard-issue hovercrafts for arbitrators. They were shaped like slick sports cars with reinforced windows, sliding doors, twin turrets beneath the white headlights, and two exhaust pipes beneath the red brakes in the back. There was a GPS navigation system on the main console showing a display of roads and green dots of other on-duty arbitrators. Dakari sat in the black leather seat in silence, parked on the rooftop of an abandoned building in Sector 7.

The city of Dain was the Republic's intergalactic capital on humanity's new homeworld: New Earth. It was still strange for Dakari to think that only two generations ago, his parents lived under Vrin's tyrannical regime thousands of light-years away on Earth, a dying world full of miserable citizens and failed restoration plans. The Terraforming Institute deemed the planet "unsalvageable" a few years back, prompting the matriarchs and patriarchs of the Republic to pass a bill to double the I.S.F's spending on the lottery: the annual, random selection of Earth's citizens to receive paid transportation to New Earth. Dakari had never seen Earth in person (not that anyone would willingly travel there), but he had heard stories. He remembered his grandfather describing the final days of the New World Order as Boris Gerumandian led a stunning revelation to bring him down. *We left the world of dust and desert behind*, Dakari's Grandfather had said, *to a world of metal and steel.*

Grandfather Minathi was not entirely wrong. The City of Dain, built on the backs of alien slaves the Republic had captured upon conquering the planet that was now New Earth, was a metropolitan spectacle of towering five-thousand-foot high-rises, winding canals of aquamarine blue, and stunning feats of Waion architecture that took everyone's breath away. That said, not all parts of the city were as picturesque as Republic postcards. Like Sector 7, for example, where the cramped arrangement of buildings stacked on top and around each other like a claustrophobiac's worst nightmare. Billboards the size of freighters shone advertisements for neurotics like glimmering stars. Blimps soared weightlessly in the sky, their massive turbines spinning endlessly in the wind.

New Earth was supposed to be paradise. Not that it wasn't. In fact, compared to the alternative, Dakari counted himself quite fortunate to be a citizen of New Earth. However, the same problems that plagued Earth were showing hints of their migration with each new skyscraper added to the horizon. Endless life meant endless expansion. The task of the Republic, then, was simple: control chaos. Simple indeed. Psychics were far from the first ripple of uncertainty AOL had caused, and it certainly wouldn't be the last. Not even a minute after that thought crossed Dakari's mind, a red dot flashed on the GPS monitor.

Speak of the devil.

Dakari accepted the distress signal and picked up the receiver. "This is Captain Dakari Minathi speaking. What's the situation? Over."

Brief static. Then the distress.

"This is Lieutenant Xing requesting immediate assistance! Confirmed psychic activity. Code zero. I repeat code zero."

Dakari's blood went cold as he shifted the wind-piercer into a higher gear. Zero was bad. Zero meant casualties. Friendly casualties. There was no time to ask questions. There was only time to move.

Two seatbelt straps stretched over Dakari's chest in an X-shape as he turned on the emergency lights and eased into the air traffic in the mid-airway space in Central Dain. Flying outside of air traffic lanes was impossible without a state-authorized free-navigation console, which were only given to arbitrators to use in desperate times. This was one of those times. The vehicle cruised down to the lower levels of the city, its engines humming like a colossal hummingbird. Crowds of pedestrians walking on the city's asphalt streets and sidewalks looked up as the shadow of the racing wind-piercer cut through the rain like an arrow in the afternoon sky. Dakari turned right and arrived near the restaurant where the distress signal came from. He released several camera drones from the side of his vehicle and watched two simultaneous cameras pop up on the main screen.

What he saw was the fuel of nightmares.

Two charred corpses lay smoking on the side of the road, their bodies black from head to toe. Dakari's jaw lowered in shock as he identified the burnt victims. The woman, identified by the burning white blouse and singed hair, was Katharine Middleton. The man a few yards from her, motionless on his knees with a severed hand and burnt body, was Samuel Middleton, Chief of the Arbitrator Department. He died in a frozen posture of supplication, his head low, his blaster lying in his severed hand in a mud puddle by the side of the road. Dakari's jaw clenched so hard that when he saw himself in the rear-view mirror he thought it might snap.

"This is Lieutenant Banner from the CDAD, reading you loud and clear," a voice from the radio said. "What seems to be the issue? Over."

Dakari's trembling hand reached for the receiver and clenched it.

"Code zero! Two casualties! Get a ground support team on Irkurian drive now!"

Arbitrator sirens wailed in the streets like dying screams. Dakari yanked back the throttle and slammed on the main pedal, shooting the wind piercer in the darkness of a nearby alleyway. Both camera drones whirred ahead of him, their lights flickering and flashing as they collected data to track the culprit of the Middleton murders. Both bodies were fresh, charred only seconds before Dakari had arrived. Whoever killed them had not gotten far. Camera drones relayed more information such as vocal commotion, disturbances, and strange movements from crowds. A red light flashed on the GPS 0.2 miles away.

"Warning: potential psychic sighting in your area," the computer said.

Dakari set a course for the disturbance and ignited the turbo. Blue fires burst out the back of the wind-piercer as Dakari turned onto main street, half a mile wide and endless miles long. Sky-seeking high-rises stretched around Dakari as his drones scoured the sidewalks and open streets. Red and blue spinning lights reflected off the glass windows of business buildings as large hovercrafts with rotating wind turbine engines arrived on the scene. Then the computer blared as the camera drones' lights flashed from white to red, narrowing on a cloaked figure trapped at the end of an alleyway. Dakari turned into the designated spot as the figure looked up into the lights and the camera feed registered on the main console.

"Warning: psychic identified," the computer said.

A young, pale, cloaked girl looked into the camera with eyes as blue as the Cypher Sea. A brown shawl covered her blonde hair. There was the slightest smile on her face as she slowly raised her arm at the hovercraft. At first, Dakari thought she was surrendering. Then he saw her eyes glow, and by then it was too late. The glow in a psychic's eyes signaled the creation of a tear: a small portal the size of a psychic's hand. The portal in the girl's hand was midnight blue. It spiraled and darkened and then flashed as a grappling hook shot out from the portal and scraped the side of Dakari's wind-piercer. All systems blared red as the vehicle teetered to the right, forcing Dakari to level it and go autopilot. The girl recoiled her arm and the grappling hook hissed back into her portal. Dakari grabbed the radio receiver as his voice echoed from the speakers of the vehicle.

"My name is Captain Dakari Minathi. Place your hands above your head! You are under arrest!" She stood motionless. "I can bring you in unscathed. Or I can bring you in scarred."

The girl paused as if she genuinely believed him. Then slammed both hands together and created another tear. The chain-linked grappling hook launched again, this time crushing the front of the windshield. Red lights blared from inside the vehicle as the hovering car lost balance again, teetering left and right, left and right. Then the girl recoiled the grappling hook, and Dakari felt the wind-piercer being dragged to the end of the alleyway where the girl gritted her teeth and reversed the direction of the grappling hook's energy.

"Activate retro thrusters!"

Blue flames spat out from beneath the wind-piercer.

"Reverse!"

They spun in the direction of the girl, halting his descent. Dakari released his seatbelt straps as the inner sirens of the vehicle blared in his ears.

"Very well," Dakari said. "Scarred it is."

He pressed a blue button beneath the console and closed his eyes. The seat reclined horizontally until Dakari faced the ceiling. Several robotic limbs lowered scales of armor over his body, slowly covering him from head to toe. A helmet fastened above his head and flashed green. Scales of white armor overlapped and fastened around his navy-blue uniform. Gloves slid over his dark dry hands. He wore an arbitrator's armor: white plates, carbon fiber interior, kneepads, and overlapping scales that raced down his arms and legs, back and chest, stretching with his movements and hardening upon contact. The CDAD badge glimmered on his breast.

"Armor attached," the computer said.

Dakari opened his eyes as they aligned with the interior display of his chrome black visor.

"Deploy."

A cable fastened into Dakari's back as the chair reversed and positioned Dakari's body to the floor. Then the lower levels of the wind-piercer opened. The rush of the wind raced against Dakari's visor as he ejected from beneath the vehicle and descended into the alleyway, the cable slowing his fall. He braced himself for landing as his kneepads softened the blow. Both boots planted in the ground and splashed in several puddles to the surprise of the young girl. With the cable still fastened to his back, Dakari retrieved his black stun baton from his belt and clicked its blue buttons. Little tingles of electricity danced on the tip of the rod as his heart raced with rage.

This girl killed the Middletons.

The girl snapped her fingers, firing another grappling hook out from a portal in her palm. Dakari raised his baton, the wrinkling chain wrapping around his weapon, yanked the baton back to vault her in his direction, then smacked her across the face with his tactical armored gloves. She slammed into the wall and fell into a puddle. She lay motionless, dripping wet, then tried to get up. Dakari shook the chain off his baton. She leaped up from the ground and created another portal, but Dakari smacked the stun baton across her face, knocking her out cold. Her body jolted, then froze. In the aftermath of their brief battle, an unsettling feeling arose within the arbitrator Captain, who now called for evac to ensure the safe delivery of the psychic. It wasn't just the fact that this girl had brutally scorched the Middletons, people he deeply cared about and loved. It wasn't just the fact that he had beaten a teenage girl with the stun baton, though the brutality of the act settled horribly within himself and he guessed he would pay for it later. It wasn't even the close call he felt with nearly losing his own life. No...it was something even more shocking, something that broke his hold on reality. He knew it as clear as day as he saw the blue in the girl's eyes and remembered why her smile had been so eerie to him. It was because he had captured this girl in the field before. And someone had

11

helped her escape.

Rupture in the Rain

When Quan awoke, it was with the frantic rush that is so common among people plagued with night terrors. He lay on a blue couch by the window, heaving in heavy breaths, drenched in sweat. The gray morning light shined dimly on his pale complexion, his bright blue eyes peering at the rain clouds brooding menacingly outside his window. Rain fell softly from the skies. In other places, it poured in thicker torrents from spouts. Quan sat up from the couch with slow movements. It hurt to move. Last night's duel had taken quite a beating to his frail body. Quan was a dueler at the Brawling Bandits. That was how he made his money. Without that money, he and his partner in crime, Alexander, who slept on the floor snoring, would be sleeping in some trash-filled alleyway, exposed to the elements and thieves. This was the better alternative, but it came at a cost.

That's the price you pay when you drop out of high school and run away from home, Quan thought. Still, he didn't regret his decision. He had no choice. He fumbled for his vape pen in his pocket, took a brief hit, and tucked it away. Not long after, the coffee machine poured him a cup of steaming black coffee. When that was finished, he slung an oversized black windbreaker over his shoulders and took a walk through the crummy, graffiti-ridden hallways of their apartment complex in District 7. He rode the elevator to the rooftop and found a nice spot on the edge to sit and smoke beneath the rain.

With both legs dangling off the edge, a torrent of thoughts arose in Quan's mind. Pedestrians navigated the claustrophobic alleyways and streets of the impoverished residential district, their heads arched low towards the screens surgically attached to their forearms. A disorganized arrangement of towering buildings surrounded Quan like a jungle of silver towers and glass windows reflecting the gray sky. A sky titan could be seen soaring above the clouds. The mere sight of a starship brought the pain of remembrance and longing. It was a symbol of why he ran away from home in the first place and threw his future away.

It all started two years ago when Quan was feeling sick at school. In pre-algebra, as several automatons whirred on their one-legged wheels to assist other high schoolers, Quan felt something churn in his chest like sour butter. It seemed to stretch and expand in his stomach. The automatons escorted him to the nurse's office.

"What seems to be the problem?" The nurse asked.

"I'm sick," Quan said. "Can I go home?"

Perhaps Quan's expression had been enough because he was sent home without a fight. He walked through the sunny suburbs of the Silverside residential district: a beautiful neighborhood with two-story houses, neat grass lawns, and wide driveways with hoverbikes and automobiles. Each house was the same as the last. And in the distance stood the expanding city of Dain. What followed was the most traumatic experience of Quan's life.

No one else was home when Quan arrived. He ran up the stairs, slung his backpack on the bed, and went into the bathroom. That was when he saw it for the first time—the glow in his eyes, as bright as flashlights. He stood like he was seeing a ghost, yet the ghost was himself. It was as if someone had stuck tiny blue flashlights in his irises, yet he could still see with the same clarity as if they were not glowing at all. Then it spread to his hands. They burned like he had pressed both his palms against a hot iron, scorching his skin with searing pain. He screamed and bent over the sink as the lines in his palms started to change. They morphed into perfect circles, and as they changed, blood flowed from the slits caused by their growth. He cried as drops of blood dripped into the faucet. He looked up into the mirror as his eyes widened with horror. He knew exactly what this meant.

He was a psychic.

With the time he had left to spare he packed as much as he could in his backpack and ran before his parents would ever know he was gone. He called Alexander that same day. There were white bandages taped around both of his hands. About a week after that incident, the lines on his hands would return to normal, as was the case for all psychics so that they could conceal their powers, but that did not make the initial change any less painful or frightening. Each time a car drove through their suburban district he panicked that his eyes were still glowing. They were not, but the fear remained all the same. Alexander picked up.

"Hello?"

"Alexander!?" Quan shouted. "Alexander can you hear me?!"

"Yeah dude, calm down."

"Do you trust me?"

"I mean...yeah. I trust you."

"Then I need you to listen carefully to everything I'm about to tell you," Quan said. "I'm ditching school. I can't say why but I'm offering you the invitation. Pack as much as you can fit in a backpack and meet me in district 7–downtown Dain."

"You're joking."

"I'm not. If you say no, I'm hanging up." Quan paused. "What do you say?"

Almost without hesitation, Alexander said yes. They met in person a week later, swapped the GPS trackers on their datapads, and purchased a cramped apartment in a lowlife district of downtown Dain.

"Why'd you choose me?" Alexander asked.

"Because I knew you were the only person that'd say yes." They stood around a glass coffee table as Quan projected an image from his datapad to a hologram. "Civarian station," Quan said. "That's where we're headed."

They looked at a holographic display of New Earth, a planet of yellow, green, and blue colors. Almost a quarter of its surface was covered with cities built by Waions and men. Orbiting the planet was Civarian Station shaped like a crescent moon. It was built by the gray wash of

Ordonotanium and directed all private traffic flowing in and out of New Earth's atmosphere. "If we can get there," Quan said. "We can leave New Earth."

"Where would we go next?" Alexander said.

"Darisin. The Marauder's Oasis."

They switched the holo panel. Darisin was one of the Republic's four outer worlds conquered after the War with the Waions. It was an all-desert planet and received its name for its reputation for attracting criminals. Its only city was Tainer, 100 square miles with sandstone walls and dome shields protecting it from the desert storms.

"Why Darisin?" Alexander asked.

"It's the only planet that'll accept people like us."

"You mean people like you."

Quan's bright blue eyes flickered ever so slightly.

"Right. The problem is that we can't get to Darisin without getting to Civarian station first. And we can't get to Civarian station without an intergalactic passport."

"How much are those?"

"5 million recs. Each."

Alexander scratched the back of his head.

"Ouch."

"90% of the Republic's fuel comes from a mining colony called Yenkalium. There's enough fuel to fund interplanetary travel for all. The problem is that we can only harvest so much so fast. Plus, the Republic's lottery efforts to transport earthlings to New Earth has made fuel the most expensive commodity in the Republic. There's no way around this one. If we can't come up with that many recs, we're not going anywhere." Quan shot a dark look at Alexander. "And don't think for a minute that I'm gonna turn myself into one of those arbitrators at the CDAD." Quan shut off the holo panel and stood up. "Come on. Let's go make some money."

And money they had made. But not nearly enough. As Quan smoked on top of the rooftop, the progress of the past bubbled up to his mind, yet it failed to comfort him. He felt endlessly stuck, the fear of the wrong decision paralyzing him. Some nights, Quan could see the blinking lights of Civarian station orbiting the atmosphere, orbiting New Earth in the blackness of night like a paradisal moon that promised all that Quan ever wanted. Freedom. A world where psychics could live in streets and not cages. Darisin could provide that. *It may be a world of criminals*, Quan thought, *but that was better than a world of people who pretended to be something better.* He valued a criminal's honesty over the professional man's false courtesy. As the last tendrils of his vape pen rose into the gray dawn, Quan tucked the pen away, then held his hand out in front of him, his outstretched palm facing the rain.

He got an idea.

With the snap of his fingers, a current of power rushed in his veins and traveled to the end of his upward-facing hand. A midnight blue portal burst above his fingertips, its edges purring with kinetic energy and vibrating like a hummingbird's wings. Each drop of rain that came in contact with the portal was absorbed, as well as the wind that went in with it. Not a single pedestrian below him looked up at him, even though all it would take to expose Quan's cover would be one call for an arbitrator, or the scum of the state, as Quan liked to call them. Arbitrators were the only reason Quan had to flee New Earth in the first place. They locked up psychics for no good reason and took them to rehab centers "for their own good." Sure, Quan was young, but he could spot a lie when he saw one. There was a reason no one knew what happened in the psychic rehabilitation centers half a mile below the CDAD. It was because nothing good happened down there.

Someone opened the rooftop door.

Quan spun around and snapped his fingers. A new portal emerged in his left hand, firing a sharp gust of wind and rain in the perpetrator's direction. He gasped and relinquished the tear with embarrassment when he saw who he had just slammed against the wall.

"Oops...my bad."

Alexander stood up with a scowl. Water dripped down the tips of his wavy blue hair half-hidden under his soaked white hoodie. His silver eyes

17

squinted with frustration. His attempt at appearing menacing, however, failed. Alexander was so skinny that his shoulder blades looked like bolts and screws jutting out beneath his clothes, the angles on his face defined and sharp.

"We've talked about this! You can use your powers, but you can't use them on me." Alexander wiped the water off his face and shook his hands. "Who knows what's gonna come out of that portal?!"

"I do." Quan demonstrated with another snap of his fingers, facing his hand towards the sky. "Rain goes in." He aimed it at Alexander and shot a lighter gust of water in his direction. "Rain goes out."

"STOP IT!"

"Sorry."

Quan shot a warmer gust of wind in Alexander's direction, blowing back his hoodie and the last bits of water off his face. The scrawny tech wizard walked past him and peeked over the rooftop to the streets below.

"You need to be more careful. Someone could've seen you."

"I am careful. What's got you so worked up?"

Alexander nervously scratched the back of his head.

"Our rent is due today."

"So? We have plenty of recs."

"I mean...we used to." Alexander pulled back his sleeve, revealing a chrome black device on his forearm. It was his datapad-the mandatory, surgically attached smart screens of the Republic. None of them seemed nearly advanced as the one Alexander sported. "Remember those attachments I was talking about last week? The ones with the EMP device? And the grappling hook?"

Quan pinched the bridge of his nose and groaned, preparing for the worst. "You didn't..."

Sure enough, there was a silver cable cord jutting out beneath the bottom of the datapad, hidden beneath Alexander's sleeve.

"I did."

Quan lunged forward and gripped Alexander by the collar of his jacket. "You idiot! A grappling hook! What were you thinking?!"

Several pedestrians below looked up, freezing their momentary feud. Quan shoved Alexander back towards the door and placed both hands atop his head of curls.

"I'm guessing that wasn't cheap."

"Not at all. But on the bright side, the dealer gave them to me at half the usual price: 10,000 recs!"

Repeating those words under his breath was like uttering a curse.

"Great. You happy now?"

"I guess so. Now I just need-"

"Forget it. You can complete your stupid shopping list once we have a stable income. Until then, we have approximately eight hours to scrounge up fifteen hundred recs for this month's rent."

"What about your share?"

"That money doesn't just sit around, dumbass! Who do you think's been paying for groceries?" Quan's attention was drawn back to the streets. "If we're going to meet this month's payment, we need to get creative."

Alexander rubbed his hands together with a sinister smile.

"I like the sound of that. Time to go phishing."

"And time for me to go for a walk. You never know what kind of loose change you can find on the streets."

Moody Mornings

An alarm blared on the dresser near Mirabelle's bedside. She smacked it against the wall. A dreadful silence took its place as the olive-skinned girl rolled back over in bed, her eyes staring blankly into the beige-tile ceiling of her dorm room. *Mondays.* She woke up with what her father used to call an "angry hangover." A splitting headache. A gut festering with rage. A mind clouded with regrets of bad decisions. She would've loved to ask her father how he cured his emotional hangovers the day after he made terrible decisions, but such desires were nothing more than wishful thinking. Mirabelle hadn't seen or spoken with her father in almost ten years.

What was worse was that last night, she had a dream about him. Though she supposed it really wasn't a dream so much as it was a memory that occurred to her during her sleep. Like most dreams, she remembered fragments of it and interspersed the parts she didn't recall with reality. The dream state was back to her kindergarten days when it seemed like she was transferring schools every week. Mirabelle lived by her father's words: "If you ever have to hit someone, hit them good," to which her mother repudiated her father at the dinner table for saying something so crass to their only child. Father defended himself saying, "She's an impurity. In this world, that means she's gotta be strong." Then she remembered her father looking at her with a wide smile. "But my daughter's strong, aren't you Mirabelle?"

She certainly liked to think so. In fact, because of this, she made sure that no insult went unpunished. Each time she was insulted at school she landed a blow worth a thousand punches. Or at least that's what she thought. Father wasn't as proud as she imagined he would be, and it was at their fourth school change that he realized he may have gone a bit too far in his advice.

"I should be clearer," Father explained as he drove her to school. "Stand up when you need to but choose your battles wisely. If you punch every kid that's gonna say something mean to you, you'll never coexist with people on this planet. You got to walk the line between releasing and retaining your anger. Don't go looking for battles. Battles will come to you, and you'll know which ones deserve your fist and which ones deserve your silence."

That became a mantra for Mirabelle's turbulent social life, but life with her family was always pleasant. There was only so much she could remember at five years old, but a few things stuck out to her the most: trips to the beach, walking on the sand, handing the coffee to Father before he left for work, helping make breakfast with mother in the mornings. Simple things, but simple was fine for her. Until, that is, it wasn't.

"Mirabelle Adeline Marshall!" Mother shouted.

Mirabelle sat in a laundry basket at the top of the stairs with her brown hair tucked in a helmet and flight goggles strapped over her eyes. She was still young enough to fit in the basket and wild enough to consider riding it down the stairwell. Father emerged from the kitchen and saw her inching the basket towards the edge of the highest step. Her olive skin hid the blush in her cheeks. It was over. She was caught. Then she smiled.

"Attention!" She said. "This is your pilot speaking! Please clear the runway!"

Mother looked at Father.

"Aren't you going to say anything?"

Mirabelle stared at Father with big brown eyes. This was the moment of truth. If both parents said no, Mirabelle had no case. But if Father said yes then he would bear half the blame. She smiled wider when she thought of that, and then, ironically, Father smiled too, waving his arms over his head, as if guiding the basket.

21

"You are clear for takeoff!"

Mother gasped as Mirabelle cheered and bounced down the stairwell. A few bounces later she flew out the basket and into Father's arms. He caught her, his eyes wide with joy as he held her like a baby, even though she was five years old. No joy could compare to seeing his daughter smile. Mother put both hands on her hips as her brow furrowed, breaking his momentary trance. Father nervously laughed.

"Sorry. We'll take this outside."

Mirabelle giggled as her father gave her a piggyback ride out back. From this height, Mirabelle could see the city of Dain over the brown fence in their backyard. It was different from most cities back on Earth. Of course, Mirabelle didn't know what those cities were like. But her parents did, so she assumed they were right. Father always told her that she should feel lucky. They won the lottery when she was only a few months old, then made the long trip through the hyperspace belt outside Mars and received citizenship to the Republic's capital planet: New Earth.

"Your mother was all worked up," Father said. They sat in the grass across from one another. "She didn't think it was safe for you to be in a cryo-chamber for the seven months it took to get here."

Mirabelle picked a few blades of grass.

"I wish we didn't get picked so early."

"Don't ever say things like that," Father said. "We're lucky we got picked at all. Billions of people are still cooped up on that dying world. You're lucky you don't remember any of it."

"But I want to remember flying."

"Ahh, so that's why you start pouting when we talk about this." Father smiled and stood up tall. "Hey. Look at me."

Mirabelle set the blades of grass down and stood up straight.

"There's nothing stopping you from flying. If you wanna be a pilot, go for it. Then you'll be just like your old man."

Mirabelle's eyes lit up like diamonds.

"Then we can fly together!"

Father smiled.

"There's nothing that would make me happier than flying the skies with you."

Footsteps echoed from inside as Mother leaned against the doorway.

"There's someone here to see you," she said.

"Can it wait?"

Mother stepped aside. A dark-skinned man in white business robes stepped forward. He had a rich man's smile—wide and frequently used.

"Sorry to barge in like this. I'm Darius Leonardo. CEO of L-Transport."

Father bowed. Mirabelle, not understanding the situation, quickly bowed too.

"I apologize for my tone. I'm honored to receive a visit from the Leonardo family."

Darius smiled.

"Care to step inside? I've heard great things about you, Aidan. I have a proposal I'd like to discuss with you."

Father looked at Mirabelle.

"This won't take long." He walked towards the door. "I'll be back shortly."

Mother walked out towards Mirabelle and held her hand as they watched Father step inside. Mirabelle thought it was strange how Mr. Leonardo seemed to be the one inviting Father inside, even though it wasn't even his home. She figured he must be a very powerful man. But Father was too. She knew everything would be alright. But things didn't turn out alright.

Later that night, a light burst into Mirabelle's bedroom. Someone had opened the door. And now someone was walking towards her. A calm, gentle, and then familiar figure approached as the light from the hallway shined on his face. But Father had lost his usual smile. She sat up as Father sat next to her on her blue spaceship bedspread. He stroked her hair.

"Mirabelle…"

He held her close and lowered his head.

"I love you."

Father held her tight. There were tears in his eyes. Mirabelle was confused, sitting idle as she saw her mother standing in the doorway.

"What's happening?"

He kissed her on the forehead then stood up.

"I'm sorry."

Father left the room with Mother. Mirabelle felt glued to the bed–paralyzed, immovable, her mind turning with unanswered questions. Then she leaped down and ran towards the stairwell. Mother was crying in Father's arms. Then he let go, walking past the empty laundry basket Mirabelle had used as a spacecraft earlier that day. He stood by an open door with a suitcase by his side. Several men in dark suits stood in their driveway with rifles. Mirabelle sprinted down the stairs.

"Daddy! No!"

Mother held her back.

"Where are you going?!" Father didn't even turn around. He kept walking as if he didn't hear her. Mother grabbed Mirabelle's arm tighter as she struggled to break free. "Where is he going?!"

Father stepped inside a massive hovercraft as the guards shut the doors. There were words on the side of the vehicle.

L-Transport.

Mirabelle struggled and cried as the four rotating turbines erupted with blue flames. The hovercraft ascended from the pavement and accelerated into the night sky. Mother relinquished her grip on Mirabelle, who quickly sprinted out the doors and fell on the grass on the front lawn. She watched the hovercraft get tinier and tinier in the sky. *That can't be it*, she thought. *Daddy wouldn't leave. Daddy wouldn't do that.* But the hovercraft never turned around, and eventually, it disappeared into the buzzing air traffic in Dain. Her lips quivered until she broke down in a terrible, uncontrollable sob. Mother knelt by her side in the grass that night and started swaying her side to side.

"It's going to be alright, Mirabelle. One day you'll understand."

Mirabelle shut her eyes as tears streamed down her cheeks.

Mother kept swaying her and looked up at the city.

"One day."

That had been ten years ago. And for some reason, on that dreadful morning before school, all the crumminess of her past returned to her with full force. She wasn't five anymore. She was fifteen. She wasn't a kindergartner. She was a flight student at the Gerumandian Academy. And she had to get moving.

She swung her legs out over the side of her bed and sat there for a minute, shoulders hunched over, hands clenching the edge of the foam mattress. The pale-white window shutters receded to the ceiling, unveiling a metropolitan sprawl of scythe-shaped spires and silver buildings rising up towards a cloudy gray sky. The glow of early morning dawn cast a soft shade on her desk, where a messy assortment of crumpled papers and unwashed coffee mugs scattered around her half-open laptop, still playing soft ambient sleep sounds from the night before. The parts of the walls that weren't a blend of beige and green wallpaper were spotted with calendars, star charts, and pictures of group photographs of memories from semesters at the Gerumandian Academy. Rain fell softly against the glass as if mirroring Mirabelle's mood. Dark eyes drifted towards the dim sunlight, absorbing the sight of Dain from the 133rd story with casual indifference. The endless air traffic seemed dead with dullness, each vehicle looking like silver bullets against the neon backdrop of New Earth's shameless billboards of commerce. With a heart heavy with disappointment, the auburn-haired girl forced herself out of bed.

Like every other weekday, Mirabelle started her morning by changing into her form-fitting combat suit, colored in shades of gold and green. She zipped up the center of the one-piece uniform and pinched the energy shield receiver at the top of her spine. A sharp tingle of static raced across her body, coating her gloved fingers and toes with a hot, vibrating sensation of electricity. That feeling was good. It meant her suit was charged and ready to bear the brunt of blaster beams and e-blades. The smell of last Friday's sweat wafted up from the shield's activation. Of course. She had forgotten to wash the uniform over the weekend because of the debate tournament. Too late now. It was better to be smelly and on time than flagrantly late. Plus, five minutes into training, everyone would be smelling like sour, electric sweat anyway. Lord only knows she had better things to worry about.

The residential hallways of the Gerumandian Academy were a blend of sleek design and comfort. Long stretches of sandy beige paint covered the walls, only interrupted by deep green wooden door frames with security-sealed mahogany doors. A similar color theme decorated the carpet, filled with a long patchwork of abstract geometric shapes and the repeating insignia of the Academy: a large **G** framed beneath two clashing battleaxes. She merged with the procession of other students in uniform and met them in the elevator. As the sliding doors closed and the compartment began its descent, Mirabelle received a notification on her datapad.

Reminder: Appointment at Warden's Office in 10 minutes.

She froze. *How could I forget?* Mirabelle wasn't going to training this morning, even though her habits had set her in motion to do so. Instead, she was being called to answer for yesterday's outburst. With that in mind, instead of following the rest of the students to the training rooms, she turned left and made her way to the administration wing of the Gerumandian Academy, praying that her appeal would go through and that she wouldn't get expelled in the process.

* * *

"Do you know why you are here, Ms. Marshall?"

The warden held a slim holopad in his hand, the indistinct letters of paperwork running down his glasses as he scrolled. The warden's office was something out of the Old Era: a rosewood desk with a green glass lampshade. He set the device aside and regarded Mirabelle with a stern expression, but she did not return his gaze. Instead, she slouched in the chair on the other side of his desk, her eyes drawn to the view afforded by the window behind *Mr. Denimander*, as the silver plaque read. Something about the man's eyes rubbed her the wrong way, condescendingly peering through his gold-tinted spectacles.

"No."

The warden raised a brow.

"Really?" He raised the holopad to his eyes and adjusted his glasses. "You don't recall punching a student in the middle of a debate round?"

Mirabelle shifted in her seat.

"He deserved it."

"Did he now?"

"He insulted my father."

"What did he say?"

She shook her head, biting her lip.

The warden sighed when he realized he was in a standstill of silence.

"Mirabelle, if you don't talk, we can't have this conversation."

"He called him an *incestuous pig*!"

The warden paused as if holding back a smile.

"And why would he call him that?"

"I don't know."

"Did you give him a reason for him to say such a thing?"

"Of course not!"

"Then why else would he have said it?"

Mirabelle's blood stopped boiling. There was no hiding it anymore.

"Because he's an impurity. Like Mom." She looked down at her shoes. "And me."

The warden leaned forward and folded his hands together.

"Well. Was he right?"

What? She thought. That couldn't have been right. No self-respecting man would ever ask a question like that to a 15-year-old. No warden at the Gerumandian Academy would have such a blind spot to consider such a low-blow insult to be true. *Right?* Wrong. And Mirabelle knew better than that. She shouldn't have even arranged the appeal. She should've taken the extra clean-up duties and let bygones be bygones. No one ever looked at her the same once they knew she was an impurity. It was true. Impurities often married other impurities. But if that was incest, then that would make any AOL human just as culpable for marrying other AOL humans. There were a million insults Mirabelle wanted to say, but any one of them would get her expelled. So she bit her lip again, closed her eyes, and took a deep breath. Father had always taught her to know which battles in life deserved her fist and which ones deserved her silence. This one was pretty obvious.

"No," she eventually said. "My parents were not siblings."

"Were?"

"I haven't seen my father in ten years. I don't know if he's dead or alive. Can I leave now?"

"What about your appeal?"

"Are you going to give it to me?"

The warden fiddled with his thumbs.

"I'm afraid not. Just don't care so much about what other people think about you."

Mirabelle stood up.

"I'd like to leave."

She shut the door and stormed down the hall, then froze. Her debate partner, Zane Minathi, leaned against the wall as if he had been waiting for her. He was a lean young man with rich dark skin, a firm jawline, and a head of nappy black hair spotted with blonde highlights. Today he wore a ragged spacer's garb, a slim white v-neck with a faded leather jacket, and baggy cargo paints dotted with neon paint stains. He had the same stern gaze as his father, Dakari, but the playfulness of his mother's personality. Something about Zane always invited honesty and encouraged vulnerability, which is why today Mirabelle fought so hard to resist the urge to spoil her feelings of frustration. This was the last place Mirabelle expected to see him, then remembered that she had told him about her appointment. She walked with him down the hallway towards the main elevator.

"You wanna talk about it?" Zane asked.

"No."

"Can you at least tell me what he said?"

"I'm not getting out of clean-up duty."

"That's not what I meant."

Mirabelle pressed the elevator button.

"I'm not telling you what Derek said."

The elevator door opened. They both stepped inside. Mirabelle chose the ground floor and watched the blue lights flash to life and shoot them down.

"Fine," Zane said. "But at least take this." It was her trophy–a mini bronze statue of Robert Dain with a syringe in one hand and a sphere in the other. "I know we didn't win the big one, but quarterfinals ain't half bad."

She took the trophy and let out a long-winded sigh.

"I'm sorry. I cost us our match."

"You're good. I don't care."

After scanning their datapads for lunch, they grabbed food and sat across from each other at an empty table while other students mingled around in the prism-shaped room. Zane padded the sides of his taper fade haircut, staring at his reflection in his gallon water canister. It was obscenely large. He set it on the ground and started eating.

"I've been meaning to ask you," Zane said in between bites. "We've been debating both sides of this resolution for a month."

"You want to know which side I really believe?"

His hands froze halfway before taking a bite of his sandwich.

"Oh, come on, Zane. You ask me this every time. You're kind of predictable." Mirabelle paused, then set her sandwich down. "Sorry. I'm in a bad mood."

"That's alright. Forget I asked."

"No. I mean…" She sighed. "Ok. Here's the thing. It's an unbalanced resolution. Robert Dain created the AOL drug. Then Vrin sold it illegally and gained a following to establish the New World Order on Earth and assume power after killing everyone on the council. He burned libraries of documents that detail whether Robert Dain helped him. We remember Dain as a saint. Our own capital is named after him."

"And you think that's wrong?"

"I don't know if it's wrong. He may have been a saint. But the problem is that the Republic could care less about doing their homework. They love Dain because they're trying to increase AOL injections for the few that haven't given in."

"Given in?" Zane asked. "You say that like they're making some noble stand."

Mirabelle shifted in her seat.

"Not everyone can take the drug."

There was so much truth behind those words that it almost pained her to speak them. Some people chose the impurity life. For others, the impurity life chose them. She would never forget hearing her mother's explanation as a child. *A genetic mismatch.* Allegedly, there was a small percentage of the population who could develop adverse reactions to AOL. That gene ran in the Marshall family. The worst part about it was that she had cousins who were AOL standard: aunts, uncles, even grandparents. She didn't know who to blame. Most days, this was nothing more than a passing thought. Other days, the feeling that all her friends would live forever while she grew old and died *terrified* her.

Great, Mirabelle thought. *Now I'm depressed.*

Zane broke that trance with a pointed question.

"Do you even know any impurities?"

Their collective pause was long enough to be noticed, but not long enough to assume that any of them were lying. Or that they even cared.

"No."

"Me neither," Zane said. "So who cares?"

They returned to eating their sandwiches. None of them said anything for a little while. She felt bad for lying. But Zane was one of her only friends. He couldn't know, and to be honest she was simply banking on the fact that Derek wouldn't say anything either. Being an impurity was one of Mirabelle's best-kept secrets. Not her biggest secret though…but being an impurity was a close second. She glanced at her trophy then stuffed it into her backpack.

"I have to go," she said, picking up her tray. "See you tomorrow."

Zane said goodbye too. He finished his food alone, hoping to stomach the regret of lying to Mirabelle about his own status as an impurity. That was something he couldn't tell anyone, one because of the discrimination he knew he'd face, but also because at the end of the day, he wasn't even sure he believed his own reasons. Zane inherited his parent's beliefs about AOL, that a life numbered was a life better-lived. Second thoughts were an understatement. He wrestled with those convictions every day.

A few minutes later he got a call on his datapad. He connected his earbuds and returned his tray, briskly leaving the cafeteria and with the trophy behind.

"Mom? You called early today."

"I know," Desta said. She expressed all the sympathy a loving mother could express to her son. "I heard Mirabelle was trying to appeal yesterday's results."

Zane sighed and rode the elevator to his residential hall.

"Yeah… it didn't do anything though."

"I'm sorry."

"It's alright. I'm over it. I can't wait to see you soon."

"I know. I'm counting down the days. When are your finals?"

"Later next week. They shouldn't be too bad this semester. Officer Hackett said my arbitrator prospects are top in my class right now. He says he might even get me an internship with the CDAD this summer."

"Zane! That's amazing! Then you could work with Dad!"

Zane couldn't stop smiling.

"I know. It's exciting. How was your day?"

She didn't answer right away. Zane thought that was strange.

"Busy…pretty busy. There's a lot going on in my department right now."

"Problems with the Chief again?" Zane scanned inside his dorm room and shut the door behind him.

"No. Other administrative stuff." She paused. "I'll be fine." Before Zane could ask again, she changed the subject. "I got a new recipe for crecan bread by the way. I'll have some ready for you when you get back."

Zane knew something was up but didn't press her.

"I can't wait." He unzipped his backpack and double-tapped the screen on his desk. "I wish I could talk more but I gotta get to studying. Love you, Mom."

"Love you too."

"Bye."

"Ba-bye."

* * *

Later that afternoon, after Mirabelle finished her afternoon classes and workouts, she returned to her dorm and showered. The heat and steam engulfed her senses, sending her mind into a spiral of thoughts. She washed, shut off the water, wrapped herself in a towel, then stood before the mirror. Dark hair clung to her face. She wiped away the fog with her hand and gazed at her reflection. Brown eyes. A dusting of acne across her forehead. A deep red scar across her nose. That was the most significant feature of all because it was the one with a story.

A story better left untold, she thought and didn't let her mind go there. Instead, as she changed into gray sweatpants and a blue tee, the events of today started to replay in her mind. The warden completely misunderstood her. *Care what people think about me?* That was not the issue. If Derek had simply insulted her, she would've finished the debate and won; but he crossed the line when he brought her father into this. Family was family. If their honor was publicly shamed, it was only right for her to defend it. And she had; now she paid the price.

She lay on her blank blue bedspread, her dark wet hair sinking into the pillow. She listened to the gentle hum of air traffic outside her window, each sound of hovercrafts a reminder of her ambitions to be a pilot as well as a darker memory: the day her father left.

10 years. 10 long years.

Nope, Mirabelle thought. She got up to her feet, refusing to let herself sulk in her own thoughts in silence. Instead, she would grab whatever books she needed and spend the rest of the day studying in the library. She would've left undisturbed too if she hadn't rummaged around in the top drawer of her dresser long enough for socks. Her hands brushed past a thin material. The second she touched it she knew what it was. A photograph. She wanted to close the dresser but instead found herself drawn to the

32

picture at the bottom of her dresser, knowing all too well that there were more inside. This was her biggest kept secret: the mystery of the missing students.

She took out a photograph from inside. It was a boy with ebony black hair and golden eyes. He wore a white uniform and smiled. There were dozens of other photographs like it, pictures of guys and girls with notes written about them on the back. A blend of old feelings and memories overcame her. Mirabelle started to feel sick to her stomach. She grabbed the picture with two hands to rip it in half, closed her eyes...and didn't do it. It always ended the same way. In the end, she always put them back in the dresser. She did the same thing with the other photographs: Brian Welldens, Jamey Ledgings, James Benedict, and Jon Jerry. There were too many to count. In the end, she put them all back in the dresser and buried them beneath a pile of folded laundry. She tried to forget their names. And more importantly–that she was the one to bear their weight.

* * *

"Then I called her father an incestuous pig! AND I WON!"

Derek pointed to the bruise on his face as his friends howled with laughter. They slapped each other, kicked each other, rolled over onto the floor until their faces were red and their abs were sore. Like a bad case of the hiccups, they randomly broke out into chuckles as they tried to go back to studying in silence. But it was hopeless. Donny's dorm room was no place for studying. Bruce knew that too. So did Derek.

Where to begin with Derek Hunt? Son of the legendary Brigadier General, Carter Hunt, a Masten Scholar, intelligent, and according to the ladies, *devilishly* handsome. Derek was one of the few people who had it all and knew it too. He admired his reflection in the mirror each night before he went to bed, taking pride in his toned physique, his sandy blonde hair, and golden tan skin. Plus, the prestige that came with his father's name made him the talk of the Academy, second to maybe only his older brother, Matthew. Needless to say, he had loved sending that impurity bitch to fumes with that message about her father.

There were times when Derek surprised even himself with how clever he was. It was all planned so carefully. He remembered watching Mirabelle tense up every time the word "impurity" was brought out in the debate. He knew who Mirabelle was because she was a Masten Scholar, like himself. *Not as good as me*, he thought. *No, not even close*. Still good enough to get some tuition money. Not that Derek needed the tuition money, but he liked the title. And he knew that for as quiet as Mirabelle was, in their weekly meetings when she cared about something, she *cared* about something. And so, when she asked to see one of their articles of evidence, after constantly slandering impurities during their crossfire for their stupidity (which the judge nodded in agreement with), it only took one little whisper to set her off. In their weekly meetings, she had once made the mistake of alluding to her father's ten-year absence. And then, with Derek noticing the way she argued for the humanity of impurities, he connected the dots, crafted the perfect insult, and fired away.

Bang.

Did he feel bad? A little bit. Did he have a choice? No. Mirabelle was kicking their asses. She had gone undefeated in preliminaries and was on her way to winning finals. If he hadn't stopped her there, she would've won the tournament. It was fair, because apparently all was fair in love and war–some earth poet had once said. And Derek saw everything as a battle. He played to win.

A Somber Celebration

Later that afternoon, Kalak, the new Chief of the Central Dain Arbitrator Department, stood by the window of his office with his hands folded behind his back. From the window he and Dakari could see the dozens of arbitrators typing away in their cubicles, some of them answering calls, some of them wandering back and forth across the large room, escorting criminals to cells, and in the rarest of cases–psychics. There was something in the center of the room that went unnoticed by veteran arbitrators but was always noticed by cadets. There was a steel scaffold in the heart of the department. Not like the ones for buildings, but the ones to execute criminals. Except this scaffold had no noose and no wood. It was made of silver and steel, with blue lines crossing the center of the elevated platform. Kalak had sentenced many criminals to death by electrocution on that scaffold. It was both a haunting reminder to the prisoners that were escorted to their cells as well as a warning against traitors. The scaffold waited for those that defied the law. But no one stood on that scaffold today.

"Beretta Keys should be standing there," Dakari said, referring to the name of the girl he had caught earlier that day. *And the girl I caught four years ago*, he thought. Though that thought he didn't mention, at least not yet.

Kalak, hawk-eyed, a man with a pale complexion, a stern brow, and a black and grey beard, did not remove his eyes from the scaffold. He watched like a resilient bird of prey.

"She's fourteen years old," Kalak said.

"She murdered the Middletons."

"We don't execute minors. End of story."

They continued staring at the scaffold in silence.

"If it was anyone else," Dakari said. "They would've gotten the circuit."

"True. But the law must make room for psychics. She will be punished in other ways. We don't have very many psychics to study these days."

"She murdered the Chief!"

"Do I look dead to you?"

Dakari paused.

"You know what I meant. The old chief. Samuel Middleton."

"And now I have taken his place. I will not spend my first day giving the press new material to slander us with. Do you really want them saying we murder teenage girls?"

"I want them to say we uphold the law. Not that we bend it when it's convenient."

"An eternity in a cell is punishment enough," Kalak said.

"Back then they used to call it a 'lifetime' in a cell."

"What's a lifetime to people who don't grow old?" Kalak looked at Dakari. "Perhaps you could tell me, seeing that you still refuse to get AOL treatment."

"Do my convictions confuse you?"

"Confuse me? They disturb me. What kind of person would reject biological immortality? A life without having to worry about old age." Kalak looked down in the main room. Not a single man or woman in their department looked over 30 years old. Their physical bodies had sailed through adolescence and dropped their anchor at young adulthood. Except for Kalak, of course. But he was given his dose a little later in life than most. "Impurities like yourself are just about as rare as psychics these days."

"Isn't it interesting how the Republic calls AOL humans normal but traditional humans, impurities? If anything, it's the other way around. Your blood has been tampered with. Mine remains pure."

"They coined the term, impurity, because aging is a disease. The only thing pure about original human DNA is its expiration date. It's never too late to get treatment, you know."

Dakari paused. *Of course I know that. You don't have to remind me.* He held his tongue though, hoping that Kalak would move on to another subject.

"I don't mean to press you, Dakari. Really, I don't. It's just that what you did out there today proves that you're one of the best of the best. If you were a lousy arbitrator, it'd be a lot easier to see you wither up and die." Kalak inspected his life-long friend, then glanced over to the wall. There was a picture of their graduation ceremony at the Gerumandian Academy. Kalak and Dakari smiled with their arms around each other. Desta, Dakari's wife, was next to them too. "But we have a history. I don't like thinking that our friendship, and your service to the CDAD, has an expiration date." Kalak reached into his coat pocket and pulled out a golden badge with the words *Deputy* engraved beneath a symbol of the CDAD. "This is yours whether you receive AOL treatment or not."

Dakari stiffened.

"A promotion?"

"Someone has to fill in as Deputy seeing that I'm filling in for Middleton."

Dakari gazed back at the scaffold. Images of the scorched corpses of the Middletons kept surfacing to his mind like ghosts.

"I don't know…it's a lot to consider."

"You're refusing?"

"No, sir. I just need to think it over. That's all."

"I'm sure you know the implications in declining a promotion," Kalak warned. "I would strongly advise you to accept. It would be a shame for a good friendship to end like this."

Dakari smiled.

"And what would be a good end?"

"A noble death in the field, perhaps." Kalak removed a pass card from his pocket and handed it to Dakari. "Or no end at all."

Dakari took the pass card and read the inscription:

Central Dain Medical Clinic: AOL Treatment.

"What is this?"

"A new future for you and your family if you want it. I had the department cover the expenses myself. Show them that card and you and your family will receive the great gift of biological immortality at no cost to yourselves."

Dakari looked at the passcard again.

"I'm not convinced the AOL drug is as free of problems as we think it is."

"It's been around for 100 years."

"You never can be too careful." Dakari looked down at his badge. "Quite a lot to consider." He handed the passcard back. "But I've already made my mind about this."

"Keep it. I feel better knowing you have the option."

"Very well." Dakari slipped the passcard into his pocket. He thought about bringing up the thought that crossed his mind earlier, about catching Beretta Keys twice, but stopped himself. He'd brought enough trouble to Kalak's mind today. No need to bother him about something he couldn't prove with evidence. Instead, he saluted. "Tomorrow I will inform you of my final decision."

"I'm looking forward to it," Kalak said. "Tell Desta I said hello."

Dakari walked back to his office, shut the door, and sat down. He rattled his fingers on the polished rosewood of his desk, eyeing a picture frame of himself and his family. The passcard weighed heavily in his coatpocket, as well as the prospect of becoming Deputy. A promotion meant more pay. In this case, however, it also meant more hours. He reclined deeply in the suspension chair and let out a deep breath, closing his eyes. In the darkness, he saw burning bodies. The bodies of his friends.

The Middletons had been close friends of the Minathis ever since Dakari and Desta joined the force. Even though Desta was working at the Eastern Dain Arbitrator Department, they had shared countless meals together over the years. Desta had even made plans with them this morning. *How on New Earth am I supposed to tell her that they're dead?* He shook his head and leaned forward over his desk with a sigh. The answer was simple. He wouldn't have to tell her at all. *Odds are she already knows.*

Someone broke Dakari's trance with a knock at the door.

"Come in."

A slender woman in a navy blue trench coat, blonde hair in a topknot, opened the door.

"Permission to speak with you…Deputy?"

Her jovial personality brought a smile to his face.

"Permission granted, Amelia. But only if you cut the formalities."

"I'm just teasing." Captain Lancaster closed the door and set the papers and the Deputy badge on Dakari's desk. They rested next to the photograph of the Minathi family. "I'm sure your wife's going to be happy."

Dakari leaned forward and grabbed the picture. It was a perfect snapshot of family life, good enough for a postcard. Father and Mother sitting on a park bench, smiling with their six-year-old son, Zane. *He's sixteen now,* Dakari thought. *This needs an update.* "Maybe. Back at the Academy, we used to tease each other about who would become Chief of our departments first. She might finally have to concede that I was right."

Amelia walked around Dakari's desk and looked at the picture with him.

"I remember this photograph. You sent it as a Christmas card years ago."

"I remember it taking a light year for Zane to sit still. He hasn't gotten much better in that aspect to say the least."

"You think he'll join the force like you?"

"That's the plan. I'm not pressuring him in that direction though. Lord only knows how dangerous our job is getting these days. Beretta Keys should have been executed."

"You know why Kalak couldn't do that."

"Do I? Why let her live? You really think an eternity in a cell is enough?"

"It was enough for Vrin."

"Vrin's dictatorship on Earth plunged billions into poverty. If Boris executed him there would've been national outrage for letting him off the hook so easily. Beretta's death would be remembered by no one. She'll be forgotten."

"Then why are you so insistent on having her killed?"

Because I caught her before. He wanted to say that more than anything else in the world. The memory of capturing Beretta four years ago was ripe with details. It had been raining that day. Commissioner Roy Andersen had been killed, and not long after, Dakari had found the culprit: a ten-year-old blonde girl with eyes as blue as the Cypher Sea. *She still has those same eyes. And smile.* Young psychics were like baby snakes; they didn't know how to control their venom. They killed everything they touched. *Just like they killed Roy Andersen, Samuel, and Katharine. Who was next?* The problem with this theory was that there was no way she could have escaped. No psychic had ever been released from the rehab centers. At least, not to his knowledge.

Dakari's eyes darkened as he searched his mind for another answer to Amelia's question. "I've seen psychics face to face. They're crafty creatures. I'm not confident a cell can hold them. And I saw what they did to Samuel and Katharine today." *I fear for my own family,* Dakari wanted to say but held his tongue. He gazed at the photograph one last time, then set it back on the desk. "I should get going. Have a good night, Amelia."

Captain Lancaster saluted, then left his office.

Not long after she left, Dakari walked down the hallways of the Central Dain Arbitrator Department, a million thoughts mulling over his mind. He listened to the typing keyboards, conversations in the glass sealed cubicles, the footsteps of white armored soldiers escorting criminals and psychics in straight jackets down an open glass hallway in the higher levels of the building. And then the scaffold. He walked past it and then paused in the middle of the hallway as he saw something else: the detention center. Its main elevator doors opened. Not even Deputies were allowed down those doors. That was all handled by internal affairs. He paused to get one last look as two guards led the psychic inside.

It was the blonde girl that had killed the Middletons: Beretta Keys. The girl he had caught. Not once, but twice. He was sure of it. Their eyes met each other in a stalemate as the doors closed. Most teenagers were terrified to go into the underground prison. But not Beretta. She was smiling.

After the doors closed, Dakari continued his long walk out of the department. But he never forgot that smile.

* * *

"Honey?" Dakari asked. "I'm home!"

Soft music played from the living room speakers as Desta cooked dinner on the stove. Several orange lamps illuminated the atrium of their apartment as the projector played today's news on mute. Dakari's eyes wandered to the screen, frozen at the cycling footage of yellow police tape on several restaurants on Irkurian Drive. The burnt bodies may have been covered on Regal News, but they were forever tattooed into Dakari's memory. The only sight that washed those terrible sights away was the emergence of his wife from the living room, who snuggled straight into her husband's arms with the stove heat on low.

Then the tears started to fall.

"I'm so sorry..."

Dakari rested his hand on the back of her head, stroking her dark cropped hair.

"I don't know how this could've happened," Desta said, sniffling. "He was off duty. How would a psychic know he was off duty?"

Because this was no ordinary psychic. He shoved that thought away. *You have no evidence for that.* Arbitrators never dealt in pure conjecture. Still, Dakari couldn't shake the feeling that this was something bigger than he imagined. It was the only thing to stay his tears.

"Let me finish dinner," Dakari said.

"I've already-"

"Please. It'll give me something to do."

She saw the look in his eyes and nodded.

"I'll open a bottle of wine."

They ate at the dinner table with an electronic candle glowing between the two of them, casting faint shadows on their somber faces. They ate lasagna in silence, an old recipe passed down from Desta's side of the family. Dakari swirled his wine glass, struggling to meet his wife's expression from the other end of the table. *We were planning to get together with the Middletons this morning.* The change of the world seemed too overwhelming to think about. He lost his appetite.

Desta's sly green eyes meandered to the badge on Dakari's chest. Then both their eyes met–lovingly. That glance meant the world to him. It was such a stark contrast to her often-menacing look, her bold gaze, one that knew the arbitrator's stare just like he did. But her gaze softened upon seeing him again. It welcomed him home.

"I'm glad you're ok."

Dakari shifted his food around with his fork.

"I was never really in danger." He paused. "I was late."

"Stop. You can't blame yourself for what happened."

He didn't answer.

After dinner, they sat on the couch, their eyes drawn to the window where Zane used to draw smiley faces when he was a baby. He used to watch the hovercrafts zoom in the upper city and the neon lights of billboards and signs. Now he was at the Academy. Desta set the bottle on the table and brushed her hair out of her eyes.

"What do you mean she escaped?" Desta asked.

"I caught her before. Four years ago."

"That's impossible. Psychics don't leave the detention centers."

"I know. That's what worries me."

"How do you know it was her?"

"Believe me. I know. I saw it in her eyes, her smile, her hair. It was Beretta."

"Why didn't you bring it up at work?"

"It wasn't the time. With the new Chief and all."

Desta nodded, quietly sipped on her wine, then set it back on the coffee table.

"Did you check the records for her name?"

"It's the first thing I'll do tomorrow."

"Why didn't you-"

"Like I said…wasn't the right time." A long silence ensued between them, their eyes drawn back to the silent screen. "Can we turn this off?"

Desta grabbed the remote and shut the news feed.

"If you're serious about this, Kalak needs to know."

"Not before I do my own research. Kalak respects me. I don't need him thinking I'm showing signs of PTSD in the field."

"Fine. If the old arbitrators followed protocol on the Roy Andersen case, then there should be photographed documentation of the psychic in question." Desta paused. "Though I hope you're wrong, for both our sakes." Her eyes meandered back to the new badge on Dakari's chest. "Deputy, huh?"

"I don't know if I'm taking it."

"Why not?"

"The higher up you go, the bigger the target is on your back."

"In that case, you should be more worried about Kalak."

"He says hello, by the way."

Desta smiled. "You two have always been so close. How could you decline the promotion now? You captured 20 psychics last year alone."

"Not everyone agrees with my methods. Times are changing."

"People always die in the line of duty."

"They're dying more than they used to."

"Wait. Don't say it," Desta said. "You're going to talk about the Last Resort Bill."

"And why wouldn't I?" Dakari said. "It's putting our officers at risk and you know it. If you don't allow an arbitrator to draw their rifle before a psychic creates a tear it's too late."

"It's not as ludicrous as it sounds. Rifles are provocative. Remember that these are mostly children we're dealing with. They're too young to hide their abilities like adults. If you point a rifle at them, they go crazy."

"This bill makes us walking targets."

"That's not true. There's always a way out."

"Tell that to Middleton."

"He was off duty!" Desta said. Then she took a deep breath. "If you resign it will break Zane's heart."

"I'm doing it for all of us."

"Then am I supposed to resign too?" No response. "We knew this going into these jobs. But someone has to do it." She smiled. "Who better than us?"

"Someone other than us."

Desta cupped her hand over her mouth, trying not to laugh.

"What?" Dakari asked.

"I love you, Dakari." She rested her hand on his. "But sometimes you're stupid."

"Stupid?"

"Did you suddenly realize today that our jobs are dangerous?"

"No. I saw it with my own eyes. I've seen arbitrators die, but not like this."

"Death is death."

"Then you're not afraid of it? Or afraid for Zane?"

"I am. But that's why I'm on the force." Desta sighed. "Let the earth poets think about death. We have lives to live."

Dakari smiled.

"You and your poetry."

"It's actually enjoyable. You should read some with me sometime."

"How romantic."

Desta leaned close until their noses touched.

"Too sentimental for a big, burly man like you?"

They kissed, but then Dakari leaned away.

"I'm out of wine."

A few glasses later, Dakari and Desta swayed gently in each other's arms as a soft jazz tune played in the background.

> *"And who are you? The girl I wed*
> *That you should love me still*
> *A thousand days will pass along*
> *And we've not had our fill*
>
> *I often said, I often said*
> *My Sweet Darling so dear*
> *That Heaven's gates, don't lead to home*
> *Less I can see you here."*

"This song was playing when we met," Desta said. "On Cypher Tower."

"How could I forget?"

"Some men forget the songs their wives walk down the aisle to."

"Maybe because we're too busy looking at the bride." Desta let her head fall gently into Dakari's chest with a soft laugh. He loved that laugh. It reminded him of their days back at the Gerumandian Academy, where they were nothing more than two recruits trying to pass exams and physical aptitude tests. Never in a million years would Dakari have imagined that he would be calling the girl from the second row his wife.

"Kind of a depressing song to walk down the aisle to," Dakari said.

"And why's that?"

"Because we don't have a thousand years."

"Maybe not." Desta smiled. "But ours will be worth thousands more."

Dakari paused.

"Kalak offered to pay for our family's treatment." Their gentle sway stopped until they stood with the fading music. "It doesn't have to be so temporary."

"What's the fun in staying like this forever?"

"You're saying you want to grow old?"

"Wrinkles don't make us old. They just remind us where we're going."

Dakari's smile started to dip like a soft stream. And his eyes matched the falling rain. He clenched the back of Desta's coat and held her tight. "Do you know what I saw out there today?" His voice quivered when he spoke. The sights of the charred bodies returned to him. "I saw you." He clenched tighter. "And me." Desta's eyes widened. Then she pulled back and tugged on the sides of Dakari's coat, gazing into his tear-stricken eyes. "The Middletons were good people...and they were burned for it." He sniffled. "Why? What would lead a fourteen-year-old to do such a thing?" He clenched her arms for support. "And why do I hate her so much for it? I *beat* her, Desta...I beat her..."

"You..." Desta paused. "You were upset."

"I was *more* than upset," Dakari said. "I wanted to *murder* her. I wanted to kill every glowing-eyed freak in this world."

"Our job isn't to kill them. Our job is to escort them somewhere safe so that they don't abuse their powers. Not all psychics are like that."

"But they can all become like that." Dakari's head bent low. "Samuel was more than a good leader. He was a good friend." He shook his head. "He didn't deserve to die."

"Who does?" Desta asked. "And as for Beretta, she's captured now. The work is done. The CDAD still needs you. You're one of the best."

"I know." He wrapped his arms around Desta. He closed his eyes and tried to suppress an irrational hatred of psychics that swelled in his heart. He felt it rise. "Thank you."

They went to bed. After Dakari shut off the lights in the living room, he thought he saw an old smiley face that Zane had drawn on the window. When he blinked, it was gone. *Nothing but a memory.* He told himself that the same was true of Beretta, that the girl he caught today was just a reminder of what had happened to Roy and nothing more. There was just one problem: he didn't believe it. Beyond that window stood a city lurking with unidentified psychics. He wanted to keep the people he loved safe. He went to bed mulling it over, and eventually drifted off into a restless, anxious sleep, where he dreamed of charred arbitrator bodies, glowing-eyed psychics, and a side of himself that he had never seen, and never wanted to see again.

A Budget for Brawls

It was Monday at the Brawling Bandits. In tonight's match, the "Viper" looked to end the undefeated record of the infamous "Underdog," otherwise known as Quan Son Jerry, who desperately needed this match to make up for this month's rent. He fought weekly here and hadn't lost a match. He didn't plan on losing tonight either. The underground arena looked like a miniature oval amphitheater with high walls to prevent combatants from getting into the stands. Quan stood at the edge of the ring and faced Viper, a middle-aged man with a slight twitch in his right eye. Both combatants wore black exoskeleton suits that covered them from head to toe, fitting tight on their bodies with overlapping reptilian-like scales. They each held an e-blade: katanas coated in thin wiring to deliver an electric shock to their opponent. They couldn't pierce through armor, but they sure did sting.

   Drunken men and women in rags and worn clothes crowded around the stands. They placed bets and cheered and booed and occasionally were thrown out for trying to get involved in the fight. Other than trying to ignore the fans, the fight was simple. Each exoskeleton, in addition to a helmet that Quan saw out of through a glass visor, had an energy shield provided by the Brawling Corps. Whoever disabled the opponent's shields first won. The reward was 15% of that night's ticket sales. Some nights, that didn't mean much. But tonight, there was a full house. If things went well, Quan could be walking home with 500 recs.

   "Beat him up!"

   "Come on, don't let this brat get the best of you!"

The buzzer blared.

It was a quick fight. Viper swung every swing like it was his last. He was angry, quick, and stupid. Quan sidestepped, dodged his blow, then bumped Viper in the back of the head with the hilt of his blade, sending him staggering into the stands. A roar of laughter emerged as Viper bumped against the side of the arena, scaring the fans away.

"You know," Quan said, dusting off his shoulder. "You're pretty slow for someone who's said to move as fast as a snake."

Viper yelled and lunged at Quan, swinging his sword like a banshee. Another mistake. He aimed in Quan's general direction, but he had no precise target. Quan slashed the tip of Viper's blade, then smacked it back towards his shoulder to sting him on his sword arm. That made Viper stagger back.

"Ah, you don't like the sting, do you?" Quan held his e-blade behind his back. "Then don't worry. I won't swing until you tell me too."

Viper yelled and charged again. Quan's body curved away from each swing in the same way that similar ends of magnets repel from each other upon close contact. He ducked and kicked Viper in the back, sending him flying towards the other end of the arena.

"That was better," Quan said. "But keep your back straight."

"Draw your blade and SHUT UP!"

Quan smiled. There was no need to carry this fight any longer. The crowd would get bored if he did. Sparks flew around Viper's armor as Quan sliced him in five different joints with five quick swings. Then as Viper staggered away Quan hit him square in the back like a baseball bat, deactivating his shields and sending his frozen body falling flat on the ground.

"Ladies and gentlemen, we have our winner! Give it up for the Underdog!"

Half the crowd cheered. The other half threw half-empty beer bottles into the arena. A few guards rushed to Quan's aid and escorted him out of the gates and down a set of stairs. They guarded the entrance to the locker room as Quan removed his helmet and handed his e-blade to his assistant.

Someone started clapping from the back of the room. It was Alexander.

"Well done! Jolly good show!"

"Knock it off." Two auxiliary droids whirred behind him and began to remove his suit. "Get the money from upstairs."

"Sheesh. Someone's angry."

Alexander left without another word. After Quan's exoskeleton was removed, he sat down on a bench and wiped his sweaty face with a warm towel. He saw his reflection in the locker room mirror. He had a lean, muscular build, necessary for any dueler. Small enough to dodge attacks, strong enough to deliver them. He started to flex his bicep, then heard someone open the door. He paid no attention to the man until his footsteps grew closer, then stopped altogether.

"You've improved."

That voice, Quan thought. *I know that voice.*

But Quan didn't turn around. So, the man kept talking.

"You've learned how to beat a man in five swings. If you had fought like that at Silverside you might have won regionals."

"You got the wrong guy."

"No, I don't. I know my old students when I see them."

Quan slammed his locker and turned around.

"What do you want, Mocroft?"

"That's *Officer* Mocroft, now."

The Officer stood tall in a forest green dress coat with shiny gold buttons and a thick stiff collar. There were several medals on his breast and an insignia stitched on his right shoulder. *Gerumandian.* He still had those same thin, piercing brown eyes and indifferent stare. And the pencil-thin mustache.

"You're a Gerumandian?" Quan smiled. "My brother not good enough for you?"

"I'm not here to talk about Jon." Mocroft tossed a card. Quan caught it. "My sources say there is a promising young dueler in the Brawling Bandits. You're being scouted by the Gerumandian Academy. Congratulations."

"Why would I want to go there?"

"It's all you ever used to talk about."

"Not anymore."

"What changed?"

"Things changed."

Alexander burst through the door and ran downstairs with a pouch full of recs.

"Quan! You won't believe how–" He froze. "Why is the mustache man here?"

Mocroft raised a brow.

"I see you still haven't learned any respect. No matter. I know my worth." He scanned Alexander from head to toe. "And it appears I know yours too. What's with your hair?"

Alexander tucked the pouch in his oversized jacket.

"We're hiding out. I thought it might be better to change our appearance a bit." Officer Mocroft laughed. "What's so funny? You here to bring us in?"

"I'm not contractually obliged to find a group of lousy runaway students."

"Then why are you here?"

"It's not every day that an 18-year-old goes undefeated in a place like this." Officer Mocroft started counting with his fingers. "Although if my calculations are correct…" He smiled. Quan turned pale. "You're barely 16."

"You can't say anything. Please."

"Why? Because then you'd no longer be able to spend your weekdays fighting middle-aged men who never realized their dueling dreams?"

"A duel is a duel."

"True. But you can't separate the dueler from the duel in the same way you can't separate the dancer from the dance. Remove the dancers and you have nothing but an empty stage."

"What's your point?"

Mocroft scowled.

"You've been dancing with amateurs. Go to the Academy and you'll face competition worthy to brag about."

The pensive officer walked away, his footsteps echoing up the stairs, then silenced altogether with the shut door. Quan threw away the card in the trash the second his old instructor was gone.

"What are you doing?!" Alexander shouted.

"We don't need him. And we certainly don't need to waste time at the Academy."

Alexander's eyes didn't leave the trash can.

"You're not one to walk away from your dreams."

Quan grabbed his backpack from the floor.

"I am if they're dead ones."

He grabbed his jacket and walked away. Alexander looked back at the trash can, grunted in anger, then reluctantly followed him out of the locker room.

* * *

In the late hours of night, the streets were wet and smelled of asphalt. A few black market vendors bargained beneath fluttering tents and silently sold augmentations, fresh fish, trinkets, datapad attachments, and clothes. No one ever looked like they wanted to be here. Their faces were scowling, their words, quick and bitter. You would have never guessed that the gift of immortality flowed through their veins. They looked as unhappy as earthlings. In these parts of District 7, everyone wore dark raincoats with big hoods. On the bright side, it made blending in no problem.

After his victory at the Brawling Bandits (and unexpected encounter with Officer Mocroft), Quan left his apartment to clear his head. Somehow they had managed to scrounge up enough money to pay their rent before the deadline. It was a victory, but a small one at that. They didn't run away from home just to meet housing payments. They were trying to save up for an intergalactic passport. In some ways, their current progress felt more like running on a treadmill than a marathon. That's why with the day's luck still in his favor, Quan hoped he could make a few extra coins with some late-night thievery.

He entered a busy alleyway with his hands in his pockets. There were large tents and cargo boxes all over the place. One man looked particularly vulnerable paying for a fish beneath a blue tarp. He saw him plucking recs out of his pouch. Quan smiled and removed his hand from his pocket, creating a tear no bigger than the size of his thumb. A sharp gust of wind shot out from beneath his sleeve and blew the pouch out of the man's hand. Several fish, a hat, and loose coins flew off the stand. He snagged a few of the man's recs while he wasn't looking and kept walking, unnoticed and undisturbed.

With one block left until he made it home, Quan made a right and crossed through a narrow alleyway. It grew quiet. Then three figures appeared at the end of the walkway, and one appeared behind him. Quan froze. A hooded man stepped forward.

"A little young to be walking around this late, don't ya think?"

Quan smiled.

"Aren't you a little old?"

None of them laughed.

"Get him."

They rushed Quan like shadows in the night. He swept the first man by the legs and watched him splash in a puddle. Quan staggered back and deflected their punches, elbowing the second man in the side of the neck. Then the man from behind shoved Quan into the wall, scraping the side of his head. The pain flared and blurred Quan's vision as the remaining figure clutched the young boy's shoulders and threw him into the other side of the wall like a ragdoll. He hit the cement hard, groaning and standing up as the four men towered above him.

"Search him."

Several hands padded him down his legs and clawed in his coat. They took the pouch of recs that he stole from his jacket and a pack of cigarettes. Quan lay defenseless. Blood trickled down the side of his forehead where the throbbing was most intense. The lead figure squatted down low, the long shadows of the alleyway hiding their faces.

"This ain't your district, kid. If we ever catch you out here again, we'll kill you."

A dim blue light shined against their frozen faces. Their features turned from smug smiles to horrified dropped jaws. They backed away as Quan stood up and created a tear in both hands, aiming it at the thieves.

"Or how about this?" Quan said, blood trickling down his brow. "I take whatever I want and I go wherever I please. You're gonna give me back those recs, then you're gonna leave District 7 for good, or you're gonna die. Understand?" They were too stunned to speak. "Understand?"

They nodded and threw the pouch back at Quan.

"Sorry about that…we'll be on our way."

"The cigs. I want those back too."

One of the cloaked men trembled forward and threw them back. Quan relinquished the tear and caught it, tucking it in the same coat pocket as the pouch of recs. "Beat it."

They ran. After they were gone, Quan felt the side of his forehead and saw a bit of blood stick to his fingertips. He washed them off in a puddle, then stuck both hands in his coat pockets. It was another day in the city of Dain and another reminder of why it was time to leave. That night Quan lay on the couch with a bandage on his forehead. He dreamed the same dream: a light in the darkness, a star of gold, a planet of power. The heat felt warm on his skin and burned away the pain of the past. Perhaps it was an omen of a brighter future. *Perhaps*, Quan thought, *it means I will see the stars myself and leave this planet for good.*

No Heroes in Hell

The sparring room at the Gerumandian Academy was a prism-shaped structure with natural sunlight peering through triangular windows from the ceiling. It shone comfortably on a forest green mat in the center of the room, where about a hundred students waited with anticipation. Officer Mocroft looked at his datapad. It was 10:00 a.m.

"Attention!" Each student straightened their posture and saluted their superior. They wore green Gerumandian uniforms. "At ease!" They set their hands back by their side and stood in solid formation. Mocroft paced around the mat in the center of the room. There were weapon racks on both sides of the wall. "Welcome to Hell's Pit."

Matthew Hunt, a tall, muscular boy stood among the veteran students with his arms crossed. He looked untamed and dangerous–a young man whose wildness had been shoved inside a vacuum and narrowed to a sharp point. It looked as if the sea breeze had swept over his sandy blonde hair and forever creased it back, with a few strands dangling over his forehead like gelled, hanging waves. He was tired of these introductory shenanigans. He wanted to fight.

"In this room, there are many different kinds of students," Mocroft said. "Some are Pit Dogs, some are veterans. Despite your discrepancy in rankings, you're all in the same age group, which means if one student is head and shoulders above the rest of you, look to that student as the standard. There will be no complaints of pairings and no refusals if you are chosen to fight. The same rules that govern the rest of the Academy apply in the dueling room: obey your superiors."

Each student remained firm in their stance. A few Pit Dogs, the lowest ranking students, gazed at the floor, preparing for the nightmare of fighting someone several ranks above them. Officer Mocroft picked up two e-blades from the weapon rack. He kept twisting them around in his hands so that the sunlight flickered across the smooth black edge of the swords. Other students would look careless doing that. Mocroft made it look easy.

"We are here to work. Your parents are paying for a soldier, so a soldier is what we will give them! Whatever you are majoring in is your professor's concern. In my time, you are infantry. If you can't accept that then you've already failed."

A grin crept over Mocroft's face.

"Who's ready to duel?"

Half the room raised their hands. Matthew gave them all a smug look with his arms still crossed. Dozens of hands shot up in the air as students demanded their right to prove themselves. Mocroft laughed. Matthew waited. Then he heard it. The shouts from the higher-ranking students crystallized into something coherent. It formed into two words until nearly half the room was chanting his name.

"Matthew Hunt! Matthew Hunt! Matthew Hunt!"

Matthew Hunt uncrossed his arms and walked through the crowd of students like an Olympian demigod. No one wanted to be on the other end of his gaze, with his menacing green eyes of violent apathy. They were a paradox of ambition and hopelessness, of fire and water. Hunger coursed through his veins. He was more muscular and taller than any other student in the room. 6'3. 200 pounds. Lean. Fast. Frightening. He bowed before Mocroft and accepted the blade. The medals on his shoulder pads glistened beneath the window light. Most students had two. Matthew had seven. Students whispered to each other as their shining example stood before them.

"…he's a Juggernaut."

"…a Masten Scholar."

"…youngest to achieve both."

"…son of Carter Hunt."

Matthew stood on the forest green sparring mat and clenched his blade, his brow narrowing, his blood rising at just the mention of his father's name. *Carter Hunt,* his famous father. Oftentimes no one cared about a wealthy man's personal life unless his personal life was wealthy too—rich with scandals and public sins so that everyone could say: "I'm not like them!" Everyone said that about Carter. Not because of his sins or scandals, but because of the sheer absence of them. *A perfect man,* they said. One to build your hopes on. *Not mine,* Matthew thought. *The man they praise will sing my praises. The man they bow to will bow to me.*

Officer Mocroft asked for a respective Pit Dog and was met with stunning but predictable silence. "No one?" Mocroft clicked a spinning dial of numbers in his palm. A combination of the ID numbers ticked and started to slow to select the next opponent.

The ticking stopped.

Mocroft showed the number.

"Luke Gruber! It's your lucky day."

Pathetic, Matthew thought. He watched the wide-eyed, scrawny opponent inch his way onto the platform like a walking corpse, trembling to his own grave. He felt insulted to go up against him and even more insulted that the Academy had accepted him. No matter. Matthew gave the audience a sly smile. He would give them a good show.

They grabbed their e-blades, activated their energy shields, strapped on their helmets, then stepped to opposite sides of the mat. Donny and Bruce, some of Matthew's closest friends, gave their own commentary from the sideline.

"Matthew's gonna kill that sucker."

"Yeah. Rest in peace, Luke."

Derek Hunt, the young brother of the Hunt sons, stood with both arms crossed.

"It's a boring matchup."

A digital clock flashed to life on the wall.

"Remember," Officer Mocroft said. "The match is three minutes long. No mercy rule. No submission. Fight until the clock stops. If a student's shield deactivates in the round, the match is brought to an immediate halt. Otherwise, the shields should regenerate themselves and be set to stun. No grabbing new weapons from the rack and no intervention on behalf of the crowd. Any questions?" There were none. "Great. Is everyone ready?"

The crowd let out a cheer. Luke gave a thumbs up. Matthew gripped his blade.

"Begin!"

With one lunge, Matthew struck first. Each time their blades clashed a loud boom echoed throughout the room. Their blades were supercharged and created a powerful implosion upon enough contact with another blade or shield. The more you hit the shield, the more powerful the blast would be, sometimes knocking them off their feet.

Sparks flew between them as their blades clashed. Luke tried to parry Matthew's attacks but started getting hit on both sides of his body. Each time he took a hit his armor absorbed the attack with a red glow. Luke gritted his teeth in pain and staggered back. He charged forward with rage, but Matthew side-stepped, dodged his blow, then whiplashed his blade across his back, sending him staggering towards the wall. He fell on the ground, then quickly leaped up and got back in the fight. Then he was smacked down on the mat again. Matthew would wait for him to get up, then hit him again, the metal scales of Luke's armor crunching against the foam floor.

It was pointless. Luke was exhausted, throwing too much of his momentum into one swing, only to miss, and take another blow to the chest. Then Matthew tightened his grip on the e-blade and slashed across the boy's helmet. It scraped across Luke's visor and zapped him. Luke screamed, held his face, and fell to the ground.

"I give up!" Luke yelled. "I'm done, Matthew! Please! I yield!"

There were still two minutes left on the clock.

"You're not done till I say you're done!"

Luke reached out for his blade, but Matthew slashed it. The sparks stung his hand. He tried backing away but Matthew slit his chest again, causing Luke to squirm and huddle into a ball. It was the most pathetic thing Matthew had seen in his entire life. He felt angry watching it. *A Gerumandian cowering in fear?* He would teach him a lesson.

Matthew brought down thunder against the boy's back, his anger drowning out the sounds of his screams and the gasps from the jaw-dropped crowd. He swung at Luke's back like he was digging ore from a mine with a pickaxe, scraping and slashing and whacking the scales of his glowing red armor, amplifying the sting. Each student watched in horror as a two-minute onslaught followed. It was like a public whipping.

"STOP! PLEASE!"

The audience was speechless. Matthew kept slashing, inflicting so much fiery pain into the boy that it would make him wish he'd rather be dead. Another slash. Against the wall, Officer Mocroft watched with a scowl. He turned away until the buzzer blared. Luke sniffled and continued to cry as he held his hands in pain, his moans and cries stunning even the most resolute Gerumandians watching in silence. Matthew dropped the e-blade and removed his helmet. He walked past them like an executioner leaving the scene of a bloody end. There was an anger in his eyes that no one could understand. It was an eye of a raging bull. Unlike his younger brother, Derek, Matthew understood that *nothing* was fair in love and war. Cheaters prospered. There was only one principle: kill or be killed.

Cautious Cadets

About a week after the Middletons were murdered and burned on Irkurian Drive, something strange happened to Dakari. He had a dream. That hadn't happened in years. He was transported back to a time when Zane Minathi was a little boy; the son any father would dream of having. He was the victim of cheek squishing from all his grandparents in Cypher, and his little brown curls were heartstoppers. Wide-eyed, enthusiastic, and respectful, Dakari treasured every moment with him. In this dream, they were sitting in the pews of the Eastern Dain Church.

The Minathis were Presbyterian Christians. Today's sermon was about an important message: AOL treatment. It was one of the most controversial topics in the church. Few people spoke of it out of fear that they would be accused of being false Christians from the side that disagreed with them. Then, one Sunday, the pastor gave a sermon on that exact topic.

"It is a great question," Pastor Chandler said. "And a relevant one too. I have prayed with many of you in private as you navigate these strange waters of the new age, where men have created a holy grail and welcomed all to drink from its chalice. The question will never go away. And yet, because of this, I don't think the answer will change." The reverend turned the pages of the Trade Language Bible on the pulpit. "Paul teaches us in Colossians 3 that we are to set our minds on things that are above, not on things that are on earth." Chandler smiled. "No matter how much the Republic wants to win over our hearts, this new earth is not our new heaven. AOL is not our salvation in the same way that Robert Dain was not our savior. In time, we will learn that whatever extra years we are granted in this life pales in comparison to the joys that await beyond. Philippians 3:20-21 also reminds us that 'our citizenship is in heaven, and from it we await a Savior, the Lord Jesus Christ, who will transform our lowly body to be like his glorious body.'"

The reverend removed his spectacles and smiled at the congregation.

"Remember, dear friends, that AOL overpromises and underdelivers. Search your heart before considering treatment and remember too the good words from Ecclesiastes, that there is a time to be born, and a time to die. If you seek AOL to escape from death's clutches, remember that to die is to be born again. If you seek AOL to flee judgment, remember that Christ has done all the work on the cross for those who trust in him. If you seek AOL to bask in the pleasures of New Earth for longer than our mortal bodies permit, remember that even the greatest pleasures of New Earth pale in comparison to the glories of heaven. Amen."

The congregation responded. Dakari sat with a swelled heart. One arm rested over Zane's shoulder, the other lay around his wife. He looked at both of them.

"Amen."

They took communion, thanked the minister for the sermon, and then walked back to their hovercar in the fifty-story parking lot. They flew home. Dakari rested his hand over the steering wheel, his wife sitting in the shotgun seat in a white blouse with roses. Zane sat in the back seat, asleep. Sunlight shone through the windshield onto their rich copper skin as they watched the world from high above in Dain's air traffic highways. It was a snapshot of paradise, a memory in the making.

"You know," Dakari said. "I've been thinking."

"Dakari, please," Desta said. "Not now."

"Not now? What do you mean not now?"

"I'd rather not talk about this."

"You didn't even know what I was going to say."

"Yes I do. You know I do."

What is with her? Dakari thought. *Is it so wrong to want to save the people I love? Is it wrong to kick death's door down a few hundred years if we end up in the same place?* Those were all the things he wanted to say. But Desta had shut her mind away from those questions, either out of fear that she was wrong, or deep-rooted convictions that she was right and that he might never understand. He drove through the upper city, passing the hundreds of skyrises. He glanced down as he noticed they passed the street corner on Irkurian Drive. Two charred bodies lay on the side of the road. He flinched, blinked, and they were gone.

"Honey?" Desta asked. "Are you alright?"

Dakari didn't answer. He gripped the steering wheel and flowed through the air traffic. With a gentle tilt of the rear-view mirror, he saw Zane asleep, his head gently bobbing to the rumble of their wind-piercer.

The dream ended.

Dakari Minathi woke up in a world where Zane was no longer twelve, but sixteen, and a student at the Gerumandian Academy. Warm sunlight filtered into his bedroom. He lay next to Desta, who slept peacefully, her dark hair curving over her face like a veil. Not many signs of older age. If anything, her smooth round face had taken on the character of an empty nester: a woman who possessed love, wisdom, and a hint of melancholy from missing her only son. Her breath was steady and sound. Dakari stroked the side of her head and gave her a kiss on her forehead.

"Your breath stinks," she said, eyes closed.

Dakari smiled.

"And a good morning to you too." Dakari kicked his legs out over the bed and stood up. "I'll get the coffee."

Desta mumbled something that sounded like gratitude and rolled over in bed. Dakari left the room. He walked past Zane's empty bedroom, the door still half-open as he left it. Dakari looked down at his datapad and figured he was training right about now.

The sight and smell of hot coffee on the bedstand woke Desta up again. The warm mug sat next to Desta's leather-bound anthology of earth poetry and the Bible. Dakari started getting dressed in the bathroom and shaved. Desta sat up from bed and took the cup in both hands. Dakari walked back into the room as he brushed his teeth and saw Desta sitting in bed, drinking her coffee.

"You gonna be on time today?"

Desta shook her head.

"Weston gave me the day off. It's been a rough week."

"You're not one to call in sick."

"I'm not sick." She stretched out one arm and yawned. "Just tired."

Dakari spat the toothpaste into the sink and set his toothbrush aside.

"You're working too hard." Dakari slung his coat over his shoulders. "And taking on too many cases."

"I can't help it. Something's piqued my interest."

"Such as?"

"You really think I'm going to give away the biggest case in my career? Sorry, tiger. Not happening."

Dakari sat next to her on the bed. "Come on. You can tell me."

"I will when I'm ready." She looked out the window and set her coffee aside. "It's all just speculation right now. Besides. It might get me in trouble."

"It's that serious?" He paused. "And you don't trust me?"

"I'm worried you'll do some digging on your own. You know I'm right."

"It's not good to go minding other people's business."

"It is my business if it's in my department."

"Then that also makes it mine if my wife's the one conducting the investigation." Dakari leaned closer. "Please, Desta."

"Fine." She sighed. "I've been doing some asking around in my department...about Beretta."

Dakari set his coffee down.

"I told you I'd look into it, didn't I?"

"You did, but I couldn't help it. You wanna know the crazy thing? There are no records on her. Nothing at all."

Dakari froze, troubled that his worst nightmares were coming true.

"You're kidding, right?"

"No. I'm not."

Dakari's smile faded when he realized she wasn't.

"Please don't tell me that's why you called in sick."

"What else was I supposed to do? Do you know what this means?"

"It doesn't mean anything yet. Maybe the records were just transferred?"

"Where on New Earth would they be transferred to?" Desta crossed her arms. "And why are you suddenly so quick to defend them?"

"Because what you're suggesting could lead to treason."

"If there's corruption within our department, we have an obligation to expose it."

"And if we're wrong we could get court-martialed in the process. We need to think carefully about how we proceed with this. There's still no proof." Desta's eyes trailed away towards the crumpled bedsheets. "There's something else you're not telling me."

Desta sat up straight. "Let me ask you a question. Four years ago. Roy dies. Beretta is captured. Do you know what happened to her after her arrest?"

"She was sent to the detention center. I saw her go down."

"And then what?"

"She was transferred over to Eastern—to your department." Desta took another sip of coffee. "Are you saying that never happened?"

"I haven't said anything yet. I just find it strange how the EDAD has been restricting access to the detention centers and that there seem to be no files on Beretta Keys."

"They can't have those files accessible to everyone."

"I know. But still. When I started searching for information on Beretta, there was nothing on her. She killed the Commissioner of the CDAD. How could anyone forget her?"

"I'm sure they've just forgotten the name. It was four years ago."

"But you remember it."

"Because I caught her." Dakari rested her hand on Desta's as their diamond rings glittered in the window light. "I promise I'll look into it. Really, I do. But I'm concerned about you arousing suspicion from other arbitrators."

Desta removed her hand from Dakari's.

"I don't think it's that simple."

Dakari's eyes darkened.

"It might be." He looked at his datapad and stood up when he saw the time. "I have to go. Promise me you won't worry about this, alright? You need a day to yourself. Kick back. Relax. I might even grab us another bottle of wine on my way home."

"For what occasion?"

"Do I really need an occasion to celebrate the love of my life?"

Desta smiled sarcastically.

"Aww, you really *are* sentimental."

"Don't push it."

They kissed before he walked towards the door. "I'll see you when I get home." With those last words, he stared into his wife's eyes. She looked back at him and smiled, this one genuine, timeless. A thought occurred to him as he saw her sitting in bed with the glow of the window. He was the luckiest man in the world.

* * *

Gerumandian classrooms were shaped like miniature amphitheaters. An instructor in officer's garb spoke from the center of the room, facing five-hundred students in silver uniforms. Silver denoted the color of those in the arbitrator school, a subset of the Academy and one of the most prestigious in Dain. Zane sat a few rows away from stern-browed Officer Hackett, who pointed to an orbital projector hovering above him, its presentation visible to all students at every angle of the room. Blue alphanumerics raced across the screen as students feverishly took notes to keep pace. It was a compilation of footage from psychics from the Central Dain Arbitrator Department–the dream destination for arbitrators in training.

"There are three ways psychics use their abilities," Officer Hackett said.

"Transmission." A security camera showed a hooded boy shoot bullets out of a portal in his hands, killing several innocent civilians.

"Retraction." A young girl absorbed blaster fire from several arbitrators by opening a portal in her hands.

"Flow." A boy absorbed a grenade in a portal with one hand and shot it out a portal in his other hand, exploding an armored vehicle.

"They do this by creating tears: dimensional rifts in matter. We call this process eidolophoresis: the process of transmitting, retracting, and flowing phenomena from the phyofrenia into reality."

Hundreds of students typed notes. Hackett changed the slide to a model of a brain.

"This is the phyofrenia. That tiny golden light beneath the cerebral cortex. It's not very bright, but it burns in all of us ever so slightly. It burns the brightest in psychics. Researchers at the Cephei Institute of Modern Science have theorized that this is what allows psychics to use eidolophoresis. The problem of studying the phyofrenia is that it can't be seen in three dimensions. We can only see its effects. The glow you're seeing is not the phyofrenia, but evidence that such a thing exists. It's like there's a light inside your head, but no source. That makes it almost impossible to study." Hackett smiled. "If you've ever wondered why the AOL drug makes our eyes a little brighter, this is why."

The slide flickered and changed. On the globe-projector, a new image showed a child's eyes glowing like headlights.

"There are two truths that every cadet will have to face," Hackett continued. "Number One: arbitrators have been the victims of 90% of psychic murders in the past twenty years. Number Two: the psychics you are hunting are often children. Remember that psychics are just AOL humans gone wrong. All psychics identified by the Republic were at one point AOL standard and only became a psychic because of their breakthrough, a term we use to refer to the mutation an AOL human undergoes to become a psychic. This event is often triggered by traumatic situations, such as the loss of a loved one, family drama, a near-death situation. A psychic has almost no control of their actions during a breakthrough. That's what makes them dangerous."

Zane raised his hand.

"Yes, Zane?"

"If psychics can't control themselves during a breakthrough then are they really culpable for their actions?"

A few students gazed back at the instructor in puzzlement. Hackett straightened his posture and smiled. "Breakthroughs only occur once in a psychic's lifetime. They are the doorway into eidolophoresis. They cannot control the door the first time it opens, but they take full responsibility for every action after."

"And how many times has someone been murdered because of a breakthrough?"

"Excellent question." The projector changed and displayed a chart of all psychic murders within the last twenty years. "Breakthroughs only account for 2% of psychic murders. Most psychics kill because they are simply unable to adapt to civilized society. Rehabilitation centers are designed to help psychics understand and control their abilities. It's a Pandora's box that once it has been opened, unfortunately, can never be closed."

A video showed a young girl with blonde hair and blue eyes burning a man on the street.

"Should you make the mistake of pitying these creatures, recall our history. This was Commissioner Roy Andersen. He was murdered by an unidentified girl in 2131. She was just ten years old."

Zane stopped typing.

"What do you mean unidentified? That's Beretta Keys."

Students stopped typing. They stiffened in their seats and turned around slowly. They hadn't done that the last time Zane asked a question, but when he saw the look on Hackett's face he understood why. He hadn't raised his hand.

"Humor me, Mr. Minathi." Hackett began a slow walk up a few rows of desks, his hands folded behind his back. "Are you a guest lecturer?"

Zane lowered his head.

"No, sir."

"Were you giving a presentation?"

"No, sir."

"Were you spoken to?"

"No, sir."

Officer Hackett stopped beside Zane's desk.

"Then why did you speak?"

Each student had now completely turned around to face him. Zane clenched his fingers to stop them from shaking and looked away. Then looked up.

"Because that slide was wrong. Her name was Beretta Keys."

"That is compelling evidence." A few students chuckled. "Care to explain why you think you're more credible than the verdict of the Eastern Arbitrators?"

"Certainly." Zane stood up. "My father captured her when I was a little kid. He–"

"I was joking." Each student tensed in silence. "Sit."

"But my father captured her!"

Hackett's scowl hardened.

"Your seat or the door. Choose."

Zane kept a harsh stare at Hackett, then slowly sat back down.

"Wonderful." Hackett walked back towards the center of the room. "Another thing to remember about psychics." Hackett caught Zane's eye. "They're incredibly stubborn."

* * *

Fieldwork was always messy, but today's situation was particularly asking for trouble. Dakari Minathi reached for his blaster, then paused. *No glow yet*, he thought. *Can't draw a blaster until they use their powers.* He and several other white armored agents cornered a ten-year-old girl at the end of the trash-filled alleyway and stared at her through their chrome-black visors. She trembled beneath the shadows of skyscrapers as bypassing pedestrians caught a glimpse at the scene from behind the arbitrators.

"Hands up!"

The girl obeyed.

"Corporal Smith," Dakari said. "Detain her at once. There's an armored car on its way. Make sure she's ready to go."

"Of course, sir."

Dakari double-tapped the side of his helmet and accepted an incoming call.

It was from Kalak.

"Sir?"

"Change in plans. We need you at Main Street."

"We're still securing the suspect."

Dakari watched as Corporal Smith tightened his handcuffs around the girl's back.

"I didn't ask, Dakari."

"Leaving a psychic before detainment isn't exactly following protocol."

"Neither is disobeying orders."

Dakari's brow narrowed.

"On my way, sir." Dakari switched channels and connected back to his squadron. "Corporal. I've been ordered to go to Main Street. Keep her safe until the car arrives."

"But there's only two of us!"

"Orders are orders. An escort vehicle will arrive in three minutes."

Corporal Smith saluted.

"Very well. Good luck, sir."

Dakari ran over to his motorbike on the street corner. He gripped the handle and turned and sped until he was cruising past other vehicles past Irkrurian Drive, a street now riddled with bad omens. He flicked the red and blue emergency lights and sped through the opening in front of him, the sirens echoing across the city. Kalak's orders had been strange and sudden, but they were still orders.

He stopped the motorbike until he stood behind a barricade of armored cars on Main Street. Siren lights flashed. In the middle of the street, a boy stared into the hollow black barrels of fifteen blaster rifles. Street-side citizens recorded the scene with their datapads. Captain Amelia Lancaster stood behind the open door of her vehicle and raised the megaphone to her lips.

"Put your hands up! You're under arrest!"

The ten-year-old boy kept turning around in circles, his blue eyes shifting from one blaster barrel to the next. Captain Amelia kept her blaster rifle aimed at the target as Dakari stopped by her side. He drew his blaster too and aimed it at the psychic in the middle of the street.

"Captain," Dakari said. "What's the situation?"

"I thought you were after the sister."

"Plans changed. Kalak said you could use backup."

"Let's hope not. He tried to use some of his abilities earlier, but since then he hasn't shown any signs of resistance."

Captain Amelia raised the megaphone to her lips again.

"This is your last chance! Hands up! Down on your knees! You are under arrest!"

The boy fidgeted with his hands. A few citizens cried out in pity for the boy.

"He's only a child!"

"Leave him be!"

Dakari kept his blaster aimed with his finger over the trigger. The boy raised his hands to his head in submission. Captain Amelia double tapped her helmet.

"Cuff him up."

Several arbitrators stepped out from their vehicles and steadily approached the boy. With one shove they pinned him against the asphalt, whipped both hands behind his back, then strapped him in a pair of cuffs. They walked him back to one of the vehicles and slammed the door. Dakari holstered his rifle.

"That was too easy. Why was Kalak so insistent on getting me over here?"

"Beats me," Amelia said. "You know the Chief gets paranoid."

"You had fifteen arbitrators here. We only had three."

"Orders are orders."

Dakari watched the armored vehicle drive away.

"I guess." He walked back over to his motorbike and froze. It was another incoming call. "Corporal Smith. What's the situation?"

A light flashed in the rear-view mirror of Dakari's hoverbike; then a thundering explosion crackled in its wake. Each pedestrian on Main Street flinched and turned as Dakari's eyes widened in terror behind his visor. The wind snapped. Plumes of black and orange smoke rose from several blocks away. The Deputy's chest trembled as the sound of splintering cinderblock and the sudden crescendo of shattering glass coalesced into a single eruption. Screams rose as civilians scrambled away from the sight. Dakari, however, couldn't take his eyes off the rising fires. It wasn't because of the way the explosion caught him off guard. It wasn't because of the destruction it caused to the surrounding buildings. It wasn't even due to the street-shrieking terror it ensued in its flames. It was because he knew exactly where that explosion was coming from.

District 7 residential.

Perhaps from his own home.

Novel News

An orange sky bloomed outside the window, barely visible from Quan's apartment. The black-haired psychic lay on the floor and threw a rec back and forth in his hands, the bronze coin catching the faintest amount of light as it spun in the air. With each push and pull from a tear in each hand, Quan bounced the coin back and forth in a state of perpetual motion, amused by the trivial use of his abilities.

"And to think that we just need a couple million more of these. That's all it would take to leave this planet."

That's the dream, Quan thought. *To leave.* To find a planet and make it his own, free from school, parents, and arbitrators. Technically he was already free from two of those things. But the arbitrators had always been the biggest threat to him. Parents and school threatened his fun. Arbitrators threatened his life.

Alexander coded on his desktop with headphones on in the far corner of the living room. He was listening to heavy metal. Quan moved over to the couch with a notepad in his lap. He tapped his pencil against his head as he watched R-Sports highlights on the projector. There was a rerun of the top ten duels of the week. And like every week, the Hunt brothers somehow always managed to snag a spot in the top five. Matthew and Derek: the two hotshot duelers from the Gerumandian Academy. They were the sons of Carter Hunt, but each commentator fawned over them like they were their sons too.

"And that brings us to number four! Derek Hunt!"

Derek beat two opponents and ended up throwing one opponent into the other.

Alexander grabbed a soda from their mini-fridge and walked behind the couch.

"That guy's pretty good."

Quan gripped his pencil.

"He's alright."

A few other highlights were shown until the announcers introduced the last clip.

"And of course, to no one's surprise, we bring you number one! Matthew Hunt!"

Quan stopped tapping his pencil. He watched with dull eyes as Matthew proceeded to sweep his opponent from beneath his legs and land a blow in his chest. They showed a few more angles of other attacks against the student, then showed Matthew slashing the boy's back as he cowered in fear on the ground. Quan leaned forward.

"Wait a minute! This is Hell's Pit! How do you get number one by beating a Pit Dog in Hell's Pit!?"

Alexander opened his soda can with a crisp click, followed by bubbling carbonation.

"Don't know, don't care." He started chugging, then wiped his mouth on his sleeve.

"It's stupid. It's poor competition."

"And your competition is better? Tell me. Do you think Viper took a trip to the local pub before or after your fight? If I'm a betting man, I'd say he liquored up both times."

"That doesn't mean this Pit Dog was any better."

"If Matthew's that bad why don't you fight him yourself?"

"We're not in the same league."

"You got that right."

"Not like that. I meant that Matthew only fights other Gerumandians." He looked back at the screen. "Apparently Pit Dogs too."

"Then become a Gerumandian." Alexander spun his chair around and faced Quan. "Oh, wait. You have bad blood with that Academy."

"I have reasons."

"Stupid ones."

Quan changed the channels on the projector.

"You're more amusing with your headphones on."

Alexander spun his chair back around.

"I can't say I disagree."

Alexander resumed coding and his heavy metal playlist. Quan grabbed a soda can from their mini-fridge. He tossed the notepad aside and changed channels. *Explosion in District 7–Several Casualties.* Skip. *My Cyborg Mom–Season 5, Episode 2.* Skip. *How to get that silky smooth skin your man will love!* Quan almost made a joke to Alexander, then stopped. He was mad at him. He had to stay mad. Skip.

L-Transport Sponsors 32nd Gerumandian Dueling Tournament.

Grand prize: Sojourner.

Skip.

Quan's eyes widened.

"Wait a minute."

He went back and read that headline again, then jumped up from his seat.

* * *

"*That's* the grand prize?" Alexander asked.

They both leaned in closer as they read the report on their monitor.

"What do you mean *that's* the grand prize?!"

"Why on New Earth would they give something so valuable in a dueling tournament with teenagers!? There's gotta be a catch."

Alexander clicked on the link for more information and started reading.

"The Sojourner is an L-36 dynamic frigate with hyperspace capabilities. It's the first commercial starship with military-grade armament and a self-regenerating power core. It has five decks with a captain's cabin, command deck, crew's quarters, hangar, engineering facilities, as well as other luxurious accommodations like fitness rooms, an observatory, and cargo holds. Leonardo Transportation Industries is proud to announce the starship as the grand prize in the 32nd Gerumandian Dueling Tournament. Its market value is equivalent to…"

Quan and Alexander leaned closer.

"150 BILLION RECS?!"

They ran around the room like wild Waions, jumping over the couch, pounding on the glass. They kept shouting that number, then paused when reality settled back in.

"What are we doing?" Quan shouted. "Sign me up!"

They hurried back over to the computer and found the registration page.

"This couldn't have worked out any better."

"Yup," Alexander said. "All we gotta do is get you enrolled in the Gerumandian Academy."

Quan froze. That couldn't have been right.

"Wait…what?"

Alexander scooted away from his desk and pointed at the screen.

"They call it the *Gerumandian* Dueling Tournament for a reason."

"I thought that just meant it was sponsored by them!"

"Fought by them too. Gerumandians only. Glad you finally have a reason to go?"

Silence. It hurt to be wrong, but it was even more painful when you didn't have good reasons to stay stubborn. About a year ago, Quan vowed to himself that he would never go to the Gerumandian Academy. He didn't want to break that vow now.

"I still have to think about it."

"Think about it?!" Alexander stood up and faced Quan. "What exactly is there to think about? They're offering a starship!"

"But it would mean–"

"Yes, going to the most prestigious military Academy in Dain, I know." Alexander studied Quan's expression. "But you're serious right now, aren't you? You would throw away our best chance at leaving for some stupid grudge you have with your brother."

"I didn't say that."

"So, I can send your application then?" Alexander crossed his arms when he saw that Quan was not going to respond. "You're nothing but talk–always have been. You say you could beat Matthew, but you won't even apply to the Academy. If you can't even do that what makes you think you could last any longer than that Pit Dog Matthew skewered on TV today?!"

"This isn't about Matthew."

"No. It's about you. You're afraid to lose."

"And I guess there's nothing wrong with you."

"No, I have many flaws, but I'm in control of them. You, my friend, are…soft. Like a coddled, spoiled, child. You've created this bubble where you always win and never lose. And the one time you did lose, you ran away. You're still running away."

"You did too."

"We had different reasons."

"And what were those?"

"Simple," Alexander said. "It sounded fun."

"Fun?"

"You kidding me? No school, no parents, no responsibilities?" Alexander sat back down and kicked his feet up on the desk with both hands behind his head. "And best of all, we're making more money than ever! I'm doing my part–you do yours."

Quan wanted to hurl Alexander across the room. He wanted to grab him by the neck and shove him into the couch. But instead, he walked over and towered over him.

"You're just a pathetic, scrawny, good-for-nothing nerd with a mouth bigger than your brain. You have no *idea* what you're talking about!"

Alexander looked unphased, his sly smile begging him to continue. Upon seeing this, Quan's anger reached a boiling point, but instead of saying anything, he walked away. "I'm going for a walk." He slammed the door and didn't look back.

* * *

Zane gazed out the sunlit window of his dorm. Mom still hadn't called. This had happened before. Sometimes her schedule changed at Eastern. Sometimes they needed to call her in the event of an emergency. But that couldn't have happened today. Chief Weston had given her the day off. There were plenty of other arbitrators on call. *So why hadn't she called?*

Fifteen minutes passed. Then thirty. He figured that maybe Chief Weston had changed his mind. Plus, Mom knew he was busy with finals anyway, so she was probably just giving him more time to focus on school. He went back to studying and figured he would call her next week.

A Load of Laundry

Boxing was like therapy. In an empty, dark training room at the Geru-mandian Academy, Matthew Hunt hammered his fists into a punching bag. Sweat flew from his body in the darkness with each lunge, his coiled hands colliding into the sand-filled bag with thundering force. No punch went untargeted. With each blow, he aimed at the familial pressures passed down from his father to him. There were no lights down here. He wore no headphones to drown the sounds of his heavy breathing, the dripping of sweat on the floorboards, or the rattling chain. Instead, he heard voices, as if they were coming out of a tunnel. He heard millions of people shouting his name. And he loved it.

And with each successive punch, the ripe memories of Hell's Pit returned to him, each lunge another blow into the young boy's back. Some people would hate him for it, but some people would always hate him, so Matthew never cared to win over the people he could never please. Another thunderous blow into the leather, the sweat splattering off his coiled fist. *What was so bad about it? The boy didn't die. A few scars never hurt anybody.* A bit of pain always made a body stronger.

A few more punches, his knuckles bruised and bloody from each blow. The bag was winning. But it couldn't win, so Matthew took a new angle. He gave that old leather bag a roundhouse kick in its center. That wasn't enough, so he leaned back, hit its pressure points, then jabbed left, right, center. He saw himself standing in the center of Cypher Stadium with confetti firing in the air. They shouted that timeless name of his. They would remember it. That sound started to grow louder and louder until he realized that someone was actually calling him.

The lights turned on.

It was his younger brother: Derek Hunt.

"Matthew!"

Matthew squinted and raised his forearm to see his brother standing in the open doorway. Sweat dripped from the tips of his sandy blonde hair. He stared at his younger brother with menacing green eyes, his muscular body glistening under the harsh lights of the room. Matthew was an inch taller, but both the Hunt brothers had broad shoulders and a muscular build. Their skin had a deep golden tan. No acne, no blemishes, no moles. They were like super soldiers. And at the tip of their spines, a dark green tattoo of an Ouroboros: a snake with a tail in its mouth. It was the family sigil, a permanent reminder of their shared identity.

"I've been calling you for the last five minutes," Derek said.

Matthew raised his left arm and double-tapped his datapad.

"I was busy."

"Tell that to the Boss."

Derek stormed out of the room.

Matthew ran both hands through his hair and punched the bag one last time.

* * *

Back in his dorm, Matthew plugged both headphones into his datapad.

"Are you awake?" Matthew asked.

"I never sleep. You're late."

"Sorry, sir. I was training."

"Sorry isn't good enough. We're on the clock."

"I know. What is it?"

"Nothing unusual. There are reports of potential psychic activity in Section A of the Academy. Could be a prank, but better to be safe than sorry."

"I'll check it out. Do you have a name?"

"Alan Jones."

"Room number?"

"Section A, room 375."

Matthew entered the name into his datapad.

"I'll look into it."

"Do it tonight."

"Tonight?"

"Did I stutter, Matthew?"

"N-no, sir–it's just–"

"Yes, you're going to have to get him faster than usual. We think a few arbitrators might investigate this case soon if word keeps spreading around the Academy. We're not going to let the state snatch another psychic out of our hands. If he tests positive, dial back this number, and bring him downtown tonight. There will be two men in a white van waiting in the alley by Pick Up Center A. They'll handle the rest."

"Understood, sir."

"Good."

Matthew hung up, then ripped the headphones out of his ears. He suited up in a navy-blue laundry uniform. He put on his cap and then called his younger brother.

"Hello?"

"Derek. Section A, room 375, five minutes. Bring Bruce with you…" Matthew looked at a laundry bag in the far corner of his room. "And some handcuffs. We got some laundry to do."

* * *

Three students in navy blue laundry uniforms pushed a white laundry cart down a beige residential hall of the Gerumandian Academy. In the late hours of 2 am, nobody would be wandering around with mandatory morning workouts the next day. That made it the perfect time for a laundry run. The rusty wheels of the cart stopped outside room 375. Derek set a handheld slickspawn sound incubator on the floor, casting a blue holographic barrier around them to prevent any sound from traveling down the hall.

"Test it," Matthew said.

"This never gets old." Derek connected his datapad to a speaker and pressed play. A random pop song blasted from a speaker beneath the cart. They let the song play for about thirty seconds. No one came out of their dorms, so Derek shut it off.

"Promise me you'll choose a different song," Matthew said, then pinned a five-millimeter kintrubon device against the wall. "Stand outside for visibility test."

Derek walked through the holographic barrier and looked back at the cart. From his perspective, Matthew, Bruce, and the laundry cart had disappeared.

"Everything checks out," Derek said, stepping back inside.

"Good."

Matthew looked at Bruce, who gave a thumbs-up, then knelt down. He pressed both palms flat against the door, took a deep breath, and closed his eyes. A flash of electricity jerked through his fingers, spreading a vibrating mass of energy around the door. It spread as slow as molasses. Then it started to glow bright blue. Bruce kept his breath steady as the substance completely enveloped the door.

"Ready?" Bruce asked.

"Ready."

He snapped his fingers.

The door glowed like a supernova and then split into millions of tiny particles so they could see inside. In the room, a male student was manipulating the particles of a chair, struggling to balance it as his body leaned from side to side. With the sound of the translucent door, Alan's roommate, Tony, sprung up from bed and scratched his eyes.

"What's going on?"

Bruce snapped his fingers. Tony's eyelids shut as he fell back on the bed, knocked out cold. Alan relinquished his telekinetic grasp on the chair. It fell with a thud.

Matthew stepped inside the room, meeting Alan Jones with a menacing stare. The young auburn-haired boy froze as if he knew his time in hiding had run out. Matthew met his frightened gaze with a long scowl.

"Bag him up."

Alan raised his clenched fist, sending the chair flying across the room. Matthew created a quick tear in one hand and shot a gust of wind in Alan's direction, reversing the kinetic energy of the chair back so it slammed the boy in the chest. In desperation, Alan shot fire out of two portals in his hands. Derek crossed his arms like an **X** and deflected the flames off a gold energy shield vibrating around his body. The flames flew to Alan's bed. Matthew grabbed Alan and flipped him over on the ground.

"Bruce! Put it out! Quick!"

Bruce raised both hands above the burning bed and shot out water from two portals, extinguishing the flames. Matthew pinned the psychic to the ground as he squirmed and struggled. Derek cuffed Alan, hoisted his head up, and strapped a wad of duct tape over his mouth, muffling his screams.

"Give him the stim!" Matthew shouted, trying to keep Alan pinned as Derek grabbed a needle from his utility belt. Shaking and sweating, Derek punctured the needle through the back of Alan's neck. The caught psychic screamed under the duct tape until the stim entered his bloodstream, dilating his pupils and knocking him out cold. Matthew placed two fingers under his neck.

"Pulse is good. Get the scanner."

Derek reached into his utility belt and gave Matthew something that looked like a thermometer with a light. He flashed it over the boy's forehead as Derek's eyes read the information being transmitted to his scanner. It highlighted Alan's brain activity as the green light scanned him several times. Matthew's heart raced. Sweat drenched from his brow as he waited for Derek's evaluation. Matthew wasn't a praying man, but every time they conducted a scan, he prayed it wasn't a stage 4 psychic.

"Stage 2 psychic," Derek said.

Matthew sighed with relief.

"Good. Let's bag him up."

They stuffed Alan Jones beneath a pile of laundry at the bottom of the cart.

Matthew put his earbuds in and made the call.

"Are you awake?"

The Boss answered.

"I never sleep."

"Good. He was a stage 2 psychic. No signs of cartography. No one was hurt but his bed was burned, and a chair was broken. We need a cleanup crew."

"A group is on their way." Matthew turned down the hall and saw two arbitrators walk out of the elevator. "They'll take care of your equipment. Go to Pick Up Center A immediately. A white van is waiting for you."

Both arbitrators entered the soundproofed visibility field as soon as the laundry crew left in the opposite direction. Matthew led Bruce and Derek to the elevator, rolling the laundry cart down the silent halls of the Academy. No one paid any attention to them. Not the students, legitimate state arbitrators, or even the automatons in the laundry rooms. They snuck out the back door without a fuss. A white van was waiting for them in the alleyway outside.

A few men in laundry suits opened the back door and walked up to the drop-off. The lead man tugged down on his hat. Matthew responded by doing the same.

"Thank you, gentlemen," he said. "That will be all."

The men stuffed the body bag in the back of the van and slammed the door. Matthew, Derek, and Bruce rolled their cart back inside and stowed it back with the others after making sure all their items were removed. Then the three boys went back to their rooms, locked their doors, and went to sleep.

A Reluctant Resignation

Rays of early morning sunlight pierced a narrow slit between the window curtains, waking Dakari from a night of sleepless angst. Remnants of last night's depression littered the room: empty beer cans and the faint, sour stench of burnt lizolai. Dakari's eyelids were heavy, and his limbs were weak. His hand slid beneath the sheets to the other side of the bed, reaching for a figure to hold. They found no such solace. Upon realizing this the forces weighing down on his eyelids lessened. Then his eyes widened with a dim horror, closing with resignation as if there was no reason to ever open them because there was nothing good in this world to look upon. And then the untouched memories of yesterday returned to him like a horror reel.

It had taken hours to fall asleep, and when he did, it was never more than a few minutes at most. He would spring up from the bed reaching out to rescue his wife from the flames. He felt like he was suffering the repercussions of forty hangovers. Nothing seemed real. And nothing looked good. It was all darkness. And each time he heard a distant siren in the city he thought of his own sirens that were turned on too late to save his wife. And as the night went on, his thoughts worsened. And the sound of the air conditioner grew more pronounced. And the ticking clock ticked. And the commotion of the city became louder. And the light of his wedding ring reflected the morning sunlight brighter. And the memories of weddings and parties and breakfasts and dinners and dates became foreign things to him. And suddenly "Sweet Darling" was a song he never knew. Or one that was filled with sadness. Nothing looked good at 4 am.

Nothing at all.

And worst of all: he hadn't even told Zane.

Yesterday's explosion had destroyed his apartment, forcing him to stay in a hotel until he arranged for a new place of residence. That building, along with its memories, had erupted in plumes of smoke. And though the hotel room was smaller, it felt hauntingly empty. There were extra spaces everywhere. An extra space in the bed. An extra space in the bathroom to brush his teeth. One less cup of coffee to make. One less omelet to make for breakfast. And yet Dakari still found himself reaching out for his wife's shoulder, stepping around spaces in the bathroom where she would normally stand, brewing two cups of coffee, making two omelets instead of one.

There was a silence in all these things that grew the most pronounced when Dakari sat down at the table in the kitchen. He looked across where Desta would normally sit. There was no one there, nothing but an empty white, high-backed chair in her stead. Dakari's hands trembled as he raised his fork to his mouth, then let it drop from his hand. A river of tears rushed to his eyes as he clenched his fists and pressed them against his lips. He kissed his wedding ring. He kissed it again.

Back in his Academy days, the Gerumandians had taught Dakari the necessity of suppressing strong emotions. There was no need for them. Despair was like the fog of war. It could come from anywhere and bury a soldier in obscurity. A Gerumandian that could not face this fog was no true Gerumandian. The great irony of it all was that he had attended that lecture with Desta sitting next to him. He could still feel her soft hand as he slipped her a note in class. And see her smile. Beautiful memories became terrible with violent emotions.

Death was always a terrible thing. It was the senseless, amorphous, faceless force that sucked all good things from a world of life and beautiful things. But with Desta's passing, it became something else. A monstrosity. An obstruction. An error in the cosmos. Its message was a phrase: *this is not the way things should be.* An ocean of unanswered questions swam in the growing darkness of Dakari's thoughts.

No, he thought. *Not another moment longer.* He couldn't let his mind drift to things that would sharpen his pain. He needed to sever them from the source. Dakari shoved his plate of food away and stood up. He grabbed his arbitrator uniform and walked out the door. There was one thing he had to do.

* * *

"I see," Kalak said. "And you've made your decision?"

Deputy Minathi sat on the other end of the Chief's desk. He looked down at the floor with his hat in his hands. There was a gaping hole in his heart. It perpetually took his breath away. Half his mind saw the Chief sitting across from him with his black and grey beard. And then the other half of his mind stood speechless in front of a mound of rubble by the sidewalk. He could still remember the smell of smoke.

"Deputy?"

Dakari blinked back into awareness.

"Sir?"

"You were mentioning your resignation. You asked me for my thoughts." Kalak stood up and looked out the window behind his office. He watched hundreds of investigators carrying out their business on the main floor. And the scaffold in the center of it all. "I wouldn't blame you. Not after what you've been through."

Half of Dakari's mind drifted away again. Yesterday's events replayed in his mind. Back in the remains of his apartment in District 7, Dakari stepped towards the rubble with bated breath, treading across shards of glass that cracked beneath his black boots. And in between the sounds of sirens and distant footsteps, he heard the shaky breath of a woman behind the layers of smoke.

"Arbitrators in this department often prepare themselves for death," Kalak said. "We sign up for these jobs risking our lives. But rarely do we have to prepare for the deaths of others."

Dakari could never understand why he thought of Desta in a wedding dress when he saw her for the last time. It was as if the smoke curved around her face in a veil. And then the way her dark hair blew over her emerald, green eyes.

"Your absence would certainly be felt. But no one is forcing you to stay."

Dakari fell to his knees and collapsed by her side. He held her close to his chest and cried out for an ambulance. None of the arbitrators ever forgot that sight. Everyone at the CDAD had strongholds they made to shield them from trauma. But in the face of his wife, Dakari's strongholds shattered like glass. All his Academy training–gone. And then came the sobs when Dakari realized that Desta had stopped breathing–when he realized that the woman whose eyes had looked so lovingly into his had lost their ability to see. Fading with emptiness. That the mother of his only child, whose voice had sung him lullabies, could never sing again. He held her close and treasured the last moments of warmth. Dakari remembered singing to her as they rested among the rubble: "That Heaven's gates, don't lead to home..." He clenched her tighter. He waited for her to finish the line, but she never would. Her soul had ascended to the skies like the smoke that surrounded them. He felt like no true Gerumandian. He felt like a man who had lost his wife. Nothing more.

"Of course, if you were to leave, there would be no coming back."

The memory had ended.

Dakari looked down at his wife's wedding ring that hung over his neck.

"I know," Dakari said. He stood up. "I'll hand over my files to Amelia."

Kalak smiled, turned around, and extended a hand to Dakari. That couldn't have been right. *A smile?* Dakari thought. *No.* His grief was getting to his head.

"It's been a pleasure working with you, Dakari. I wish you the best of luck."

Dakari's heart beat out of his chest. He paused, then shook Kalak's hand. "Thank you, sir."

Dakari wasn't in the mood to say goodbye. He walked quietly down the halls of the Central Dain Arbitrator Department and stepped into his office. Amelia stood behind his desk with a folder of papers.

"Have you made your decision?" She asked.

Dakari nodded. "I have. I wasn't aware you already had my forms."

Amelia looked away.

"These aren't your papers." She flipped through each file, one by one. "But they might change your mind about handing those other ones in."

Dakari raised a brow.

"What are you saying?" Amelia's blue eyes glanced at the door, which Dakari gently closed. He walked over to the desk, but Amelia held the folder closer to her chest. "Amelia, what's going on?"

"If I show you this, you can't tell a soul. It might cost us our jobs."

"I'm not planning on sticking around."

Amelia set the folder on the desk.

"You might after you see this."

Dakari cautiously looked at Amelia, then opened the folder.

* * *

In the prism-shaped cafeteria at the Gerumandian, Zane Minathi sat alone. Students waited in long lines curving along the marble white room and took their trays to their tables. Zane kept checking the time on his datapad. 12:11. She was 11 minutes late. He started eating and waited in silence, occasionally listening to two students debate the nature of psychics at the other end of the table.

"My pastor said they're demon-possessed. He said it's God's way of cursing humanity for trying to mess with immortality."

"That's not what my pastor said. He told us that the AOL drug represents the kingdom of God being fully realized, which made Robert Dain the second coming of Christ."

"What about Vrin?"

"He was the anti-Christ."

"But he's still alive."

"He is?"

"Yeah. He was sentenced to an underground cell for the rest of his life."

"Wait. I got it mixed up. My pastor said that Dain *and* Vrin are both Christ."

"I hate to break it to ya, but your pastor's a heretic."

Before Zane could chime in to give his thoughts, he saw Mirabelle, dressed in her white and blue flight uniform, walking to the table with a tray of soup.

"Well, well. If it isn't Mirabelle Marshall," Zane said. He took a sip from his gallon water canister and let out a sigh as the auburn-haired flight student took her seat across from him. She smiled.

"You didn't double-tap."

"What?"

Mirabelle took a sip of her water glass and tapped it twice on the table.

"Take it to the dome."

Zane groaned in remembrance and eyed the gallon canister with resignation.

"Come on…please don't make me do this. You were late!"

"But this was your game. You started this."

"But you were late."

Mirabelle looked at the canister again and started laughing. It was monstrously large as if Zane thought that his walk to class would be a marathon in the deserts of Darisin.

"That canister could feed a family of five."

"Or one *very* thirsty boy."

"Stop wasting time and chug."

Several other students around the table overheard the crime and turned Zane's way. With the eyes of Table 47 watching him, Zane ceremoniously stood up and raised the canister in the air.

"Ladies and gentlemen! I have committed a great crime! And now I will pay the price!" The canister crisply clicked open as Zane flicked the lid and raised it above his head.

Several other students started pounding their fists and chanting: "Chug! Chug! Chug! Chug!" Then other students from other tables turned around and shouted: "Take it to the dome! Take it to the dome!" And soon enough, a crowd was watching Zane. He kept his eyes on Mirabelle as he kept chugging and swallowing a gallon of water. She tried to hold her laughter and looked away in defeat as Zane finished the canister and flipped it to the side over the table. Not a drop left its lid. The crowd cheered as Zane bowed, then returned to their meals like nothing ever happened.

"Thank you, thank you, everyone. You're too kind."

"Impressive," Mirabelle said.

"Don't flatter me. I'll have my revenge."

"And I'll eagerly be waiting for it."

They both smiled, then resumed their meal in silence. After finishing their food, they pushed their trays across from one another. Zane slid a toothpick between his lips.

"You finish your finals?"

"Yeah," Mirabelle said. "You?"

"Almost. I got a group project due tomorrow."

"You started?"

"Not yet. It's with Dr. Lekovar so it should be fine. Plus, I talked with my partner yesterday and he sounds smart."

"Who is he?"

"Does Alan Jones ring a bell?"

"Not at all."

"Eh, doesn't matter. I figured he got a head start so I'll swing by his dorm tonight."

"Sounds fun." Mirabelle took a sip of water and set it back down.

"Does it though? And take it to the dome. You didn't double-tap."

Mirabelle groaned. "Stupid game." She finished the rest.

"That was quick," Zane said, then looked away and tapped the table. "I have a question."

"Shoot."

Zane kept averting his gaze from her.

"There's a rumor going around the Academy. About you. About Derek. About what he said to you. Why you punched him."

Mirabelle raised the glass to her lips, but it was empty. She set it back down.

"You want to know if it's true?"

"I want to know what he said. Gossip has a way of stretching what was said."

Mirabelle looked at Zane, their eyes finally meeting.

"I want to know what they're saying first."

Zane sighed. No backing out now.

"They...they said you were born out of incest. And that the reason you don't date anyone is that you're in love with your brother."

"I don't have a brother!"

"I know that! You only asked for what they said. I'm telling you."

Mirabelle pinched the bridge of her nose in frustration. She could care less about what "they" said about her, whoever they were. But Zane. She cared about what he thought of her more than she liked to admit.

"That's not exactly what he said."

"Then what, *exactly*, did he say?"

Mirabelle's eyes drifted to other tables. A few people met her gaze, snickering, smiling, then whispering to their friends. If social status was a game, she had lost a thousand times over, but a rumor spread by a Hunt brother would not die easily. Some students felt ashamed if their eyes met, looking away the second a connection was struck to forget that it happened at all. But Zane still sat with her. And he returned her gaze.

"I'd rather not talk about it." Zane nodded. "Not here. Not now."

He lifted his head up.

"When?"

Mirabelle smiled.

"Tell you what. Forget these people. Movie night. My place. Tonight." Then her smile started to wane. "Wait...I forgot about your project."

"Forget the project. It'll be done before 7:00."

"That won't be enough time."

"It will be for me."

"What if you need to double-check your answers?"

"I'll get it right the first time."

"And what if you don't?"

"Mirabelle. I don't care about a stupid project." Their eyes met again. And Zane's hand rested across the table where Mirabelle's could have been had she not pulled it back by her side. There was something he wanted to say, but he didn't say it. So he said the next best thing that was closest to the truth. "I will be there at seven. Mark my words."

"Marked." She paused. "I'll see you then."

They went their separate ways. Neither of them could stop smiling.

* * *

"I don't believe it," Dakari said. He stood over his desk and examined the layouts again. The papers were standard routes CDAD vehicles used in emergency situations. He compared the two routes side by side. One showed the recommended route to get a vehicle from District 7 to the CDAD Headquarters. The other showed the route that Corporal Smith took the day he was blown to smithereens outside the Minathi apartment complex. "This doesn't make any sense."

"I drove both routes myself," Amelia said, tracing her finger along the page. "These estimates are accurate. The standard route is approximately three miles. The route that Smith took was 3.5. He took a two-minute detour while in possession of a dangerous psychic." Amelia paused. "Only he never made it back."

"What about blockades?"

"They were only used on Main Street." Amelia pointed back to the standard route, the one that would have avoided his apartment. "This route was open."

Dakari collapsed back on his chair. He didn't know whether to feel angry or confused. "Why would you look into something like this?"

"Something didn't seem right after you mentioned Kalak calling you away so abruptly. And then there was the official investigation. They reported that the cause of the explosion was a breakthrough. Of course, that's all speculation, seeing that every arbitrator who interacted with that

91

psychic died in the crash." Amelia paused. "Did that psychic create any tears before you kidnapped her?"

Dakari rubbed his fingers together, looking away.

"I don't think so. I'd have to look at my body cams."

"But they were recalled."

Dakari clenched the wedding ring that hung over his neck.

"What exactly are you implying, Amelia?"

Amelia turned around before opening the door to leave.

"Reconsider your resignation. There's one more investigation I might need your help with." Amelia opened the door. "I'll see you around, Deputy." She left the room.

Dakari froze as he stared at the papers. He closed his eyes, his hands trembling as a red rage erupted inside of him. He wanted to find Corporal Smith and gun him down, but he was already dead. He wanted to go back in time and shoot the psychic that caused the eruption at his home, but she was dead too. With no target for his vengeance, the rage inside of him intensified. Unless he was wrong. Unless there was a puppet master behind the scenes. Unless Desta's findings were more than what Dakari believed them to be. Then Amelia would be right. There was one more investigation, one stone left unturned. With that thought, Dakari grabbed his resignation papers. He stared at them and recalled his wife's encouragement to stay. He thought of the way they danced, the way they talked, and then the abrupt way she had died.

Dakari stood up and ripped the resignation papers into shreds.

Late Night Lingering

The Odyssey wasn't the most prestigious nightclub in District 7, but it was certainly the most affordable, and one with scanners that couldn't detect the encryption in Quan's fake ID. From the outside, the street side bar was a glimmering spectacle of flashing neon lights against a dead merchant's strip a few blocks from Main Street. A line of jacket-covered pedestrians wound around the street corner as the bouncer scanned their datapads. A heart-pounding bass rumbled in Quan's chest as he was admitted entry, his underage eyes devouring the sight of disco lights, crowds of dancers, and loud gatherings in booths surrounding the circular walls of the establishment. A marble ebony bar with crisp white overhead lights looked out onto the dance floor. An automaton served drinks, several people danced among the interchanging neon lights, and private booths housed couples, businessmen, and university students passing the time. Most people, however, just sat there scrolling themselves to death on their datapads. Their heads were so accustomed to the downward arch that it felt strange to do anything otherwise. Quan found himself doing the same thing, instinctually, then stopped. He ordered a gin and tonic and found an empty booth to pass the time.

Sometimes he started to go insane being cooped up in that apartment with Alexander. They were buddies from tier school, but that didn't mean they were immune to cabin fever. Alexander made a living pushing buttons on machines but made enemies by pushing people's buttons. That made Quan angrier than anything else. He didn't need anyone to tell him what to do with his feelings. They were his feelings after all.

With distant conversations echoing in his ears, Quan sat in his raincoat in an empty booth. He sipped on his drink and watched. A husband danced with his wife. A girl entertained advances from a man at the bar. Two businessmen shook hands and left their booth to go their separate ways. Behind their personalities, behind their exterior presentation, there was something that Quan could see about these people that they couldn't see in themselves. There was a faint golden light in the center of their brain. Sometimes when Quan looked at a person, he saw this light, as if he had x-ray vision. He saw it for a second and not a second longer. It burned brighter in some people than others. But in some people, it bloomed like a flower.

It bloomed the brightest in psychics.

He stared at the dim reflection of his pale face. He blinked twice and saw it: a bright golden glow behind his eyes, floating gracefully like a flower in the center of his brain. He felt disembodied, detached, and suspended. Light from the world around him grew dark except for the light in his brain. Then he blinked again, and it was gone.

Someone broke him out of that trance.

"Thought I'd find you here," Alexander said, sliding into his booth. He sat across from him with a smile. "You were trying to find other psychics, weren't you?"

Quan looked away.

"You can't go one night without letting me do something on my own, can you?"

Alexander typed in an order of drinks into his datapad.

"You think I'm here because of you?" An automaton whirred over to their booth and delivered Alexander a beer. "Some people just go to clubs to drink." Alexander raised his glass. "Cheers to us. Because we're awesome."

Quan kept his hands folded on the table and scowled.

"How did you find me here?"

Alexander smiled like a schoolboy who had been caught stealing. "I added a tracking device to your datapad."

"I want you gone."

"Gone? I just got here!"

"Not out of the bar..." Quan leaned close to Alexander. "Out of my life!"
Alexander set his beer down.

"That, my friend, would be your biggest mistake yet. You need me. I
need you. It's mutual. And calm down." Alexander's face went pale. "Your
eyes are starting to glow."

Quan's heart skipped a beat. He stared at the glass on his datapad. Sure
enough, parts of his eyes were glimmering blue. He buried his face in his
hands and leaned over the table, hiding his face from view. He waited a
few moments, then looked up.

"Better?" Quan asked.

"Better." Alexander slid his glass across the table. "Drink."

Quan nodded. He chugged a few gulps of beer then slid the drink back.
He didn't even realize he had already finished his gin and tonic before
Alexander arrived.

"What am I gonna do?"

"I mean, I can always remove the GPS."

"I'm not talking about the GPS! I'm talking about our ticket off this
planet." He looked around the bar. "Someone could've seen me and that
would've been the end of it. I'm tired of hiding. I'm tired of running. I'm a
loser."

"You don't have to be. And luckily for us, you have a way out. Join the
Academy. Win the tournament. Get the ship."

"But what if there's another way?"

"Why would you need another way? The Gerumandian Tournament is
eight months away. Unless you can think of a way to get another starship
of that caliber in eight months, I'm all ears. But even my best ransomware
couldn't make a million in that span of time. There's no question. You
enroll at the Academy."

"And what if I see Jon?"

"You could always just kick him in the balls?"

Quan shrugged.

"I guess so."

"See? You're less of a loser already."

"But…"

"No buts. You apply. You commit. You decide."

"People aren't computers, Alexander."

"Tell me about it. Computers are way better. Less emotions, more obedience, twice the fun."

"You're still not tracking. Back in Silverside, wasn't there anyone you hated? Someone you couldn't stand being around?"

"I'd like to think that I'm perfectly ambivalent towards everyone and everything."

"That's not true. You hated Olivia Chandra."

"Because she was annoying!"

"Or because she beat you in the regional robotics competition. Now imagine if I asked you to work with Miss Chandra on some new project."

"No."

"See? You're more human than you think."

"Fair, but if working with her was the choice between staying on this planet and leaving it, I'd be her best friend. And you're telling me you're not willing to go to the Academy because of a stupid grudge with your brother?"

Quan looked down at his wristband. Engraved on the rubber material of the band was a simple message: *Never Give Up.* "We made a promise to each other that the day we decided to go the Academy, we'd go together."

"I've said it a million times and I'll say it again." Alexander took another sip of beer. "That's a stupid reason."

Quan pinched the edge of the rubber band and flicked it back onto his skin.

"You don't get it. It wasn't just that he left without me. It's where he left me." Quan unrolled his sleeve back down over his arm. "Home wasn't exactly great."

Alexander coiled his fists and stood up.

"Then don't let your stupid brother hold you back from doing what you've always wanted to do! Jon's ruined your life enough. Don't let him ruin it anymore."

"And what if I see him there?"

Alexander smiled.

"Then kick him in the balls."

Quan and Alexander stubbornly glared at each other like two drill sergeants in a staring contest. Then they smirked and erupted into laughter. They were too high off their dreams to hold any grudges. They walked home side by side. Alexander hummed a tune and gave his number to several ladies walking towards the club. Quan steered him away and led him towards the apartment. He looked at the city lights above him. There was no going back now. He was going to the Gerumandian Academy.

Absent Alan

Later that evening, Zane hummed a tune under his breath and walked at a jovial pace to room 375 in Section A of the Gerumandian Academy. Zane was always throwing projects like this together last minute. The difference between himself and other procrastinators was that he was good at it. He used what he liked to refer to as his "innate genius" and got an A when he had only worked a quarter of the time other students put into their projects. He'd have to work extra hard tonight though if he was going to have time for "Movies with Mirabelle." He had a statistical analysis of crime-ridden districts in Dain due at 8 a.m. tomorrow morning.

"Let's hope Alan's already started," Zane said, then knocked.

A guy with frizzy black hair and bags under his eyes opened the door. He yawned.

"Can I help you?"

"Yeah. Is Alan here? We have a group project due tomorrow."

"Alan?"

"Uh, yeah. Your roommate?" He paused. "You're 'Sleepy Tony' right?"

"Is that what they call me?"

"Sorry. I didn't–"

"Ah, no. It's fine. I just get tired in class sometimes."

An awkward moment of silence passed.

"Right. But back to Alan. Is he here?"

"I don't know who you're talking about. I don't have a roommate."

Zane raised a brow, this time unable to hold back a weak laugh.

"Funny. Can you just let me in, please? We seriously have to get started."

Tony stepped aside.

"Be my guest."

Tony shut the door, letting him into a room that smelled of sweat and smoke. Zane realized he wasn't kidding around. There was only one bed, one desk, and one drawer in a room that was supposed to fit furniture for two students. It was as if Alan's things had been taken away.

"You're serious, aren't you?" Zane asked. "You've never had a roommate?"

Tony rolled around in his bed and said: "Yeah man...gotta sleep."

Zane double-checked his datapad. Section A, room 375. This was the one.

"Thanks anyway, Tony. I'll see myself out."

Tony waved as Zane shut the door. The most likely scenario was that he had gotten the wrong number. He didn't blame his own memory. He liked to think he had the mind of a sponge; like his Dad. He thought it would come in handy when he was serving on the arbitrator force, so like any arbitrator, he conducted his own investigation on the case of the mysterious room number. He knocked on every door in the hall and was met with an array of similar responses.

"Alan?"

"Never heard of him."

"No Jones I know of on this hall."

"Leave me alone."

The last door slammed in Zane's face. He took the elevator down to the first floor and walked into student services. There were white marble floors, beige walls, a few leather chairs in the lobby, and sealed wooden doors on the offices of the Academy psychiatrists and counselors.

"Can I help you?" A woman asked.

"Yes," Zane said, leaning against the front desk. "Can you give me the room number for Alan Jones? We have a group project, but I think he gave me the wrong room number."

"You didn't just try texting him first?"

"I don't have his number."

"When's the project due?"

"Tomorrow."

"Sounds like you're off to a great start."

"Yeah, yeah. Can you just look him up for me? We need to get started."

"Don't any of your friends have his number?"

"No. None of us know him. We have a project due on–"

"I gotcha, sweetie. Just gimme a second." Zane sighed with relief as the woman started typing. "Name?"

"Alan Jones."

The woman kept typing. The computer screen reflected a list of names in her glasses as she scrolled down on the touchpad. She shrugged her shoulders.

"I hate to tell you this, kid, but you've been duped."

Zane raised a brow.

"Why's that?"

"Alan Jones doesn't go to the Academy."

* * *

There was a knock on Mirabelle's door. Mirabelle looked at her datapad. It was 6:27. She set her curling iron down and double-checked to make sure all the snacks were set out on her desk. These days she didn't have too many guests over in her dorm, so she wanted to make sure she didn't screw this up. *Calm down. It's not like this is a date or anything.* She opened the door. It was Zane Minathi, heaving and leaning against the door frame like he had just spent the last few hours running a marathon instead of working on his group project.

"You're here early," she said. "And apparently tired too."

Zane stormed inside and slammed the door. She backed away.

"Uh, Zane? What's going on?"

"I must be going crazy, Mirabelle," Zane said. The brown hues in his eyes were wide. There was no hint of a smile or joke. He looked like he had seen ghosts rising from a grave. "I seem to be the only person at this entire Academy that remembers Alan Jones." A long pause. His eyes focused on hers. "Don't tell me you don't remember him either."

The words floored Mirabelle with overwhelming shock. A host of memories and strange feelings arose within herself. She fought with every ounce of willpower in her body to not look at that damn dresser against the wall.

"Please tell me you're joking," she said.

"Joking? Why would I be joking?"

"You do that a lot."

"But not about things like this! This is serious!"

She fidgeted with the end of her sleeves. Then started laughing.

"What's so funny?"

"This isn't happening." She walked over towards her desk, a throbbing pulse beating her brain. "You want something to eat? Or drink? I don't know what movies you're into but I'm sure we can find something."

Zane gripped Mirabelle's arm. She glanced at his clenched hand in shock, her eyes meeting his. Beneath the dim fluorescent lights of her dorm room, Zane's face looked pale.

"Don't touch me," she said.

"You're lying. You know exactly what I'm talking about."

Mirabelle paused, her eyes frantically moving in disarray. She shoved Zane's arm away and walked towards the wooden dresser.

"Screw it."

She flung open the top drawer, dumping dozens of socks and photographs on the floor. They were pictures of students. Each snapshot seemed to smile at Zane with a sinister eeriness as Mirabelle put the socks away, then assorted each image. Interspersed with each image was a list of names. It was jarring for Zane to see. There had to be at least three dozen pictures of strangers and foreign faces.

"Ok, now I want you to tell me you're joking," Zane said, the frames forever gazing at Zane with frozen smiles. "You're starting to scare me."

There it is, Mirabelle thought. *A trap door on the floor.* With one laugh, one smile, one sigh of resignation, she could put this whole case away. In fact, maybe with Zane, she'd have the strength to burn these photographs and get back to her normal life, a life free from late nights mulling over whether to invite anyone else into her strange world or to keep this mess a secret to rot in its obscurity. But each face grinned as if expecting her to proclaim their names. If someone else had known of their disappearances, someone else would have reported it. *Except for me.* For years this had been a battle she believed merited her silence. Today it wasn't.

"It's not a prank," she said. "But I wish it was."

Zane stepped carefully around the photographs. He grabbed one of a girl in a white uniform. Note: Jamey Ledgings. Black hair, blue eyes. Last spotted in the Lounge. Second Semester. 2133.

"Mirabelle? Who are these people?"

They stood in the silence of the cluttered room that freed them from having to put problems into words. Then Mirabelle shattered the silence, her utterance a final declaration that meant she could no longer turn back. The cat was out of the bag. The Pandora's box was opened.

"You wouldn't believe me if I told you."

Zane crossed his arms.

"Try me."

Die-hard Delinquents

"We've got a problem, boys," Matthew said. "Someone remembers Alan Jones."

It was a late and loud night in Derek's dorm, but after that announcement, everyone went silent. With everyone having finished their finals, Bruce, Derek, and Donny were having a little celebration. They snuck in some alcohol and were playing rounds of Cyborg Wars on the Square. Matthew had no plans on seeing these delinquents until he received a call from the Boss about the updates of their situation. Alan Jones had been safely transported. But someone was looking for him.

Before anyone could respond Matthew shut off the projector.

"Does the Boss know who?" Derek asked.

"No. Thankfully, they were only secondary remembrances. Someone says the name Alan Jones, the name passed through their mind, and then they move onto something else."

"Then there must've been a problem with the data sweep."

"They checked that too. Records are gone. Plus, all the remembrances showed up on Alan's old hall and student services, which means that this wasn't a problem with the mind snare. Someone was looking for Alan, someone immune to the Boss' tricks."

"How can you be immune to mind snares?" Donny asked.

"Same way you are," Derek said. "Psychics can't use mind snares on other psychics. I forgot you're new. Matthew? You wanna explain the rest to him?"

Matthew sighed in annoyance and looked at Donny. That smug bowl-cut bastard was always asking stupid questions.

"They gave you the rundown, right? You know the rules?"

"I think so."

Matthew grabbed Donny by the collar.

"What is that supposed to mean?"

"It means I was scared during the meeting, alright?"

"If you went through the initiation you should know. How about a refresher in case the Boss gives you a private job, which literally happens all the time!?" Matthew let go of Donny and pushed all the empty beer cans off the table. "I'm going to describe this in a way that your buzzed brain will understand."

Matthew placed three empty solo cups on the table. He filled two cups with beer and left one empty. "See the cups of beer? This is your brain."

"On drugs!" Derek shouted, laughing at his own joke. Bruce laughed too.

"Actually yes. It is your brain on drugs. The AOL drug to be specific. It stops us from aging, it prevents us from contracting diseases, and allows you to live conceivably forever unless you forget to eat your breakfast or get run over by a car."

Matthew grabbed a pint of lizolai from the table and squirted a drop into the first cup. The blue chemical dispersed and started to fizz.

"However, some people who received the AOL drug started to undergo mutations in their DNA, which gave rise to the psychic gene. No one really knows why this mutation evolved, but it did, and that's just something we all have to live with." Matthew gestured to each cup. One was empty, one had beer, and the other had beer and lizolai. "Psychics can do a lot more than create tears. Some can erase memories, but they can't do it to everyone. It's like this pint of lizolai. When I put a drop in this cup of beer, it gives the drink a bit of a kick. The lizolai is the mind-snare. It works on AOL humans because it's compatible and mixes with the drink. Psychics can manipulate the minds of AOL humans because they both have a phyofrenia–it's just significantly weaker than ours. If a psychic is powerful enough, they can tap into this doorway of the mind and destroy symbols that represent a memory. Find the core representation of Alan

Jones, destroy it, and you destroy anyone's memory of him too."

"Then why doesn't this affect psychics?" Donny asked.

"Because our phyofrenia is strengthened, prohibiting access from another psychic. It's the same reason why I can't mix two drinks of lizolai. You don't get a tastier drink–what you get is an overdose and a quick death. Or you can think of it like a door. AOL humans have an open one. For psychics, the door to the phyofrenia is closed."

"Ok," Donny said, taking a sip of the mixed drink. "Then that means that the person who remembers Alan Jones is a psychic."

"Not exactly." Matthew grabbed the empty cup. "This last cup represents the mind of an impurity. They don't have a phyofrenia because they don't have the AOL drug. In that case, there's nothing for this little drop of lizolai to mix with. There's no chemical reaction, which means they're immune to mind-snares just like us."

"Why do you keep calling them that?" Donny asked.

"What? Impurity?"

"Yeah. Someone told me it's offensive."

"I don't care. It has nothing to do with who you are as a person, your sex, or the color of your skin. It's all determined by the blood in your veins and the chemicals in your brain. Impurities are the ones arbitrators should put in asylums, not us. They're the reason some people still have cancer, physical deformities, and graves six feet under the ground. Only a fool would voluntarily reject AOL."

Matthew stood up.

"Our suspect is either a psychic or an impurity. Let's hope it's a psychic."

"Why?"

"The parents," Matthew said. "Oftentimes the parents of psychics aren't psychics themselves, which means the Boss can make them forget they even had a child in the first place. Of course, the Boss has to alter the memories a little bit, make them think differently of the kid they have photographs of around the house, but once the core memory of that person is gone, it's amazing how much the brain deceives itself to stay sane. Making a parent forget they had a child is the better alternative. But impurities…"

Donny's eyes widened with horror.

"They don't actually kill them, do they?"

"It depends. Impurities are drawn to each other like magnets. If you're an impurity, you often have friends that are impurities too. There are a lot of loose ends." Matthew tapped his datapad. "But let's not jump to any conclusions. None of the secondary remembrances gave us any names, but we do have some descriptions. Young black male, maybe 15-16, nappy black hair with a taper fade haircut. We'll search the directory and then send a list of the names to the Boss to see which ones he can see."

Matthew stood up.

"Party time's over. You can get wasted over the summer, but it's imperative that we find the suspect as soon as possible, seeing that he's so interested in finding our transported friend." Matthew shot a dark look at everyone before leaving the room. "Our obligations to the Boss are more important than anything else. Remember that."

Matthew shut the door.

The party ended.

The second Matthew left the room, Derek's mind churned with ideas. *An impurity, huh? I got just the person in mind.* He left the room shortly after. He didn't tell anyone where he was going. And especially not Matthew. There were great rewards to be earned for catching people who caused secondary remembrances. And even though he knew the suspect was a male, Matthew was right. Impurities fed off each other's craziness. If there was another impurity on campus, Mirabelle Marshall would know.

Internal Investigations

In the "Fireside Diner," Amelia Lancaster sat alone by the window in a black dress. A red and gold Ogata droid strummed a gentle tune with his harp in the background, but that did not make Amelia feel any more relaxed. Her back stood straight, her shoulders low, her eyes scanning the holopad in her hands. Dakari Minathi entered the restaurant and followed a waiter to the table with the woman. He thanked her, then took his seat.

"Were you followed?" Amelia asked.

"Of course not," Dakari said. He removed his raincoat and set it on the chair next to him, revealing his collared shirt underneath. "Why do you ask?"

"The Chief's intrigued by your decision to stay."

"Then let him be intrigued. Kalak's got too many things to worry about."

They ordered their food and started eating. Halfway through dinner, Amelia slid the holopad over to Dakari's side of the table.

"What's this?"

"It's a record of companies the CDAD has conducted business with over the last 12 months. I don't know why you think it's important, but here it is." Dakari nodded and scrolled down. "You gonna tell me what you're planning on doing? Or at least why you wanted this list specifically?"

Dakari highlighted a few companies by double-tapping their names.

"What do you want me to say, Deputy? That Desta's death wasn't an accident?"

Amelia took a sip of her water to collect her thoughts.

"Not exactly. I traced those routes because I wanted to know if there were any other options. We're too early into this to make an inference like that."

"Bingo."

Amelia reached for the holopad, but Dakari tilted it away from her.

"Hold on," Dakari said. "Before I show you this, let me ask you a few questions."

Amelia straightened her posture.

"Very well."

"You went to the Gerumandian Academy, same as me. What were the two truths about the force that every arbitrator had to know by heart?"

"90% of psychic murders are targeted at arbitrators."

"And the second?"

"Most of those psychics are children."

"Combine those two truths in addition to severe punishment for the premature shooting of psychics and what do you get? An arbitrator force that is supposed to keep the streets safe from psychics but gets court-martialed for doing their job."

"To be fair, Dakari, some of those changes are good. Fewer children are being shot."

"Fewer psychics are being shot. They want you to see these things as innocent kids."

"Because they're not *things*. They're people. And some of them are innocent."

"Then how do you explain this?" Dakari pulled out a folded piece of paper from his pocket. Amelia opened it up. It was a chart. "Arbitrators weren't always the primary victim of psychics. They used to be random and less frequent. Then a kid got shot on the side of the street."

"Clara Murren. I remember that."

"Everyone does. There were protests for weeks. They demanded justice for Clara despite the fact that she killed four innocent civilians, but it didn't matter. No one cared about who she was after they saw her corpse. Almost overnight the arbitrators became the monsters. That's when the 'Last Resort' bill was passed, severely restricting what arbitrators could do to psychics. But the murders didn't go down after that bill. It was the other way around. They skyrocketed by a hundred-and-fifty percent."

Amelia double-checked the chart.

"Explain this to me," Dakari said. "Why would psychic murders increase after measures were taken to ensure their safety?"

"Maybe the arbitrators didn't follow those measures."

"Maybe, but that's not my point."

"Then what are you saying?"

"If psychics hated the CDAD so much, why weren't they killing us before the 'Last Resort' bill? There's no evidence that they were organized. As far as we know, psychics to this day live separately from one another. It wasn't psychics who passed the bill. It was AOL humans."

"Who wanted to make sure that psychics were treated more humanely."

"That's one way of looking at it. On the other hand, if I wanted to find a way to make arbitrators defenseless, this is it."

The hairs on the back of Amelia's spine stood up.

"I see."

"There's more, too. How much do we know about the psychics we catch? Nothing. And where do they go after they're caught? Rehab centers with top security clearance. Even if she were still alive, I could never interrogate the girl who caused the explosion if I wanted to. That's all handled by internal affairs."

Dakari finally slid the holopad over to Amelia.

"Though you might find it interesting to see who else has access inside." Amelia took the holopad and looked at the companies with circles over their names as Dakari continued his explanation. "Someone has to transport supplies to the underground detention centers. With each captured psychic, new supplies and testing kits arrive to conduct experiments on the phyofrenia. From the looks of it, there's one company the CDAD has contracted to deliver those supplies."

Amelia found the last circle and looked up at Dakari.

"L-Transport."

"They deliver shipments every month and each time a psychic arrives at the center. The way I see it, there may be a few cooks in the kitchen."

Amelia tucked the device in her purse and folded her hands together.

"It's an interesting find, but I don't see what it offers us."

"It gives us some leads." Dakari stood up from his seat. "We don't have clearance, but now we know who might. I'm going to conduct a more thorough investigation on L-Transport. There's no way we'd ever get clearance to enter the detention center from the CDAD, but if L-Transport is delivering supplies, they must be using bodyguards. I'm going to see if I can find them. In the meantime, I want you to find the autopsy reports of all arbitrators killed by psychics since the Last Resort bill."

"Why's that?"

Dakari straightened his cap on top of his head.

"Samuel Middleton and Desta had something in common. They were both impurities." Dakari tossed a few recs on the table and slung his coat over his shoulders. "I apologize for leaving so soon, but…" Dakari thought of Zane. "I have to make a call." He left without another word. And with a heavy heart of what awaited him next.

* * *

Zane Minathi leaned against the wall of Mirabelle's room, his mind dizzy with possibilities. The world, as strange as it was, had always followed a set of consistent principles. What Mirabelle was saying about missing students seemed to break all the rules.

"What do you mean they just disappear?" He asked.

She handed Zane a cup of coffee as they stared at the taped photographs on her wall. It was easier to see them that way instead of gazing at the floor.

"They're just gone. It's as if they never attended the Academy."

"That's impossible."

"Is it though? The Academy forgot about Alan Jones."

"I mean, yeah…that's strange. But all these other students? Something at this scale would attract attention fast. There are too many variables involved: teachers, friends, and especially parents. It's not like these students don't have social lives. If students were really going missing, parents would be all over this."

"Unless they didn't remember."

"What?"

"You said it yourself. You felt like you were the only person at the Academy who remembered Alan Jones. No one on his hall remembered him, not even his roommate, and there were no records of him at student services."

"Then how do *we* remember him? That seems like a huge problem."

"It is," Mirabelle said. "But I'm betting it's a problem they don't know about or else we wouldn't even be having this conversation. Or else–"

"We'd disappear too. I get it." Zane sat down on the edge of Mirabelle's blue bedspread, trying to collect his thoughts. "Why haven't you told anyone about this?"

Mirabelle froze, her eyes wandering around the floor. She took a seat next to him in silence. Her glossed lips were pressed with indecisiveness when her eyes raised up to meet his. Faint lines on her face revealed the forgery of her expression that was otherwise resting in a state of contemplative sadness.

"I mean…" She looked up at Zane. "Would you?"

"Of course."

"No, I mean, if you were the only person who remembered. If I didn't remember Alan, you'd start to go a little crazy. Maybe Alan never went here. Maybe he never existed." Zane raised a brow. "What I'm saying is that it's not that simple. I never felt comfortable sharing this because I didn't know if I was going insane. Your parents might be arbitrators but mine are not."

"Then let's get my parents involved. I'll call my Mom and Dad right now."

"Zane, don't. Please don't do that."

"Why not?"

"If these people have the power to erase memories, wipe records, and make people disappear out of thin air, what good do you think calling an arbitrator will do? There are already plenty of them on campus. If they weren't subject to losing their memories too, they would've been all over this case long before you and I knew it was happening."

"Then what do we do?! Why are we the only people who can remember anything?"

They looked into each other's eyes as if searching for the answer in each other that they couldn't find in themselves. They sat in silence.

"I don't know," Mirabelle said. "But I wish I did."

"People need to hear about this."

"Not yet. Our secrecy is our biggest advantage. If you want to be brought into my world of madness you need to play by my rules. We need to know who's behind this before it goes public. Don't tell your friends, your instructors–not even your parents." She extended a hand. "Deal?"

Zane shook her hand.

"Deal."

* * *

Derek froze when a student his age stepped outside Mirabelle's room. He had been waiting outside in the hallway for only a few minutes, but this was the last thing he suspected. *Mirabelle has friends?* They awkwardly paused and stared at each other as the door closed. Derek tried to hide the surprise and shock on his face. *Wait a minute...that's him*, Derek thought. Black male. 15-16. Taper fade haircut. *He's the impurity.* He knew it without even asking for the boy's name. He knew it because he was Mirabelle's debate partner. He had seen him before.

"Can I help you?"

"You already have," Derek said. "Sorry, I mean–this is Mirabelle's room, right?"

He raised a brow.

"Wait a minute, Derek Hunt? We debated you in Quarterfinals."

"That's the one."

The boy coiled his fists.

"You called Mirabelle an incestuous pig!"

Derek let off a wild smile. "Guilty as charged." Then his smile faded. "But that's why I'm here. To apologize."

"I didn't know the Hunt brothers knew the word 'sorry.'"

"We are full of surprises. Take care..." Derek held his hand out in silence, awkwardly waiting for a name. The boy paused, then shook Derek's hand.

"Zane."

They shook hands as Derek's smiled widened.

"Take care, Zane. See you around."

Derek stood in front of Mirabelle's door and looked down the hallway. He raised his hand to knock, then set his arm down when Zane was gone. There was no need to pay her a visit and certainly no need to apologize. He had all the answers he needed. Or almost all the answers. He waited a few moments, then walked down the hallway, tailing Zane from a distance.

* * *

Zane shut the door to his dorm, his head spinning with questions. He sat down at his desk and opened his laptop, then immediately shut it. *School?* He thought. *How can I do school with students going missing?* Knowing that his partner was one of those students made things worse. He couldn't concentrate. It was almost 9:00 p.m. And he still hadn't even started his statistics project. He opened his computer and stared at it with dull, indifferent eyes.

"I'm going to fail."

And how would he tell his teacher that his partner had disappeared? Would she believe him? And why was Derek acting so strange? He gave up and closed the computer. Then his datapad buzzed. It was his father. He sighed with relief. *Thank goodness. Maybe he had answers.*

"Hey Dad. You wouldn't believe how crazy my night has been."

There was no response on the other end.

"Dad? You there?"

On the other end of the call, at the hotel, Dakari sat on his bed and buried his face in his hands. *He doesn't know*, Dakari thought. That made it even worse. He had suspected that Zane had seen something on the news.

"Dad? Why aren't you saying anything?"

There were few things that Zane feared. His father's silence was one of them. It was unnatural for a man of his intellect and assertiveness to be at a loss for words, and so when he was, a terrible ache strangled Zane in the gut. His legs gave up on him as he collapsed on the bed and sat down. Something terrible occurred to him. In the shock of disappearing students, Zane had forgotten all about his mother's missed call. He kept shaking his head. And when the silence continued, Zane wished it could go on forever, because he knew nothing good would follow it. Nothing trivial followed the silence of a man of many words. Zane shut his eyes so tight that he wished they wouldn't open again. He tensed as he heard the crescendo of his father's trembling breath. Then, like a whisper, his father managed:

"Turn on the news..."

"Why?"

A longer pause.

"It's about Mom..."

Zane rose, staggering towards the projector, waving it to life with the motion of his hand. He read the headline and nearly dropped from terror. Then he cried too.

* * *

Derek removed the audio amplifier from the wall outside Zane's room. That was enough. He couldn't listen to it any longer. He had never heard a young man cry, let alone sob. It was pathetic, but only at first. Derek felt something different as the boy's conversation with his father carried on. There was great pain in Zane's voice as he begged his father to tell him it was all a lie, that his mother wasn't dead, that he would see her next week, that she would have another batch of crecan bread made for him. Derek saw his mother once a year, always during formal occasions. He didn't understand the closeness that Zane had felt with his mom and the pain

114

that her absence had brought him in her passing. It made him angry, then pitiful, and then sad. There was a part of him that wanted to know what that was like. The love at least. Part of him felt guilty for being a fly on the wall of someone's sadness.

He walked away.

On his way back to his dorm, a few students saw "the great" Derek Hunt walking alone, with his hands in his pockets and his head held low. Derek didn't even notice their stares. If he had, he would've stopped and resumed his otherwise powerful posture. But his mind was torn. No. Tormented. It was one thing to call an impurity an incestuous pig. It was an entirely other matter to *kill* them. And that would be required if it was true. Derek knew that. And then that would mean that Zane's death would be on his hands. A death. He was used to playing a game with people's memories, but people's lives were a whole other matter. And he hated the fact that he wasn't strong enough to do it. He felt like less of a Gerumandian. Less of a Hunt. He entered his hallway and paused when he saw Matthew leaning against the wall.

"You look like you've seen a ghost." Matthew smiled. "Want to tell me about it?"

Derek walked past him.

"I don't know what you're talking about."

Matthew grabbed Derek by the jaw and raised his head up.

"Are you mad!? Look at you!" He shoved him away. "You look pathetic. I don't think I've ever seen you this sad in my entire life." Matthew crossed his arms. "Where did you go?"

"Nowhere."

"Ahh, so you did go somewhere."

"If I did it's none of your business."

"Your business is my business." Matthew's eyes scanned his younger brother like a lion inspecting its prey. "You're going to walk me down to your room. You're going to tell me where you went and exactly what you saw."

Derek's brow narrowed.

"Not today."

Matthew started laughing as Derek walked away.

"So that's how it is huh? You found him and you want to keep the glory all for yourself? Very well. Keep your secrets." Matthew smiled as his brother slammed the door in his face. "You can't keep them for long."

* * *

In less than a week, the Gerumandian Academy would send students home for the summer. That gave Mirabelle and Zane a week to solve the mystery of disappearing students. But there was one problem: Zane had gone off the grid. Mirabelle had tried calling him, texting him, searching for him at class and during lunch. He was nowhere. That's when Mirabelle felt an all too familiar, haunting feeling.

What if they got him too?

Whoever "they" were.

They were scheduled to meet at her room later that afternoon, but since Zane hadn't been answering her calls, she paid a visit to his dorm instead. She knocked. Nothing. She knocked again. Nothing.

"No...no this isn't happening." She raised both hands to her head. "Zane if you're in there! Please! Open up!"

The door opened. She froze. Immediately she noticed something different about him. He hid half of his face behind the door as he reluctantly looked at her. There were bags under his eyes as purple as plums. They were bloodshot red. He wore a ragged undershirt and gym shorts. He looked like he hadn't left his room in 24 hours. He raised a cigarette to his trembling lips and smiled. It was the saddest smile Mirabelle had ever seen.

"What's up?"

Mirabelle was speechless. She stood there feeling dumb for not saying anything. What could she even say? Where would she start? Zane's smile waned. He grew angry.

"What do you want?!"

"Zane…"

He tried to slam the door, but she shoved her leg through the opening.

"Zane, *please*. Let's talk."

Their eyes locked onto each other's as they struggled against the door.

"Don't do this to yourself," Mirabelle said. "Please. Let me in."

Zane's anger increased, then, in a slow, gradual decline, it left him again. His eyes lowered. He stopped leaning against the door, allowing Mirabelle to sneak in. She gently shut the door, then faced Zane. He raised the cigarette to his lips again as his eyes looked down at the floor. She snatched the cig from his hands.

"You've never smoked a day in your life. Why now?"

Zane closed his eyes. There was a mound of crumpled tissues on his desk. Without asking a thing, Mirabelle wrapped her arms around Zane and held him close. He tried to push her away, then wrapped his arms around her too. She didn't know why, but she didn't need to. Some things couldn't be put in words. She figured she would find out soon enough. When she did, she understood everything. The world was falling apart at the seams, and they were descending into the madness together.

A Fast Farewell

"What was she like?" Mirabelle asked.

They sat side by side on the edge of his bed. There had been a few deaths in the Marshall family, but nothing as drastic as what Zane was going through. She couldn't even imagine. Losing anyone was hard. But losing a mother in the way Zane had seemed unbelievably horrible. It left her with no words of consolation. If they were out there, she didn't know them. Instead, she felt like it might at least be better to bring up good memories of his Mom, at the very least hoping to share the burden.

"She was wonderful." Zane rested both hands in his lap, his eyes aimlessly gazing at the floor. "I called her every week."

"Really?"

"Yeah. My grandma used to tell me that most sons forget about their mothers the day they leave for the Academies. But I didn't want to be that kind of son. My mother was too good to me. I wanted to let her know I still cared."

Mirabelle smiled.

"I'm sure she knew that."

Zane nodded.

"I know she did. But...it still stings." He coiled his fists. "And my father. He let a whole day pass before telling me! She had been dead a whole day!"

"Zane—"

"Mirabelle, don't pretend you know what that's like."

"I don't have to. I lost my father when I was five years old."

He lowered his eyes.

"I'm sorry."

"You did nothing wrong. I'm sure your father took this pretty hard. He probably wasn't sure how to put it in words."

"He couldn't even say the words. He just told me to turn on the screen."

There was nothing Mirabelle could say to that. Nothing at all.

Zane looked over at her.

"I need you."

Mirabelle blushed. *To be needed?* Who had ever needed her? For some reason, it felt more to her like an honor than a chore, despite the fact that she had willingly made a living out of shutting people away before they could do the same to her. But now that had changed. At that moment, she believed that he genuinely meant what he said, and for a brief minute, Mirabelle's heart rose with the warmth of making his life better and his grief manageable.

"What?"

"This case. These students. I want to know what happened to them." His hands trembled. The richness of his brown eyes had faded into something on the brink of collapse. "I will waste away without this case. What better way to distract myself than exploring a mystery that can't be solved?"

Mirabelle smiled.

"We'll figure it out."

Zane looked away.

"Part of me hopes you're right." He paused. "Part of me hopes you're wrong."

* * *

Things didn't magically get easier for Zane overnight. In fact, they didn't seem to get easier at all. Zane woke up each morning staring at a dull ceiling with a pit in his stomach. He thought trying to solve the mystery with Mirabelle would ease things, but it was only a distraction. Each time he left her room and was alone again, the ache returned, as if it had been bottling up for hours, waiting to release its pain in one crippling moment.

He wandered back to his room, closed the door, then fell on the bed—only to wake up the next day and do it again. And again. And again.

He failed the statistics presentation because he never showed up. Dr. Lekovar ended up excusing his absence and final due to "extenuating circumstances," but Zane didn't care about grades anymore. He just wanted his Mom. *But she's not here*, Zane thought. *Momma didn't raise no loser.* Mom was a Gerumandian. Dad was a Gerumandian. *I am too.* That meant he was going to throw away that last pack of cigarettes and get back to business. He was an arbitrator. And there was a case to be solved. That didn't mean the pain went away. But it was better than sitting in his room doing nothing. That being said, the case was going nowhere.

It was the most painfully fruitless work they had ever done. Mirabelle was starting to realize that whoever was behind the disappearing students was extremely thorough. There were no records of these people. On Wednesday night they met in Mirabelle's room and posted all their theories on a whiteboard. Empty energy drink cans, old catalogs, and markers covered the floor.

"Ok, so we have two theories," Mirabelle said.

"One theory," Zane muttered. "The second one was a joke."

"You don't think the Waions are kidnapping students and wiping their memories? Like that earth film…"

"Men in Black?"

"Yeah! It's like *Men in Black* but reversed! This time the aliens have the neuralyzers and they're using it on people."

"Again. I was joking. Neuralyzers don't exist and all the Waions are underground slaves."

"Well…" Mirabelle walked back to the wall. "There's really only one more. It's the psychic one. Some of those journals I read mentioned telekinesis, but what about telepathy?"

"There are no confirmed studies of that," Zane said. "As far as we know, psychics are only able to manipulate things around them. They also lose energy fast in the same way we get tired from physical exercise. I can't imagine how much energy it would take to erase the minds of thousands of people. That would take an enormously powerful psychic, certainly someone too powerful for us to stand up against."

"So we just give up?"

"Did I say that?"

"Sounds like you did."

"Well, I didn't, ok?" Zane stood up. "I think we're both just a little tired. We've been doing nothing but reading for the past three days. Why don't we call it a night and do something fun?"

"Fun?" She asked. *"Fun?* How are we supposed to have fun when people are disappearing? How are we supposed to just sit around and watch movies when the Academy's boiling us all alive?!"

"Why don't you tell me? You seemed to do it for years."

She gritted her teeth, holding back what she really wanted to say.

"I did that because I had no choice. If I hadn't kept this a secret, there's a good chance these people would've taken me too."

"What people? Mirabelle—we don't even know who's behind this."

Mirabelle turned around and faced the board.

"That doesn't mean the answer isn't here though. We have to keep looking. What do all these people have in common? Why would someone target them? Why would they be singled out among everyone else in the Academy?! Why?!"

Mirabelle's eyes grew bloodshot red. Her fists coiled with anger as she tightened her grip on the marker. Zane sighed.

"You're not talking about those students, are you? You're talking about us."

She dropped the marker.

"Yeah. I guess I am."

They sat down on the bed. Neither of them said anything for a while. The gears in both of their heads were fired. Countless hours of trying to make meaning out of photographs left them exhausted with an empty feeling in their stomachs. They kept their fears to themselves, that fear of being wrong, that fear of failing. It was all there as they lay side by side, staring at the ceiling in silence as the nighttime air traffic echoed outside Mirabelle's dorm. And it was as the energy wore off that their fears bubbled back up to the surface where words could start to make sense of them.

"I'm an impurity," Mirabelle said.

Those words took her breath away. It had all come out so sudden, so thoughtlessly. Her face blushed red as she gave part of herself away. That was the truth she had always wanted to hide, but it was the truth she needed to share because in doing so she realized why Zane wasn't surprised. In the span of a few seconds the dots were connected.

"Me too," he said.

It was the happiest moment of their lives and the one good feeling that shed light on Zane's dark days. A warm fuzzy feeling blossomed in their chests as they looked up at the dull ceiling, but from the gaze in their eyes, you would've thought they were looking at the stars. Their eyes held the few remnants of humanity, the ones that couldn't beat disease, deformity, or even death. It was that collective feeling of being a misfit that made them feel just a little bit less lonely. Zane left the pain of his mother's death in the background as he held tight to her memory. Mirabelle felt settled with her father's absence and accepted the scar on her face.

"An impurity," Zane said, tasting the sound of the word on his tongue. "What a strange thing to call us." He paused. "Why do we have to live with the slurs people have given us?"

Mirabelle looked over at Zane.

"We don't have to."

Zane looked at Mirabelle.

"I guess so." He paused. "Why didn't you get treatment?"

That question was a bit harder to answer, but it had to come out now.

"Because I never had a choice." She paused. "My parents said I'm genetically incompatible with AOL."

A long silence filled the space between their words.

"I'm sorry."

"It's ok." Mirabelle rolled over in bed until she was facing Zane. "What about you?"

Zane's expression was indecisive. "Because when I know my days are numbered, I make them count. That's at least what my father always told me. Guess I kind of just…accepted it, ya know?" He slid his hand across the blue bedsheets, absentmindedly tracing his finger along the seams in the cloth. "Guess that makes us both crazy."

"Why's that?"

"Because you can't get the drug. And I'm just stupid."

Mirabelle looked at him and laughed her most genuine laugh in years. It wasn't that the joke was even that funny. It was just perfectly timed, a perfect moment of release for someone who had been trying to crack the mystery of the Gerumandian Academy for years and had made as much progress as a tortoise trying to reach the end of a treadmill, for a girl who felt isolated knowing that she would die and that her friends would live on for maybe hundreds of years. And it was cathartic for Zane. He felt a weight slip off his shoulders with each laugh.

"Yeah," Zane said. "We're so crazy we think students are disappearing!"

Mirabelle laughed so hard she rolled over and fell on the floor. Zane was barely able to catch his breath as he walked around to help her up. He found her giggling against the wall, her hair a tangled mess. She grabbed Zane's hand as he helped her up.

"Wow." She wiped a tear from her eye and pushed her hair back. "My bad."

"Your bad? That was awesome!"

She smiled. Her auburn eyes seemed to shine like diamonds in the light of her dorm room. And Zane loved looking into them. They stood there for maybe a little longer than they both initially intended to. They looked perfectly at peace, perfectly rested, lost in each other's eyes. Under normal circumstances, the moment would've died, and "awkward interaction" would've taken the stage. But Zane saved the moment. He quickly typed a song into his datapad. It was "Sweet Darling:" a slow, smooth, R&B jam. It was Zane's father's favorite song.

"Can I show you something?" Zane asked, both hands out as if to dance. Mirabelle's eyes looked wild with excitement, her heart beating faster than she could handle. "Come on. From one detective to another."

Mirabelle smiled and gave Zane her hands.

The song played:

"And who are you? The girl I wed
That you should love me still
A thousand days will pass along
And we've not had our fill."

They stood in the center of the room, swaying back and forth like in times when old couples used to dance when people used to grow old. But it was fitting for them, because while the world stayed young, they were growing old, aging each day until death called them home. They danced close, occasionally a step out of place or a beat too soon. But they danced to the beat of their own hearts in a gentle sway.

"I always said, I always said
My Sweet Darling so dear
That Heaven's gates, don't lead to home
Less I can see you here."

"My parents used to dance to this when I was a kid," Zane said. "I always thought they danced when they were happy, but later my dad told me they danced when they were scared. They danced to the tune of the recession in 2125, the tax act of 2128, and my mom's miscarriage in 2130. In these moments they were afraid, but they danced to drive the fear away." Zane paused. "Are you afraid?"

Mirabelle wrapped her arms around Zane's waist, and then their dance became sort of a swaying hug, holding each other and rocking back and forth to the gentle music coming from Zane's worn-out speakers. She nestled her head into Zane's chest and lay there for a moment, perfectly at peace and perfectly afraid.

"I never said, I never said
My Sweet Darling, I fear
That all this life is all there is
So keep me close and near."

"Yes," she whispered, the sound of the music fading from her ears. All she could hear was the sound of her own shaky breath and the steady beat

of Zane's heart. He kept his arms around her, holding her tight. "Are you?"
Another pause.

"Yeah," he said, still swaying to the beat of the music. "But we're going
to be ok. I promise." Mirabelle gripped Zane even tighter, holding him
closer as the music reached its climax. She wanted to tell him something
but found herself unable to speak as she drowned in a wave of emotions.
So instead, they danced in silence. They danced until their fear faded with
the song's last note.

* * *

Back in his dorm room, Derek threw his headset on the ground. He had
bugged Mirabelle's room. He had heard everything. Their jokes, their
laughs, their dance. There was no way he could go through with this. Not
only had Derek found Zane, but he discovered that Mirabelle was catching
onto them too. Two impurities. Two students who needed to die. He
bounced his leg up and down nervously in his chair and eyed a duffel bag
in the corner of his room. He unzipped the bag and peered inside. There
were several capsules and a large syringe with a label printed on each piece
of equipment:

AOL Treatment.

Derek zipped the bag back up again. He was running out of options—and
time. With only two days left before the Academy sent students home, if
they didn't find the suspect soon, the Boss would get involved. Or Matthew
would find Zane first. They were only looking for a male, which meant
that Derek assumed he could leave Mirabelle out of this. That meant this
treatment had to work. It was the only thing he could do. With that thought,
he grabbed the duffel bag, opened the door, and stepped outside.

The Monster Behind the Mask

Later that night, Zane stopped by the Lounge for a quick snack before returning to his dorm room, high off warm feelings. A few students mingled in chairs and couches sprawled around the cozy recreational space, conversing with one another as Zane scanned his datapad on the vending machine and typed in the three-digit number for a protein bar. He hummed "Sweet Darling" under his breath as the bar dropped into the tray, letting his mind return to the colorful memory of his dance with Mirabelle. The way he held her, the way they had swayed in each other's arms. It made him so...*happy*. It was so much more than that. They had struck a connection beneath the orange fluorescent lights of her dorm. No real progress on the case for missing students had been made, but Zane didn't really care. He left Mirabelle's dorm with something far more valuable: the feeling of being known and loved.

Strangely enough, his first impulse was to call his mother. Then a thorn of pain pierced the center of his newfound happiness, as is so often the case in moments of pure euphoria, leveling him back to reality. But the pain could not overwhelm him. Instead, as he rode the elevator back to his dorm, his heart churned with a blend of joy and sadness, love and grief. Sometimes the grief struck Zane with a gravitational pull strong enough to bring him to his knees, but the moment he shared with Mirabelle seemed to stretch him in the opposite direction. The pendulums of human experience weighed heavily inside Zane as he struggled to live in the in-between.

I could call Dad, Zane thought as he walked down the hallway to his dorm. *He could use some good news.* That arose a whole new host of questions. If he called his father, would he tell him about the missing students too? Surely, it couldn't hurt to try to get him involved as well. These brief moments of worry, however, were overlayed with the image of Mirabelle's dark brown eyes looking lovingly into his. If that was all he could see for the rest of his life, that would be more than enough. He scanned his datapad to the reader by the door handle and stepped inside his dorm.

The second the door shut behind him, he knew something was off.

"Hello, Zane."

Zane froze as the door closed behind him. A figure leaned back in a chair in the center of the room, half-hidden by a shadow brought about by the dim light above him. This wouldn't have terrified Zane so much had he been expecting visitors or had a roommate, but he had neither. He had a single. Furthermore, he hadn't given his room passcode to anyone, not even Mirabelle, meaning that this person had broken in. He eyed the bed.

"Don't even think about going over there. I already found your blaster."

That was when Zane saw the barrel pointed directly at him in the shadow. He still couldn't see the figure in the dark, but he could tell he was wearing a mask and a voice amplifier over his mouth.

"Have a seat."

There was another chair in the room. Zane hesitated because he only owned one chair, then figured that if this person was willing to bring a chair, maybe they would be willing to talk. He sat down where the lighting could still shine on him.

"Pretty ominous setup," Zane said, trying to mask the terror throbbing in his right temple. "I'd say 'I like what you've done with the place' if you didn't keep aiming that blaster at my face."

The man chuckled.

"That's good. You got a sense of humor. Maybe we can make a deal." The masked man leaned forward. He was wearing a navy-blue laundry uniform. "I know you were looking for Alan Jones."

That's impossible, Zane thought. *We didn't tell anyone.* His mind swam with anxiety but his face wore a mask of confidence. He recalled every arbitrator interrogation technique he knew. It was do or die now.

"Then you should also know that I've figured it out," Zane said. "I know who you are."

"I know a bluff when I see one. If you knew who I was, you'd be with Alan."

"Dead?"

"Good. You don't know. That should make things easier."

"If your operation is so airtight then why do I remember him?"

"There are exceptions."

"You mean, mistakes?"

"I meant what I said. This isn't the first time something like this has happened, and as long as there are more psychos like you, you won't be the last. There's a fine line–"

Zane kicked the gun out of the man's hand and sucker-punched him in the face. He howled as the gun flew towards the bathroom. Zane tried to get up but found himself stuck, not out of fear, but literally immovable. Some kinetic energy overcame him and made gravity feel a million times stronger. It was as if all his nerves froze in place. He managed to turn his head around and saw the face of the figure in the dark, his mask and voice amplifier lying on the floor. It was a calculating boy with sandy blonde hair. Matthew Hunt. His eyes glowed bright green. He had his arm outstretched and strained as if he was using every ounce of his strength to keep Zane fixed. He looked afraid.

"You're behind this!?"

"Leave the blaster in the bathroom and we'll talk."

"You're a psychic!?"

"Zane! I won't ask you again! Sit down!"

"You really expect me to believe that? You're holding all the cards. It doesn't matter if you have a blaster. Your hands could do the trick no problem."

"So could the other guys outside your door."

Zane's heart skipped two beats.

"Have a seat."

The kinetic energy was relinquished. Zane gasped and lost balance, then put his hand out on the wall to keep himself steady. He felt nauseous as Matthew brought his chair closer to the light. They both stood, gasping for breath. Zane's training told him to go for the blaster solely because he knew his chances of escaping with his life were slim, but the investigator side of him told him to have a seat. There could be answers, and if that meant ending this case, it would be worth the risk. This was bigger than himself. This was about every other student gone missing. Without breaking eye contact with Matthew, he gently sat back down in the chair.

"How'd you find me?"

A few strands of Matthew's sweaty blonde hair hung down over his forehead. The glow from his eyes had disappeared.

"That's not important."

"It is if you want me to cooperate."

"You're not exactly in a position to negotiate."

Zane paused.

"Not exactly. Before I thought you were lying when you said you didn't kill those students, but now I know you were telling the truth. Your eyes are still innocent. You don't know what it's like to kill someone. You don't know how it changes you."

Matthew smirked.

"And you do?"

"No. But my father does."

"Ahh, yes–Deputy Dakari Minathi. A fine arbitrator. Great at tracking down psychics. Not great enough to catch me, but still good nonetheless."

"Give it time. In the end, they always find you."

"If you get your detective skills from your father then I highly doubt it."

Zane's eyes narrowed.

"You'd really rather not kill me. You would've done it already if you wanted to."

"I appreciate the compliment." Matthew smiled. "And yes. I'm not here to kill you. I'd much rather make a deal."

"Like those other students? You make deals with them too?"

"Some of them, yes. Others were not as *cooperative*."

"Does your father know you're a monster?" Matthew's proud persona shattered, for half a second, but that was all Zane needed. "Being the son of that famous General, I'm sure he's expecting a lot from you."

"And what makes me a monster? I didn't kill Alan Jones. I removed him. Tucked him away somewhere safe. If you think about it, what I do is no different than what your father does. We catch psychics and lock them in little cells, not at the CDAD. But somewhere else. Somewhere better."

He thinks I'm a psychic, Zane thought with a smile.

"Is that it? You found out I'm a psychic and wanted to make me disappear?"

Zane's Dad had taught him how to read facial cues from an early age, particularly the eyes. But Matthew was good. The only thing that had tipped the scales was the mention of his father. Since then, his eyes were immovable, as fixed as stones.

"If you were a psychic, we wouldn't be having this conversation," Matthew said. "It was too obvious after looking over your parents' files. You're one of those impurities. That's why we need to talk. The old mind tricks don't work on you."

Zane smiled.

"I wouldn't look so happy," Matthew said. "It makes this harder for everyone. We can only wipe the minds of AOL humans. Unfortunately, your inability to conform to common sense has put us in a strange predicament. If I were to kill you or even make you 'disappear,' there would be hell to pay, especially considering that your parents are both investigators." He paused. "Or I guess it's just your father now."

Images of his mother flooded Zane's mind, instinctively causing him to lunge forward. Matthew froze him again with the wave of his hand. Zane's face contorted with anger. He gritted his teeth and tried to reach forward, but it was pointless. With the flick of his hand, Zane was pushed back down into his chair. A feeling of nausea overcame Zane when he started to follow Matthew's train of thought. He couldn't hold a bluff anymore. He started sweating and his heartbeat raced.

"If I killed you, I'd have to kill your father and any other impurities he knows. It'd be a nightmare. No one wants that, Zane. You don't want that."

Zane shook his head.

"How dare you compare yourself to my father?! He would never do this."

"No. He's done worse. At least I don't beat fourteen-year-old girls with stun batons," Matthew said. "Try to understand where I'm coming from. I bet you don't know what happens inside those rehab centers, but it wouldn't be hard to take a guess. You think those psychics are glad to be there? You think they're treated well? Where do you think the studies come from? They treat us like *animals* and they always will. At least we're trying to give them a new life. We erase minds because if the state found out they'd shut us down. They'd end this whole operation and every psychic ever born would be sentenced to a life of solitary confinement and become a lab rat for the Republic."

Matthew leaned forward.

"But you wouldn't understand, would you? You've been conditioned from a young age just like everyone else to think we're *freaks*. I hear how they talk about us on the news. They call us mutants and monsters. It doesn't matter if we promise to withhold our powers or use them for good. They won't believe us because they're not willing to take that chance. They'd rather stick us in a cell and call it quits. How many psychics has your father killed? How many do you think he's sentenced to a life of imprisonment?"

Matthew's eyes were red with anger. He gripped the arms of the chair so hard his veins looked like they were going to burst. Then they relaxed.

"It doesn't matter," Matthew said. "Because you don't care. Your empathy only reaches so far. At a certain point, we all need scapegoats. We can't have a united Republic without aliens to enslave. We can't have a united humanity without psychics to torture and oppress for being involuntarily mutated. None of us chose this."

Zane's mind raced through a million different scenarios of how this might play out.

"Then what do you want from me?" He asked. "Why tell me all of this?"

Matthew stood up from his seat. His uniform boots echoed as he picked up the blaster from the ground. Zane closed his eyes and prepared for the end until he felt the blaster drop into his lap. He opened his eyes. Matthew sat in the chair and sighed.

"If you shoot me, my boys outside will finish you off, which means they'll also have to finish off your parents too. If I shoot you, they'll also have to gun down your father because there will be too many loose ends, too many minds we can't erase." Matthew raised two fingers and pointed them towards his own skull. "However, let's say there was a third option, one where no one asked any questions."

Zane stared at the blaster, horrified. It made him want to vomit.

"You can't be serious."

"If there is another way, I'm all ears. But you and I both know you can't keep this a secret. This would be the case of your father's lifetime. You might be able to keep quiet for a time, but eventually, you'd slip up. There's nothing you could say that would make me believe otherwise. You know I'm right."

Zane couldn't stop looking at the gun. Tears filled his eyes. He remembered that dance his parents did. He remembered his father teaching him self-defense in situations when he came home from work. Those memories evaporated into tears, but Zane wouldn't let them fall. They just stayed there in his eyes.

"You could win me over to your cause," Zane said.

"I thought about that one too. The only problematic variable would be your motivation. There's a reason our gang is comprised of psychics. They have nowhere else to go. Their lives hinge on the secrecy of our operation. Yours doesn't. As soon as you leave this room there's nothing stopping you from calling your Dad. Then he'd tell his arbitrator buddies, then it'd make the news, and then there are too many minds to erase. You might want to help us now, but even you don't know what you might be thinking when you no longer have to worry about losing your life."

Matthew leaned forward and grabbed the blaster from Zane. He displayed it before him.

"If you really wanted to keep Dad alive, you'd bite the bullet. In a way, you already have. Impurities like you gotta think about death every day, right? I mean, sure we could all get hit by a hovercraft, but those things are up to chance. Your life's a clock, ours is a game of cards. You play them right? You'll be in the game a long time."

Zane held back tears. He thought about Mom. Then Dad. He thought about calling him—maybe even the arbitrators. It was true. He had to face the reality of death as an impurity, but he was still young. He wasn't ready to knock on death's door. And yet now he felt like he was standing on the edge of a cliff, and below him, a dark fog-filled canyon. He wasn't ready to jump. There was so much more life he wanted to live, so much more he wanted to do. He thought of Mirabelle. The way they had held each other. The way they danced.

"Zane?"

He shook his head and came back into consciousness.

"Zane. You need to make a choice."

"No! You've got it all wrong. Your footprints are all over the scene. They'll find you! And my mental state? I've got no record of depression, no suicide warnings. They won't believe it. No one will."

"Your Mom just died, Zane. Anyone would believe it. I mean, if I wanted to, I could just shoot you right now and have the arbitrators frame it as a…" He stopped talking. It was true. This entire time with the arbitrators arriving on the scene, it didn't matter how Zane died. They could shape the scene however they wanted. Zane swallowed a lump in his throat when he saw the blaster in Matthew's hand.

"Give me the blaster, Matthew."

"Why the change of heart? Suddenly so eager to kill yourself?"

"Not as much as you are unwilling to do it. You don't want blood on your hands. I can keep talking all I want. You won't do a thing! You can't live with yourself as a monster, so you pin it to the arbitrators instead. But you're no different than they are. You're worse! The truth is that you could've just hidden your abilities if you wanted to, but you can't have that. You're one of the Hunt brothers. You're perfect not because everyone tells you, but because you tell that to yourself. If you kill me, that voice in your head goes silent. You face who you truly are."

Matthew breathed heavily with anger. He shook while holding the blaster between them, seeing his own life and Zane's life flash before his eyes. At that moment, he realized something: one of them wasn't leaving this room alive.

"You have to do it," Matthew said. "Or daddy goes too."

Before Matthew could even react, Zane had sent a text to Mirabelle saying: *The missing students are psychics.*

Then Zane did something daring. With as much force as he could muster, he punched his left arm, right in the center of his datapad, shattering the screen into fragments of glass. A flash of pain seared in his body with its internal destruction, the electric shock flaring his hand. But the deed was done. The text was sent and the datapad was broken. Mirabelle would know the truth, or part of it that he could send before Matthew would realize what he had done. Yet he would have no idea who he sent the text to. None at all.

"I can't do that, Matthew."

Matthew's eyes widened with horror upon realizing what Zane had done... then narrowed with anger, his fingers clenching the blaster tighter.

"I know."

* * *

Derek stood outside Zane's dorm. He closed his eyes, then flinched as he heard a blaster fire inside. He stood in the sound chamber with Bruce and Donny, each of their heads held low. Derek took a deep breath as Matthew opened the door and wiped the end of his blaster with a blood-stained rag. He looked at Derek and stared into his soul.

"Repeat after me," Matthew said. "There was no other way."

Derek swallowed a lump in his throat.

"There was no other way."

"What's done is done."

"What's done is done."

134

Matthew nodded, then patted Derek on the shoulder.

"Well done. You did good today. Your honesty will be rewarded."

Matthew walked away as several arbitrators arrived on the scene. And all the while Derek's eyes remained fixed on the carpet. An ache crept in his belly. He started to feel nauseous. He knew that at the end of the day, though Matthew had fired the blaster, the death of Zane Minathi was on his hands. And he hated himself for it. He wanted to die.

An Inconsolable Intermission

The funeral service for Desta and Zane Minathi was held on a grassy hillside, far from the city of Dain. Several gray tombstones scattered the green slopes, shaded by springtime trees. White-armored arbitrators carried two closed caskets down an open isle of black chairs, causing everyone in attendance to stand up and remove their hats. Only a few weeks had passed since their deaths, the grief still fresh and ripe. The sight of those coffins hoisted above his fellow officer's arms wrought a wellspring of silent tears from Dakari's eyes. It was a sight he could never imagine, a reality too terrible to believe. Kalak watched by the Deputy's side, his hat placed in the center of his black suit, his eyes holding a distant sadness. Amelia Lancaster stood in that row as well, her expression fraught with grief. Then there was Mirabelle Marshall, eyeing the casket of Zane as streaks of black mascara started to drip down her olive-skinned face, avoiding the makeup that covered her scar. The sun shone brilliantly in the blue sky as if mocking the tragedy it illuminated.

The slow procession of arbitrators was accompanied by no music and no words. Instead, soft sobs echoed in the audience. The scaly white boots of armored officers crunched the wet grass. Then the sounds of shovels digging up dirt as Dakari watched his wife and son get buried six feet underground. God seemed to be buried with their bodies, or at least a God that Dakari could believe in. There seemed to be nothing in this world that could console such senseless tragedy.

Five high-ranking armored officers raised their rifles into the sky, far off into the distance. Both the Minathis would receive a proper arbitrator's funeral. Even though Zane had never graduated and never officially joined the force, they deemed him worthy of the send-off given his parent's reputation and the officer he was destined to be had he been afforded the time to realize his dreams. Each hand in the crowd was raised to salute as the rifles fired and the caskets were lowered. Some hands were steadier than others. Dakari's hand trembled. He couldn't stop staring at their headstones and the ominous dates beneath their names. Amelia started to weep. Mirabelle turned away as the caskets were lowered. She pinched herself to stop the tears, but they fell down her cheeks like rain.

People started to walk away as soon as the burial was over. Modern funerals held no spoken words, no eulogies, no formal partings. They stood for the burial and then walked their separate ways because, in this world, death was too terrible to be dealt with. It was the most unnatural of forces, the great error that had been corrected by AOL. Most people left without saying a word because there was nothing to be said. What could you possibly say to a man who lost his wife and son in the span of a week?

"He would've made a fine arbitrator," Kalak said. "God only knows how well Desta served us too."

Dakari stared at both graves, the dirt now piled over the caskets. There was only so much tragedy and heartbreak a man could take. It was like treading water in a bad storm. Desta's death nearly drowned him, but with the help of Amelia and the determination to avenge her death, Dakari was able to break through the black, raging waters and gasp for breath at the surface. But when he got a phone call from the Gerumandian Academy, saying that his son had committed suicide, just a few days after hearing of Desta's death…that was a dark day. And the day was still dark. He was back beneath the current of the storm, so entrenched in the waves where sadness could not reach him. There was only numbness, his mind's last defense to preserve his own sanity.

"That's why we gave him an arbitrator's funeral," Dakari said.

Kalak straightened his cap on his head.

"He was a good kid." Kalak set a bouquet of flowers in between the two graves. "A shame that so often the good ones go first." Kalak put a hand on Dakari's shoulder. "Stop by my office sometime. There's something we should discuss." He paused. "And...I'm sorry for your loss."

Kalak walked towards his patrol car and left the hillside. Amelia offered her condolences too and left shortly after, each departure adding another layer to the cemetery's growing silence.

Mirabelle stood a few feet from Zane's grave. One hand held the strap over her purse. The other held a damp tissue, now stained with black ink and tears. She set it back in her purse, then froze. Her fingers brushed the edge of a photograph. She forgot she had even brought them. The missing students. The investigation. And the most damning evidence of all: a text from Zane himself. *The missing students are psychics*, he had said. She walked towards Dakari and stood by his side, trying to approach as quietly as possible to not disrupt his thoughts.

"Mr. Minathi."

She paused. This man was broken. His back was slightly arched. There was stubble on his face from where he would normally shave. And his eyes, with dark bags beneath them, were pressed heavily by flat eyelids. Mirabelle couldn't decide whether Dakari was heartbroken or whether he felt nothing at all. Then he looked her way, forcing something that could barely be called a smile.

"I hear you were good friends with my son." He made eye contact with her. "I'm glad to know he was surrounded by good people."

Mirabelle couldn't return the glance.

"I just..." Dakari covered his mouth with his hands. "I keep asking myself: if I hadn't told him over the phone. If I had waited a day longer..." Dakari closed his eyes. "What would've changed?"

Mirabelle held the side of her arm. She pinched herself.

"I don't think anything would've changed."

It wasn't a lie. But it felt like one. Dakari shook his head.

"No. I know my son. He had no reasons other than the reasons I gave him."

Mirabelle's fingernails dug into her skin. She couldn't tell him. She had told Zane, and then he died. If she told Dakari, he would die. End of story.

Go home, she thought. *Walk away.* But she couldn't. Her feet wouldn't move. Her conscience split into two halves. *Tell him and put his own life in jeopardy. Walk away and let him believe he's responsible for the death of his son.* She closed her eyes and did the only thing she could do. She wrapped her arms around Dakari and hugged him. He looked down in shock, leaning away, then slowly accepted her gesture of kindness and hugged her back. They both stood in silence. Then Mirabelle started to cry. Dakari patted her head and fought back tears of his own. Mirabelle sniffled and leaned closer.

"Are you bugged?" She whispered.

Dakari opened his eyes.

"What?"

"Can anyone hear our conversation?"

Dakari was too shocked to move. The last few arbitrators that were in attendance were far from the gravestones, approaching their vehicles. He looked down at Mirabelle. "No," he said. "No one can hear us."

"Are you sure?"

Dakari's brow narrowed with anger.

"Why?"

"Because if someone can hear us, we're both dead."

"Mirabelle, no one can hear us. What are you saying?"

She spoke in a haunted whisper.

"Zane didn't take his own life." Tears streamed down her face. "He was murdered."

* * *

It was late in the afternoon. A brisk wind swept up the cemetery hillside. The afternoon sky bled orange, red, and blue, framing the city of Dain with a backdrop of colors. Mirabelle and Dakari sat on a bench overlooking the headstones of Zane and Desta. They were the last living people in the cemetery. Mirabelle took a photograph back from Dakari and slid it into her purse.

"You were afraid to tell me," Dakari said. "Why?"

"I was worried that what happened to Zane might happen to you."

"Don't worry about my safety. Worry about yours."

"But I still don't know how they found him...or who 'they' even are."

Dakari let out a long sigh. "This is worse than I imagined."

"What is?"

"I'm starting to think the problems plaguing both our lives might be connected." Dakari looked back at the headstones. "Desta started to ask a lot of questions at Eastern. The next day there's an explosion at her apartment. Zane learns about missing students at the Academy. The next day he..." Dakari coiled his fist into a ball.

Mirabelle's eyes trailed aimlessly on the ground.

"And what about me?" She asked, feeling almost guilty in saying those words. "How am I still alive?"

"I ask myself the same thing," Dakari said. "Maybe we're the lucky ones."

"If this is luck then I don't like it."

"Neither do I."

"So what's our next move?"

"*Our* next move?" Dakari asked. "This isn't your fight."

"Are you kidding me?" Mirabelle stood up. "I gave you this information."

"And it's helpful, but no one else needs to get hurt."

"I've been keeping this a secret for *years*. I've known about it longer than you have. If they didn't catch me then, they won't catch me now. I can help."

"You're right. I apologize." Dakari stood up. "Sometimes I just wonder. Enough blood has been spilt trying to bury this secret. At what point is it not worth it? There's a point where I'd rather not see any more good people die."

"I know what you mean," Mirabelle said. "But what do you think Zane and Desta would do?"

Their headstones were silent, but even then, they seemed to give a clear answer.

"They wouldn't rest until this case was solved," Dakari said. "But you need to lay low. I'll keep a low profile at the CDAD and see what I can find on these students. If it's true that psychics are behind this, then Zane may have just given us our next course of action."

"And what's that?"

"We need to find a psychic."

They sat on the crest of the hillside in silence, watching the wind rustle the leaves of full-grown trees, brushing the tips of grass against the backdrop of a blooming sunset. At that moment, Dakari lamented that such a beautiful world could be spoiled by so much death…and the pain it left in the living. They sat on the hillside for hours before going their separate ways, their grief only cushioned by the purpose it gave them and a case that still needed to be solved.

A Search in the Skies

About a month after the Minathi funeral service, Alexander and Quan packed their bags and stood in the doorway of their apartment for what felt like the last time.

"If things go well," Alexander said. "This may be the last time we see this place."

Last month's activities had consisted of the usual brawling and thievery, but instead of spending the remaining time at nightclubs and in front of entertainment projectors, the dynamic duo crafted a stellar application for Quan to enroll at the Gerumandian Academy. On the day of their departure, they wore matching tuxedos for the Masten Scholarship interviews later that evening. They had packed their suitcases with all their belongings except the couch, refrigerator, and desks.

"I hope you're right," Quan said.

And that was it. Without looking back, they made a quick walk to the subway station and hopped on the shuttle. They were finally going to the Academy. Inside an L-Transport shuttle, they sat in awe as they gazed at the city of Dain from high in the sky. They passed other hovercrafts in the upper city air traffic. The glass windows of each building reflected a golden sunset. Citizens sat at rooftop restaurants, walked in airway tubes from building to building, and mingled in outdoor clubs. It seemed like a great world. But it was one that Quan knew could never be his. To disrupt this trance Alexander handed Quan a printed version of his resume.

"Go over this so you don't look like an idiot in the scholarship interviews," the blue-haired tech maestro said. "You got into the Academy, but we can't afford it. If you don't get this, we go back home."

"It still says, 'Quan Son Jerry?'"

"What did you expect?"

"Anything but my real name."

"There's no reason you shouldn't use your real name. It's not a crime to drop out of high school. Besides, I found a way to explain that too."

"Anything else I should know?"

"Yeah. Don't screw this up."

Quan slid his resume into his backpack.

"Thanks."

A few minutes later, the Academy emerged into view outside their window. Alexander rushed to the window and got up from his seat.

"There it is!"

They pressed their faces against the glass like little kids arriving at a theme park. The Gerumandian stood out as a giant among other buildings, with three massive towers jutting towards the sky like spires. Several parts of the towers curved like scythes from the re-used Waion architecture. Each window was circular and shined like a sea of shimmering glass. It looked like it could easily house 100,000 students, if not three times as much. Part of the building's design almost resembled a mountainous cathedral amidst an assortment of blank rectangular buildings. An airfield stood behind the main campus where jets took off and left the atmosphere. The Gerumandian symbol, a **G** framed beneath two golden battle axes, rested in the center of the building. A statue of Boris Gerumandian himself stood among fountains in the main entrance where cars came and went. The shuttle released plumes of white smoke, hissed, and made its descent at the drop off. Several other passengers walked out the open doors. Alexander set his luggage on the sidewalk and stretched his arms. He looked up at the 5000-foot-tall campus and felt dizzy.

"I can't believe we–" Alexander turned round. Quan stood in the doorway of the shuttle with his luggage in his hand. "Hey! You coming?"

Quan looked at the wristband on his arm. The words still read: *Never Give Up.*

"Jon's going to be here somewhere."

"Hey, kid!" The driver honked. "I got more stops! Make up your mind!"

Quan looked at the driver, then back at Alexander, and then at the towering Academy above him. It felt surreal standing before the campus of his dreams, at a place where legends like Chas Rodo and Ledarius Tartaren had fought and trained. Those legendary duelers lived lives Quan envied to the depths of his being. And now he had the chance to join their ranks. At that moment, the threat of seeing Jon paled in comparison to the glory that awaited him.

"What do I have to lose?"

With one step forward, Quan left the shuttle.

Alexander smiled. "That's the spirit." He put his arm around him as they walked up the steps. "Now let's go get that scholarship."

* * *

Someone knocked on Dakari's office door.

"Come in." It was Amelia. "What do you got for me?"

She shut the door and set a folder on Dakari's desk.

"I found those autopsies you were looking for." She watched Dakari flip through the pages. "You were right. They're not all impurities, but enough to make the targets statistically significant."

Dakari set the papers back down, stroking his chin in puzzlement. The last month had consisted of a single principle: stay busy enough to prevent his thoughts from taking him to places his mind could not handle. Insurance was still paying for a hotel a block away from work, preventing a long commute. Some days he walked home. Some days he slept in his office, though only on the rarest occasions.

"This doesn't make any sense. Why target someone based on their blood type?"

"In fairness, that's the same justification we use to hunt down psychics."

"That's because psychics are human superweapons. Non-AOL humans are just about as powerless as a human gets." Dakari stood up. "No matter.

It's a pattern, and maybe one that means something."

"And what do you think that is?"

"Not sure." Dakari put on his CDAD coat and buttoned up the middle. "But I might have a lead at L-Transport."

"You're going now? With no search warrant?"

"This isn't an investigation yet," Dakari said. He turned on his holopad, revealing several contracts. "Each month L-Transport renews their contract with the CDAD. I'll be tagging along to see if I can get some answers."

"You really think they're gonna let you do that?"

Dakari gestured to the four silver stars stitched to the sash on his shoulder.

"They won't have a choice."

Amelia smiled, then saluted.

"Be careful, sir."

"Will do."

Dakari Minathi walked down the stairsteps of the CDAD, a wide sprawl of Main Steet unveiling itself before him, and approached three arbitrators standing outside a hovercraft. It was an L-25 model, military-grade, large enough for ten troops or more. Lieutenant Banner, a plump man with faded blonde hair, stood outside the open doors and talked with his men, then noticed Dakari heading their direction. He saluted.

"At ease," Dakari said.

"Forgive me, sir. We weren't expecting you."

"I heard you were meeting with L-Transport this afternoon. Mind if I tag along?"

Each arbitrator exchanged a glance. Lieutenant Banner cleared his throat.

"We're just renewing the terms of our agreement with Darius. It's a business trip."

"I understand. I'd just like to meet the man we're conducting business with."

After a brief hesitation, Dakari Minathi was given permission to board. They left shortly after. Dakari watched the Central Dain Arbitrator

Department shrink in size as they ascended into the skies. He knew Kalak was down there somewhere, maybe even watching them from a window. He felt his wife's wedding ring and his son's dog tags hanging beneath his shirt. He prayed he was doing the right thing.

Stuck-Up Scholars

The Great Hall was one of the most impressive rooms at the Gerumandian Academy. Its ceilings stretched several stories high, adorned with glorious wartime frescoes and portraits. Dying Waions covered the scenes, illuminated by the glow of a Gothic chandelier hanging from the center of the ceiling. Beneath the spectacle of light, a wide wooden table filled the space of the room where several officers, military veterans, and donors sat comfortably in the midst of important discussion. The Masten Committee was expecting scholars soon and shared their thoughts on the prospective students. A door opened, ushering in swift silence. Every man and woman at the table stood up and saluted as a broad-shouldered man in a green military jacket entered the room. His footsteps echoed across the marble floor as he made his way to the head of the table. He stood with a straight back and a hardened look on his leathery-shaven face. His eyes were as green as the grasslands of New Earth but as dark as the most dangerous forests. Within his countenance was the world's most perpetual scowl, and on his chest, a golden imprint of the Ouroboros.

It was Brigadier General Carter Hunt.

"At ease." He removed his cap covering his trimmed blonde hair. "Have a seat."

The Masten Committee obeyed. They discussed the schedule for the following weekend and assigned roles to different members of the Committee. It was the middle of summer, which meant that the Gerumandian Academy was at less than a tenth of its normal enrollment. They reserved plenty of rooms for interviews and demonstrations, then started assigning bunkmates to students. And then came the most important part: interviews.

"That settles it for David," Carter said, checking off a box on the holopad. "What about this last one? Quan Son Jerry."

Officer Mocroft's ears perked up. He looked up from his holopad.

"What was that?" Mocroft asked.

"Quan Son Jerry," Carter said in his grating voice. "It says here that he attended Silverside High School in the suburbs of District 3. Quite the dueling resume for an 18-year-old. He even spent some time in the underground dueling arena in his spare time."

Mocroft smiled. *18-year-old, huh?*

"Is that so?" Estra Harlyn, assistant chairman of the Masten committee, smiled. "That's unusual for someone of his age to venture out into other areas."

"He's pretty old for a sophomore in tier school," Sergeant Williams said.

"It says here he was held back twice in the sixth grade," Carter said. Meanwhile, Mocroft covered his mouth with his hand, trying not to laugh at the litany of lies. "That seems to be when he started turning his life around. Other than that, he's nothing special. He's got a normal family life, no real troubling circumstances. Any takers?"

Mocroft raised a hand.

"Why not? I'd like to see what all the fuss is about."

"Very well." Carter tucked the holopad away. "It's settled then. Soon the chefs will prepare the opening meal. In the meantime, it might be a good idea to go over the files of the students you'll be interviewing. Not long from now, the other Masten scholars will be joining us, and then..." Carter smiled. "The selection process begins."

* * *

A few hours later, Quan twiddled his thumbs in an empty reading room in the library. The walls were white, the silence eerie, the boredom swiftly overcoming the young dueler awaiting his interview. He sat up straight as the second the door opened. Then his jaw dropped when he saw who had stepped inside, closing the door behind him with a smile.

"Never thought I'd see you here," Mocroft said, taking a seat from across the young boy. He set his holopad on the table and scrolled down his notes.

Quan rolled his eyes and groaned.

"You gotta be kidding me."

"Not happy to see me? Isn't that why you applied?"

"I didn't do it for you."

"Not a great way to start an interview with your superior."

"You already know everything about me. Why choose me?"

"Because I know that the second this interview is over, you're going to avoid me like the plague. I'd like a few questions answered."

"And what if I told the committee you skipped the interview questions?"

Mocroft's eyes widened, then he roared with laughter. It was kind of amusing for him to see Quan grow from an elementary school dueler into the person he was today. Though he had grown in size and stature, he still saw the same child in his bright blue eyes.

"Where's your bargaining power? I know enough about this fraudulent resume of yours to send you back to that backwater alleyway you crawled out of."

"It's not all fake."

"I'm a patient man, Quan. But even my patience has its limits."

"Fine. What do you want to know?"

Mocroft shut off the holopad and leaned back in his seat. There were many things he wanted to know. Being Quan's old dueling instructor at Silverside, he had seen the boy go through many highs and lows. In the hallways, he saw how he interacted with his friends and even his brother when they were still on speaking terms. He saw him with girls at dances and in the woes of breakups. Whatever was going on in Quan's life, he brought it with him into the dueling ring. That had been over a year ago. There was a lot Mocroft wanted to catch up on. Naturally, the biggest question of all rose to his mind.

"Why did you run away?"

Quan crossed his arms.

"Why do you care?"

"You were the shining star of Silverside High School, a student that any teacher would dream of having." Quan tried to keep himself from laughing, but Mocroft continued. "There were other superstars like you at Silverside. Your brother was one of them. But they were power-hungry stuck-up scholars. You were a good kid."

"If you want me to be nicer you can just come out and say it."

"You're missing the point."

"Am I? I didn't know the Gerumandians loved nice people."

"They don't. That's why most of my students are monsters."

"Whose fault is that?"

"It's hard to say. I'm a dueling instructor. I see a student for no more than thirty minutes a day." Mocroft sighed. "There are a lot of posers in this world, but at the end of the day I could see that you cared about giving back. That all changed when Jon left."

"And how'd you expect me to respond?! We were supposed to go to the Academy together! But they wouldn't take both of us. They wanted him, regardless of the fact that I was just as good, if not *better* than he was."

"And that was it? That made you run away?"

Flashback: a young Quan stood in the mirror, bloody hands, tear-filled eyes. The breakthrough. The trauma. Those things couldn't be said. He needed to say something else, something true, but tangential to what he was permitted to say.

"No. I ran away because on that day I learned a hard truth. People don't get what they deserve."

"But they do reap what they sow. Not every story ends in a happily ever after, but that doesn't mean good things aren't worth fighting for." Mocroft smiled. "Funny. For someone who spent his entire life winning, you sure don't know how to lose."

There was a sudden silence between the two of them. Mocroft typed something into his holopad when he realized that Quan was done sharing. "I'm going to do everything I can to get you into this Academy because

I believe in second chances. I also know there was more behind your disappearance than your brother's broken promises."

"Is that what this is?" Quan asked. "You want me to make peace with him?"

Mocroft froze.

"You mean you never heard?"

Quan tried to feign disinterest but failed. He leaned closer.

"What do you mean?"

"Your brother doesn't go to the Academy. He vanished about a year ago."

"Vanished?"

"One day he was here, the next day he was gone. No one knows why he left or where he went." Mocroft grabbed his holopad and stood up.

"Hold on." Quan pinned the door shut with his fist. "Why haven't I heard about this?"

"You're the one who stopped talking to him."

"Does anyone else know?"

"Of course. It was the whole buzz of the Academy for days."

Chills ran up Quan's spine. He started to feel dizzy.

"Where would he go?"

"Not a clue. I didn't know him well. But I know someone who did. There's a girl at the banquet tonight you should meet named Mirabelle Marshall. She and Jon were lab partners." Mocroft opened the door. "If I were you, I'd try to stop running away from this world–it could use you."

The mustache man, as Alexander was so fond of calling him, shut the door, leaving Quan alone in a stunned and stupefied silence. The weight of running into Jon slipped off his shoulders, but it was replaced with a mystery. *Where could Jon have gone?* There seemed to be only one person who might have that answer. Some random girl named Mirabelle Marshall.

A Bewildering Banquet

In the upper city, Dakari Minathi and four other arbitrators arrived at the Leonardo Estate: a sprawling penthouse that looked more like a palace than a home. The front courtyard stood behind steel gates, sprawling with lush vegetation, exotic flowers of pink and purple, a towering fountain circled by cobblestone paths, and several landing pads with L-Transport hovercrafts. Beyond the high walls surrounding their estate were sleek diamond-blue roads spotted with black street lamps. It was as if someone had placed an entire neighborhood above high rises and building complexes for several miles in each direction. It overlooked the city of Dain with other famous estates just across the glass-enclosed walkways. They strolled through the courtyard as several servants escorted them past a statue of Darius Leonardo himself. He stood with a proud gaze to the sky. The real Mr. Leonardo, not the marble sculpture of himself, stood beneath the golden doorframe of his home wearing the usual white business robes that fell gracefully on his shoulders. He had a dark complexion like Dakari but had eyes of violet. He welcomed the arbitrators with a smile.

"Good evening, gentlemen," Darius said. "Can I interest you in any beverages?"

"A pleasure to see you, Mr. Leonardo," Banner said. He was dressed in his navy blue trenchcoat uniform like all the other arbitrators. The only thing that set him apart was the hint of nervousness that ran across his face. "Unfortunately, we can't drink on the job."

"Ahh, forgive me. Where are my manners?" Darius eyes meandered over Lieutenant Banner's shoulder, landing on a middle-aged copper skinned man with a look of resolute seriousness cast over his expression. "I see we have a new face here. Care for a tour?"

"That won't be necessary," Banner said. "This shouldn't take long."

"Actually, I'd love a tour," Dakari said. "Who am I to turn down hospitality?"

"Wonderful! Right, this way then."

Banner and a few other arbitrators exchanged a glance, then followed Mr. Leonardo inside. The front doorway opened up to a sprawling atrium of fifty-foot high ceilings. Large portraits of the Leonardo family decorated the walls, each of them casting proud glances below at the observers who craned their necks to look upon them. Large marshmallow-white couches surrounded a glass table in the living room with lapis lazuli curtains resting gracefully in hooks by the windows. There was a stage for performers and a pool on the overlook outside, a private movie theater, and enough bedrooms upstairs to house several families. Their tour ended at a large wooden table in the dining room, where each arbitrator took their seat across from the founder of L-Transport himself, who regarded the navy blue arbitrators with folded hands and a courteous smile.

Banner slid his holopad across the table.

"These forms are for the L-25 engines we use in the hovercrafts."

Darius smiled and accepted the device in his hands, scrolling through the paperwork.

"That was the first model we started commercializing. Even the Republic Military uses them now." He scanned the terms of agreement and signed several more forms. Then paused. "That's new." Darius showed the arbitrators the screen. "What's this one?"

Banner retrieved the device quick enough, preventing Dakari from catching a glance.

"It's a new project we're working on based on the highspeed railways in downtown Dain." Banner slid the device back to Darius. Their movements were subtle but deliberate. There was something on that form they didn't want Dakari to see. And in their eyes, he could see the fear of Darius' loose tongue, of not knowing what he might say or how he might respond.

There was a call on Dakari's datapad. He silenced it immediately without looking.

"An underground railway system beneath the CDAD?" Darius asked.

"We'd renew the contract on a monthly basis if you change your mind," Banner said, his voice so hideously courteous. It was a stark contrast to the brash, bad-mouthed officer Dakari knew behind closed doors. "It's no secret that people who work in the CDAD are being targeted at alarming rates. If certain people discovered you're involved in this, it might put you in danger."

Darius laughed.

"You don't think I realized that when I started selling L-25 engines to the Republic? I know the risk." Darius kept reading. "Oh. You'd want to use L-Transport cargo ships for—"

"The transfer of precious cargo," Banner said. "Precisely."

Dakari tried to hide his puzzlement.

"I'm not sure I understand the novelty of this," Dakari said. "L-Transport cargo ships have been in our records for several months."

"Maybe hovercrafts with my engines have, but I have not authorized the use of any L-Transport vehicles for CDAD operations."

Dakari was silent. He had strong evidence that suggested otherwise. Numerous transponder codes within the CDAD charted L-Transport vehicles in the detention centers. Either Darius was remarkably forgetful, or someone was keeping information from him. He tried to press the issue but felt his datapad vibrate again. It was another call.

"I think you might be getting a call, *Deputy*," Banner said. "Perhaps you should step outside and answer it. We can handle things from here."

Their eyes met in a subtle stalemate. Dakari stood up from his chair and followed a servant out to the front courtyard. He double tapped the screen on his datapad. It was Kalak. And he wasn't in a good mood.

* * *

Derek Hunt combed back his wavy blonde hair in front of the mirror, doing his best to avoid making eye contact with himself. Even months after the death of Zane Minathi, whose very name conjured a claw of pain inside himself, a flash of guilt would strangle Derek, an irrefutable feeling that could not be reasoned with. It was like someone had him at gunpoint; but that someone was himself. All he could do was raise his hands and hope the inner gunman would walk away and torment some other poor soul that had done bad things. That wasn't going to happen anytime soon. Derek's guilt traveled with him where he went. And yet he still fed himself the same lie Matthew forced him to repeat on the night the deed was done:

What's done is done. There was no other way.

Someone knocked on the door.

"It's unlocked," Derek said, swiping his hair back again.

Bruce entered the room. He had gelled his auburn hair and wore his green and gold Gerumandian dress suit for special occasions, the same one Derek wore as well.

"We better head downstairs. We got dinner with the prospectives in five."

They left and took the elevator downstairs.

"You sign up for the overnight deal?" Bruce asked.

"Yeah," Derek said. "You?"

"Same. But to be honest I'm not looking forward to bunking with someone for an entire weekend. I just hope I don't get someone weird. Or pretentious."

"Same."

On the ground level, the hallways of the Academy were silent. Derek and Bruce were used to it by now. During the summer, the campus was a ghost town. They quietly slipped into the Great Hall as Officer Mocroft gave a speech. Each of the prospectives stood behind their chairs on the main table. The whole room was draped in gold and green, the wartime frescoes looking as regal as ever. Derek scanned the room for his father but saw no such figure. Instead, he saw Carter Hunt's portrait on the walls, skewering a scaly green Waion with a spear.

They joined a group of the current Masten scholars in the corner of the room where they waited to be called. Derek sat on the couch and looked to his right. It was Mirabelle. She sat silently in her white uniform. He couldn't even bring himself to look at her after what he had been apart of. He couldn't even begin to imagine how she felt. *I bet she still thinks he committed suicide*, he thought. That made him feel even worse.

Officer Mocroft gestured towards them.

"And now, we'd like to welcome our Masten scholars up to the table."

Mirabelle straightened her collar and stood up as the students walked over to the table. Derek stood up and followed suit. *There's no way she knows I was involved*, he thought. *Stop being so paranoid. Plus, there was no other way.* He repeated this mantra to himself as he smiled and waved at the prospectives. *Little do they know, they're waving at a murderer. They're waving and smiling and talking to the man who killed Zane Minathi.* He hoped he didn't look as dead as he felt and took his seat.

* * *

At the same Derek's conscience was eating himself alive, Quan's eyes went wild at the embarrassment of riches that surrounded him in the Great Hall. *A free meal?* Quan thought. *This is paradise.* It was fancier and more expensive than he was accustomed too. He cut a piece of steak with a golden knife and kept pausing to see his own reflection. He looked around the room, almost thinking about tucking it away for later. Then he realized that might destroy his scholarship chances, so he set the knife back down. Table manners were going to be a problem. He kept mirroring the movements of other students around him. He felt out of place even though he wore a suit like everyone else. He was terrified someone would call him out for not setting his knife on the right side of the plate after cutting his steak. He set the fork and knife on the same side to be safe.

An olive-skinned girl with dark hair and a scar across her nose sat across from him.

"Your knife is on the wrong side," she said.

Quan nervously laughed and switched it over.

"I knew that. I was just testing you."

"No, you weren't." There was a pin on her dress with the words *Masten*. "I'm already a scholar." She extended a hand with a deadpan look. "Mirabelle Marshall."

His eyes widened. He froze as he lifted his fork to his mouth, then dropped it completely. A few officers looked his way as he shook Mirabelle's hand.

"Quan Son Jerry."

Her deadpan looked vanished from her expression. She squinted her eyes and got a closer look at Quan, making him feel a bit uncomfortable. *I know that name*, she thought. *Or at least the last one.* They both let go of each other's hands.

An awkward silence passed. Quan kept shoving food in his mouth, more concerned about having an excuse not to talk than keeping a false facade of manners. He swallowed.

"So…" Mirabelle said. "What brings you to the Academy?"

Quan took a sip and set his glass back down once. Mirabelle's eyes lit up, then lowered with a hint of despondency as he cleared his throat to speak. *He didn't double tap.* That thought hurt. A lot.

"I'm a dueler. And I need money to–" Quan let out a belch that sounded like the croak of a dying frog. A few heads turned his way. Mirabelle snickered and tried not to laugh as Quan's face grew as red as a tomato. Luckily, the only people that looked his way were other students. Most instructors were too busy listening to conversations to notice him. "My bad." He looked across the table. "You think they heard that?"

"You better hope not. Don't give these people any reason to reject you."

"You don't think Gerumandian officers would find it amusing if I burped in their face?"

"Try it."

"Nah, I'd get in too much trouble." Quan started looking at the instructors at the other end of the table. "What about that guy? Weird nose. Pointed mustache."

"Officer Mocroft?"

"More like Officer Mc-Soft. You ever have him for a teacher?" Quan cut his steak. He started cutting faster. "I had him for interviews. Seems like a dud if you ask me. I'd rather watch paint dry than listen to his lectures."

She almost dropped her fork due to speechlessness, then leaned forward. "You are *exactly* like your brother."

Quan immediately stopped cutting his steak.

"What did you say?"

"Jon Jerry. He was your brother, wasn't he?"

Quan started cutting the steak again. This time even faster.

"I don't know what you're talking about."

"Yes, you do."

"No. I really don't."

"Then why are you getting defensive?"

"I'm not getting defensive!"

"Yes, you are!"

"Well—so are you!"

"But you started it!" Mirabelle said. They weren't really yelling as much as they were intensely whispering. It was harsh enough to indicate their anger at each other but not loud enough to be noticed by other instructors. Though a few did look their direction with some surprise at the tone with which they spoke to one another.

Quan took a bite of his steak and pointed his dripping knife at her.

"You have no proof. Jerry is a common last name."

"I don't need any proof. He wore that same wristband."

That was the last straw. Old memories and old grudges bubbled with volcanic intensity to the surface of Quan's mind. He tensed his fist as a tsunami of hatred overcame him. He dropped his fork and stared intently in Mirabelle's eyes. He pointed his finger at her and curled his lips as he tried to think of something hateful, something *terrible* to say to her. All that came out was:

"I have to use the restroom!"

A few students looked back as Quan got up from his chair and stormed out of the Great Hall. Mocroft, who had been watching him, shook his head and sighed.

* * *

In the restroom, Quan leaned over an empty sink. A few strands of his black hair hung over his eyes. He swiped them back into place.

"You sound just like your brother. Stupid girl."

He tried to calm himself down. *Deep breaths*, he told himself. *Deep breaths.* He didn't understand everything about his abilities, but there was one thing he knew perfectly: the eyes of a psychic can glow during periods of intense emotions. It didn't happen often, but sometimes in a fit of rage, Quan's eyes would shine as bright as headlights. He saw the faintest glimmer, not something a casual person would notice, but to an eye trained to spot psychics, someone could notice the intensity. He needed to be more careful. Even the name of Jon had awakened something in him. He thought about punching the glass. Then he thought that would be dramatic. And stupid. Really stupid. A few deep breaths later, he stood up and straightened his collar, then slid his wristband beneath his sleeve.

He returned to the Great Hall, slipping in without much notice. He took his seat and ate his food without another word. And of course, not once did he glance at Mirabelle. And she didn't glance at him. By the time the dinner was over, Officer Mocroft stood up and gave the biggest announcement of the night: bunkmates. Students were paired off with another Gerumandian to bunk before interviews the next day. Quan patiently waited for his name to be called.

"Quan Son Jerry," Mocroft said, taking a moment to make eye contact with him for dramatic effect. "You will be rooming with Derek Hunt."

The blonde-haired bastard looked over at Quan with a smile, who did not return the gesture. *Great*, Quan thought. *This day just keeps getting better and better. First I meet someone who knew Jon. Now I'm stuck with Carter's golden child.* To anyone else, the pairing would have been a dream come true. To Quan, the Hunt brothers would always be obstacles in his way to the Gerumandian Dueling Tournament. Though now that Quan thought about it, he realized it may not be the worst thing in the world. There was an old saying to keep your friends close and your enemies closer. In that regard, what better way to stay close to your foes than to become their bunkmates? Maybe it was a little too close for comfort, but it did afford Quan a unique opportunity: to learn about Derek Hunt, and in the process, learn his weaknesses too. With this thought, Quan happily joined Derek on the other side of the room, walking towards his dorm with a sly smile.

Random Roommates

"Here is it," Derek said, holding the door to his room open. "Home sweet home."

Quan set his luggage by the bed and stretched out his arms. His skinny, blue-haired, loud-mouthed friend followed suit. Derek hadn't spent more than ten minutes with them, and it was already a nightmare. They wouldn't stop talking. Especially that guy with the modified datapad. "Ok, can you please tell me who this guy is?"

"That's Alexander," Quan said. "He's just a friend."

"I don't care if he was your brother. He's not on the list."

"If they don't know, they don't know," Alexander said. "And what they don't know don't hurt em. I'd appreciate it if you just kept this one on the down low. I'm technically not allowed to be here."

"Exactly. That's my point."

"But my good-spirited muscular friend, I *need* to be here. We're in a moving phase right now."

"Can't you just...I don't know. Go home?"

Quan and Alexander exchanged a glance, then erupted in laughter. They kept shaking their heads and started unpacking some of their belongings onto the bed.

"I don't know what's so funny about that," Derek said. "Plus, I don't have a place for you to sleep."

"Not a problem," Alexander said. "A nice space on the floor is fine. I brought a pillow." He chucked the cushion into the corner and dusted off his hands. "Now that that's settled, I'm gonna go look for some food. Got any vending machines?"

Derek was too stunned to respond.

"Uh, yeah. There's one down the hall. Knock if you need to come back inside."

"Thanks, bud." He patted Derek on the shoulder and left the room. The younger Hunt brother closed the door behind him. "Hey man, I'm not tryna be that guy, but your friend wasn't on the list. Who is he really?"

"He's a friend." Quan kept setting his shirts on the bed.

"And do your friends typically tag along on your scholarship invitations?"

Quan zipped his luggage. "Ok, don't tell anyone but uh...Alexander is homeless."

"What?"

"Yeah. He follows me everywhere I go. I can't get rid of him. You know...since he has no home."

"That would make sense."

"But he's a great guy. He won't get in your way and he's too obsessed with his datapad to mess around with anything in your room. Trust me. Let him stay until the weekend is over and you won't even notice he's there."

"And then what? He's just gonna sleep on the floor of your next dorm?"

"Yeah. He's enrolling this fall too, but since he didn't get an invitation for the Masten Scholarship, he'll be bunking with me until then. That's allowed right?"

"Pretty sure it's not."

Quan shrugged his shoulders.

"Well, if you could just not tell anyone that'd be great."

It was a bit awkward and abrupt, but Quan had his fingers crossed that it would work. Quan looked around the room. It was a standard Academy double: two beds, two desks by the window, and one bathroom. An Ouroboros banner of green and gold with a snake devouring its own tail hung from the wall; the Hunt family sigil. The rest of the room was littered with gym supplements and duffel bags filled with protein canisters, BCAAs, supplements, and pre-workout tubs. And then there was something else, something strange.

Traces of gold pixels hung in the air for seconds at a time like a winding stream. They were there one moment and gone the next. Some spots in the room were brighter than others, but they were there. Quan reached out to touch them and discovered that they disappeared upon blinking. He looked over at Derek who was sorting a few papers on his desk. Then Quan blinked and peered at the back of Derek's buzzed blonde head, trying to see something inside. And then he saw it. Blooming like a flower, a ray of golden light flickered inside his cranium. A shirt fell from Quan's hand.

I can't believe it! Derek Hunt is a psychic.

"I don't know how to say this," Derek said, setting a few papers in the drawer. "But Alexander's gonna have to leave. It's just protocol."

"Protocol, huh?" Quan traced his finger along the psychic particles that kept bouncing back and forth between his vision. "And what might the Academy's protocol on psychics be?"

Derek raised a brow.

"Same as everywhere else. Call em if you…" Derek's eyes widened. He followed Quan's gaze and saw where his fingers were tracing. There was nothing there but air. But that didn't mean that was all there used to be. Derek's blood went cold. "…see em."

"Interesting." Quan made eye contact with Derek. "That's very interesting. You might even say something like that would receive a greater punishment than an extra roommate. Wouldn't you agree?"

Derek tensed up. *What on New Earth is this kid referring to? Why is he being so cryptic?* There was no way he could've known he was a psychic…none at all.

"Yeah," Derek said. "Good thing that's not a problem we have to worry about."

Quan saw the golden aurora flash inside Derek's cranium one more time, just to be sure.

"Yeah," Quan said. "Good thing."

* * *

163

Later that afternoon, Derek paid a visit to Matthew's dorm.

"He knew I was a psychic," Derek said.

Matthew leaned against the wall with his arms crossed. He had spent the whole day in the dueling chambers training for the tournament later this fall. He was tired. He wanted to sleep, not deal with his brother's paranoia.

"That's impossible."

"No, it's not. The Boss warned us about a psychic like this before."

"That doesn't mean he's the one."

"But it could be."

"Why are you so insistent about this?"

"He tried to blackmail me! He knows. I could see it in his eyes."

"Stop worrying. I'm calling it a bluff. And if you're right, it means he won't say anything because he's probably a psychic too. He wouldn't want to draw that much attention to himself."

"How can you be so casual about this? Shouldn't we bag him up?"

"Run a test first."

"When?"

"When do you think genius? You guys are sleeping in the same room! Do it tonight." Matthew sighed. "It's remarkable how unprofessional you are sometimes. You need to stay cool. There's no confirmation he's a psychic so there's no need to get anyone else involved. Understood?"

"The Boss always said there was a psychic that had a power like this. If he's the one, it's game over."

Matthew pointed.

"The door is over there."

Derek reached for the door, then stopped.

"What about his friend? I won't be able to scan Quan if he stays in my room."

Matthew eyed an empty bed in his dorm.

"Send him up here and I'll take care of the rest. Goodnight."

Derek stormed away and slammed the door behind him.

* * *

Back in her dorm room, Mirabelle sat on the edge of her bed and stared at her dresser at the far end of the wall. The Jerry name had triggered a wellspring of memories and emotions within herself. Disbelief was chief among them.

"It can't be him."

There was only one way to know. Mirabelle walked across the carpet and stopped in front of her dresser. She took a deep breath and closed her eyes. It opened just as easily as it did each morning, and when she pushed a wad of socks to the side, she saw the tiny reflections of missing students smiling at her. And now Zane smiled at her too. She sifted through the photographs. She had to know, and when she found Jon's photograph, the truth lay in her hands as clear as day.

She looked at the photograph at the older boy with black hair and golden eyes.

Jon Jerry.

Then she looked at the picture of Quan on her datapad. Black hair. Blue eyes.

Quan Son Jerry.

There was no doubt in her mind. They were brothers. Jon Jerry's disappearance was the outlier among the other cases for one simple reason: the Academy still remembered him. Perhaps that meant that it was unrelated to the case she was trying to solve, but because it was still a disappearance, she lumped it into the same categories as the others. And now she had to find out the truth of what happened. The photograph fell to the ground as light as a feather. Mirabelle grabbed her coat and ran for the door.

* * *

Someone knocked on Derek's door. He flinched, readying himself in a combat position, then froze. *What are you doing? Calm down.* Easier said than done; but it had to be done. With a few deep breaths, Derek opened the door, then felt a wave of shock overcome him.

"Mirabelle?"

She did not look happy to see him.

"Where's Quan?"

"He just stepped out to take a call. I think he said he was going to the rooftop." Mirabelle walked away. "What's the–"

"It doesn't concern you." She kept walking. By the time she had left Derek's line of sight, he shut the door, collapsed on the bed, and covered his eyes with his hands. Then he sat up and threw his fist towards the wall. A sharp gust of wind shot out a portal in his hands, knocking over his duffel bags, spilling all his supplements onto the floor in a fit of rage.

* * *

After wandering through just about every hallway in the Gerumandian Academy, Quan rode the elevator up to the rooftop. He talked with Alexander on the datapad as he listened to the hum of the engine below his sneakers. He felt better to be back in his maroon t-shirt and jeans instead of a dress suit. This was more his style and more comfortable too.

"I don't think it's that big of a deal," Quan said. "I mean, I'm staying with Derek, you're staying with Matthew. If anything, this means I have an advantage! See if you can learn any of Matthew's dueling secrets! Some people are saying he might join the tournament."

"Yeah, because he's totally going to tell me that. He doesn't like me."

"How do you know?"

"I just know. He's got scary eyes."

"Find out what you can. But don't make it too obvious."

"He'll see right through me!" Alexander paused. "Where you headed now?"

A few seconds later, there was a chime as the elevator door opened to the rooftop. A girl was leaning against the railing, facing Quan. It was Mirabelle Marshall.

"Oh crap," Quan said, stepping out of the elevator. "I gotta go."

"What? Wait, Quan!"

Quan ripped the earbuds out of his ears and stepped outside the elevator. The two newfound rivals stood in silence as the sliding doors closed. A gust of wind swept up the sides of the Academy tower sitting 5000 feet above the ground. In the distance, the air traffic of Dain became nothing more than a gentle hum, the pedestrians and cars below reduced to silence. Mirabelle's hair fluttered in the wind as she looked at Quan with reluctance, her scar like a shadow across her face in the afternoon sunlight.

"Wow." Quan laughed. "First you disrespect me. Then you stalk me."

"Disrespect...what are you talking about?"

"Fine. Maybe you didn't know. But you definitely stalked me."

"Why would I–"

"How'd you know I was gonna be here?"

"I asked Derek."

Quan raised both arms.

"Case in point!"

"I had my reasons."

"Oh?" Quan crossed his arms. "Do tell."

Mirabelle shook her head with annoyance and grabbed something out of the coat pocket of her yellow leather jacket. It was a photograph. "You know who this is, don't you?"

Quan didn't move, then took a few steps forward. With the sun setting in the distance, he saw the light fall upon half the image while the other half lay in a shadow. He took it from her and lay the image flat for a better look. Mirabelle watched his reaction as he handed the photograph back to her, his eyes gazing off into the distance.

"Well?" Mirabelle asked. "Do you?"

Quan rested his forearms over the rooftop railing and looked over the edge.

"Why do you care?"

Mirabelle leaned next to him, her gaze wandering through the metropolitan maze.

"Then I was right."

"You didn't answer my question." Quan looked her in the eyes. "Why do you care?" She didn't respond. "No, like, seriously. What does it matter to you? Why do you have a photograph of Jon?"

Of all the ways Mirabelle expected this encounter would go, this was certainly not one of them. Quan seemed maniacally committed to his stubbornness. The tone in his voice was irritating, and the way his eyes scanned her like one of those people who believed everyone in the world was out to get them—it nearly drove her mad. The lines in his forehead were always scrunched in resolute seriousness beneath his mop of wavy black hair. As much as she wanted to mock him, she knew she needed to take the high road if she wanted to get any useful information out of him.

"People like your brother don't last long at a school like this," she said. "They disappear." She tucked the image away and hid both hands in her coat pockets, tensing up in the cold. "Then they're forgotten."

"What's that supposed to mean?"

Pain flashed through her veins so fiercely at that moment that she honestly wanted to die. The only thing she could think about was the similar conversations she had had with Zane not even a month ago. Those wounds were so fresh within her that they continued to bleed at even the slightest remembrance of his person—a person who had been so full of life and vitality that to lose him felt like losing a part of herself she could never hope to recover. When she did muster the courage again to speak, the words came out with the slow heaviness that is so accustomed for people dealing with overwhelming grief.

"It means I wouldn't have come to see you if I didn't think that you'd be next."

Quan's eyes stared blankly without the slightest apprehension.

"Next? Stop being so cryptic. Spit it out."

"It's not that simple. If I tell you...they might come looking for you too."

Quan laughed. Mirabelle thought it was the most inauthentic laugh in the world.

"You're crazy."

"No, I'm not."

He shrugged his shoulders, then turned around. "Yup. Forget this. I'm out."

Mirabelle faced him as he walked away.

"That's it? You really don't care about what happened to him?"

"Nope." Quan pressed the elevator door. It started humming.

"So, you didn't come to the Academy to look for him?"

"Of course not."

"Then why did you come here?"

The elevator door opened. Quan nearly stepped inside but turned around instead.

"You ever heard the phrase: 'mind your own business?'" Quan inched towards her as tension rose in his voice. "I don't know how you knew about Jon, but quite frankly, I couldn't care. If he died, serves him right! He finally got what he deserved! But I never did. They never talked about *Quan*! Jon was always the better one! Wasn't he!? They always cared about him, didn't they!? They *never* cared about me!"

The reflexive anger had risen so instinctually within Quan that he hadn't even realized the throbbing in his temples and the blue glow reflecting in Mirabelle's dark eyes. She shuddered back in fear as Quan's eyes burned bright blue like flashlights. The knee-jerk reaction to "Jon Jerry" had caused him to slip again. He had done it. He had let his anger go too far, activating his abilities. Mirabelle backed away to the railing as the newly discovered psychic backed away too, his eyes dimming and returning to their normal color. They looked at each other in silence for what seemed like minutes until Mirabelle broke the ice.

"You're a psychic."

Quan buried his face in his palm. *You idiot. You came all this way to the Academy just to throw everything away.* The dread that overcame him was indescribable. It felt like death.

"That…that wasn't supposed to happen." Mirabelle walked towards the elevator and pressed the button, ignoring his pleas. "You won't tell anyone, right? I mean, that's my biggest secret."

Mirabelle paused. A unique opportunity had presented itself with Quan's burst of irritation. *Dakari had said we needed to find a psychic...this might be just the person we need.*

"If you want that to stay a secret: follow me. We should talk."

The elevator chimed open. Quan froze in frustration. He had no choice and he knew it. Every nerve in his body squirmed with discomfort. But he stepped inside.

"Fine. Lead the way."

Paranoid Projections

It was raining. The coffee machine hummed on Mirabelle's desk. Quan received his mug and sat down on the edge of the bed. She leaned against her desk.

"I figured it might be a late night," she said, cupping a hot mug in both hands.

"Hopefully not too late." Quan took a sip.

Mirabelle sipped too. Beneath the dim orange lights of Mirabelle's dorm room, their voices were replaced by the faint sound of falling rain.

"So, what's up?" Quan asked. "You here to tell me that students are disappearing? And that somehow I'm next?"

Mirabelle lowered her eyes.

"I'm not sure."

Quan set his mug on the bedstand.

"Then what are you trying to tell me?"

"I'm gathering my thoughts."

"Oh, great. Then can I leave?"

Mirabelle set her cup down by her desk.

"Not yet."

"So, you're blackmailing me?"

"What? No. No one is going to find out you're a psychic. I have no motive to turn you in and I'm not asking for your help. I'm just asking you to listen."

Quan scooted against the wall aside from Mirabelle's bed.

"Fine. I'm listening."

Mirabelle told Quan her story. In many ways, it reminded her of the first time she had shared this story with Zane just several months ago. She told him about the mysterious disappearance of Alan Jones, the way that no one else seemed to remember his existence, and eventually Zane's death.

"The media framed it as a suicide," Mirabelle said, noticing Quan's inattention. "But I knew Zane better than that. He wouldn't have taken his own life."

"How do you know?"

"Because I know."

"I mean, his Mom died."

Mirabelle opened her datapad and showed Quan a text from Zane. *The missing students are psychics.* "He sends me this text with no warning and then he's dead. Why would he text me that and kill himself?"

"Maybe he learned something terrible."

"Zane was not a coward."

"I never said he was. But some things are too dark to live with. Think about it. His Mom dies, he uncovers the mystery, but it's too terrible to be believed, so he takes his own life."

"This isn't too terrible to be believed. It's the answer we were looking for. Plus, his Mom's death wasn't an accident either. She uncovered something at Eastern."

"What would you rather believe?"

"That's not the question we need to be asking."

"It might be. What if you're wrong? What if Desta's death was just due to an accidental explosion? What if Zane's death had nothing to do with this mystery and more to do with missing his Mom? That seems plausible to me."

"You're done asking questions."

"Because I might be right?"

Mirabelle didn't say anything, then stared at Quan. In that instance, her annoyance strangely turned to pity. Instead of seeing him purely as a cocky, insolent bastard, she saw another side to him. Quan looked like someone trying so tirelessly hard to be someone else—someone large and important.

His eyes would always trail away from the person he was speaking to. If there was a window nearby, he was looking at it. But rarely was he looking at you. He would dramatically lean against the wall, his arms crossed, or his hands in his pockets. There were always long dramatic pauses between his responses as if he was waiting for some imaginary camera to film him speaking, like his entire life was some documentary. Mirabelle had to pinch herself several times to not laugh at his attempts to speak and walk like the legendary dueler Chas Rodo. He tried to be a westward-looking man who ended up looking more like an ever-ungrateful, silently whining child.

"No. Because you're wasting my time." Mirabelle handed him the photograph of Jon. "Was your brother a psychic?"

"I don't know. We weren't very close." There were scattered documents on the floor. "Wait. If no one remembers these students how do they remember him?"

"That's what I want to figure out. I don't think your brother was captured. I think he ran away."

"Why would he do that?"

Mirabelle shrugged her shoulders.

"I don't know. He was Dr. Marini's top student. He showed up on time every day. Then one day he stopped showing up. If he were captured, no one would remember him. But they do." Mirabelle turned towards the window revealing a city masked in the falling rain. "If your brother's a psychic, I imagine he's still out there somewhere. I can't say the same for these students though. I don't have the slightest idea of what happened to them."

"But all of these other students...how do *you* remember them?"

"Zane and I theorized it was because we were impurities."

"What about me?"

"You're a psychic. You're not normal either." Mirabelle's tone darkened. "Something must've happened with Jon to make him run away. If they were after him–"

"Then they'll come after me too, yeah I get it." Quan sat down on the bed. "But you don't even know who *they* are."

"Not yet. But there might be a way." She paced around the room in thought. "We know the missing students are psychics, but we don't know who's taking them. However, if we give them a psychic to take…"

Quan's eyes widened when he followed her train of thought.

"You're gonna use me as bait!?"

"Nothing will happen to you! I know an arbitrator. He can protect you."

"You must be pretty naïve if you think arbitrators will work with psychics."

"Maybe not all of them, but this man will. I won't let him harm you and in return, we'll forget we ever saw any of your powers."

"I didn't come to the Academy to solve mysteries. I'm here to join the tournament, win the Sojourner, then leave."

"And you could do that after you help us."

"What makes you think either of us will live?! Look what happened to Desta! Look what happened to Zane! What makes you think these are people we should cross? Why are you so insistent on fighting other people's battles?"

"Because they made it my battle the day they killed Zane!"

"*If* they killed Zane!"

"He would want me to finish this."

"You can't speak for the dead," Quan said. He paused. "Lemme ask you something. What do you want most? More than anything in the world?"

"To expose the people who killed Zane."

"Besides that."

"I want justice before anything else."

Quan looked at the star charts on the wall. "I don't think that's true." He walked over to her desk. There was a picture of her father. "Who's this?"

A new wound was opened in the tapestry of Mirabelle's scars. She froze.

"No one."

Quan smiled.

"Ah, so it is someone."

Mirabelle snatched the picture away, then paused. There was no sense in hiding it.

174

"My Dad went missing ten years ago. I want to find him."

"Then there's your fight. This one isn't yours. And it isn't mine either." He paused. "You want my honest opinion? Let this go. Burn these photographs. You'll never be able to focus if you don't. And just because you evaded these people last time doesn't mean you'll be so lucky again. The world shouldn't expect any kindness from those who have been wounded by it. Someone else will figure this out."

"And what if someone doesn't?"

"Then this world gets what it deserves. Goodnight, Mirabelle."

He closed the door, leaving her with nothing but a sobering silence.

* * *

Derek opened his eyes to the delightful sound of Quan's snores. That meant the person he needed to scan was finally asleep. A dim light entered the room from the window, revealing the nighttime skyrise. He grabbed his scanner and crept towards the suspect's bed. *This could be the one*, he thought. *The one to end it all.* The prospect of being free from this group with one last scan gave him too much hope. He didn't know what to do. It overshadowed his guilt and made him feel like a better person, as if being free from Matthew would atone for his sins.

It was a simple job: get the scan, collect the data, and confirm if he was a psychic. But there were a few problems. The only times that Derek had ever used the scanner was on unconscious suspects that had been drugged. He had no idea if the scanner even made a sound. The device was a long white tube with a light at the end. He bit his lip, cringed, and looked away as he tapped the button. To his relief, it was silent.

A green light flashed across Quan's forehead. He didn't move. Derek kept the scanner steady as he relayed the information back to his datapad. Brain waves flashed across his screen as the data compiled together. He listened for the click. Adrenaline coursed through his veins. His pulse rattled. His heart skipped a few beats when the click finally came.

He read the data, then nearly dropped the device in shock.

* * *

"So, it's true," Matthew said. "The cartographer exists."

It was 3:00 a.m. The Hunt brothers stood on opposite ends of Matthew's dorm. It continued raining, but it felt as if all the rain on New Earth had stopped for good. That report felt like the end of the world for Matthew and the start of a new one for Derek.

"A stage 4 psychic to be more precise," Derek said. "A new mutation. It's exactly the one the Boss was talking about, the reason we're even here."

"You don't have to tell me what I already know," Matthew said. He leaned against the wall with his arms crossed, his eyes lost in the darkened city.

"Should I make the call? We can bag him up tonight while he's sleeping."

"Does anyone else know about this report?"

"No one outside this room," Derek said.

"Good."

Matthew snatched the scanner and chucked it against the wall. It shattered to pieces. Derek stared at its remains, horrified as the report was erased from his datapad.

"Are you insane!?" Derek shouted.

"Why keep a record of something we already know? We both saw the same thing. There's no sense in letting that report get in the wrong hands, especially since you're rooming with the guy. I'm surprised he isn't already onto you."

"He was asleep! He has no idea."

"Good. I'd like to keep it that way."

Derek raised a brow, his eyes drawn back to the fragments of shattered plastic and glass on the carpet floor. Matthew had moved too fast and suddenly. The destruction of the device made no sense. None whatsoever.

"What exactly are you saying?" Derek asked.

"I'm *saying* that if no one knows...then no one knows."

"You said it yourself: if he's a psychic, we bag him up."

"I was being hyperbolic. Obviously, now that we know what kind of psychic he is, we may have to tailor our approach a little differently."

The stars started to align. Derek crossed his arms with a scowl.

"You mean until you earn the immaculate soldier." Derek laughed. "You won't turn him in until you win the Gerumandian Dueling tournament."

Matthew tried to ignore the brunt of his brother's condescension with a scowl.

"I'm just saying that considering what this means, if you need to tie up any loose ends, you better tie up those loose ends."

"If the Boss found out we were hiding a stage 4 psychic it'd be our end."

"Which is why not the Boss, not Bruce, and not even Donny is going to hear about this." Matthew walked close to his brother and stared him down. "Nothing will happen as long as we stay quiet. Still, that doesn't mean we can forget about him entirely. For starters we'll have to find a way to get him enrolled at the Academy, seeing that he's actively botching his chances at becoming a Masten scholar with his etiquette."

"And then what?"

"Don't worry. I got something for you to do. We'll have to keep a close eye on him, make sure he doesn't accidentally use his abilities and get snatched by the state." Matthew's eyes mischievously landed on his brother. He smiled. "What better way to keep a close eye on him than to be his friend? That might give you a chance to atone for finding Zane Minathi."

Derek's blood boiled with anger. He raised a finger at his brother.

"You pulled the trigger."

"And you found his room. We'll split the blame 50/50. How does that sound?"

Derek tried to punch Matthew, but the older brother caught the younger fist.

"Oh, you *are* a soft one, aren't you?" Matthew threw Derek back. He lingered in anger, then stormed towards the door. He paused when he saw Alexander passed out on the bed with a blindfold tied over his eyes.

"What did you do to him?" Derek asked.

Matthew smiled.

"We have to take precautions. If he's as close with Quan as you said he is, then we need to make sure the Boss can't manipulate any of his memories.

I had a Gray Eid give him a mirage. When he wakes up, he won't remember a thing. And the Boss won't be able to tamper with his mind either."

Derek shook his head in disbelief at the lengths his brother took to keep Quan's true identity hidden.

"You can't keep this a secret forever."

"I don't need forever. I need five months. Goodnight, Derek."

Derek slammed the door on his way out.

Matthew went to bed. Smiling.

A Sketchy Stowaway

Dakari Minathi stood in Chief Kalak's office with both hands folded behind his back. His superior gazed out the window with his back turned to the Deputy. He watched the other arbitrators with a steady eye and paid particular attention to the metal scaffold in the center of the room. The Chief's gaze could strike fear into any man or woman in the department. In a world where gray was becoming a color of the past, there was something strange about Kalak's perpetually aging but ageless face, a blend of black and gray. It was stuck in time but showed remnants of age. Half in this world. Half in a world that was nothing more than a memory–a memory that lived in Dakari's DNA, in an age where men grew old and died.

"I find myself in a difficult position," Kalak said. "You were promoted to be my assistant, but lately it feels like you're my internal investigator. Care to explain why?"

Dakari kept his posture straight and his expression firm.

"I don't see what the issue is, sir. I sat in on a meeting. Am I wrong to want to learn more about the people we do business with?"

"Yes. Because it's not your business."

"Then whose business is it, sir?"

Kalak turned around.

"We run a tight operation here. With more psychics threatening our Republic, it's imperative that information critical to the psychic detention centers stays within a very select group of people. If that information got into the wrong hands, there's no telling what kind of coordinated attack our department could experience."

179

"Like an underground railroad?"

"That as well as other things, yes."

"And what about Corporal Smith's route on the day Desta died?"

"I know nothing about that."

"Really? You don't know the roads your squadrons travel?"

"I am vaguely familiar, but I don't know the details. Do you know why?" Kalak paused. "Because it's not my business."

"And what about when your officers don't do their jobs? Or they do them poorly?" Dakari leaned over Kalak's desk. "If your wife died, would it be your business then? How many more people would have to die for you to consider this *your business?*"

Kalak tensed.

"Is that a threat, Mr. Minathi?"

Dakari removed his hands from the desk.

"After the funeral, you told me to come by your office. You said there was something we needed to discuss but you never followed up on it."

"Because you never came by. Perhaps you should have."

"What did you want to tell me?"

Kalak smiled.

"I know that you and Amelia have been examining records of arbitrator deaths since the release of the 'Last Resort' bill. I know you've been tracking L-Transport flight logs every time a psychic is arrested. I also know that you've become quite interested in the two truths the Academy so adamantly teaches its students. It wouldn't take a genius to connect a few dots on what the two of you might be plotting." Dakari swallowed a lump in his throat as Kalak grabbed a portrait of his family. He looked at it with a smile. "No. The truth, Dakari, is that I wanted to talk because like you, I have a theory of my own about why these arbitrators died."

"And what might that be?"

Kalak set the photograph down as his brows narrowed.

"Because perhaps they lacked trust. Or, like Icarus, maybe they flew a bit too close to the sun." Kalak smiled. "I've always wondered. When Icarus fell from the sky, do you think he made a thunderous, ceremonious fall that made ripples across the seven seas?" He looked at the scaffold. "Or was it nothing but a splash?" Dakari stood speechless as Kalak patted him on the shoulder. "I hope you keep that in mind the next time you take a trip to L-Transport."

Dakari's heart sunk as he made the long walk back to his office. He called Amelia, but she didn't answer. He stopped by her office. She wasn't there. *No*, Dakari thought. *It's too late.* She was already at the Leonardo Estate. Immediately upon returning to the CDAD Dakari had scheduled a follow-up appointment where Amelia and Mr. Leonardo could meet alone. He had to stop her–and he had to do it fast. He slung his coat over his shoulders and raced down the hallways of the CDAD. Dakari spotted an arbitrator chatting with another officer by the steps of the facility.

"Get me a hovercraft. And do it fast."

"On it. And where to, sir?"

"The home of Darius Leonardo."

A few minutes later, Dakari took off in a hovercraft. Kalak watched him fly away. He made a call.

* * *

Quan sat across the Masten Committee in the Great Hall. He was sharing a table with some of the most important people in the Republic. He sat on one side while they inspected him, questioned him, and wrote notes. They each wore medal-covered coats or million-rec dresses. But he kept his composure. He had faced bigger threats than questions.

"I've noticed that wristband on your arm," Colonel Arthur said. "You wear it wherever you go."

"That's correct, sir."

"Can you show us what it says?"

Quan raised his arm and felt the old material of the rubber wristband. It was inside out, but when he stretched it, there were words underneath.

"Sure," Quan said. A few of the more attentive officers noticed the way Quan's chest rose and fell slightly faster than before. They saw his eyes hesitant to look at the words himself. But nevertheless, Quan pulled back his sleeve, raised his forearm over the table, and turned over the wristband. "It uh…" He cleared his throat as he stared at the yellow letters. "It says never give up."

There was silence. A few officers exchanged glances.

"That was Chas Rodo's slogan during the 22nd Gerumandian Tournament."

Quan turned the wristband inside out again.

"Yeah…it was."

"What's the significance? I ask because that's not the first time I've seen that wristband," Colonel Arthur said. "Your brother wore the same one."

Quan sighed. If anything, his outburst with Mirabelle had made him a bit more prepared to deal with topics like this, even if they were a little bit riper with inattentiveness. That was the worst part about old wounds. The longer they went unattended, the more they hurt when they returned.

"Back when we were kids, Jon and I made a promise. Ever since we saw Chas Rodo and Ledarius Tartaren win the tournament it became our dream to do the same. We promised each other we would join the Academy and win the tournament together." Quan paused. "Then Jon left."

"And then what happened?"

All Quan could think about was running away.

"Nothing. I carried on with my life and I've been trying to get here ever since."

"And what about your brother?"

"I don't know. We haven't spoken since."

The committee went silent.

"The Jerry name has a troubled history here. On the one hand, Jon was one of the Academy's top students. But then again, he also threw several semesters' worth of tuition down the drain. How can we believe that you won't follow in his footsteps?"

Quan's eyes narrowed.

"Because I hate my brother. And I'm the better dueler."

"We understand that but–"

"No," Quan said. "I don't believe you do."

All seven members of the committee looked up from their holopads. He knew he had their attention, albeit risking offending the respect of the officers. But they needed to know the truth. And he would tell it to them. Carter Hunt leaned forward. Not with a scowl, but a slight smile.

"I lived in his shadow for years. He had better stats than me because he was older, but if you compare our performance at the same age, I beat him in every category. I was happy for Jon when he got accepted, then frustrated only to find out that I had been rejected. You can imagine even more so my anger when I found out he threw everything away. I am not my brother. I will not make his mistakes. I am Quan. Not Jon, and I certainly won't take responsibility for his errors. I'm ready to get back in the game."

It was a longshot, certainly an answer that the board was not expecting, but one that captured their attention. Only time would tell if it worked.

"That will be all," Carter said. "Send in the next person on your way out."

Later in the day, there was a skills showcase. Students prepared a demonstration of a talent they wanted to pursue at the Academy. Some laid out plans for aeronautics projects, others for arbitrator studies, but most showcased their dueling abilities. Quan strapped on a headset in the simulation chamber and selected a scenario he had performed with his own simulation system at the Brawling Bandits. Several Masten scholars and committee members watched from a glass room above. In his spare time, Quan had read the standard requirements for recruits. They only had to beat two opponents on a level two difficulty. Quan faced three opponents set to level four.

He chose a double-bladed weapon from the rack and started the simulation. The lights around him darkened as three orange holographic enemies charged. He parried the attack of the first, ducked under the collective assault of the other two, spun around, and disabled the first hologram's shields. It disintegrated as he used both edges of the blade to fight off the other holograms as they cornered him. Quan pressed both feet against the wall and lunged forward, cutting down both enemies in the process.

Admiral Leithart smiled behind a wall of glass.

"Impressive."

Matthew Hunt crossed his arms.

"Nothing I haven't seen before."

"But more than we've seen from any of the other prospectives," Officer Mocroft said. "He's light years ahead."

They asked him to run a few more scenarios, to which Quan eagerly accepted. They noticed the fluidity of movements that he had begun to perfect over the summer, the way he balanced the blade, the force of his strikes, and the timing of his parries. He fled from fights he would lose and charged into scenarios he would win. When he finished his last simulation, he removed his headset, and the lights came back on. He bowed before the board of directors and walked out without a word.

Momentary Milestones

Several servants led Amelia through the courtyard of the Leonardo Estate. No one else had joined her except the pilot, who remained in the cockpit with the hovercraft prepared for takeoff if things went bad. Amelia didn't have any reason to believe such things would happen, but now that she saw his house, that changed. Darius was a rich man. And she had come here to tell him he was wrong. He stood beneath the doorway in white robes as his bald brown head glistened in the sunlight.

"You must be Miss Lancaster. To what do I owe this pleasure?"

Amelia bowed, then stood up straight.

"Nothing more than a few minutes of your time."

They sat across from each other at the dining table. A few servants poured Amelia a glass of water. She was dressed in her navy blue trench coat, the CDAD badge glimmering above her breast. They poured Darius a glass of wine. Darius tapped his golden-ringed fingers on the table and studied Amelia closely as she brought out her holopad and displayed two separate files on the screen.

"You came alone," Darius said. "Why?"

"Because if others were here, they wouldn't want you to show me this."

"Then is it wise to show me?"

"It is if you want to know the truth?"

"What truth?"

"That you're being swindled by the CDAD."

Darius sat straight.

"That's a serious accusation. I assume you brought proof?"

Amelia slid the holopad across the table.

"Do you recognize any of these forms?"

Darius leaned over and inspected them.

"Of course, I signed this one earlier today."

"Which is supposed to grant the CDAD use of L-Transport cargo ships, correct?"

"Where are you going with this?"

"There was no need to sign those forms. The CDAD has been using your ships for years. See for yourself."

Darius inspected the other form closely. Amelia nervously waited on the other end of the wooden table, twiddling her thumbs. The message from Dakari was simple: show him the forms, show him the fraud. They had spent the last several weeks inconspicuously examining the charts of vessels docking in the underground railroads and found strange patterns that proved L-Transport vehicles had been used before. It did not seem to make any sense then why Banner had asked for those forms to be signed. That is unless Darius was being honest and truly forgot. That seemed impossible, though. No one could erase someone's mind so easily. *Maybe in another world*, Amelia thought. *But not in this one.*

Footsteps descending down the turnpike steps broke her trance. A young, handsome, teenage boy with dreadlocks curving down his face like a lion's mane rounded the corner, shocked to see an arbitrator returning his gaze. Amelia smiled and waved. He didn't.

"Who is this?" The boy asked.

"Not now, Kairo."

"We already had arbitrators over. Why is there another one in our house?"

Darius looked up at his son with a menacing stare.

"You will apologize to Miss Lancaster. And then you will return to your room."

Kairo walked around the table to where his father was. Amelia tensed as he leaned over his shoulder and peered at the holopad.

"Did you hear me!? I said LEAVE! NOW!"

Years seemed to pass in the silent standoff between Darius and his son,

Kairo. Their eyes were locked in a perpetual stalemate of two scowls. Amelia couldn't believe how the Leonardo son had such confidence to speak to his father that way, and then stare him down like he was a peer. Then, in a moment of stunning revelation, Amelia saw the reason behind the young man's confidence.

With the snap of his fingers, Kairo's eyes glowed like headlights. Darius' body went limp as he slouched in his chair, his eyelids shutting closed. He passed out as his head hit the table. Years of training told Amelia to reach for her blaster in the presence of a dangerous psychic, but the shock of the moment overwhelmed her instincts. She froze as the boy turned towards her from the other side of the table with haunting brown eyes. "You were so close. But my father doesn't need to know about these forms yet."

"You're behind this!"

"I am one piece in a large puzzle."

Amelia's heart raced.

"Why are you telling me this?"

Kairo smiled.

"Because when my father wakes up he won't remember anything." He aimed his fingers at her. "And neither will you."

He snapped.

Amelia froze, her hand inched for her blaster, but it was too late. A faint gray fuzz overcame her brain, blurring her vision. She felt like she was going blind. And then everything went black.

* * *

Thirty minutes later, Dakari spotted the hovercraft on one of the landing zones at the Leonardo Estate. He leaned over the pilot's shoulder as their vehicle sped up.

"Drop us there."

"We don't have clearance!"

"I don't care! Do it now!"

"Very well, sir."

The main engines died down as four landing thrusters flipped towards the ground and brought the vehicle to a slow, gradual descent on one of the empty landing pads. Dakari saw several servants spot them and run out from the courtyard. Dakari yanked the lever and opened the landing bay doors. He stormed down the ramp and emerged into the sunlight as several servants raised their rifles in alarm.

"Please state your business at the Leonardo Estate. We were not informed of your arrival."

Dakari flipped open his wallet and gestured to his badge.

"I'm with the CDAD. I'm here to bring my assistant home."

The servants exchanged a glance, then reluctantly led him through the main gates. They led him past the fountain and beneath the main arch. Darius and his son, Kairo, stood inside the living room with Amelia by their side. It was almost as if they were waiting for him to arrive.

"Dakari Minathi!" Darius smiled. "Didn't think we'd be seeing each other so soon."

"Neither did I." Dakari glanced at Amelia. "I apologize for the intrusion but there's been a change in plans. I'm here to bring her back to our headquarters."

"That shouldn't be a problem," Amelia said. "We just finished." She turned to Darius and bowed. "Thank you for your hospitality."

Darius bowed in return. Dakari sensed something strange in their behavior. There was a look of perfect peace in her eyes. It was unsettling.

"It was my pleasure," Darius said. He waved as the servants escorted them out of the home. "Take care!"

Dakari walked by Amelia's side and turned around one last time. He caught the gaze of Mr. Leonardo's son under the archway. He could've sworn that he was smiling.

* * *

Back in the CDAD hovercraft, Dakari and Amelia sat in the main cabin away from the other arbitrators.

"What happened back there?" Dakari asked. "You can cut the act by the way. We're alone."

"What act?" Amelia asked. "I don't know what you're talking about."

Dakari laughed.

"Very funny." He double-tapped his record and pulled up a memo from their last meeting. "Last time Banner met with L-Transport they created a new contract to service an underground railroad. They also authorized the use of L-Transport cargo ships. Did you show Darius that the CDAD was already using those ships?"

"No. I didn't know the CDAD has ever used L-Transport ships."

"You didn't–" Dakari scowled. "I'm not kidding around, Amelia."

"Neither am I."

"We've talked about this. The whole point in making that visit was so you could show Darius the contract is meaningless. We've been using his ships for years."

"I wasn't aware of that."

"What do you mean you weren't aware of that?! We've been planning this for months!"

"Why are you being so cryptic?"

Dakari's eyes widened in sudden apprehension. *Impossible*, he thought. *There's no way they could've gotten to her too.* Something about this situation was terribly wrong. *No shit captain obvious.* It wasn't just the fact that Amelia had no recollection of their plans. It was the fact that whatever happened to her at the Leonardo Estate couldn't have taken longer than a few minutes. He tried to figure out how to extract the information out of her but was suddenly worried if she was comprised. He needed to be as vague as possible.

"Amelia?" Dakari asked. "Why were you sent to the Leonardo Estate?"

"To verify the contract between the CDAD and L-Transport."

"And is that the only reason?"

"Yes."

Dakari paused.

"And who exactly sent you there?"

Amelia paused as if trying to remember.

"Chief Kalak of course."

Dakari's eyes widened with horror. He leaped up from his seat and stormed into the pilot's cabin. He leaned over the pilot's shoulder and watched as they approached the main hangar of the CDAD. He saw Kalak standing outside the facility talking with a group of arbitrators. He eyed the hovercraft as it veered towards the building and made its descent. A newfound fear came upon Dakari as the landing bay doors opened, the fear that this little game of cat and mouse had come to an end.

* * *

"Where have you been?!" Kalak shouted.

Dakari and Kalak walked side by side through the main corridor, past dozens of busy cubicles with service workers answering calls. The scaffold still stood in the center of the main room. *It waits for you*, a haunting voice told Dakari. He shrugged this thought aside. *Not if I'm careful*. That was easier to believe earlier. It was becoming harder to believe now.

"I was out, sir."

"Out? What the hell does that mean?"

"I brought Amelia back from the Leonardo Estate."

Kalak stopped, forcing Dakari to stop too.

"Do you want to lose your badge, Deputy? You may have superiority over other officers, but there's still one man you have to answer to, understand?"

"I do, sir."

"Then prove it." Kalak shoved a holopad into Dakari's arms. "There's an investigation team up in the 27B surveillance room. I suggest you go take care of your own business before minding anyone else's. You got another psychic to catch."

Kalak walked away without another word. Dakari watched him leave. Half of him was relieved he still had his badge, that Amelia was alive, and that he was alive too. But the other half of him knew how close he was to death. He was closer into this case than Desta had ever gotten. And if he wasn't careful, he wouldn't get any further.

He walked to the surveillance room and shut the door. There were three other investigators in the darkroom. They were reviewing a flagged surveillance tape from the Gerumandian Academy sent yesterday.

"What's the situation?" Dakari asked.

"Potential psychic activity at the Gerumandian Academy."

"Play the tape."

Dakari grabbed a cup of coffee from the back and watched, half his mind still in shock over almost losing his job. The suspects were one male and one female, both about fifteen years old. They stood on the rooftop balcony of the Gerumandian Academy. They were arguing, yelling. Then their inaudible conversation was cut short when the boy's eyes burned bright blue like flashlights. They left the rooftop shortly after that. The angle was from the security camera on the top of the main Gerumandian building, too high to view with good detail.

"That's it?" Dakari asked.

"We have no footage beyond that, but their–"

"Rewind. Zoom in on their faces."

Another investigator typed into the computer and pinched the screen. They stopped at an angle where both suspects were standing on the rooftop.

"Run a face scan."

Two green boxes narrowed in around their faces, then registered through hundreds of comparative scans with several potential matches.

"Filter out non-Gerumandians."

A match came up for the girl: *Mirabelle Marshall.*

Dakari almost spat out his coffee. He thought back to seeing her at the funeral months ago. The headstones. The gunshots. The tears. They came back to him like a torrent of ripe memories. That old anger returned to him again–and the promise that Dakari and Mirabelle had made with each other. They hadn't spoken in months. Maybe this was the nudge they needed.

"Sir?"

Dakari shook his head and came out of a trance.

"Sorry," he said. "What about the boy?"

"Doesn't look like he attends the Academy. We have no ID on him."

"No sense in waiting around then." Dakari grabbed his coat and threw it over his shoulders. "If we find the girl, we can find the boy. Either way, there is confirmed psychic activity at the Gerumandian Academy, giving us probable cause to launch an investigation on Mirabelle Marshall and the other unnamed suspect. I'm going to conduct a low-profile, private investigation myself to avoid attention from the press. As of right now, not a word of this investigation to anyone outside the room, understood?"

"You got it. Good luck sir."

Dakari shut the door and headed back towards the hangar, leaving a room of confusion and silence for a place of answers. At least, that's what he hoped for. That's what kept him moving. This case was wearing on him. And if he didn't make progress soon, he figured that his time would be cut short.

Forgotten Findings

Six students remained in the Great Hall, but one more had to go. Quan nervously watched as the Board of Directors made their last choice of elimination beneath the shining light of the chandelier. The last six prospectives sat at the other end of the table with bated breath. They were motionless. Quan tried to hide his smile. The other prospectives had joked that he wouldn't last the first day with his manners. And yet here he was, one elimination away from earning a full ride to the Gerumandian Academy. Quan thought it was funny. Those students had made the mistake of assuming that table manners were more important than talents. Maybe at another university. But this was the Gerumandian Academy. When your life was in another soldier's hands, which would you choose? The one who knew where to place a knife on a table? Or the one who knew where to place a knife in your enemies?

"David Becker," Colonel Arthur said, standing up to shake the student's hand. That was another funny thing. Each student was sent off with the manners that failed to get them their scholarship. "It has been a pleasure getting to know you. We hope you still choose to enroll at the Gerumandian Academy this fall and wish you the best of luck with your arbitrator reform projects."

David shook the man's hand, stood up, and was escorted out of the Great Hall.

Quan bit his lip to hide his smile. He knew what the Colonel would say next.

"That means from this moment onward, the five of you are the official

2135 Masten Scholars. Congratulations."

Each committee member stood up in applause. Quan shook their hands as he proceeded with the others down the line. He made eye contact with every one of them, expressed his gratitude, and then approached the man at the end of the line: Officer Mocroft. There was no smile on his pale face. He eyed Quan like every other student.

"Congratulations."

Quan shook his hand.

"Thank you."

Then Mocroft said something to Quan that he had not said to anyone else.

"I vouched for you. Don't screw this up."

Quan smiled.

"I won't."

He left the Great Hall. He kept a calm pace until the elevator opened on his floor, allowing him to sprint with excitement and knock on his own door like a madman. Alexander opened the door with a glaze in his eye.

"Please tell me you got it. I don't want to pack."

They didn't have to pack, Quan told him. They were staying. They celebrated with some beer Alexander had smuggled into his suitcase. They clanked their cans together and drank. They played music in the background, but the high of their momentary victory didn't last long. It was interrupted by a text from Mirabelle Marshall.

I heard you got accepted!! Congrats! If you're free, swing by my room. There's someone I want you to meet.

Alexander noticed Quan looking intensely at his datapad and leaned closer.

"Who's that?"

"Some girl from the Masten Scholars."

Alexander raised a brow.

"A girl's texting *you*?! What are you doing here with me?"

"It's not like that. She's annoying."

"Nah you just haven't talked to a girl in ages." Alexander pushed him towards the door. "I'd be a bad friend if I let you stay here, so you're leaving."

Quan lowered his datapad.

"Fine. But don't do anything stupid."

"I can't promise anything."

"Then promise me this: move our things out of Derek's dorm into ours. Room 565. Floor 37."

"Why do *I* have to move to our new room?"

"Because *I* got us the scholarship. Room 565. Don't forget it."

"I won't."

Alexander shut the door.

On my way, Quan texted. He threaded his arms through the elbow-patched sleeves of his blue leather jacket and closed the door on the way out. The soreness of yesterday's dueling demonstrations ran deep in his bones, the tightness in his muscles loosening on his walk to Mirabelle's dorm. It felt good to walk, but it was a long one–long enough to give him space to think. He hated space to think. He liked the bliss of swiping his datapad and the speed of dueling. He passed dozens of rooms before making his way to the elevator, nearly all of them empty. It was strange to think that Jon had lived in one of them about a year ago. And now he was off the grid. That at least made him more at ease. He didn't have to worry about running into him at a corner or seeing him in class. This place would be his. He was determined to make it his. Not even the Hunt brothers would stand in his way. It felt good to walk through the hallways of an Academy he wouldn't have to pay a dime to attend. This euphoria, however, was short-lived. The scholarship was a means to an end. It paled in comparison to the true prize: a place on New Earth's largest stadium, the chance to become the object of the world's envy, the poster child of someone else's dreams, and then the keys to a starship to leave it all behind.

To what world? There were five other planets in the Cephei Star System. *Anywhere but here.*

He knocked on Mirabelle's door, but someone else opened it instead. A bald darker-skinned man in a navy blue arbitrator coat stared into Quan's soul with black eyes flickering with the wildfire of hell. There was anger in his firm gaze, as well as resolute sadness as if the man was bottling all of his emotions with fierceness. Mirabelle sat on the bed. Quan froze as the man showed him his badge. Instinct told him to run.

"My name is Dakari Minathi. Are you Quan Son Jerry?"

Quan looked at Mirabelle.

"You set me up!"

"It's not what you think!"

Without waiting for an explanation, Quan sprinted down the hallway as fast as his legs could carry him. His heart raced as he heard the arbitrator racing behind him. He spammed the elevator button, then turned around and created a tear in both palms.

"Hold on!" Dakari shouted. He raised both hands, revealing no weapon. "Set those portals aside and let's talk."

"I bet you'd love that, wouldn't you?" Quan said, waiting for the doors to open. "Then you could bring me back to the CDAD like all those other psychics, right?"

"If I wanted to arrest you, I wouldn't have come alone."

Quan considered this for a moment and saw Mirabelle approaching from the far end of the hallway. They stood exchanging glances in silence until the elevator chimed and the doors slid open. "Why should I believe you?"

"Because I need your help," Dakari said. "She does too."

Adrenaline coursed through Quan's veins. He kept his arms aimed towards Dakari. The open elevator doors seemed to taunt him with opportunity. *Run you fool*, he thought. *What are you doing?* He didn't know. Years of scouring the streets told him to flee. But at this Academy, there would be nowhere to hide. He would have to hope that Dakari was telling the truth, and as he accepted this, Quan dropped his arms by his side, then followed Dakari back to Mirabelle's room.

"You did the right thing," Dakari said.

They stepped inside Mirabelle's room as she shut the door.

"I guess we'll find out," Quan said, crossing his arms when he returned his gaze to Mirabelle. "I thought you said you weren't going to turn me in."

"I didn't," Mirabelle said.

"Then I suppose this is just a friend of yours."

"She's telling the truth." Dakari handed a folded piece of paper to Quan. "A security camera sent us footage yesterday of a potential psychic sighting on the rooftop of the Gerumandian Academy. You need to be more careful."

"Then why didn't you just come straight to my room instead?"

"Facial scans only picked up Mirabelle, so I thought I'd pay her a visit first."

"This is Dakari Minathi," she said. "Zane's father."

Quan lowered his eyes. Part of him knew this man had experienced great pain, but it was still hard to see him as a man. The arbitrator symbol on his chest aroused only anger. Men like him had dragged his kind into chains in underground cells. Part of Quan felt bad for his suffering. The other part of him believed he got what he deserved. But still, a father was a father, no matter the actions he had done. Perhaps he deserved some pity.

"I'm sorry for your loss," Quan said.

"No need to apologize. In fact, you're just the person I'm looking for. Have a seat. This might take some time to explain."

Mirabelle gestured towards the chair in the room. Quan sighed, then reluctantly sat down to hear Dakari unveil his plan.

* * *

"No way," Quan said. "I won't do it."

"Be reasonable," Mirabelle said.

"This man wants me to turn myself in at the CDAD! How is that reasonable?"

"Because the CDAD has footage of you using your abilities," Dakari said. "If I don't bring you in someone else will. Wouldn't you rather have it be me than someone else?"

"I'd rather stay here."

"You won't be able to. They'll find you."

"It depends. They identified Mirabelle's face, but what about mine?"

"Like I said. The cameras didn't focus on either of you until your eyes glowed. By that point, the glow in your eyes hid your facial features from the camera angle."

"Which means technically you can't see my face...which also means you don't need to bring me back. All you need is a psychic."

"Oh, of course!" Dakari said. "Why didn't I think of that? We just need to find another psychic at the Gerumandian Academy! Where should we start?"

Quan leaned back in his chair with a scowl.

"I wasn't joking."

Dakari crossed his arms. "Fine. Then tell me: how do you honestly expect us to find another psychic before sundown?"

"Derek Hunt."

That perked Mirabelle's interest.

"What?"

"Derek Hunt is a psychic," Quan said. "I saw it with my own eyes."

"What do you mean?" Dakari asked. "Did he create a tear?"

"No. I can sense psychic energy. I saw remnants of psychic activity in his dorm room."

"That sounds like a cop-out."

"It's not."

"Then how do you know I'm not a psychic?" Dakari asked.

Quan blinked twice. "Because there's no glow behind your brain." He blinked again. "You're not even an AOL human. You're both impurities."

Dakari's eyes widened in surprise. Mirabelle wasn't amused.

"Nice try," she said. "But I already told you that."

"But you didn't need to! I already knew!"

"Enough," Dakari said. "We won't entertain this."

"I'm being serious! There's a golden glow behind the brains of all psychics. I can see it behind my eyes every time I'm in the mirror. I saw the glow in his room!"

"That's impossible," Mirabelle said. "Psychics can only create tears."

"Not exactly," Dakari said. "Some studies have suggested that psychics are mutating. But that still doesn't mean he's telling the truth."

"I can prove it."

"How?"

"Capture Derek. If he's not a psychic, you can capture me instead."

"That's not exactly proof as it is a deal. It would be the perfect time for you to escape, wouldn't it?"

Quan placed his wrists together.

"Then handcuff me here until you find him. I'll be waiting."

"You have the scholars' banquet in two hours," Mirabelle said.

"Then you better work fast."

"And why should I take him over you?"

Good question, Quan thought. He needed a good answer.

"Because you don't need me at the CDAD. You need me here." Dakari and Mirabelle exchanged a glance. "Think about it. If the missing students are psychics, you need a psychic to lure these people out from hiding, but you also need to capture one to show the people at the CDAD that you did your job. Bring Derek in to save your skin and I'll help you find the people that killed your son."

"How do I know you're not working for them?"

"Let's just say that working with others has never really been my strong suit."

"Then why'd you come to the Academy?"

"To win the Sojourner. I'm registering in the tournament this fall."

"The Sojourner? What would you do with a ship like that?"

"Simple. I'd leave. That way I can get scumbag arbitrators like you off my back. We're not all monsters, you know."

"That may be true, but it's the monster inside you I'm worried about–the one that hasn't woken up. But I suppose even if every dog has its day, surely a psychic can too." Dakari looked at Mirabelle. "Thoughts?"

Mirabelle gazed at the photographs of missing students taped to the wall.

"Derek may be innocent with regards to the rooftop footage, but he's not a good person. It wouldn't be the worst thing in the world for one of the Hunt brothers to go behind bars."

"Then you support it?"

"If Quan isn't lying…then yes. I support it."

Quan looked up at Dakari.

"Then you're letting me go?"

"Not quite. If it's true that we're the only people immune to these memory games, then I need both of you on call until I learn more from Derek. I'll send a dispatch unit to apprehend him. I need you both to stay out of trouble. After ascertaining Derek, I need to learn what happened to Amelia's memories at the Leonardo Estate. It might be our first clue to figure out what's happening here."

"Wait," Mirabelle said. "You said the Leonardo estate? As in Darius Leonardo?"

"I did."

"That's the man who took my father away from me. When are you going back?"

"Not anytime soon."

"Then can you take me there?"

"No. It's too dangerous. And besides, we've only gone on business trips."

"This *is* a business trip. Personal business."

"What do you mean?"

"I can't exactly say." The photograph of Mirabelle and her father became eerily present to her. She looked away. "I just need to speak with Mr. Leonardo. For other reasons."

"You'll get your chance," Dakari said. "But we have bigger battles to fight for the time being. Kalak will fire me if I made another trip there. He's already gotten onto me once."

"Then promise me this: the next time you're there, ask about what happened to Aidan Marshall."

Dakari paused, his eyes trailing to the photograph on Mirabelle's desk. It didn't take a genius to connect the dots to what she was asking, so out of kindness, he agreed.

"You have my word." Dakari grabbed his hat from the desk and set it atop his bald head. "I'll see you all soon." Dakari looked at Quan, then at Mirabelle. "And make sure he doesn't do anything stupid."

Quan bit his tongue to stop himself from speaking, then watched Dakari shut the door, leaving them in silence. The second the arbitrator was gone, a new side of Quan emerged.

"I hope you're happy now," he said. "You may have just cost me my freedom."

"This wasn't my fault! Dakari would've gone looking for you anyway. If anything, I'm the only reason you still have any freedom."

"Oh, so I should just bow down and worship you, huh?! Oh, thank Robert Dain for Mirabelle Marshall! Where would I be without her!?" He leaned close to her. "You'll pay for this. Somehow, someway." He walked away. "Goodbye, Mirabelle."

He slammed the door. Mirabelle sat in silence. She didn't move. Any remnant of pity she had for Quan was gone. She hated him and hated even more that she had to work with him. And then there was her father. Once again, she was one step closer to finding him. And the world kept pushing her back.

* * *

Alexander zipped up their last suitcase and set it by the door of their new room.

"That everything?" Quan asked.

Alexander wiped the sweat off his forehead.

"Everything!? I just unpacked everything and now we're packing again?! What happened in there?"

"Let's just say that I'll feel a whole lot safer once we leave."

"What about the Sojourner? And your scholarship?"

"We'll have to find another way to leave New Earth. I wish I could say more, but I can't." Quan grabbed his suitcase. "I'm going to go outside and make sure the coast is clear. Whatever you do, don't come out until I text you, alright?"

Alexander rolled his eyes.

"Yeah, yeah. I'll just wait around. Apparently, it's all I'm good for."

"Thanks."

Quan stepped outside their room and shut the door. He felt his heart race as he looked back. Standing there was like watching a funeral from far away. Both his hands trembled as he started to walk away from the room to leave his friend behind. He had planned on leaving Mirabelle the second Dakari threatened to force him to stay, but never in a million years could he have envisioned leaving Alexander too. A gut-wrenching feeling curled in his stomach. He tried to shove it away by closing his eyes, but it remained. He knew this was the only way. If what Dakari and Mirabelle were saying was true, then Alexander was a liability. If someone could get information from his mind concerning his whereabouts, it would all be over. At that moment Quan felt like he was walking all alone, surrounded by an all-encompassing black fog. For the first time in his life, he learned what it was to be truly alone. But he knew he had no other choice. He took another step.

"Going somewhere?"

Each nerve in Quan's body screamed as he jolted and looked in front of him. The tall menacing arbitrator stood beneath the dim lights of the beige hallway. He didn't exactly look pleased.

"Dakari?"

"You're not a very good liar."

No sense in lying to him again, Quan thought.

"What do you want?"

"I want you to reconsider."

Quan's anger returned in full force. He felt his hands burn red like lava.

"You don't know the first thing about me."

"Maybe not, but the last few hours have shown me that you lack integrity. You lied to my face and Mirabelle's." Dakari sighed. "Then again, you did give me a lead, and I can't be the one to control your destiny. You gotta choose the path you walk yourself."

"You mean…you're not going to try and stop me?"

"Of course not. I'm going to let you choose."

"Then I choose to leave."

"Why do you even want to leave?"

"Kind of ironic of you to ask me that question."

"You could always just hide your abilities."

"I've tried that for years. It doesn't work."

"Why not go home?"

Quan gripped the handle of his suitcase just a little bit tighter.

"Home? What home? I spent my entire life living a lie. My birth parents are dead, my adopted parents don't even want me, my brother left for the Academy without me, and to top it all off, I'm a psychic in a world where I'm seen as nothing more than a monster. Give me a reason why I should stay, and I'll give you ten more reasons why I should leave!"

"And you don't think that power gives you some responsibility?"

"You don't get it. I'm not wanted here. I owe this world nothing."

"And what about me? Don't you think I thought the same things when I learned what happened to my wife and son?" Dakari felt the ring under his jacket. "I feel that rage every day. But if you let that anger turn into apathy, you'll become just like the people who made your life a living hell."

"You mean people like you? How many psychics do you think you've put behind bars in the last ten years? And among those, how many do you think have already lost their minds by rotting in an underground cell? I'm leaving whether you like it or not."

"And where will you go? If you leave the Academy you have no chance of winning the Sojourner. That was your ticket off this planet, wasn't it?"

"It was. Until you threatened to arrest me."

"Then allow me to rephrase things. Give me five months of your time."

Quan considered this.

"Five months?"

"There are five months until the tournament, right? Which means you'll at least be around the Academy until November."

"Yeah, but it's not like I won't be doing anything. I'll be training."

"I'm not asking you to do a lot. I just need you to work with Mirabelle if we run into problems. As things stand, the only people who know about this are the three of us. And if things go well with Derek, we may not even need you at all." Dakari paused. "Five months."

Their eyes met in a tense stalemate.

"How often are you gonna call me in? What would you even have me do?"

"I'm not sure. That depends on how much I learn from Derek and how much Mirabelle and I can do on our own. If I'm being honest, the only time I foresee bringing you in is if we need something done that only a psychic can do, and whatever that is, I promise I'll have your back."

"Which means?"

"No detention centers. No arrests. You have my word." Dakari extended his hand. "Do I have yours?"

Quan looked down at his hand, then up at Dakari. Something about this whole situation felt weird. It was against what instinct told him to do. But the tiny prospect of doing something good lit a spark inside him. It wasn't enough to change him, but it was enough to get him to shake the man's hand.

"Five months. Not a day more."

"I wouldn't dream of it." Dakari let go and walked down the hall. "Take care kid. You've got a banquet to catch."

Quan watched Dakari leave. He looked back at his dorm room, wondering whether he had just made the biggest mistake of his entire life. Either way, it didn't matter. With a quick tug, he pulled his luggage behind him and opened the door.

"There you are," Alexander said, springing up from the bed. "We leaving or are we not?!"

"We're staying," Quan said, opening up his luggage. "I can't explain now."

"Why not?"

Quan grabbed his suit and threw it on the bed.

"Because I got a banquet to catch."

A Tempestuous Traitor

In the Great Hall, old and new Masten scholars alike gathered for the acceptance dinner. Mirabelle kept glancing over at Quan's seat as an awkward silence passed over the table. Matthew sat with a smug expression on his face. Officer Mocroft impatiently stroked his pencil mustache as other decorated veterans awaited their last guest. Then the towering doors of the Great Hall opened. Everyone in the room turned around. Mirabelle let out a long-awaited sigh.

It was Quan Son Jerry.

"Sorry I'm late." He straightened his tie. "I found out some of the elevators here go sideways and well…" Quan smiled. "I couldn't resist."

The entire table erupted with laughter. Officer Mocroft kept shaking his head and tried to hide his smile, watching as Quan made a table of military veterans laugh like they were cadets again. Matthew kept a straight face with both hands folded in his lap. Derek looked over at his brother, his face saying: *I told you so.* Matthew ignored him and raised his glass to his lips. He carried on with the dinner, pretending that Quan wasn't even there.

* * *

"There's nothing to worry about," Matthew said. He walked back to the elevator with Derek in their forest green dress suits. "Pretend like you don't know."

"But we *do* know," Derek said. "Someone is going to find out."

"Only if you're paranoid."

205

"How can I not be? The Boss ordered us to turn in a stage 4 psychic. How can I be calm when we're going against those orders?"

"We're not. We're just delaying the day we turn him in."

"But the tournament is five months away! What if someone gets him first?"

"Do you hear yourself, right now? It's like I'm talking to a child." He shook his head. "I'll turn him in the day I win the tournament, you have my word."

"Your word means nothing to me."

The elevator door chimed and opened.

"Your ride is here," Matthew said. "Goodnight, Derek."

Derek stepped inside as the doors closed behind him. He felt like his brain was spinning with a million worries and fears. He felt hungry even when he was full. He was only eager to turn Quan in because he knew that he would be the last one. No more laundry loads. No more dead students. They would leave the Academy for good. Their mission would be finished. And then he wouldn't have to walk the same hallways that Zane used to walk. He wouldn't have to see Mirabelle, whose very existence reminded him of his greatest sins. He had done things worth the price of Hell's admission, but at least with the AOL drug he had eternity to suspend his judgment. The only Heaven he believed would accept him was one away from the Academy. This place would never look the same. It was forever marred with the blood of Zane Minathi. Blood that was as much on his hands as Matthew's. He was so lost in thought that when he opened the door to his room, he didn't see the other people waiting for him inside.

There were five armored arbitrators. Derek froze as he stared at their black visors. It was as if they were in a western standstill, waiting for someone to make the first move. His heart pounded inside his chest as the lead arbitrator stepped forward.

"My name is Deputy Dakari Minathi. Do you know why I'm here?"

Minathi. A name worth a thousand emotions. Derek's eyes widened with disbelief as he stared into the dark man's eyes. They were just like Zane's, except they were angry. Derek felt like his feet were glued to the floor.

His heart pounded as he realized why they were here. Somehow, they had found him. They knew what he had done. And now Zane's father was here for vengeance. It was the only theory that made any sense to him.

Dakari's expression changed when he saw something in Derek's face that gave his guilt away. Then he watched the boy fall to his knees and cry out.

"It wasn't my fault!" Derek shouted. "Matthew did it! Not me! It was *him!*"

Dakari gripped the boy by the collar and yanked him to his feet.

"Did what!? What are you saying?!"

Derek's eyes swelled with tears. He didn't have to say anything. A haunting realization overcame Dakari as he looked into the boy's eyes, which widened upon meeting his.

This boy killed my son!

The red rage rose. Dakari threw Derek to the ground and whipped out his stun baton. He clicked it to full charge as Derek crawled to the corner like a child. He clubbed Derek across the face as blue sparks pulverized his body. Dakari saw the world through a crimson shade as he beat him with his stinging baton, relishing each thunderous blow against his suit. Derek convulsed on the ground and blacked out. Part of him prayed he had died.

* * *

"No press," Dakari explained to Officer Mocroft. A team of arbitrators carried Derek into the back of Dakari's patrol car. Raspberry lights flashed in the courtyard as hovercrafts arrived. Other board members were nudged away from the scene by patrol members.

"I'm not sure that–"

"I don't think you heard me properly. I said no press. *None.*"

"Can I just ask who it was?"

"No. Not until we get a full report from the station."

Officer Mocroft sighed.

"Very well. Good luck, Deputy."

"As you were."

Dakari walked down the stone steps of the Academy entrance. Amelia debriefed him on the situation as they walked back to his patrol car. "They've sealed off 8th street but there are some camera drones nearby. They don't know who the suspect is yet."

"That's all that matters. I want a–hey! Get out of my vehicle!"

Sergeant Xing stood up and saluted by the open door.

"Sir! I have orders to deliver the psychic back to the CDAD as soon as possible."

"And who gave you those orders?"

"Chief Kalak, sir."

Dakari cursed under his breath.

"I can drive him back myself, Sergeant."

"Understood, sir."

Dakari stepped inside his armored patrol car as Amelia held the door open.

"What about the girl?" Amelia asked.

"She's innocent. I have a written memo you can give to internal affairs later if you want. Make sure no one bothers her. She's not a psychic."

"Understood. Have a safe drive, sir."

Amelia closed the door as Dakari drove down the winding streets of the Academy. He passed several other vehicles and saw arbitrators setting up yellow tape on other entrances. In the distance, several cars from media outlets drove towards the scene. Dakari turned on both blinkers and sped up. He wasn't going to let this operation go wrong. And even more important, he was going to find out the truth about what had happened to his son.

* * *

Derek woke up in a tiny white room, sitting at a table beneath beaming ceiling lights. He was in a straitjacket. A tight strap ran up his crotch over his pants. He tried to put his arms over his head but encountered tight resistance. An overwhelming, nauseating sense of claustrophobia overcame him. There were bruises all over him. It drove him mad not being able to move. He squirmed and sweated profusely as the thought of staying in one position for the rest of his life began to drive him insane. He lifted his eyes up from the desk as they adjusted to the brightness above him. Then he flinched as a towering figure slammed both his hands on the table and leaned close to his face. It was Dakari Minathi.

"What happened to my son?"

Derek leaned away, his mind swimming with a million questions.

"How did you know?"

"I've met a lot of murderers. I know the look."

"B-but I didn't kill him."

Dakari slowed down. There were still several unknowns about this case. Technically Derek had never used his abilities back at the Academy. In this case, Mirabelle had the alibi that revealed Derek to be the kid from the cameras, but it was now a gray area whether that gave Dakari the right to beat him with a stun baton. He already felt bad about that. *God, I have anger issues.* No denying that. It was the chance of cheap justice that had made him reach for his weapon. Previously, he wasn't sure he would ever come close to finding Zane's killer, but the way this boy had pleaded with him told him otherwise. The way this blonde-haired bastard had said: *"Matthew did it. Not me."* There was real guilt in that whining voice of his. He had heard something like it before.

"Then how did you know he was murdered?" Dakari asked.

"Because my brother did it!" Derek lowered his head and squinted his eyes. "It was Matthew...not me."

The seasoned arbitrator took a long pause, inspecting the way Derek's eyes kept trailing away. "Why do I get the feeling you're trying to convince yourself and not me?"

Derek's lip started to quiver. He looked pathetic.

"Because I gave Matthew his room number! But I had no choice!"

Dakari scoffed.

"That's the biggest lie this world has ever told. Why is it your choice to put on your shoes in the morning but not your choice when someone else's life rests in your hands? Why do you have the agency of choosing from a menu but not choosing to pull the trigger to end someone's life?" Dakari leaned across the table. "Is it your choice that's taken away? Or the strength to make the right one?" Derek looked away. Nothing of his posture indicated that he was going to respond, so Dakari continued the interrogation. "Who ordered you to do this?"

Derek kept shaking his head.

"If I told you they'd kill me."

"Your life's in my hands, not theirs. And I'm still undecided."

Derek swallowed a lump in his throat. He stared at the floor. If he gave Dakari any information now, his chances of being saved by the Boss were over. But if he told Dakari, he might finally get the redemption he longed for. He closed his eyes and uttered the words that would seal his fate or save it.

"The Boss."

"Who?"

"The Boss. We don't know his name, but he's the one that gives us orders."

"Like kidnapping psychics?"

That seemed to perk Derek's interest. He raised his head up from the table with confusion. "How'd you know?"

"That's not your concern."

"No, you don't understand. There's no way you could know about that. No one knows about that operation! *No one!*"

"Then maybe these friends of yours aren't as clever as they think they are."

"They're not my friends," Derek said. "I never wanted any part of this. I was pressured into this job the moment I enrolled at the Academy. I was only ten. I didn't know what I was doing."

"Does this Boss have any other names?"

"Not one we know of. We know nothing about him except that his word on everything is final. He's the mastermind, but he's also the most anonymous of us all."

Dakari pressed his clenched fists into the cool metal table. "Why did

Zane get involved?"

Derek's eyes remained dark and distant.

"He knew too much."

Dakari leaned away from the table. This was too much for him. He couldn't do it.

"Derek Hunt, you're going to rot in a cell for the rest of your life."

He reached for the door.

"Wait! I can help! You can't turn me in! They're going to kill me."

Dakari turned around.

"And why should I care?! Did you spare my son when he begged for his life?!"

"I've told you a million times. I DIDN'T DO IT!" Derek started to cry again. "Please! My conscience has suffered enough."

"Oh!" Dakari shouted. "Your *conscience* has suffered?! Well, forgive me for hurting it more! But it doesn't seem I've done much damage, seeing that your conscience was never strong enough to save my son!"

Derek kept crying as Dakari towered above him.

"You're pathetic."

He almost walked away before Derek stopped him again.

"You leave this place without me," Derek said, sniffling. "And you won't leave it alive."

"Is that a threat?"

"No." Tears and snot streaked down the boy's face. "It's the truth. The Boss has people all over the Republic. Even in your own department. You wouldn't know the first place to look without me, but I can give you the leads. I can help you bring the Awakening down."

"The Awakening?" Dakari asked. "So they're the people you work for."

"Yes. The gang I was in is just a proxy. We're just one of many scattered across the Republic doing the Boss' dirty work."

Dakari paused. The boy was clearly telling the truth, but he was being too vague.

"I'm going to get us some more time. If you're going to talk, you need a cell."

"I wouldn't do that."

"Why not? Don't you see how this is going to work? You're going to tell me what you know about the Awakening and I'm going to keep our investigation ongoing."

"It won't work like that. Like I said, we have people in your department. As soon as they realize I've been captured they're going to take over this case. I guarantee it."

"Who will? Kalak?"

"I don't know who. But arbitrators help us clean up crime scenes all the time."

"Then I'll pay an extra visit to your cell."

"You wouldn't get clearance."

"I think I'd find a way to make it work in your case."

"You're missing the point. I wouldn't be any safer in a cell than I would be out there." Dakari no longer felt safe. The boy's tone had changed from petulant pleading to resolute seriousness. He felt like he was being watched. "We're both dead men strapped to a time bomb. Sooner or later they're gonna blow us up."

"Is that why you're telling me all this?"

"No. Not a day goes by where I don't regret the things I've done. I've wanted a chance to atone for what I did and now I have my chance."

Dakari analyzed the suspect. He had already let one psychic go today, and he had nearly run away. And now he stood across the table from a psychic partially responsible for the murder of his son. But he knew how to read the boy's eyes. There were no lies. And if the deaths of Zane and Desta had proved anything, it was that death strikes when you're closest to the sun. Dakari was flying higher than ever. If Derek was right, he needed his help. He grabbed a pair of keys from his belt and started undoing the chains.

"Wait, you serious? You're letting me go?"

"I'm letting you work with me. Do you understand the difference?"

"I think so."

"Good," Dakari said. With one last turn of the key, the chains came loose.

"Because if this is going to work, we need to move fast."

Derek stretched out his arms. With ease, the tight binds of the straitjacket slipped off his shoulders. Derek sat in awe as he raised both palms before his face. And Dakari watched Derek realize his freedom. He looked at his palms and then at Dakari, whose heart now beat out of his chest as sweat ran down his brow. If he had made a mistake, he wouldn't live long to learn from it. But Derek didn't retaliate.

"I'm ready," Derek said. "Lead the way."

An Evanescent Escape

Matthew received a call when he arrived at his dorm. No caller ID. That was bad. That meant it was the Boss. There were only a few times in his short career at the Academy when he'd received an unannounced call, none of them good. He answered without hesitation, pacing around in his room with the faint hopes that he was not about to be discovered as a liar. Had he put too much trust in Derek? Had that bastard brother of his snitched? If he did, there would be hell to pay, but knowing the kind of power the Boss held, he'd be dead before he had the chance to get his revenge.

"Are you awake?" Matthew asked, doing his best to quell the fear in his voice.

"I never sleep," the Boss said. "Where's Derek?"

"What do you mean?"

"Are you an idiot?"

I don't believe it, he thought. *Did Derek run away?*

"I...I'd like to think not," Matthew said.

"Then you must be blind, seeing that there was an army of arbitrators at the Gerumandian Academy a few hours ago."

"They didn't tell us anything!"

"Then take a guess."

Matthew's legs nearly gave out underneath him. The Boss continued speaking.

"Some reports are saying they have footage of him using psychic abilities from the night before. Would you know anything about that?"

"What? That's impossible. I was with Derek for almost the whole night."

"They say it occurred on the rooftop at 19:04 hours."

"Derek wasn't on the roof then. He was with me."

"Then why is he the one locked up?"

"How should I know? It's not my fault that he was…" Matthew stopped. He thought about his treachery, and Derek's desire to reveal it.

"That he was what?"

Matthew sighed. He didn't have long to fabricate a story that would lead the Boss down a road of alternative discovery, but if he didn't, one question would lead to another, and soon enough, the entire Academy would know that a stage 4 psychic resided in the dorms.

"I'm worried that I might get in trouble for saying this, sir."

"Then rest assured, you're already in trouble. You might want to say anything to help your case because right now you're just about as dispensable as the next psychic."

The gears in Matthew's head turned with mischief. *How do you tell a lie to the most powerful man in the world?* He thought. It was simple. *You tell the truth. Then you bend it to your will. Truth is the molten steel. The lie is the shape of the sword. And all swords have a destination. They are forged to pierce hearts.*

"I believe that Derek had information pertaining to a stage 4 psychic but destroyed the evidence to stall for time."

There was silence on the other end. The sword was drawn. The lie was placed. Time would tell if he had struck the flesh of his assailant with a true blow or merely slashed the wall beside him with dull noise.

"That's quite an accusation," the Boss said. His voice was calculating and cold.

"It certainly is," Matthew said. He walked over to a bag where he had stored the broken scanner from the night before. "But I can prove it. He broke the scanner with the information last night. I saved the remains and was planning to report his treacherous behavior later today. Unfortunately, it seems Derek turned himself in."

"Did he tell you who the stage 4 psychic was?"

"No." Matthew paused again, his mind scrambling for an explanation.

Remember. Tell him something tangentially true. The key was to bend steel, not break it. "But I imagine he's somewhere at the Gerumandian Academy."

The Boss paused, each second of silence a kind of Armageddon. Matthew felt like he was standing beneath the feet of God, waiting for his verdict of final judgment.

"I will handle Derek Hunt," the Boss said. "In the meantime, your orders are to conduct low profile psychic scans of all students that were present at the Academy during the scholarship weekend. You're lucky there's only a couple thousand and not full enrollment. But work as fast as possible. Do I make myself clear?"

Matthew eyed the bag of the scanner's remains. He almost couldn't believe that it had worked. But then again, this wasn't the first rodeo. Like many others of unchecked ambition, Matthew learned a lot about lies. He knew when to nod in the midst of political conversations, and like a chameleon, he knew how to change his colors with clever sarcasm to belittle the "opposing side" in a way that made him seem to know more than he was willing to say, and yet if asked to say anything more, he would appear as empty as a fraternity keg at the end of pledge week. The dueling ring was Matthew's world. Anything outside of that was subsidiary. If the Academy wanted him to support a political party, he'd be their poster child. He'd happily be anyone's pawn if it meant he got to keep playing chess. Some people would call him a sellout, but those people didn't matter. They'd bitch and complain while Matthew made millions and won the hearts of millions more. The mere fact that he already had enough power to end someone's life with just the words from his mouth made him feel large, important, and god-like. And now he had just lied to his own boss. In a way, the AOL drug, his psychic powers, his family name, and his academic reputation formed his apotheosis. If he couldn't die, who was to say he wasn't a god already? The bathroom mirror was his altar, and the man in the glass was the object of his undeniable praise.

"Yes, sir," Matthew said, then hung up the call.

Carter's golden child lived to fight another day.

* * *

It was a sight no arbitrator expected to see. Dakari Minathi walked down a hallway with the same psychic he had beaten with a baton not less than two hours ago. Some employees did a double-take and went back to work as the seasoned deputy waved back to them with a smile. *Nothing to see here boys*, he thought. *Nothing but treason.* There would be no turning back from an action like this. Releasing a psychic from detainment would end any chances of wearing the badge again, but by this point Dakari felt that he had enough reason to suspect that the department he worked for was deep in the weeds with the case he was trying to solve. Someone had erased Amelia's memories, and Dakari would bet a whole lot of money that even if Kalak didn't do it, he probably knew who did.

With only about a minute's walk left to the main hangar, an arbitrator in full body armor pushed off from the wall and stood in between their path to exit. A blaster rifle was tucked in the holster on his side, ready to be drawn.

"Deputy, why have you taken the psychic out of custody?"

Another arbitrator cornered them from behind, causing other workers to raise their heads over their cubicles to see the commotion. He had hoped he could at least make it to the hangar without anyone asking questions, but then again, it was Derek Hunt he was walking with. And he wasn't wearing cuffs.

"I have orders from the Chief to transfer him to another department," Dakari said.

"Then why isn't he in cuffs? That seems like a major oversight in general safety."

Dakari looked back at Derek. It was too late to talk them out of this now.

"It might. But even if he was cuffed, you wouldn't let me leave, would you?"

The arbitrators went silent.

"I'm afraid not, sir. Hand over your gun as well as the psychic. Under direct orders from Chief Kalak, you're under arrest."

Derek snapped his fingers. Before each arbitrator could retrieve their rifles, Derek pointed one hand at the arbitrator in front of him, and another at the one behind him. Dakari ducked as two laser blasts flung out of the portals in Derek's palms, pulverizing both arbitrators and sending their bodies flying across the station. He followed Dakari closely as they maneuvered their way around cubicles. An alarm system with red lights blared from the high ceilings of the station as another squadron of arbitrators cocked their rifles from the glass walkway above.

"Don't kill anyone!" Dakari shouted.

"Don't worry! It's set to stun!" Derek's eyes widened. "Get down!"

Derek clenched both fists, cocked them back, then slammed them together. He created two different portals in each hand and started to rotate them in front of his body. He absorbed the blaster fire in one portal and shot it back out the other, cracking the glass on the upper railway and sending several arbitrators tumbling onto the ground.

"Come on!" Dakari shouted. "We need to keep moving!"

Derek relinquished both portals and followed Dakari down a narrow tunnel. The deputy fired two blasts at several arbitrators in front of them and ran past their fallen bodies. They sprinted down a hallway of spinning red lights. With the swipe of his datapad, Dakari unlocked the doors to the hangar. They leaned over the main walkway and saw dozens of vacant hovercrafts, and then dozens of more arbitrators guarding them. And then to make matters even worse, the hangar bay doors began to close. With each second, the sunlight in the hangar grew dim as laser blasts bounced over their heads. Another squadron of arbitrators ran down the hallway they came from.

"Seal that door!" Dakari shouted.

Derek nodded and started rotating his hands as if he was molding a lump of clay. He extended the particles from the wall until they stretched over the doors. He clenched his fists and returned the particles to their normal state, creating a wall to seal off the tunnel and the arbitrators inside.

At the same time, the hangar doors closed.

"What do we do?!" Derek shouted.

"I can bypass the lockdown codes if you can secure a hovercraft. Can you get through these guards?"

"Yeah but–"

"Then do it! Now!"

Dakari advanced down the glass corridor overlooking the docking bay and fired several suppressive rounds at the arbitrators below. He ducked as laser blasts flew over his head, giving Derek enough time to create another tear and fling an EMP grenade out from his fists. It rattled on the ground below and disabled several arbitrators, sending them to the ground like statues. Derek deployed an attachable energy shield from his fists, attached it to his chest, and turned it on. A clear holographic coating raced over his body. Then with the turn of his hand, he grabbed an e-blade out from a portal and vaulted onto the main floor below.

Dakari scanned his datapad to the control room.

It blinked red.

"Access denied."

"What?!" He punched the glass door. Inside, several officers backed towards the end of the wall and pulled out their blasters. He kicked the door. It wouldn't budge. "Derek!"

On the main floor, Derek moved like a samurai. Blaster fire bounced off his energy shield as he used the edge of his e-blade to knock several arbitrators flat across the floor, stunning their suits.

"I'm a little busy!"

"I need a grenade!"

"You serious!?"

"We don't have time, just throw it up here!"

Derek rolled across the ground, slashed an arbitrator in the chest, then snapped his fingers, launching a grenade up towards the top walkway. Dakari caught it, dropped it below the door, then dove back across the bridge and covered his head. Glass shards imploded as the door to the control room burst open. Dakari leaped up from the ground and fired several stun rounds through the smoke, then heard the guards inside fall down. He quickly navigated across the control panel, bypassed the code, then deactivated the lockdown. The metallic hangar doors crunched and opened with rays of bright sunlight.

Derek knocked down the last guard and yanked the lever of the nearest hovercraft. They both stepped inside the vehicle and took their seats in the cockpit.

"Where are we going?" Derek asked. He watched as the main engines erupted to life as the hovercraft doors closed. They flew out of the hangar. Dakari eased up on the controls as they blended in with the air traffic.

"Somewhere safe," Dakari said. "At least for now."

* * *

In the hangar, Chief Kalak stood over the bodies of several disabled arbitrators. Several medical teams carried them away on stretchers while a repair unit blocked off the main hallway with yellow tape. Remnants of smoke rose to the skies as several firefighters finished dousing the flames on the building. Amelia approached Kalak and Banner with both hands folded behind her back.

"You wanted to see me, sir?"

"I did. I know you worked closely with Dakari. We're not claiming you had anything to do with this, but we are interested if you know where he might've gone."

Amelia lowered her head.

"I have no idea. He cut off communication with me."

"Do you have any idea why?"

Amelia stared at the landing zone of the missing hovercraft.

"Not a clue. He kept pressing me about the Leonardo Estate. He told me I was sent there to find something but never told me what that was."

Kalak smiled.

"That will be all, Amelia. You're dismissed."

She saluted her Chief and returned to her station. Lieutenant Banner smiled.

"I'd say that the Boss was successful then," Banner said. "No need to worry about her. Don't know how you're gonna cover up this mess though."

"I'm in conversation."

"What's that supposed to mean? I mean, this is Carter Hunt's son we're talking about here. If they find out he's a psychic–"

"They won't. I've got a speech prepared for the media later tonight."

"You want to give me a truncated version?"

"Dakari Minathi helped an *unidentified* psychic escape the CDAD."

"Someone was sure to identify him."

"Then why don't you tell the Boss to do what he does best? I doubt only a handful of people saw him. That's enough for us to deal with this in-house."

"And what about the psychic from the Academy?"

"False Alarm. Happens all the time." Kalak smiled. "It'll be business as usual there because it's the summertime. The problem is that eventually, people at the Academy are going to wonder where Derek went running off to. Thankfully that's not our business, seeing that Derek Hunt was never here, nor did we take him from the Academy." Kalak paused. "I'll have the Boss use a few mind-snares if they trace Derek's disappearance to us, but I'm not worried too many people will go down that rabbit trail."

"You seem pretty optimistic."

"I have good reason for it. Dakari Minathi is out of the CDAD." Kalak sighed. "A runaway impurity and a deranged psychic. It's all a perfect storm. For too long I've let my friendship with Dakari get in the way of seeing him for who he is."

"And what would that be?"

"A liability." Kalak eyed his blaster holstered to his right side. "But rest assured. I won't make that mistake again. I want patrols scouting the city on the double. As of now, Dakari Minathi is an enemy of the state. Use any means necessary to find him."

With those words, Kalak made the long walk back to his office, humiliated by what two people had made of his department. He vowed it would never happen again.

A Radical Revelation

Later that night, Dakari Minathi and Derek Hunt ate chow mein in a cramped apartment in District 3. They were exhausted. After hours of traveling and eliminating their tracks, getting rid of the hovercraft, and then creating disguises, they made their way into a poor apartment complex before the news of their traitorous deeds went viral. That didn't surprise them, but it was jarring for Dakari to see his name on every news outlet in the Republic. For some reason, Derek wasn't mentioned. They were still in great danger. But in an apartment with nothing but sleeping bags and floor mats, they felt some semblance of security on the 33rd floor with hundreds of other rooms surrounding them.

"Thank goodness they have delivery," Derek said. He kept eyeing the news feed on his datapad while he ate.

Dakari kept eating. A few minutes later he set down his chopsticks.

"You gonna finish those noodles?" Derek asked. The bald arbitrator gave them over without a fuss. Derek scarfed them down.

"Are you finished?" Dakari asked.

"Yeah."

"Then if you don't mind, I'd like to ask you some questions."

"Right now?"

"Seeing that the Republic has issued a 5 million rec bounty on my head, time isn't exactly a luxury we have. I'd like to do this sooner rather than later." He paused. "They didn't mention you though. I guess they're covering your tracks." Dakari set his bowl aside. "Anyway, you agreed to help."

"You're right. Ask away."

Dakari clicked his pen, grabbed a notepad, and flipped the page.

"Jamey Ledgings. Brian Welldens. James Benedict. Alan Jones. Jon Jerry. Do you recognize any of these names?"

Derek's shoulders slumped. His green eyes were dark and distant.

"Yeah. With exception to Jon, those are several students we've rescued over the years."

"Rescued? Others might say captured."

"They're all psychics. We're saving them from people like you. No offense."

"I thought you said your Boss has arbitrators working in my department."

"He does. But it's easier if we get them at the Academy first. If they're taken to the CDAD, we have to smuggle them out of the detention centers and erase any records of their presence at the department."

"And you've been smuggling them using L-Transport cargo ships, haven't you?"

"Yeah. They use the underground railroads to snatch psychics right beneath your noses."

"Who's they?"

"A powerful group of psychics gathered to fight against the tyranny of the state. They're called the Awakening."

"How did you get recruited?"

Derek sighed. It was not a story he wanted to tell. But he told it nonetheless.

"It started with Matthew. A few years ago, he was caught using adrenaline stimulants at the Academy. He was about to face expulsion. It was all over, until the next day, everyone forgot about the incident entirely. It was like it never happened. Later that day he got a call from someone called 'The Boss.' He said they had been eyeing Matthew for a while and wanted him to join. Obviously, Matthew accepted the offer. Two years later, I got dragged into the operation. I didn't want to do it, but then again, I didn't have much of a choice."

"How many people are a part of this operation?"

"Too many to count. I've heard they're all over the Republic. Some of them are doctors, some are lawyers, some are teachers, some are arbitrators, and some are even students. But they're all psychics, each of them sworn to the preservation and evolution of the psychic gene."

"And these psychics you capture...where do they go?"

"Telaris."

"I thought that planet was abandoned after the Battle for New Earth."

"Makes for a perfect hideout. The Awakening is using the military outposts on that planet as a training ground for psychics. They're taught to weaponize their abilities. Matthew told us there are thousands of them there, waiting to be used on the day of the 'Great Awakening': a coup d'état to overthrow the Republic."

Dakari stopped writing. *A coup of psychics?* This was bigger than anything he imagined. He looked out the window and saw the midnight traffic of the city of Dain, the thousands of pedestrians walking through the city streets. The thought of thousands of psychics burning that city to the ground haunted him.

"Then if they have the numbers what are they waiting for?" Dakari asked.

"The rabbit hole goes deeper than you think," Derek said. "There are other groups besides the Awakening, groups of psychics hiding in the shadows. The other two are Exodus and the Gray Eids."

"Explain."

"Keep in mind, the only things I know about these groups are what I've been told from the Awakening. From what I know, Exodus is the opposite of us. Whereas the Awakening wants to see a world of psychics, Exodus wants to remove the psychic gene entirely with a drug that could eliminate the phyofrenia for good. They see it as a power that will never go unchecked. They're the reason that sneaking psychics out of the detention centers is a hit or miss operation. 50% of the psychics go to the Awakening, the other 50% go to Exodus. Both groups have sworn a truce on a first come first serve mentality, but besides that, they are sworn enemies."

"What about the Gray Eids?"

"They're the most obscure group of all. They're a self-proclaimed neutral group of psychics. Octavian founded them in 2105. He was the most powerful psychic to ever live. He wanted to bring balance to the Awakening and Exodus by spreading news of the psychic gene to the public. Before the Gray Eids, no one even knew that psychics existed because every time someone discovered them their memories were erased. Octavian, however, found a way to bypass the mind-snare for standard AOL humans by creating a mirage: a deflection of the subconscious that protects an individual from accessing their memories. It didn't take long. Once Octavian started randomly giving these mirages to people, news of psychics spread like a wildfire."

"In other words, the psychic gene existed long before thirty years ago."

"Some suspect that the psychic gene is as old as the AOL drug itself." Derek paused. "But that's neither here nor there. The point is that if the Awakening started a coup d'état to overthrow the Republic, they'd be met with a counterattack from both Exodus and the Gray Eids and probably end up losing."

"Then it's just a race to see who can get the most psychics."

"Or a stage 4 psychic."

Dakari's eyes widened.

"You mean, there are different kinds of psychics?"

"Four kinds, although the public is only aware of stage 1 psychics. These psychics create tears." Derek made a small portal in his palm with the snap of his fingers. "Stage 2 psychics have the power of alteration." Derek relinquished the tear. Then he lifted his chopstick, spreading it apart into tiny blue molecules. "They can deconstruct the matter around them to its most basic form." He returned the chopstick to its original form and set it down. "And then there are stage 3 psychics. They have the power of manipulation. They're the nasty ones because they can erase your memories."

"Why can't they do this to psychics or impurities?"

"Impurities don't have a phyofrenia and psychics have a strengthened one, rendering any attempt at a mind-snare futile. Every AOL human has an underdeveloped phyofrenia, too weak to perform psychic abilities, but present enough to be manipulated."

"I'm guessing you're a stage 2 psychic then." Derek nodded. "What about a stage 4 psychic? What's so special about them?"

"That one is a little harder to explain." Derek paused. "You need to understand the difference between Our Plane and the Other Plane."

Dakari clicked his pen again and finished writing a few more notes down. "Go on."

"Our Plane is the world around us. It obeys the laws of physics, it's visible to the human eye, and it's made accessible to all five senses. The Other Plane is the world we can't see, a world of dreams, memories, and thoughts. It's only accessible through the phyofrenia. It is a plane of reality that exists simultaneously to the world we touch, taste, smell, hear, and see, but instead of obeying the laws that govern this plane, the Other Plane exists according to the rules we give it. It is an empty dreamscape that connects all the phyofrenia together. A mind-snare occurs when a psychic enters the phyofrenia of someone else and destroys an object representing a memory they wish to eradicate. Often this is done by disrupting the energy of the phyofrenia by applying pressure to someone's temples, but some psychics have found a way to do this remotely. We believe this is how the Boss erases the minds of so many people without ever revealing himself to anyone. And the only reason we know anything about the Other Plane is because Octavian traveled there himself."

"How did he do that?"

Derek paused.

"We don't know. He disappeared ten years ago. What we do know is that every AOL human is susceptible to mind-snares because of their phyofrenia. Think of it as a garage of the mind. It's an empty space of ideas, filled with meaning and objects by the subconscious. But at the end of every phyofrenia is a doorway, linking that person to the Other Plane. Stage 3 psychics can access that doorway and eliminate memories at will. They cannot eliminate the memories of other psychics, however, because, for us, that doorway is protected."

"And what does this have to do with a stage 4 psychic?"

"Remember Octavian? He found something that could change the course of history. Because Our Plane and the Other Plane are parallel to one another, things you might find in the Other Plane resemble real things in this world. If you destroy a symbol that represents someone's childhood, that childhood memory will be destroyed. A long time ago Octavian found something in the Other Plane: an incredibly powerful source of psychic energy, something as large as a planet. It was then verified by Octavian that what he found was the Krymenodon: a bastion of psychic energy and the homeworld of the plant that gave us the AOL drug. Psychics are still humans, and because of that, they are bound by human limitations. But on the Krymenodon, it is theorized that even one psychic could create entire fleets with the wave of their hand. I almost passed out by creating a few tears, but on the Krymenodon, that power would be limitless."

"And it would be the tipping point for the Awakening to launch their coup."

"Exactly. The problem is that the Awakening doesn't have any stage 4 psychics. Our leader can sense the Krymenodon in the Other Plane, but he cannot see Our Plane at the same time. That makes it impossible for him to translate the coordinates of this planet to us because the ratio is skewed. Stage 4 psychics, on the other hand, can sense psychic energy in Our Plane and the Other Plane simultaneously, and therefore find the Krymenodon."

"Then why don't they just go after Octavian?"

"Like I said. He disappeared ten years ago. We're looking for someone like him."

Dakari stopped writing and looked up from his notepad.

"And you're telling me that Quan is the one you've been looking for?"

"I ran the scan myself. It's him."

Dakari stood up and dropped his notepad. His stable grip on the world, one with rules and principles and things that made sense, was slowly starting to fall apart in the wake of what Derek was telling him. It was as if someone had pulled back a curtain, revealing the way things were as an illusion to cover up what really was. Psychics were one thing. Psychic societies were another matter entirely. Planets of power and coup d'états were problems too big for his mind to handle. He had joined the force for justice, not conspiracies. And to think now that he was caught up in the biggest one of them all.

"Does anyone else know?" Dakari asked. "About Quan."

"Yeah," Derek said, lowering his head. "Matthew does."

Dakari cursed under his breath.

"Then it's over. They probably got him on a ship to Telaris as we speak."

"Not exactly," Derek said. "Matthew might work for the Awakening, but his allegiance is first and foremost to himself. He knows that the day the Awakening finds a stage 4 psychic, he's going to be shipped to Telaris to plan for the coup. Matthew doesn't want that. Not yet at least."

"What is he waiting for?"

"The Gerumandian Dueling Tournament. The immaculate soldier. He thinks that's the only way he'll win back Dad's affection."

"You really buy that?"

"That it will buy Dad's affection? No. But Matthew believes it. And if you knew him you would believe me too. He said it himself. He's going to keep Quan a secret until the title is his, and then when he wins he's going to turn Quan in."

Dakari chuckled.

"So you're telling me that the only thing stopping the Awakening from finding the Krymenodon is your brother's desire to win the dueling tournament?" Dakari just shook his head. "What a crazy world we live in."

Derek looked out the window. Darkness settled above a city of skyscrapers and hovercrafts. "A crazy world indeed."

Dakari looked at Derek.

"You mentioned there was a way for AOL humans to have resistance to mind-snares?"

"Yeah," Derek said. "It's a service provided by Gray Eids. If you know how to contact them, they'll give that person a mirage–at a price of course."

"Do you know how to contact them? There are a few people I have in mind."

Derek lifted his datapad.

"Then give me their names. I'll make the call."

Suspicious Students

It was two hours past midnight. And Mirabelle still couldn't sleep. She tossed and turned, staring at the ceiling. Sleep required the brain to be silent. But hers wouldn't shut up. Part of the problem was seeing Dakari again. It reminded her of Zane, the way they had laughed, danced, cried. The room was haunted by his absence. Sometimes her eyes would water at this hour of the night when she thought of him, but she clenched her bedsheets and closed her eyes to drive her sorry tears away. *Stop it. You're better than this.* She thought of something else. She was now one degree removed from meeting the man that took her father away. She wanted justice for Zane more than anything, but the prospect of seeing her father again gave justice a run for its money. But she wasn't going to choose. She would do both of those things. She was sure of it. That was enough to put her to sleep.

* * *

The next morning, Dakari called Mirabelle and Quan on a private channel. There was a lot to take in. Dakari could barely get in a word without being cut off.

"Matthew killed him!?" Mirabelle shrieked. "Why didn't we capture him instead?"

"Because I didn't know that until I got to the CDAD," Dakari said. "And there's nothing we can do now. We're fugitives. Or at least I am."

"How are you so...calm?"

Derek chimed in.

"He wasn't calm yesterday."

An awkward silence passed.

"Right," Dakari said. "Anyway, there's more."

Dakari mentioned the Awakening, Exodus, and the Gray Eids. Mirages. Stage 4 psychics. Octavian. The Krymenodon. And finally–how Quan was the key to it all.

"Derek says that Alexander already has a mirage," Dakari said. Quan sat next to Mirabelle and leaned closer to the datapad. "That means he's safe from mind-snares."

"That's not what I'm concerned about," Quan said. "If Matthew already knows I'm a stage 4 psychic then I need to leave."

"Derek doesn't think it's a good idea."

"Why not?"

"If Matthew finds out you're gone, he'll tell the Awakening."

"Or he'll just let us go," Mirabelle said. "It only buys him more time, right?"

"Not exactly. Matthew is only willing to keep you a secret so long as you're in his sight. If you leave and the Awakening learns that Quan was at the Academy, it will look bad on him. Matthew's desperate, but he's not that desperate. In other words, you're on a tight leash. Matthew's the only reason you're not on a one-way trip to Telaris."

There was an eerie silence among the four of them.

"But there is some good news," Dakari said. "The Dueling Tournament is on November 10th. That gives us five months to work on a plan, assuming Matthew doesn't tell anyone, and you don't give him any reason to think you're running away."

"Then what's the plan?" Mirabelle asked.

"If it's true that there are two other groups of psychics out there, the Gray Eids and Exodus, then we need to find a way to contact them. Derek said that the Gray Eids won't get involved because of their neutrality, which means Exodus is our best bet."

"Why would they help us?" Mirabelle asked. "You said they're sworn to the eradication of the psychic gene."

"But not psychics themselves. There's a difference. The Awakening will use Quan as a tool to get to the Krymenodon. Exodus might protect him to ensure that doesn't happen. I don't see any other option. The CDAD is infested with Awakening members, meaning they can't protect you. But Exodus just might."

Quan leaned towards the datapad.

"That wasn't part of our agreement. I didn't say I'd join Exodus after our five months. I said I would leave."

"And last week I didn't know you were a stage 4 psychic. Things changed." Dakari sighed. "But you're right. We didn't shake on six months or a month with Exodus, we shook on five months at the Academy."

"What if we can't find a way?" Mirabelle asked.

"We don't need to," Quan said. "Think about it. Both the Awakening and Exodus are looking for me. If I leave, they don't have anyone to search for."

Dakari was silent. Mirabelle slowly looked over at Quan with one brow raised in confusion. Quan just stood there, his face slowly blushing when he realized how stupid he sounded.

"Yeah, that's a great point Quan," Derek said on the other end. "I'm sure they'll just give up as soon as you leave the planet."

"Then we'll fly fast! Ok? You know what I mean. If we leave it'll make their search a lot more difficult. That's all I'm trying to say."

Mirabelle started laughing.

"You're a *moron*. And who's going to fly the Sojourner? You?"

"I'll figure it out."

"Let's remove Quan from the equation," Mirabelle said. He crossed his arms. "We're still moving forward with the plan to expose the Awakening and we're starting to get more evidence. If Exodus is opposed to the Awakening, then at least we have some common enemies."

"Which brings me to the backup plan," Dakari said. "But none of you are going to like it."

"Why's that?" Quan asked.

"At the CDAD, 50% of psychics go to the Awakening. The other 50% go to Exodus. If for some reason we can't find a way to contact them..."

Quan's heart skipped a beat.

"You're not suggesting–"

"I am. If we don't find a way to contact Exodus within the next five months, Derek or Quan has to turn themselves in and hope they get caught by the right people."

Quan leaned in closer.

"I'm not turning myself in."

"I thought you might say that. In that case, Derek will. Let's hope it never comes to that. In the meantime, lay low. I may have lost my badge, but there's someone I know in the arbitrator department who hasn't. I'm going to see if we can get her a mirage." Dakari paused. "Good luck."

Dakari leaned against the edge of the wall as Derek typed into the datapad.

"What was the name of that woman again?" Derek asked.

"Amelia Lancaster. Tell them to hurry. We may not have a lot of time."

* * *

Mirabelle sat on the edge of her bed and shut off her datapad.

"You know you could at least pretend like you care," she said. "I don't even know why Dakari made a deal with you if you're just going to be this stubborn."

"You don't get it, Mirabelle." Quan stood up. "I have no stakes in this."

Mirabelle paused. She studied Quan's blue eyes and remembered their glow of anger on the rooftop. She didn't say anything. She just looked.

"Who made you this cold?"

"I don't have to tell you anything."

"Whatever." She paused. "How long have you been out in hiding?"

"Not long enough."

"But long enough to forget what it's like to be a friend." Mirabelle sarcastically smiled. "Do you ever get *lonely* hiding out by yourself?"

"I'm not alone."

233

"Ahh, that's right. You have a homeless roommate. What was his name again?"

"Alexander."

"Do you two get along?"

"I'd like to think so."

"What's that supposed to mean?"

"Things are cordial."

"Cordial? Lemme guess. He doesn't even know about any of this, does he?"

"Why should he?"

"You don't want to tell him that some random psychic gave him a mirage in the middle of the night while he was sleeping?"

"Would you?"

"I guess not." She shrugged her shoulders. "Still. It's strange. You'll have to tell him eventually. If Matthew has his eyes on you then Alexander's lumped into this too, whether he likes it or not." Quan stood there with both hands in his pockets. "You're not even listening, are you? You're just dying to leave."

Quan's eyes widened. Then they lowered. To tell the truth, he was exhausted. None of this made any sense to him. To think that he was the most wanted man in the world just because of some ability in his brain made him frustrated beyond belief. He wanted to pursue his own things on his own time, not fight someone else's battles.

"You wouldn't understand."

"Then help me understand."

He sat down next to her at the edge of the bed.

"It's not just that I don't want to be here–like in this room," he said. "I don't even want to be at this Academy. In this city. On this planet." He looked out the window. "The same city you see in need of saving is the one that told me the only place I belong is in an underground cell."

Mirabelle noticed that Quan was tugging against the wristband on his forearm.

"What about your family?"

234

"Family?" Quan laughed. "If you could even call it that. My parents died in a car crash. I was too young to remember so I never really had the chance to care. But my adopted parents...I cared about them quite a bit. Maybe too much. Then I realized they only adopted me to make replications of themselves. They couldn't have kids, so Amanda pressured Daniel to adopt me and my brother. He wanted us to be engineers, but we liked dueling." Quan paused. "He didn't."

"As Jon and I got older and Daniel realized his adopted sons weren't going to be cardboard copies of himself, his alcoholism got worse. There were a lot more fights at home. Daniel would yell. Amanda would cry. Then Jon applied to the Gerumandian Academy. Daniel lost it, and then Jon just left." Quan fidgeted with the wristband again. "We wore these wristbands to remind ourselves of our dreams of being Gerumandians. We planned on transferring together."

Quan clenched his fists.

"It was bad enough being in that home, but without Jon..." Quan shook his head. "It was a nightmare. And then to top off everything about a year later I learned I was a psychic. You know the kinds of things my father used to say about psychics on the projector?" Quan just kept laughing. "It was like the perfect storm. I was the wanna-be Gerumandian adopted psychic son that Daniel never wanted. I ran away about a year after Jon left and never looked back."

Mirabelle sat with both hands in her lap.

"Looks like you're still running."

Quan looked over at Mirabelle.

"There's a freedom of being on the run that you would never know until you've tried it." He looked over the star charts on Mirabelle's wall. "You want to know what that kind of freedom is like. How many nights have you gone to sleep wishing you could do something other than read books and study the lives of others?"

Mirabelle looked at the charts, then at the photograph of her father on her desk.

"Not as many nights as I've thought of seeing him again."

"Then maybe now you can understand why I want to leave." Quan stood up. "I have nowhere else to go." Quan left the room, then shut the door, leaving Mirabelle in a stupefied silence. She wasn't angry this time. She didn't know what to feel.

* * *

Later that night, in a dark alleyway outside the Gerumandian Academy, Bruce and Donny met with Matthew in private. They were trying to make sense of a senseless situation. Donny kept swiping his blonde hair to the side while Bruce stood motionless against the wall.

"You're kidding," Donny said. "There's no way Derek would betray us."

Matthew revealed a broken scanner from his pocket. He tossed it to Donny. "Derek knew that we'd all be shipped to Telaris the moment the Awakening found the psychic, so he destroyed the evidence to stall for time."

"Do we know who it was?" Bruce asked.

"No. He didn't tell me."

"Then why'd he show you the scanner?"

"He wanted to verify if the readings were correct. I said they were, and then he proceeded to destroy the evidence in front of my face. There was nothing I could do."

Bruce took the bag from Donny and examined it.

"Yup. That's his scanner alright." He tossed it back to Matthew, who tucked it back under his coat. "I just don't understand why. Derek showed no signs of treason."

"Traitors rarely do," Matthew said.

"But what was his motive? Why would he do something like that?"

"Who knows? Either way, it doesn't matter. Our job isn't to figure out why Derek betrayed us. Our job is to search the Academy for the psychic Derek scanned."

"How do you know he's here?" Donny asked.

"None of us saw Derek leave the Academy that night, right? He was at the meeting." They all nodded. "Then whoever he scanned had to be at the Academy too."

"What if it was one of the prospective scholars that didn't get the award?"

"Someone else is going to handle those students." Matthew opened his datapad. "The Boss got me a list of every student enrolled for the summer and the new Masten scholars. We scan every single student on this list until we find the stage 4 psychic."

Bruce and Donny groaned.

"Are you serious? That's going to take months."

"It is. But if we work fast, we can finish this by the end of the year."

"Can you send us the list?"

"Sure thing." Matthew almost hit send, then saw "Quan" about a hundred names down. He edited the document, then shifted Quan's name to the very end of the list: student #2578. He felt at ease, then pressed send. "Hope you boys got some energy left in you." Matthew smiled. "Cause we got some laundry to do."

A Miraculous Mirage

Dakari paced back and forth in their apartment in District 3. Derek was on his 50th pushup before Dakari interrupted him for what felt like the 50th time.

"You're sure this is a good idea?" Dakari asked. "What if it's a trap?"

Derek sat up, drenched with sweat.

"I already told you. The Gray Eids are completely neutral. Think of them like a corporation. They offer a service, and we pay them a price."

"You clearly haven't studied history if you think corporations are neutral."

"Just trust me, ok?" The blonde-haired hunk looked down at his datapad. "They're probably completing the operation any minute now."

Dakari looked back out the window.

"Let's hope they know what they're doing."

* * *

In District 6, Amelia Lancaster grabbed a bag of groceries from her car in the underground garage. She closed the door and walked across the cement floor in boots and a street-style dress with a light jacket. Before she stepped inside the elevator, she tapped her datapad. The car chimed and locked. Then the elevator arrived.

She shut the door to her room with the groceries and paused. There was a draft in the room. It was cool. Someone had opened the window. She set the bag on the kitchen counter. All the lights in her house were off, with only the faintest amount of light coming in from the balcony. It was open.

She reached for her blaster inside her boot, then felt a needle stick into the side of her neck. She collapsed on the floor.

* * *

"And what about her memories?" Dakari asked. "Will they come back?"

"Only because I asked for their retrieval," Derek said. "The next time Amelia wakes up she'll remember everything. And no one can use a mind-snare on her again."

"Will the Boss know?"

"No. The mirage will cast a projection. She'll be completely safe as long as she pretends like nothing is going on."

"And what about the message? Will she get it?"

"Word for word."

* * *

Amelia woke up in her bed. There was a strange dull ache in her head that got worse every time she tried to sit up. Streaks of her long blonde hair spread around her pillow. She groaned and raised her arm over her eyes.

"Was I drinking again?"

A few minutes later, the pain subsided, allowing her to sit up with relative ease. She sat upright in bed for a while, listening to the distant traffic of the city, the noise of pedestrians on the streets below. Then she kicked her legs out over the bed. For some reason, she had never taken her boots off. She walked out of the bedroom and saw a bag of groceries on the kitchen counter. There was a note taped to the brown bag. She reached out, then her hand froze.

Flashbacks sprung upon her mind like gunshots. She remembered sitting at a diner with Dakari. The records. L-Transport. The Leonardo Estate. Darius. Kairo. The weight of these forgotten memories almost made her fall.

"Dakari…he tried to warn me."

She grabbed the note. She unrolled it from the side of the bag, sat down on the couch, then turned on the light. She read every word. The second she finished, she followed the instructions on how to contact Dakari.

* * *

"I don't believe it," Dakari said over the datapad comms. "Kairo Leonardo is a psychic."

"And it looks like he's got his father wrapped around his finger," Amelia said. "I guess they wipe his memory every time they renew the contract for cargo ships."

"Why go to all this trouble to use nonstate vehicles?"

"State vehicles are tagged. L-Transport vehicles are not. I'm sure someone might get a little suspicious if they saw state hovercrafts stopping by Telaris every month."

"You have a point." Dakari smiled. "It's good to hear your voice again, Amelia."

"Likewise. I'll do what I can to investigate the detention centers. It looks like our other case was solved. Psychics were targeting impurities because whenever the Awakening slipped up and someone found out, they were the ones who still remembered. It's good you got out of there when you did."

"I couldn't agree more. But at least we have someone else at the CDAD who can keep digging for answers. Don't leave any traces. And don't rush things. Five months isn't a lot of time, but it's enough time to pace ourselves so that we don't arouse any suspicion. Understood?"

"Got it. Goodnight, Deputy."

Dakari smiled.

"Last time I checked, that was your title now. Congratulations on the promotion."

"Thank you."

"Stay safe."

With that, Dakari ended the call.

Puzzling Predicaments

Things worked out nicely for Quan with the Masten Scholarship. Quan and Alexander were living in a double. However, because Alexander wasn't enrolled on paper, Quan had to bring him meals every day to keep him fed. It was like having a pet who did nothing but stare at his computer all day. He tried to keep Alexander in the dark for a while about the case of the missing students, but boredom was taking over. That meant he was starting to ask questions–like how they were going to leave New Earth.

"What do you mean?" Quan asked. "It's simple. We take the Sojourner."

"I know that genius. But who's going to fly it?"

They almost dropped their forks from the sheer realization of their own stupidity. They sat there for a moment in silence. Quan stirred his food with his fork, then set it on his desk. Alexander did the same. A few minutes passed in silence.

"That's a…" Quan laughed. "That's a good question."

"Ya think?!"

Quan stood up.

"Don't look at me?! You didn't think of it till today either!"

"At least I thought of it." He paused. "But we may be in luck." He pointed to his computer. "I've been making some money in my spare time. Slightly illegal, but for a good cause. Maybe I can purchase a pilot to ya know–fly us around?"

"I don't think pilots are cheap. Plus, who's gonna agree to a one-way trip?"

Quan walked over to the window and crossed his arms. Then a light bulb went off in his head. He turned around with the widest smile Alexander had ever seen from him.

"Actually. I might have someone in mind."

* * *

There was a knock on Mirabelle's door. She opened it, her face expressing disappointment upon seeing Quan, then surprise as she saw his blue-haired friend in a white hoodie standing next to him. She held the door open slightly.

"Can I help you?"

Quan cleared his throat. Mirabelle grew suspicious at how happy they both seemed. "Actually, yes. We have a..." He exchanged a glance with Alexander. "A proposition we'd like to discuss with you."

"A proposition?" Mirabelle scoffed. "That's rich." She looked at the guy with blue hair. "I'm guessing you're Alexander."

"And you must be Annabelle. I hear you fly planes."

"It's Mirabelle. Come on in."

They stepped inside as Mirabelle shut the door behind them. Alexander's eyes darted across the room. He gazed at the star charts on the walls, the papers and empty coffee mugs on the desk, and then the mysterious photographs on the floor.

"Nice place. I like the mess. And your scar."

Mirabelle sighed.

"Cut to the chase."

Alexander raised a brow and turned around.

"I wasn't being sarcastic. Studies show that sometimes a good mess can fire up the creative juices in your brain, increase productivity, and improve your workflow. Plus, everyone knows that scars are cool." Alexander squatted down and picked up one of the photographs from the floor. "Quan! This is your brother!"

Mirabelle facepalmed herself.

"You didn't tell him?"

Quan shrugged.

"I didn't think I needed to."

"Tell me what?" Alexander asked.

Mirabelle looked at Quan.

"You gotta tell him now."

"I don't want to."

"You have to."

"Fine. Alexander, sit down. This might take a minute."

Alexander skeptically eyed the two of them, then took a seat on the edge of the bed. Mirabelle began the story from the few missing students she discovered at the Academy. She talked about keeping it secret, then meeting Zane, and then his death. She recapped how they used Zane's transcription to discover that Matthew was kidnapping psychics from the Academy. Then Quan explained the rooftop incident with Mirabelle, his exchange with Derek, and then Dakari's discoveries at the CDAD. He talked about Derek's arrest, their escape from the arbitrator department, and now their hideout. He mentioned the Awakening, Exodus, the Gray Eids, and their desire to find a stage 4 psychic.

"In other words," Quan said. "Their desire to find me."

It took about an hour to retell the whole thing, and by the end of it, Alexander was visibly exhausted. He collapsed on the bed as his head spun with a million thoughts and revelations. Quan had the luxury of being told the developments of this operation over the course of a few days. Alexander, on the other hand, had those findings condensed in an hour. Instead of saying anything, he just started laughing.

"Just our luck, I guess. We finally find a viable way off this planet and you become the 'chosen one.' I take it back. You shouldn't have told me anything." Alexander tightened the straps on his hoodie and walked towards the door.

"Where are you going?" Quan asked.

"Anywhere but here," Alexander said. "I don't want to be waiting around when Matthew comes knocking on your door." He opened the door. "Sayonara."

Mirabelle nudged Quan.

"And I thought you were stubborn."

Quan created a tear and shot a gust of wind and rain from his hand, slamming the door. It ruffled Alexander's hoodie over his head. He pulled it down and slowly wiped the rain off his face. "How original."

"And how typical of you! How could you just walk out on us like that? You didn't even let me finish. I'm still planning on joining the tournament. Besides, we haven't even told Mirabelle our proposition yet."

Alexander paused, then stroked his wet chin with a smile.

"You know, that might actually work." Alexander's eyes lit up like diamonds. "Matthew won't turn you in before the tournament, right?"

"Right. He needs to keep a close eye on me."

"And what better way to stay in his sight than by joining the tournament? And what better way to flee from the Awakening than in the Sojourner!?"

Mirabelle crossed her arms and narrowed her brow.

"It's perfect," Alexander said, placing his arm over Quan. He pretended to unveil a landscape in front of him with an outstretched arm. "It's your destiny to win the tournament. You'll beat Matthew at his own game and fly away a champion! Then you'll have nothing to do with the Awakening, Exodus, or the Gray People!"

"The Gray Eids," Mirabelle murmured.

"Whatever," Alexander said. "Don't you see? Your ticket away from the Awakening is in the tournament. Not even the most powerful psychic in the world could catch you in that ship. You'd be a free man. Isn't that what you always wanted?"

Quan saw the landscape Alexander was displaying in front of him. He saw new planets and stars and a life free from madness.

"It is," Quan said. "It still is."

Mirabelle cleared her throat.

"You forgot one thing. Neither of you knows how to fly a spaceship."

Quan and Alexander smiled like middle school pranksters caught in the act.

"Hence our proposition." Alexander put his arm over Mirabelle's shoulder and pointed to the star charts. "Like I said. I hear you fly planes."

"No way. I'm here to help Dakari. Not you."

"You can help both of us. We can't leave until the tournament anyway."

Mirabelle's heart rose. For that brief instant, she felt weightless–like her dreams were finally in reach. Then she lowered her gaze, holding the side of her arm.

"I don't know."

"I don't know much about you, Mirabelle." Alexander looked at her aeronautics t-shirt. "But I imagine you didn't plan on staying at this Academy forever."

She nudged Alexander away.

"Well duh. No one does."

"But you know what I mean. Sure, everyone plans on graduating, but lots of people plan on staying in this same city for the rest of their lives! But you! You don't want that. Think about it! We're all runaway scoundrels. This Academy doesn't care for us. Why should we care about them?"

"I don't care about the Academy. But Zane–"

"Yes, yes. Zane was a saint and served his purpose but *newsflash*! He's dead! And quite frankly you will be too if you wait around here another–"

Mirabelle backhanded Alexander across the cheek. Quan flinched. It sounded like a whiplash. No one moved. Half of Alexander's face grew red as he raised his trembling hand. Each nerve on his face flared in pain. He tried to speak but stuttered, then said:

"I have committed a social error and would like to apologize."

Mirabelle pointed towards the door.

"Get out."

"But–"

"OUT."

Quan and Alexander scurried out of the room like scared children.

Mirabelle slammed the door and locked it.

Alexander and Quan stood outside for a minute in silence.

"You think–"

"No," Quan said, walking away. "We're gonna have to find someone else."

Alexander lingered a bit longer, then followed Quan with his head held low.

* * *

Things changed after that conversation. There were enough things to keep at least two of them busy. Quan and Mirabelle had daily workouts to attend to and weekly meetings with the Masten Scholarship Committee. Back in her dorm, Mirabelle made a check on each calendar day she studied. The aeronautics exam was scheduled to take place on November 20th –ironically, a week after the Gerumandian Dueling Tournament. Each time she went to the library to study, a voice told her that it was all for nothing.

And then she kept thinking about the "proposition." She had been shunning Alexander for weeks after his infamous "social error," but the thought of flying the Sojourner was too alluring to forget. It was on her mind almost as much as her father's absence or Zane's death. She even dreamed about it a few times.

Mirabelle verbally denied the proposition but started spending more time in the flight simulation room anyway. She researched the model of the Sojourner and matched its specifications to the simulation. Each time she stepped into the chamber she felt the exhilaration of being a real pilot. She saw herself following in her father's footsteps and even pictured him smiling at her, wherever he was. And each night as she laid her head to rest, she saw a picture of all the planets she wanted to visit taped on the wall. That made her smile. And then she saw the pictures of missing students laid out on her desk. She thought of Zane. That took the smile away. There was no escaping the ghosts at the Academy. They haunted her every time she walked its vacant halls, wondering if she might be the next to go. And then she thought of her father. She remembered seeing the L-Transport hovercraft take him away, and then the news that L-Transport was responsible for transporting psychics. She couldn't help but think that his disappearance was somehow connected to this. All these things were tied up in an amalgam of wants, some unrelated, some tied in the same knot. She was clueless as to where to start.

At the same time, Quan continued his dueling lessons with Officer Mocroft. He was sorting through the same challenges. Each time he struck Mocroft's blade he saw the pictures of those missing students and the others that might go missing if he left. He remembered Dakari Minathi's warning in the hallway. He missed his next lunge as Mocroft swept under Quan's feet, knocking him on the ground.

"Something on your mind?"

And then there was the biggest mystery of all: Jon Jerry. No one had a clue where he was, but no one bothered erasing the memories of his existence either. It was the elephant in the room. But it was one he was afraid to bring up. He felt like no one had any answers anyway. He looked back down at his wristband. It was flipped on the right side this time.

Never. Give. Up.

Quan stood up and readied his blade.

"No. I'm fine."

Mocroft didn't buy it but prepared himself in a fighting stance nonetheless.

"Again."

Quan lunged forward and continued their fight.

These were the thoughts that plagued Quan and Mirabelle, while Alexander idly passed the time doing whatever came to his mind. The summer days grew repetitive and short. They were sitting ducks. Dakari hadn't called in weeks. Mirabelle checked off more boxes and found herself crossing the last mark on her calendar. They were now three months away from the tournament. It was August 9th. That meant they had about a week before Academy orientation. With that last mark, Mirabelle set her marker away, shut off the lights, and hopped in bed.

Then her eyes opened when she heard a knock on the door.

"Not now! I'm trying to sleep!"

"Please? This won't take long."

Mirabelle perked up from her bed. That voice wasn't Quan's. It was Alexander. She walked across the room in her pajamas, turned on the lights, and opened the door. A red rage overcame her the second she saw him.

"This better be good."

"Mirabelle–"

"Don't *Mirabelle,* me. You may as well have spat in Zane's grave with what you said. Goodnight."

"Mirabelle, wait!"

Alexander stuck his leg in the door and howled as Mirabelle tried to slam it.

"I'll kick you," she said.

"Please don't. I just want to talk."

Their eyes met in an angry stalemate. Mirabelle leaned closer in the gap in the door and spoke with her jaw clenched and her teeth gritted in anger. "I don't want to talk. Understand?"

"Just give me a chance." Alexander's silver eyes were wide. "Please."

Mirabelle paused. They eyed each other for a few more moments. Then Mirabelle yanked the door open, throwing Alexander's momentum into the wall. He stubbed his foot, howled in pain, and hopped up and down as Mirabelle walked back to her chair.

"You have five minutes."

"Ow! Thank you. Ow. Thanks."

They sat across each other in chairs.

"I wanted to apologize," Alexander said. "I was insensitive last time we talked. I had no right to speak on Zane's behalf." He paused. "Or yours."

"You don't have to apologize for the last part. I made my stance perfectly clear."

"Right." He swallowed a lump in his throat. "Anyway, I think I've figured out a way for us to have our cake and eat it in two." Mirabelle laughed. "Did I say something wrong?"

"The expression is to have your cake and eat it *too.* Not in two."

"I knew that. Just testing you."

"Go on."

"You said you wanted to stay to bring justice to Zane and the others who have been taken, and for that I commend you."

"I said no sarcasm."

"I mean it! Really. I do. And in no way do I want to take away from what you're doing." He paused. "In fact, I think I can help."

"I'm intrigued."

"Good. I think you'll be a whole lot more interested in the plan itself."

"I've already heard your plan."

"Not this one. You said that the Awakening operates under highly controlled variables, right?"

"What do you mean?"

"They can wipe the memories of thousands of students, but I'm guessing they can't wipe everyone's mind, certainly not in the millions."

"I doubt any psychic could do that."

"That's my point. Derek said it himself when he was explaining things to Dakari. The Awakening keeps these disappearances to a minimum because if too many people know, there would be too many minds to erase."

"Right."

"Then what we need is not a phone call to Exodus, but a stage big enough to display our evidence. What kind of platform offers that minute of uninterrupted silence where the whole world is watching, and everyone patiently listens to your last word?"

"I think I see where you're going with this. You want to use the Gerumandian tournament to share our findings with the world."

"Bingo. Quan wins the tournament. He gives the acceptance speech, and suddenly billions of people know the Awakening exists. They'll never see it coming."

"You're forgetting something."

"What's that?"

"Evidence," Mirabelle said. "We have nothing more than a few photographs and some eyewitness testimonies. If anything, it might draw the wrong kind of attention."

"That's where I come in," Alexander said. "Using the data we have so far I'll hack into the Gerumandian databases and search up files on missing students. Then, if you're willing, I'll use the transcription Zane sent as the icing on the cake."

"They'll probably just cut the broadcast."

"Leave those details to me. This isn't my first rodeo."

"I think you underestimate the integrity of R-Sports security."

"And I think you underestimate me. How do you think Quan got considered for the Masten Scholarship as a high school dropout?"

Mirabelle's eyes widened.

"You didn't!"

"I most certainly did. Like I said. Leave the tech to me."

Mirabelle looked down at the photographs.

"That actually might work." She looked back at Alexander. "But what's the catch? I'm guessing you're not doing this out of the kindness of your own heart."

"You're right. I'm no saint. This is where *you* come in."

"Me?" Mirabelle paused. "Oh, right. The proposition."

"You could fly it, couldn't you?"

"Are you kidding me? I can barely fly standard-issue jets. The Sojourner is a frigate. I don't even know if I could get it off the ground."

"But you could if you learned."

"What makes you think that?"

"Most students your age don't read manuals for dynamic frigates in their spare time." Alexander pointed to a textbook on the Sojourner on her desk. She blushed.

"I was just curious." Then her brow narrowed. "No. I refuse."

"Why?"

"Because it doesn't feel right!"

Alexander rolled his eyes.

"But it's perfect. Zane gets justice, Quan and I get to leave, and you get to fly."

"Dakari wouldn't approve," Mirabelle said.

"He might change his mind."

"No, he wouldn't."

"People aren't always what they seem, Mirabelle." Alexander looked out the window. "Besides, I think you're just as selfish as I am."

"We are *definitely* not the same."

"We're more similar than you think. You just haven't had the chance to prove it yet. We both have dreams and we both have responsibilities."

"But you ran away. I chose to stay."

"For now. But what if something doesn't go your way? What if the Awakening figures out where we are?" Alexander shrugged. "I'm just saying. It's something to think about."

"You think I really want to spend the rest of my days in space with you guys?"

"It doesn't have to be just us." Alexander stood up. "Bring anyone you want! I don't care. At least then we'd all be safe. No school, no stress, no worries. We could have a whole planet to ourselves, build a city on our terms. Plus, we'd finish our fight on New Earth. Exodus will hear about the Academy and step in to save other psychics."

Mirabelle raised a brow.

"You sure about that?"

"No. But it's worth a shot. And unless you can come up with a better plan that meets all our needs, I say we take that chance." Alexander opened the door. "Think about it. It might be our best alternative."

He shut the door. After he left, Mirabelle walked to her desk with the Sojourner manual. She looked up at the star charts and then at the photographs. For the first time that summer, she realized that maybe Alexander wasn't so crazy after all.

Renegade Redemption

If the days felt long for Quan, Mirabelle, and Alexander, they felt even longer for Dakari and Derek. They never left their apartment. All their food was delivered to them. Cabin fever was an understatement. Derek couldn't sit still. He worked out three times a day doing body exercises but being separated from his normal routine drove him mad. And there was another thing. He was locked in the same room with the father of the son he conspired to murder. They hadn't spoken of it since the interrogation. Perhaps there was no need to. But some days, as the silence between them lengthened, Derek was compelled to bring it up. One morning he blurted out exactly what was on his mind.

"How can you forget the things I've done?" Derek asked.

Dakari was perplexed. He set his bowl down and wiped his mouth with a napkin.

"Who says I forgot?"

Derek's heart sank.

"I just assumed that since we're working together—"

"That what? That I would forget what happened to my son?"

Derek couldn't look Dakari in the eyes. A hot feeling of shame lurked in his gut.

"I will never forget. I think the word you're looking for is 'forgive.' It's not the same as forgetfulness, though we often think they're one and the same." Dakari paused. "If we forgot the ways we've been wronged what reason would we have to forgive?"

Derek's shoulders slumped. He failed to maintain a strong façade as he felt his bones grow weak. The strength of his body could not support the fragility of his psyche. *Pathetic! Pathetic!* He kept telling himself. *Stop wallowing. Look Dakari in the eye and tell him you don't care. He may have been wronged, but he's a bad man for holding this grudge on you.* And yet at the same time, his voice told him that shame was all he should feel. *You're the bad man,* he told himself. *You're the one that did the wrong.*

"But that doesn't mean I don't forgive you," Dakari said.

Derek's inner voice went silent. He looked up. There was an old memory of heartbreak in Dakari's eyes. A rugged memory of being a husband and a father.

"What?"

"I forgive you," Dakari said. "And it's not because you weren't the one to pull the trigger. It's because you now know what you did was wrong." Dakari looked away. "I'm sorry too."

"You have nothing to apologize for."

"That's not true. I knew you were telling the truth the first time you told me Matthew killed him, but I didn't care. I was angry. And you were an easy target."

"It's not as bad as what I did."

"You're missing the point. We all got dirt on our hands. You messed up big. I messed up big. Some of us get caught, and some of us take our sins to the grave. But we all got something. Some are just better at hiding it. At least you acknowledged it."

Derek looked at the floor. The chains of his conscience were shattered. A great big weight had been lifted off his shoulders. He felt like he could fly.

"I don't know what to say."

"Then don't say anything. We've lingered on the dead long enough."

* * *

"That's great, Amelia." Kalak reclined in the back of his office chair as his new assistant, Deputy Amelia Lancaster, debriefed him on their last captured psychic. "And how have you been adjusting to your new position?"

"I'm managing," she said. "It's a lot of work, but there are a lot of good people in this department to help with the workload."

"That there are." Kalak took a sip of coffee, exhaled, then set it back down. "Any news on the hunt for Dakari?"

"Nothing yet, sir. He's off the grid."

"A shame. It would be nice to bring traitors to justice." Kalak stood up. "But then again, justice rarely is black and white in this world. Sometimes heroes die like pawns and the scoundrels go on unscathed. But Mr. Minathi will not escape the law so easily."

A door opened. It was Lieutenant Banner.

"Sir! There's something you should see."

"Pardon me, Banner. I thought Lieutenants were supposed to have manners."

The plump balding man straightened his back and saluted.

"Permission to come in, sir?"

Kalak squinted his eyes.

"Permission granted."

He stepped inside the room and closed the door.

"There's been an update in the Gerumandian psychic case."

"Really?" Kalak asked. "How timely."

"We reviewed the footage from about a month ago. Something isn't right."

"I'll have a look," Kalak said.

Amelia remained seated as she watched the Chief walk around his desk.

"Should I wait here, sir?"

"Nonsense. Why don't you tag along?" Kalak smiled. "It might be good to have some extra eyes."

She joined them in the surveillance room. Lieutenant Banner shut all the blinds to darken the room. He typed into his computer and pulled up a file.

"This is the same footage Dakari's investigation team reviewed about a month ago," Banner said. He double-tapped the file, then elongated the video by pinching it with his fingers and stretching the holographic image against the wall. It showed a sunny afternoon with an upward view of the rooftop. A girl with auburn hair leaned on the railing. Another figure stood near her, but the moment he was in view, his eyes shone bright blue. "See that? See the color of his eyes?"

"Yes," Kalak said. "They're blue. What's your point?"

"Remember the psychic Dakari caught? His eyes were green."

Amelia tried to hide her surprise. On the one hand, she found it amusing that they refused to mention Derek's name. On the other hand, they had just found a new detail that could get them closer to finding Quan.

"The psychic in this footage isn't the one Dakari caught. It's someone else." Banner zoomed in on the boy's face. "We can't see any of his features because the lights in his eyes are so bright. That's why none of the face scans work. But anyone who's studied psychics closely knows that any glow during eidolophoresis mirrors the color of a psychic's eyes. Dakari knew psychics better than anyone in this department. He deliberately brought in the wrong psychic."

Kalak was unamused.

"Don't you think this information would've been helpful *before* we knew Dakari was a traitor, not after?"

"You're missing the point. What I'm saying is that there's no way Dakari could have known that he was a psychic. He had help." Banner rewound the footage again and paused. "And I'm assuming it was from this guy right here." He pointed at the blue-eyed psychic on the rooftop. "There's still a psychic at the Gerumandian Academy."

"I see." Kalak smiled. "Great work, Lieutenant. I'll be sure to look into it."

With those last words, they went their separate ways. The moment Amelia got home, she plugged in her headphones, connected to the channel, and called Dakari.

* * *

Dakari and Derek were speechless.

"It's true," Amelia said. "They know you got help and now they're after Quan."

"Can you stall the investigation?" Dakari asked.

"I wish, but they'll suspect something. I don't have any more second chances."

Dakari groaned and stood up.

"There's gotta be a way to stop them. There *has* to be."

"I'm sorry to say this Dakari, but we've been outplayed."

If Dakari had hair on his head, he would have anxiously ran his hands through it. Instead both his hands rested flat on his head as he sighed with resignation, his mind scrambling for a way out of this mess. Then Derek spoke up.

"There might be a way," Derek said. "But you're not gonna like it."

Silence took over the room. Amelia turned up the volume as Dakari sat up.

"If you have an idea then say it."

"Amelia said it herself. They're not necessarily looking for Quan. They're looking for an answer to how you got help. Kalak and Banner obviously have ties with the Awakening, and they're worried someone might have information on their psychic spies. If I were to clear the air, they might stop looking."

"What do you mean?" Dakari asked.

Derek stood up.

"If you want another three months in hiding, I have to turn myself in."

"And what good will that do!?"

"It's a win-win situation. If I turn myself in, I'll be interrogated by Kalak or Banner. That'll give me a chance to explain how I'm the one that asked you to turn me in and faked the footage using contact lenses to draw attention from the arbitrators but conceal my true psychic identity on screen from the Awakening."

Silence filled the room. Dakari couldn't believe what he was hearing.

"You can't be serious."

Derek smiled.

"It gets better. Then I'll be shipped to the underground detention center, where I have a chance of getting rescued by Exodus. In either scenario, our plan advances."

"Assuming they don't kill you first."

"They won't," Derek said. "I'm not exactly expendable."

Dakari stroked the ends of his bushy beard.

"Your story might be a stretch, but if you get them to believe that you faked the footage, they might drop the case." Dakari's smile faded. "But you're forgetting something. If they don't believe you, you'll draw even more attention to Quan."

"Yeah. And one other thing. There's a good chance I might get captured by the Awakening in the underground railroad. They're not known to be merciful to traitors."

An eerie silence crept into the room.

"Amelia?" Dakari asked. "How long until they begin their investigation?"

"They looked worried. I wouldn't give them more than a day."

Dakari sighed.

"Derek, you don't have to do this. We can find another way."

"No need. I've made my decision." Derek faced the window. "I'm going in."

* * *

Not long after Derek left, Quan, Alexander, and Mirabelle huddled around a speaker and listened patiently as Dakari updated them on their situation. Then Quan's patience waned.

"Derek's out of his mind!" Quan said. "It's a suicide mission!"

"He already left," Dakari said. "This is our best shot. It's almost guaranteed to give you more time at the Academy and if things go well, it might also lead us to Exodus."

"That's extremely optimistic coming from someone like you," Quan said.

"And you seem more interested than usual. Something change your mind?"

"If Derek gets captured, he might talk. I don't need the Awakening coming after me when we're only three months away from the tournament."

"Derek won't talk. And he already left. He said it'd be better this way. I'm sorry I couldn't get ahold of you sooner." Dakari paused. "He wishes you all the best of luck."

With those last words, Dakari hung up, leaving everyone in the room with a sour taste in their mouths. No one said anything for minutes. They all sat there motionless until Alexander leaned away from the wall.

"I fear this isn't going to end the way we want it to." Alexander opened the door. "I'd pack your bags if I were you. If things go bad, we may have just lost our three months." He left the room as Quan lowered his head. Mirabelle stared off into space, hoping that Alexander was wrong.

* * *

That next morning, Banner stepped outside the front doors of the Central Dain Arbitrator Department. There were clear blue skies, busy airways, and streets buzzing with cars and pedestrians. Banner joined Kalak outside as he stood at the top of the stairs, waiting for their hovercraft to arrive.

"A beautiful day, isn't it Banner?"

"Indeed. A beautiful day for justice, that is."

They smiled, then flinched as an explosion erupted a block away. Plumes of smoke rose to the skies as a car flipped over onto the main street and rolled towards the CDAD. Its metallic hood flipped over and scraped the sidewalk like nails on a chalkboard. Car sirens blared as Kalak, Banner, and every other arbitrator reached for their rifles and aimed them at a hooded figure walking across the street. He showed no fear as the arbitrators ordered him to put his hands on his head. He obeyed and lowered his hood.

Kalak smiled.

"Derek Hunt." Kalak leaned towards Banner. "Forgive me, Lieutenant, but we may have to postpone our trip to the Academy. My day just got a whole lot better."

Derek never took his eyes off Kalak as two arbitrators shoved him into the ground, then dragged him up the steps of the facility.

* * *

It was an all too familiar situation. The white lights. The white walls. The faint buzzing overhead. And of course, the straitjacket. Derek sat at the other end of the table, his long blonde hair pinned in a ponytail, and faced Chief Kalak, who eyed him with a particular distastefulness. He folded both hands and pursed his chapped lips. Banner leaned against the wall behind him.

"I'm curious," Kalak said. "When you destroyed that car, who did you think was going to pay for it? I'm assuming you don't have much money seeing that you haven't been to a barber in months." Kalak smiled. "You have impeccable timing, by the way."

Derek scowled.

"I haven't been in contact with Dakari if that's what you're referring to."

"Even if I did believe that I'd still be curious to hear what split you two apart."

"He betrayed me. I turned myself in because I knew something that could end us."

"Who is 'us?'"

Derek eyed Banner, then looked back at Kalak.

"I mean, I just assumed it was true, but I guess I have to ask: are you awake?"

Banner and Kalak met Derek with a silent stare. Those seconds felt like eons in time as Derek waited for their response with bated breath. Then, simultaneously, they both said: "I never sleep."

Derek's fear vanished or at least was quelled when he learned his suspicions were true.

"You're one to talk about traitors," Kalak said. "Seeing that you betrayed your own brother."

"What are you talking about?"

"Don't be a fool. Matthew told the Boss everything. You discovered that there was a stage 4 psychic at the Academy and destroyed evidence of their existence. He doesn't know why you did it, but once you knew the consequences, you turned yourself in. You thought you'd be safer here than at the Academy. You were wrong."

Derek's eyes widened with excitement.

What a lame story, he thought. *Matthew's making my job too easy.*

"Then I guess you must've figured out how I faked the footage."

Kalak and Banner exchanged a glance.

"Matthew didn't mention that. As far as we know, the footage is authentic."

Derek smiled.

"Interesting..."

"Unless of course, we were wrong, and you have evidence to suggest otherwise."

"I just thought that renowned arbitrators such as yourselves would connect the dots. I mean, how else do you think Dakari found me? I knew that if the footage showed myself, they'd just send someone from the Awakening after me, so I just put on a nice pair of contacts..." Derek blinked. And when he did his eyes shown bright blue. "And what do you know? Blue eyes. It turns out I was right. Once I saw that some other guy was investigating me, I knew it wouldn't be hard to break him. I got him to break me out and then ghosted him. Imagine that? Apparently, you got swindled too."

Derek reveled in their frustration as Banner slammed his fist against the table.

"If we got swindled then what the hell are you doing back here?!"

"I got tired of running."

"And you'd prefer a quick death?"

"You can't kill me. I'm too valuable to lose."

"Then why are you here?"

Derek's smile faded. He looked as resolute as any other Gerumandian.

"To tell my side of the story."

Kalak crossed his arms.

"Do tell."

"It's true. I scanned a stage 4 psychic. But it's also true that I was too drunk to remember who I scanned."

A volcano of rage erupted inside Kalak. His face burned red.

"Your humor is growing less amusing by the minute."

Derek laughed.

"The only humorous thing about all this is that you asked teenagers to do a grown man's job!"

"Tell me what happened or I'm shipping you away," Kalak said.

Derek smiled. The lie was in place. Now he just needed to kindle it.

"It was the night before the Masten Scholarship Awards. Students were nervous and wanted to lay low. Me and the boys invited some of the prospects up to our rooms. There were lots of people there. Some old students, some new, some that weren't even students. People were filtering in and out by the hour. I have no idea who was there and who was not. We got a bit drunker than we anticipated and, in my dorm, one of the students grabbed my scanner from my utility belt. They ended up scanning themselves and then left the scanner on my desk. Later that night, the next thing I know I have a reading for a stage 4 psychic on my datapad.

"Matthew didn't believe me. He accused me of making a fraud, but it was real. I have no idea who scanned themselves, but I swear on my life, a stage 4 psychic was in that room. I destroyed the evidence because no one would believe me. Then Matthew accused me of treason after I destroyed the evidence when he didn't believe me the first time around! At that point, I knew it was over. So instead of waiting around for Matthew to tell the Boss, I plopped these contacts in, got into an argument with Mirabelle because I have a thing for getting on her nerves, and then waited for the arbitrators to get me."

Kalak and Banner were motionless, completely stunned. Then angry.

"How stupid do you think I am?" Kalak asked.

"Say what you want, but I had no choice. I was going to get in trouble either for letting someone use my equipment or destroying evidence. So, I ran."

Banner scratched his chin.

"And then you came running back."

Derek nodded.

"Yes. I came back because I thought that if enough time passed between then and now, maybe I'd get another chance."

"A chance at what?"

"At finding that stage 4 psychic. At redeeming myself for my wrongdoings."

Traitors and Truthtellers

Quan swung his katana up in a vicious arc, missing his dueling instructor, Mocroft, by an inch, only to receive a thundering blow to his side, knocking him against the wall. A bright red mark glowed on his exoskeleton suit as the force of the collision made him go limp. He leaned against the wall. This was their 20th match today. In the earlier rounds, Quan won with ease, but the real trick was to win when you were tired. With sweat dripping from his brow and pooling up in his armpits, Quan heaved in heavy breaths and dropped his blade.

"You're getting better." Mocroft stashed their weapons in the silver lockers along the wall. "But it's going to take more than practice fights to convince the instructors that you deserve enough bids for the tournament."

Quan perked back up as if he was never exhausted.

"What? But you said I improved!"

"And that's true. If talent alone was the gateway to the Dueling Tournament, you'd have no problem getting in. But there are lots of talented duelers at the Academy, and most of your competition has been training here for years."

"Then you're saying I gotta kiss up to all the other instructors, huh?"

"No. I'm saying you need to capture their attention."

"But there are only three weeks left before registration."

"Not to mention the fact that you're a Pit Dog," Mocroft said.

"A what?"

"You're pretty bad with details. A Pit Dog. It's your rank, kid. All students start at the bottom of the barrel, and as you probably guessed, no Pit Dog

263

has ever been eligible for the tournament. They're not worth an instructor's time."

"So no matter how hard I train I still might not get a bid?"

"I shouldn't be the one to have to tell you that. If it makes you feel any better, all the training in the world wouldn't guarantee a victory in the Final Four. There are always other competitors just as hungry as you are."

No there aren't, Quan thought. *Not a chance in this world.* For better or worse, Quan had built a fulcrum of hopes resting upon a victory in the Gerumandian Dueling Tournament. It wasn't just a dream, it was *the* dream, a childhood fantasy with years of sleepless nights and imaginings on what it would be like to fight on the world's biggest stage.

"I don't care how many other students want this," Quan said. "They don't want it as bad as I do! I'll do whatever it takes to get enough bids! I'll put in twice as many hours as those kids. I'll talk to every instructor if I have to, but I'm not leaving this place empty-handed!"

Mocroft met Quan's enthusiasm with a blank stare.

"Listen to yourself. You sound like a child."

"I'm just saying–"

"Too much. Your ambition exceeds your skill level."

"I'm not changing what I want."

"You don't have to. But you do need to take things a step at a time. The officers at the Academy see you as a Pit Dog. If you want them to see you as anything different, you might have to fight a dog bigger than your size."

Quan smiled.

"Hell's Pit."

Mocroft smiled back at him.

"Maybe you're better with the details than I thought. Take care."

With a newfound spirit, Quan jogged out of the training room. He sprinted down the hallway for what felt like the last time. In some ways it was. Everything about this place would change. The emptiness of the summertime would soon be replaced with an Academy packed with students as a new semester started. But Quan was ready. He couldn't wait to show the world what he was made of.

* * *

In the interrogation room at the CDAD, Kalak sat across from Derek, who was still in a straitjacket, while Banner inconspicuously shook his head.

"No," Banner said. "We don't even entertain this."

"I'll hear him out." Kalak gestured for Derek to continue.

"Think about it," Derek said. "You never issued a warrant for my arrest. As far as my instructors know, I've taken the summer off. If you reenroll me back at the Academy, it'll be business as usual. Plus, I can help Matthew find the stage 4 psychic."

"You're awfully optimistic that your brother will forgive you after what you did."

"I don't need him to," Derek said. "If you send me back, he'll have no choice but to go along with it. You said it yourself. They need to scan over 2,000 students. Even if they split it up and find a way to scan one student a day, that's going to take months. They need all the help they can get and since I'm the one that found the initial scan, I should be the one to get it back. If you kill me, you're wasting a psychic. If you let me help, we can find this psychic in half the time it's going to take them now."

Banner nervously looked at Kalak and Derek.

Kalak leaned back and pensively folded his fingers together.

"Face it," Derek said. "You got nothing to lose."

The Chief of the CDAD stood up and walked around the table. He towered over Derek and gazed at him with his menacing eyes. The younger Hunt brother swallowed a lump in his throat and shuddered as Kalak reached into the back of his utility belt. Derek turned away and closed his eyes, then heard a clink of the chain behind his back.

"Congratulations," Kalak said. "You're a free man."

* * *

Later that day, Banner walked with Kalak back to his office.

"Are you out of your mind?" Banner asked. "You really believe that story?"

"Not entirely. But I have it under control."

"How is letting him go under control?"

"Simple," Kalak said. "Someone isn't telling the truth. Derek's story has complicated things, but at the end of the day, he's right. We can't scan students using arbitrators because it will draw too much attention, but those boys can. We need them for the time being and can dispose of them later."

Kalak stepped inside his office. Banner shut the door behind them.

"And what if they're both lying? What if they're working together?"

"You don't know the Hunt brothers well if you'd think they'd work together."

"Then how is sending Derek back a good idea?"

Kalak dialed a few numbers into his datapad.

"Because they're both skewing the truth. The moment they're together again, their stories will clash, and the truth will come out. Plus, we'll probably get closer to finding the psychic than if we just disposed of Derek or left Matthew alone."

Banner shrugged his shoulders.

"Not a bad idea. But what if this whole process repeats itself?"

"Meaning?"

"What if they find the psychic again but hide them?"

Kalak smiled and finished dialing.

"Don't worry. I got that figured out too. We'll be enrolling two students back at the Gerumandian Academy this year." Banner's eyes widened. "Let's hope Beretta's had a good time on Telaris. It's time to bring her home."

An Ordinary Orientation

"Welcome to Cypher Stadium," Mirabelle said.

There were few times when Quan felt like his eyes deceived him. This was one of them. A stone, dome-shaped stadium, with a capacity of 250,000 students, filled with VIP suites, and a jumbotron suspended in the center of the structure, captivated Quan's attention. It was one of those feats of architecture so massive that your eyes got lost in every glance. On the center platform in the middle of the stadium, Quan saw several arbitrators lined up in a row to guard tonight's speakers. Drones buzzed in the air. Quan imagined himself standing in the center, with every eye watching him.

"This is where they have the tournament," Quan said.

Mirabelle thought he looked like a kid stumbling into an amusement park.

"Yup. And if we're lucky, this is the place the world will know the truth."

They took their seats in silence. Not long after, Matthew strolled into the stadium with Bruce and Donny by his side. A few students looked their way and pointed them out. It was hard to miss the prize of the Academy himself.

"Ugh," Donny said, looking around the stadium. "Don't tell me we have to add all these students to the list too. We're not even halfway done."

Bruce elbowed Donny and yelled at him as quietly as possible.

"Will you shut up?! You want to let the whole Academy know what we're doing?"

"If it means getting some extra helpers, I'll tell anyone."

Matthew walked away.

"Let's go find a seat."

A few lights in the stadium started to dim, shifting the focus to the center. Conversations died down as everyone sat in silence.

"Ladies and Gentlemen. Please rise for the Republic National Anthem."

250,000 students rose from their seats. Republic soldiers marched out of the four main tunnels carrying flags from one of the four main academies. Then a fifth soldier emerged down the center with the Republic flag bearing the symbol of a white **R** on a black shield. After the soldiers placed the flags by the stage, a marching band and choir played the anthem. Then a woman in a white dress with black silky hair approached the podium.

"Good afternoon and welcome to the 32nd opening convocation of the Gerumandian Academy!" She paused as over half the crowd applauded. "My name is Estra Harlyn, vice president of the Gerumandian Academy. I am privileged to be with you all as we celebrate the beginning of a new school year. I also have the pleasure of introducing a man who needs no introduction at all, the founder of the Gerumandian Academy and leading military commander in the Battle for New Earth. Please welcome: Boris Gerumandian."

Everyone stood to their feet and greeted the esteemed commander with thunderous applause. The other three executive council members, Malus Irkurian, Andrew Luken, and Daniel Haven, stood up and applauded as well. Boris Gerumandian waved to the crowd with an outstretched hand. He wore a forest green suit with medals stitched to his coat. People whistled and cheered. Boris showed his wide smile. From the jumbotron, he looked like a giant among men–his broad shoulders and burly biceps seeming to burst through the arms of his coat. A faded scar raced across his left eye.

Boris approached the podium.

"Thank you," Boris said, his voice bellowing through the mic. The applause continued, then slowly faded. "Thank you. Thank you all so much." Everyone sat back down. "It really is a pleasure to speak with you all on such a momentous occasion. Each year we hold this convocation is another year where we get the chance to establish a defense for the values we believe in: freedom, equality, and the safety of this Republic. I always say that a nation only dies in its sleep, but as long as we stay committed to our values, our leaders will never slumber. If we have learned anything in these past 100 years, it's that we are not alone in this universe, and those who inhabit it are not particularly willing to join our cause.

"Each of you may have enlisted in the Academy for different reasons. Not all of you will brave the intergalactic frontlines. Some of you will be arbitrators, some pilots." Quan nudged Mirabelle in the shoulder. "Maybe even duelers." Mirabelle looked back at Quan. "Regardless of where your paths take you, each of you will be Gerumandians–people that model the Gerumandian code of excellence. No force in this universe is as powerful as the bonds each of you will share, the trials you will undergo, and the people you will become when you step on this stage yourself and receive your badges."

There was a buzz in Quan's head. He had an idea as he stared at the stadium filled with 250,000 students. A wide smile crept on his face as he blinked his eyes and searched for psychic energy. He couldn't believe his eyes. With the exception of Matthew and his friends, there wasn't a single psychic in the entire room. He saw Matthew and his friends' heads glow a few rows away from him. But then he saw another glow in a place he wouldn't have expected. He looked at the several war veterans sitting near the podium. Each head was as empty as the last until he paid close attention to the last man in the row: Carter Hunt. There was a golden glow inside of him as bright as the sun.

Quan blinked again. It was still there.

"...wish every student here the best of luck in the new year. Thank you."

The Gerumandian students gave Boris a standing ovation.

Mirabelle noticed that Quan wasn't getting up.

"Quan? You good?"

Quan quickly shook his head out of a trance and stood up with them, dumbfounded that he had missed almost the entirety of Boris' speech. Orientation was finished. Students started to leave the stadium and headed back to the shuttle for their dorms in masses. Carter Hunt stood up and started shaking the hands of the people next to him.

"Yeah," he said. "How bout some dinner?"

It was enough to defer the issue, but Quan remembered what he saw.

Brigadier General Carter Hunt was a psychic.

* * *

Someone knocked on Matthew's door. He opened it, and immediately thought he was staring at a ghost. Derek Hunt stood in the doorway in a green Gerumandian uniform. He had his blonde hair back in a ponytail and stood with his arms crossed. Something had changed. He looked happy. He looked like he had nothing to fear, which meant that Matthew probably did.

"You got some nerve coming back here, ponytail."

"Apparently you don't pay attention."

Derek stepped inside as Matthew shut the door behind them.

"Oh, Kalak told me everything." Matthew shook his head and scoffed. "I can't believe they went through with this. This makes the CDAD look like a joke."

"Don't worry about them. The Boss has that covered." Derek revealed a scanner from his pocket. "We got more important things to do."

Matthew shoved Derek's arm away and leaned close.

"What did you tell them? There's no way they reinstated you."

Derek shrugged his shoulders.

"Why don't you ask the Boss yourself?" Derek stopped next to Matthew on his way out. "But I recommend that you don't try to make any corrections to the story I've told them. Otherwise, I might add something I forgot to tell them—something about who really destroyed the evidence in the first place."

Matthew's hands coiled into tight fists.

"What do you want?"

"The same thing as you." Derek opened the door. "Time."

* * *

"That's it?" Dakari asked. He sat on the floor of the empty apartment, alone. Several boxes of takeout were spread across the room. Patches of black hair seemed to fight against the baldness atop his head. "They just let Derek go?"

"It certainly seems that way," Amelia said. "Whatever he said sold them."

"There's no way it could be that easy. We need to talk with him."

"Not yet. They're going to be watching Derek closely now. If they discover he has any trace to you, it's over."

Dakari sighed. The days were starting to weigh down on him. Each day he mindlessly paced around the room, waiting for the next bit of information, ordering his next meal, then returning to the floor to sleep. It was more silence than he was used to. He found his mind drifting back to the old days when all was well in District 7. Each time his wedding ring reflected the sunlight from the tiny window, he thought of Desta. And each time he thought of Desta, he thought of Zane. This case was his only distraction from the silence.

"What about the detention centers?" Dakari asked. "Any luck there?"

"None. They only give a select number of individuals in our department clearance. I've even tried escorting a psychic there myself, but they never let me through."

"And L-Transport?"

"Nothing there either. I can't get in on another meeting without drawing suspicion. I'm worried I've exhausted my usefulness in this operation, sir. It might be time to get you back in the field."

"I'm not sure there's anything I could do that you can't do already. Unless...hold on. Kairo Leonardo."

"What about him?"

"We know that he's a psychic and is somehow controlling his father behind the scenes. If we can find proof that he's a psychic, you can authorize an arrest that wouldn't arouse any suspicion."

"But I couldn't get any evidence without going to the Leonardo Estate. I don't have the luxury of going there anymore."

"Maybe you don't. But I do." Dakari looked out the window. "I got an idea."

A Pitiful Pit

Nothing could completely prepare Quan for the first day of classes. The hallways were busy and packed with students in white, silver, and green uniforms. He had a busy schedule. A morning workout at 5:00, breakfast at 7:30, then class from 8:00 to 12:00. It had been almost two years since Quan had sat in a classroom. But this was all a part of the plan. If he wanted to be eligible for the tournament, he couldn't risk facing academic probation. Strangely enough, one class all Gerumandians had to take was earth poetry. Quan didn't see the point in it, but he couldn't get out of it. One poem he had to read was "Home Burial" by Robert Frost. It was about a husband and wife who had to bury their deceased child. Quan hated it. When class was over, he sprinted back to the training room. He changed into his dueling gear and carried his helmet, following the rest of his squadron and a group of upper-ranked students into a sparring room with Officer Mocroft. It was the match he had been waiting for: Hell's Pit.

Each Pit Dog kept looking at each other as the upper-ranking students scouted out their prey from the other side of the room. They were still waiting for someone to join them, but Quan didn't know who. He figured it didn't matter. While the other Pit Dogs were trembling with fear as Mocroft gave his opening speech, Quan was ready to face anyone. The upper students snickered. But Quan would give them no reason to smile. By the end of the day, he would make sure they knew his name.

"Any volunteers?" Officer Mocroft asked.

Without hesitation, Quan stepped forward.

"I'll do it."

Officer Mocroft smiled.

"Very well. We have our Pit Dog." He faced the other crowd and handed Quan his blade. "And who will dare to challenge this mutt?"

The one the upper-class students had been waiting on finally arrived. The tall blonde-haired student stepped forward. It was Matthew Hunt.

"I will."

Silence. Students parted to the side and revealed the challenger standing in the middle of the crowd. The silver scales of his suit glimmered as he kept his green eyes fixed on the Pit Dog, who now stood frozen. Some of Quan's swagger had been taken away now that he watched the best student in the Academy step on the mat.

"It might be wise to let other students participate," Mocroft said. "Seeing that this isn't your first time."

Matthew didn't look at Mocroft. He looked at Quan.

"It's a new semester," Matthew said. "I'm eligible."

The seasoned instructor sighed and handed Matthew an e-blade.

"Very well. Combatants! Shake hands and ready your weapons!"

Mocroft explained the rules while Quan and Matthew shook hands. Quan flinched at his grip. Matthew crunched his hand and smiled, then leaned in close and whispered: "I am going to *break* you."

The hairs in Quan's ears tickled, then sent chills down his body.

"You'll try," he retorted.

"Try?" Matthew's smile faded, as did Quan's. "You have no idea who I am."

Matthew shoved Quan's hand away. A dark impenetrable gloom surrounded Quan's mind as he walked back to his side of the mat, the camera drones and students watching his every move. His pulse raced. He had seen the power rankings before. There was no question that Quan would have to face challenging opponents, but Matthew was ranked number one. *Who cares?* Quan thought. *It's just a ranking.* He believed that in the past. He didn't believe it now.

Quan strapped on his helmet, sealing it to his suit as Mocroft finished his speech and directed them to opposite ends of the map. Some of his breath fogged the visor as his energy shield activated. He clenched the hilt of his e-blade and saw Matthew standing on the other side. Even though they couldn't see each other's eyes behind their visors, he knew Matthew was looking at him. Officer Mocroft started the ten-second countdown.

The buzzer blared.

Matthew advanced. Quan raised his sword as his brain waves flatlined. He knew he was supposed to circle your opponent before he circled you, but his legs were frozen. They wouldn't move. But Matthew was. And he was moving fast. Now he was here!

Quan parried Matthew's attack, then spun around. He backpedaled towards the opposite end of the mat. Matthew slashed in wide, sweeping arcs, causing Quan to cave in behind his sword and deflect each blow with a ringing clang of sparks and steel. Each collision sent tingles in his sparking hands. He gritted his teeth and kept backing away as the crowd watched in silence. Matthew pitched forward seconds after a fast swing and struck Quan in the side with a thundering blow. The Pit Dog howled in pain, and as he then tried to retaliate with an attack of his own, Matthew caught his forearm and used his momentum to throw Quan across the ground. Quan tumbled over the mat, tucking his blade close to his chest as students cheered for his downfall.

Matthew outstretched his arms and paced towards him as Quan got up to his feet.

"You're worse than I thought!" Matthew said. "Oh well, fun's over."

A newfound competitive spirit flashed in Quan's veins, causing him to rise. He tightened his grip beneath the rain guard of his electric sword and thrust forward. Sparks flew as their blades clashed and echoed inside the training room. Quan's anger was enough to get back in the fight, but not enough to win. They both moved fast, lunging and side-stepping and swinging their e-blades across one another's bodies. Quan saw Matthew leave his left side vulnerable. He swung, but Matthew pinned his blade to the ground, then punched Quan in the helmet.

"That all you got?" Matthew asked. He dodged Quan's next attack and then kicked him in the chest. "I thought you were Silverside's pride and glory!?"

Officer Mocroft's expression darkened.

The Pit Dog staggered back, but Matthew kept pressing him. Matthew moved with a speed that Quan had never encountered. He side-stepped, dashed, lunged, and struck Quan's chest with a powerful blow, hunching him over his back. Matthew punched Quan with the hilt of his blade, then swung his arm back and slashed him across the visor, whiplashing the young boy to the ground. Quan's body jolted and shook. He fell on the mat and looked up to find Matthew, who then struck Quan again, ringing his ears and blurring his vision. Quan jerked as he tried to get up but felt the sting of Matthew's blade strike different joints on his body. Then the Pit Dog grabbed his blade, rolled over, and blocked Matthew's next attack. The clang of steel brought a deafening silence of surprise to the room of wide-eyed spectators. Quan stood up and shook his head to try and stop the ringing in his ears. He steadied his blade, but the room was spinning. Blood trickled down the side of his head. And he kept jittering. He couldn't think straight. But he kept standing.

Matthew said something inaudible, then advanced. Quan lunged forward and wheezed as the Hunt prodigy repeatedly stabbed him in the chest. Each shock felt like a jumbo-sized bee sting. He was pressed against the wall. Then Matthew gripped Quan by the helmet, bashed his helmet into his, and threw him on the ground. The poor sod fell like a ragdoll. His body went limp as the blade dropped onto the mat. The crowd gasped and shuddered back. Officer Mocroft gazed at him, then turned away. Matthew landed one last thundering blow in the center of Quan's back as the buzzer blared. He blacked out immediately after.

* * *

An aching soreness ran deep in Quan's body. He sat hunched over his bed, his shoulders low, his body wrapped in bandages, his fingers trembling and jittering from the e-blade aftershocks. R-Sports highlights played on the screen. They were showing the top ten highlights of the day. Someone told

Quan he was going to make the cut, but not for the right reasons. That walk from the infirmary to his dorm was the longest walk of shame of Quan's entire life. What was supposed to be his great turning point turned out to be his greatest failure, rivaling his loss in regionals at Silverside. He felt the same things. He had only been a freshman back then, but he remembered the hundreds of disappointed faces, the lowered heads of his "parents," and Mocroft's slow walk out of the arena. And now at the Academy, news of his failure spread around the hallways like a wildfire.

Someone knocked on his door, then opened. It was Mirabelle.

"Hey."

Quan looked at his bruised hands.

"Hey."

Mirabelle pursed her lips.

"You gonna let me in?"

Quan nodded. She closed the door and stopped before the projector.

"And now at number one, we have none other than Matthew Hunt! If you thought his other duels in Hell's Pit were one-sided massacres, you haven't seen nothing yet!"

"Why are you watching this?"

"Because I need to see it."

"No, you don't."

Mirabelle grabbed the remote and turned the footage off. Quan didn't stop her and let her sit next to him on the bed.

"I made a fool of myself out there."

"What did you think was going to happen?"

"Maybe I'd put up a good fight at least."

"He's the best student at the Academy. Don't lose sleep over it."

"But how? Only one person can win the Sojourner. You know who that person is?" Mirabelle didn't answer. "The best."

Alexander burst into the room.

"How'd it go?"

Mirabelle shot him a dark stare as Alexander saw Quan in bandages.

"Oh. Nevermind then."

"Leave," Mirabelle said.

Alexander nodded and shut the door on his way out. She looked at Quan, and when she did, she did so with new eyes. In the few months that she had known him, she had noticed the wild, energetic spirit that possessed him. His eyes were often restless, his voice loud and prone to thoughtless outbursts or stubborn acts of defiance for things that he didn't like. He would always be doing things with his hands. Creating tears. Flicking coins. Tapping his fingers by his side. But now there was nothing. He looked as dead as the combatant he had been watching on the screen.

Mirabelle wanted to relish this moment. Quan had not been kind to her. There were times in her dorm and on the rooftop when he had outright abandoned Mirabelle in her moment of vulnerability. He had laughed at her cause. He had uttered endlessly the vanity of trying to bring justice to the dead. And Mirabelle had never taken those things lightly. The anger those words brought to her lingered in her soul and dried up in her bones. She longed for the day his arrogance would catch up to him–and it had. But she did not relish it. She pitied him and the look in his frozen, despondent blue eyes.

"You may have lost today," she said. "But you'll get another chance."

"That doesn't matter. He's still the best."

"That might be true today, but maybe not tomorrow. Or the day after, or the next week, or even the next month. None of those days will matter. All that matters is who's the best when it counts." She put her hand on his, causing him to turn towards her in shock. "You still have time."

Their eyes met for the first time during their conversation. That was when Quan saw it. He was surprised he had missed it all these months. It was her eyes. Dark, auburn eyes–the same color as her hair. They were filled with honesty, wide and focused on *you*, and no one else; at least at the moment when you were with her and only when she was looking at you. But it was there…and it made Quan realize that maybe Mirabelle actually cared for him. He felt embarrassed to look at her because her eyes said: "I am someone you can bring your problems to. And I will keep them safe. Forever." By looking at them, Quan acknowledged he had problems.

Maybe that isn't such a bad thing.

"I thought you didn't care about the tournament," he said.

"And I thought you didn't care about helping me and Dakari."

"And Derek," Quan said.

Mirabelle's eyes darkened. She turned away, breaking the trance.

"I'm afraid we may never see him again."

Alexander barged into the room.

"Hello! We have a visitor!"

"Not now!" Mirabelle said.

The door opened anyway, and in came the blonde Gerumandian brute. With a ponytail.

"I heard you needed my help?" Derek asked. "Am I wrong?"

Quan's jaw dropped to the floor in disbelief. As did Mirabelle's.

* * *

Derek told them his story. It was the first time any of them had seen him in person since he joined their cause. Quan always knew he was helping them indirectly with Dakari, but now he saw him up close. He was like a mini-Matthew, only "mini" was a bad way to put it. He was two inches shorter but other than that, he had the strength and cold bravado of a Gerumandian. He leaned against the wall with his arms crossed, bulging his biceps through his uniform as he explained how he convinced Kalak and Banner to let him go. Quan and Alexander listened eagerly as if forgetting Derek's past mistakes. Mirabelle was not quick to forget who he really was. The things he had said to her, about herself, about her father, and even more importantly, the things he had done that led to Zane's death. *And yet if Dakari could forgive him*, she thought. *What's my excuse?*

"What about you?" Derek asked, looking at Quan. "Alexander told me you needed my help with something. Some kind of *proposition?*"

Alexander rubbed his hands together and feverishly smiled.

"Not just any proposition. THE proposition."

"Not anymore," Quan said. He sat on the same spot on the bed. His shoulders hunched, his eyes low. "I lost any chances of being eligible for the tournament after my match with Matthew today."

"You fought my brother?"

"It was in Hell's Pit."

"Let me say this again: you fought my brother?!"

Quan sighed.

"I volunteered first."

"That was your first mistake. Choose your battles wisely, especially the ones that others see. People forget losses, but they rarely forget failures." Derek paused. "Why are you even trying to join the tournament?"

"We've been thinking about *alternative* solutions to our problem with the Awakening," Alexander said. "Plus, Quan and I only enrolled at the Academy to join the tournament. We're trying to get the Sojourner."

"Who's going fly it?"

Alexander pointed to Mirabelle.

"Who's going to get it?"

Alexander pointed at Quan. "You." Then he pointed at Derek. "And you."

"Explain."

"Let's face it," Alexander said. "Our chances of contacting Exodus are slim to none. Plus, our fate rests in the hands of your deranged brother. I'd rather take our fate in our own hands by winning the tournament and escaping with the Sojourner."

"And what about Dakari? You just gonna leave him behind?"

"We agreed to five months. Not five years. This isn't our fight."

"You tell that to Dakari?"

"No, of course, we didn't 'tell that to Dakari.' He doesn't know about this yet."

Derek stepped forward.

"Anything you tell me, you tell Dakari. I won't listen to another word."

"But we're going to tell him! We just need to phrase it in a way where he can't say no."

"Call him," Derek said. "Or I leave."

Alexander paused.

"You serious?"

"Do I look like I'm joking?"

Alexander sighed.

"Alright. Let's make the call."

Not long after, Mirabelle dialed for Dakari. They all crowded around her as she sat at her desk and turned the volume up to speaker mode.

"What is it?" Dakari asked.

"Alexander has a…proposition," Mirabelle said. "And Derek won't hear him out unless you're on the call too."

"Why's that?"

"You have a right to know," Derek said. "It's not exactly a light commitment."

"Very well. Have the blue-haired boy tell me his proposition."

Alexander leaned closer to the datapad.

"It's simple. You want to expose the Awakening. We want to leave New Earth. The tournament lets us do both. We register Quan and Derek. They advance through preliminary rounds, win the Final Four, and then use the ending ceremony to expose the Awakening in front of millions of people. Then, once our job is done, we take the Sojourner and travel wherever space takes us."

"What's so special about the ending ceremony?" Dakari asked.

Derek smiled as he caught onto the plan.

"Millions of people will be watching," Alexander said. "If my understanding of mind-snares is correct, one speech like that will leave too many minds to erase."

"Then why can't we just submit the story to a news outlet instead?"

"Good point," Alexander said.

"It wouldn't work," Derek said. "The Awakening has plenty of people in the media. No outlet would accept a piece like that with the right people watching."

"Then why would it work for the broadcast?"

"I'll set up a firewall in the broadcast room," Alexander said.

"And then you relay the broadcast with the evidence?"

"Yup. I can also use any records you find from L-Transport."

"That's not a bad plan," Dakari said. "I like it."

"Then you'll let me join?" Derek asked.

"Why wouldn't I? You are your own man. You gotta make this choice yourself." Dakari paused. "What will it be, Derek? What do *you* want to do?"

Mirabelle, Quan, and Alexander anxiously turned around. He stood against the wall in silence, then saw the three people he could now call his friends.

"A chance to expose the Awakening and get revenge against my brother?" Derek smiled. "How could I refuse?"

A Tantalizing Toast

"A toast to my father…no scrap that," Matthew said.

He stood before the mirror and erased the opening line of his speech. The eldest son of Carter Hunt, the one who bore the family name on his broad shoulders, who strolled down the Academy's halls like they were his, often had a Hunt's prideful gaze in his eyes. There was no pride today. For a moment's glance, he appeared to himself as normal as everyone else. Then he straightened his back, clenched his jaw, and wrote another line. Tonight was the Banquet of Rising Gerumandians. It was an event the Academy hosted annually to spotlight the best students in front of the Republic's biggest donors. There were promotional videos, speeches, and a few demonstrations of what Gerumandians were capable of in duels. And of course, there was a moment at the end that brought Matthew more angst than anything else—the toasts.

Earlier that day, Derek gave a few recs worth of his opinions. They had been walking back from the weight room when he said it. "How optional is a toast if all the other students are doing it? Sorry Dad, I just don't love you as much as my friends love their parents."

Derek laughed. Matthew didn't. It had been a week since Derek's return. It wasn't hard to get him adjusted to the team, especially since the Boss put them under direct orders to cooperate with each other. But from time to time, Bruce and Donny raised questions about the differences in Matthew and Derek's stories, to which they both respectively shut their opinions down. But Matthew wasn't worried about that. He was worried about the toast.

This was the scariest thing Matthew had experienced in years. *Of course, Derek's not nervous,* Matthew thought. *Dad already loves him.* Matthew spent the entire afternoon writing. Nothing about their choreography would be remembered. But the toast was for his father. He saw him maybe once a year–typically at an event like this.

That was the price to pay when your father was a famous wartime General. The absence and the spotlight. It wasn't something to be pitied (not that Matthew wanted pity) but it was one of many burdens to bear. He never forgot what this Academy expected from him when he arrived as an innocent ten-year-old. He remembered his dad dropping him off on his first day, squatting down in the courtyard so that they were at eye level. He remembered him scowling.

"Rise to the occasion, Matty," Carter said. He wore a brigadier's jacket adorned with medallions. There was not a smile on that tan leathery face of his. And his eyes. They saw not a child, but a machine. A super-soldier. "The immaculate soldier is yours. Go get it. Go make your daddy proud."

"I will," Matthew said.

Carter frizzled the top of Matthew's sandy blonde hair and smiled.

"I'm glad to hear it. You're my favorite. Always have been."

Matthew wrapped his arms around his father's bulky chest and squeezed, not wondering why his father never said he loved him. Not wondering why he never saw his mother like all the other kids at school. Being the favorite was enough.

That day he walked into the Academy and showed his talents. He was a giant among other ten-year-olds. No one could match the hunger in his eyes. He knew that hunger was everything for a Gerumandian. Something changed in Matthew when he stepped into the ring. He was faster, stronger, and smarter. He moved with the quickness of a child and the caution of a veteran. He had a strong frame and knew how to use it. He was so good he was fighting 14-year-olds by the end of the first semester.

"Carter trained him well," Boris said to one of the other instructors.

And yet, as strong as Matthew was, in those days he was good-spirited, always giving advice and lending a hand after each duel. He saw his fellow

Gerumandians not as opponents, but as fellow soldiers.

"Watch your footwork," Matthew said, helping a student who had lost his footing. "You're moving a bit slow to your right."

Because of this, he was liked by instructors and students alike. Things were going well until Matthew was declined his promotion to Adept at the end of his second year. *Two years as an Apprentice,* Matthew thought. His undefeated streak was broken. Students were learning his moves, and Matthew was fine with that. The friends he made softened his losses. He was content. But less hungry too. Carter didn't like that.

"An apprentice?" Carter said, pacing in the luxurious living room of their skyrise. It didn't feel like a living room. It was as dark as a closet. The only light in the room was a roaring fire. Matthew was 12 then but he still felt small in front of his father. "You spend an entire year at the Academy and you don't even advance a single rank?" Matthew stood there in the living room, speechless. These were the first words his father told him since seeing him again. "I'm disappointed."

During these conversations, Derek would sit at the end of the hall in his room, crouched with his ear to the door, flinching every time he heard his father's voice break out or the crack of a belt in the living room. Sometimes he heard howling, pleading, crying. Then it would stop. And then Matthew would come barging into the room, diving into bed, burying his face in the pillow, crying until he could sleep.

That was when Carter started playing a different game.

One night, Matthew crept down the hallway and saw Derek and his father by the fireplace. He remembered the dim lights of the living room, the sternness with which his father spoke as he reclined in his chair, looking at Derek who stood by him, fidgeting with his fingers and struggling to maintain eye contact with his father.

"I think you and I have gotten off to an unfortunate start," Carter told Derek, who was ten years old. "You see, Derek, I've been so preoccupied with your brother that I've hardly given you the attention you deserve. I want to apologize for that. You're getting older. And you'll be at the Academy this year, same as your brother. But between me and you, I think your brother might be getting involved with the wrong sort of folk, the type of folk who distract him from the real reason he's supposed to be there."

Matthew crept a little bit closer in the hallway.

"You've always had lower expectations for yourself because you're the youngest. But you're more powerful than you think. You got your daddy's genes." Carter smiled. "That means that you got a lot to fill, but it also means you got a lot to work with."

Carter paused and lowered his voice as if making sure no one else was around.

"I want to tell you something, Derek. But you can't tell a soul. Not even your brother. Understand?" Derek nodded again. Then, slowly, his father leaned forward with a devilish smile and a twinkle in his eyes. "You're my *favorite*." Carter rustled the top of Derek's hair as his son's eyes lit up like diamonds, his tiny face forming into a beaming smile. "I told Matthew the immaculate soldier was his. I told him he was the favorite too. But now I'm not sure. It can be yours. And if you want it. Go get it."

From that moment on, Matthew was never the same. The steady hunger that drove him to be better turned him into a beast. There were no more "fellow soldiers." No more comrades. Matthew trained until he bled. He trained until he sweat every ounce of water in his skin. Each time he heard wind of his brother's success it drove him mad. Derek was chopping through Pit Dogs like butter, advancing to Apprentice in one summer, just like his brother. Some even say he did it *faster* than Matthew. But who was counting? Derek was. So was Matthew.

They were hungry for the immaculate soldier–the title given to the highest performing competitor in the Gerumandian Dueling Tournament. Chas Rodo received that title, but Ledarius Tartaren never did. Both were good duelists, but one was better. One was the best. These were the things Matthew thought about as he struggled to write his toast.

He lost all concentration when Derek barged into his room.

"You ready?" Derek asked. "Mocroft wants us at Cypher Tower early to practice the choreography again."

Matthew straightened his tie in the mirror.

"I'll be down in a minute."

Derek left the room. Matthew had no idea that Derek had been talking behind his back. He had no idea Derek had become allies with Quan. *It will stay that way*, Derek thought. *No need for Matthew to know.*

They arrived at the penthouse in their green Gerumandian uniforms. Officer Mocroft double-checked the energy shields on their collars and ran through the choreography with the students. Thirty minutes later, the parents and donors entered the elaborate suite and took their seats at a long white table. The students stood with their backs straight in a line as Officer Mocroft welcomed the guests in. Matthew's heart stopped when he saw his father walk into the room in his brigadier general coat.

Carter Hunt hadn't aged a day. That perpetual scowl was still there, his brown eyebrows narrowed, his dark eyes skeptically eyeing the students in line. The Ouroboros, a snake with its tail in its mouth, was stitched on his breast. Matthew looked away before his father could make eye contact with him, then quickly looked back as Carter took his seat. He didn't know if his father saw him.

Officer Mocroft began the demonstration. It was a standard duel. Matthew and Derek each fought separate competitors and showed the proper fighting techniques. They performed it flawlessly. When it was over, they bowed before the table. The parents and donors stood up and cheered, blown away by their performance. Carter Hunt stayed in his seat and sipped on a glass of champagne.

"Students, please go back to the dressing rooms to change so you can join us for dinner," Mocroft said. "Now I'd like to welcome the man of the hour: Boris Gerumandian!"

The entire table, including Carter Hunt, stood up from their seats with applause. Boris, the real giant among men, stood up from the head of the table and shook Officer Mocroft's hand. The medallions stitched to his coat glittered beneath the light of the chandelier. Carter noticed every one of them and took another sip.

"Thank you," Boris said. "Thank you all so much."

The students left and changed into their dress suits as Boris began his speech. A few minutes later, they took their seats at the table across from their parents. They ate with golden silverware. A few promotional videos played on the projector for the donors. When it ended, Officer Mocroft stood up.

"And now, without further ado, our students have something prepared for the parents in the room." Matthew wiped his forehead with a napkin as Officer Mocroft gestured for him to stand. "Each of our students had the option of preparing toasts for their parents. I'd thought we'd start with the Academy's best and brightest–Matthew Hunt."

Matthew accidentally bumped into the table as he stood up from the chair. It seemed to grow eerily quiet now that he was standing. Carter sat no more than six feet across him, his brow flat and dull over his eyes. Looking at him was like looking at a soulless husk of a man, like a machine that was always calculating something about you that you weren't aware of. But Matthew was determined to make him proud. Maybe even smile. He raised his glass with slightly trembling hands.

"A t-toast to my father," Matthew said.

Carter's eyes widened. *It was the stutter,* Matthew thought. *He heard it.* Then something unthinkable happened. Before Matthew could say another word, Carter got up from his seat, bowed to Boris, and walked away. The table gasped and murmured to one another as Matthew stood there, speechless. Carter left and never looked back. Officer Mocroft tried to save the mood of the room as everyone grew concerned. Matthew sat back down. The banquet carried on.

Matthew stared out the window of the limo in silence on the way home, the rest of the speech tucked away in his jacket. Later that night, when he got back to his dorm, he tore it into a million pieces. A soldier like him wouldn't shed any tears. Instead, he walked to the registration booth in student services. An automaton behind one of the desks noticed him walk through the sliding glass doors.

"Can I help you, sir?"

Matthew's brow rested as flat as his father's.

"Bring up tournament registration. I'm signing up."

The automaton nodded and slid a holopad across the desk. Matthew signed his name, then left the room without ever looking back.

A Familiar Face

News of Matthew's registration spread faster than Quan's failure. And then the next day, news of Derek's registration spread even faster. Derek received more attention because of how odd it seemed. Derek Hunt was entering the 2135 tournament with the same Pit Dog Matthew had left nearly hospitalized a week before. It was so unexpected that it made Matthew's announcement look like nothing more than old news. "A Pit Dog?" People would say in the hallways. "He can't be serious." "No one in their right mind would do that." "It's all a joke. He'll withdraw soon." But he didn't. Derek was as committed to the tournament as he was about having Quan as his partner. A press conference was held the day after the registration deadline, officially making their announcement public. They met that afternoon with all the confirmed participants. With only three weeks before the tournament, Derek and Quan took their seats at the panel in their green uniforms. Camera lights flashed in their eyes as they sat down for questions.

"There's been some speculation that bringing a Pit Dog on your team is nothing more than a publicity stunt. What do you have to say to critics who think that you're purposely throwing the tournament away?"

Derek grabbed the mic with a corporate smile, his hair swept back like waves of gold.

"First of all, no one throws a tournament away because you only get one shot. Second, this is no ordinary Pit Dog, and his name is Quan. Third, ranks are more often measured by time spent at the Academy than they are by skill. Because Quan is new to the Academy, no one knows his weaknesses."

"But he got destroyed by your brother!"

Quan looked over at Derek, who ignored the question.

"We have as much of a chance of winning as anyone else. Maybe even more."

Students registered in the tournament were given a three-week absence from classes to spend more time training, which meant that Derek and Quan had plenty of time to strategize and stay in top shape. Not only that but each team was given the opportunity to bring other students onto their training squad, giving Mirabelle extra time to help Alexander track down files that they could use as evidence for the Final Four.

"Would you mind introducing your support team?" A Regal News reporter asked.

Quan and Derek exchanged a glance. Mirabelle and Alexander were on the panel for formality's sake, but they hadn't planned on having them speak.

"Uhh, sure," Quan said, clasping Alexander on the shoulder. "This is Alexander. He's uh…he's our comedian." Alexander gave a thumbs up. Then Quan turned to his right. "And this is Mirabelle. She's uh…she's my therapist."

Mirabelle pinched Quan's hand beneath the table, waving towards the reporters with a smile, then whispered: "I'm going to kill you."

"Yeah," Alexander said, leaning down the row. "Lately Mirabelle has been giving Quan advice on how to stop wetting the bed. Turns out that eliminating one glass of water a day can really do the trick!"

Several reporters laughed as Quan and Mirabelle yelled at Alexander. Derek stood up and groaned.

"That will be all, thanks."

Later that day, they met in private and defined their plan.

"We probably shouldn't meet for a few days," Derek said. "I'll have some explaining to do for joining the tournament with Quan, but if we play this right, I think we'll make it. See you guys around."

And that was it. Four friends. One plan. And three weeks to finish it.

They had finally debriefed Dakari and Amelia on the updated plans and got everyone else aboard. For the first time in a long time, everyone had hope. And hope was a rare thing.

* * *

Five minutes later, a press conference was held for Matthew Hunt. He never showed up.

* * *

Banner and Kalak walked down the tunnel to the hangar at the CDAD.

"The Republic Dueling Tournament?!" Kalak shouted. "What are they thinking?!"

"I just got the news too, sir," Banner said. "It looks like they both joined."

Kalak felt sweat stains creep around his armpits. He sighed.

"They say the AOL drug stops aging, but I feel like I'm getting older every day. I thought it was just Derek we had to worry about. Those brothers are as lousy as ever."

"What should we do, sir?"

The gray and black-haired Chief opened the door to the hanger and led Banner on the walkway. "The Boss isn't going to like this, but the Hunt siblings are still the best chance we got. They're the only psychics at the Academy that understand the bagging system and the scanners. If we got rid of them it'd just take longer, and if we sent in the arbitrators, we'd attract too much attention, potentially scaring the psychic away."

Kalak stopped as the main hangar doors opened. A luxurious L-Transport carrier activated its retro thrusters and made a gentle descent onto one of the landing pads.

"But the Hunt brothers are clearly wasting our time," Banner said. "If they have time to join the tournament, they certainly don't have our best interests in mind."

"I didn't say the Hunt brothers. I said *siblings*."

Vents of steam were released from the main doors of the cargo ship. Several landing pads jutted out from the ship and lowered a plank onto the floor. A beautiful blonde girl walked down the ramp. She had the confidence of a princess but the gaze of a warrior. The end of her blonde ponytail swayed with each step as her tactical boots echoed on the metal floor. She wore a tight graphene combat suit with shield straps over her shoulders. And her eyes, unlike both her brothers, were not green but blue. They shone with the brightness of a tropical coast but harbored the storm on a wild sea. They were raging like lightning and haughty–hesitant to look at that which was unworthy to be looked upon. She dismissed her assistants the moment they arrived and strolled past them.

Kalak smiled.

"Beretta Hunt has arrived."

* * *

In a dark alleyway at the Gerumandian Academy, Derek and Matthew smoked a pair of e-cigs as it drizzled overhead. The smell of smoke and wet asphalt filled the overhang as Matthew leaned over the railing.

"Why join with him?" Matthew asked.

Derek raised the e-cig back to his lips, inhaled, then exhaled with a smile.

"It's the last person they'd suspect, right?"

"And what happens if he finds out we're after him?"

"We have plenty of reasons to stop that from happening," Derek said. "Unless you change your mind, we have nothing to worry about."

"You never alluded to joining the tournament before. Why now?"

"Why not? If the world ends in three weeks, why not see what I'm truly capable of? Unless you have a problem with that."

"Why would I have a problem with that? Do you think you're a threat to me? You may as well have shot yourself in the foot by joining with a Pit Dog."

"Just like you did by joining without a partner."

"I'll be the first. No one's ever won the tournament alone."

"And for good reason. No one ever will." Derek tucked the e-cig into his coat pocket.

"They might not like both of us joining the tournament," Matthew said. "If we want to maintain a good reputation with the Awakening, one of us should drop out."

The sound of footsteps echoed out in the alleyway. They both turned to look.

"You boys give yourselves too much credit." A hooded figure approached them. Then, when she stepped into the glow of the dim light, they watched in shock as she lowered her hood, revealing her face. "You lost your chance at redemption a long time ago," Beretta said.

Derek and Matthew felt their blood go cold. They saw the shimmering blue eyes of their sister stare into their souls. She was only a year younger than Derek and about a head shorter than Matthew, but there was something she had that they didn't. She was on Father's good side.

"I'm just teasing," she said. "Lighten up."

None of them had seen her in years.

"Beretta?" Matthew asked. "What are you doing here?"

"I heard there was a train wreck in need of fixing. I'm good at fixing things."

"I thought you were on Telaris," Derek said.

"I was. But no more questions. I'll be taking that list and overseeing the scans from now on. You have 1,102 suspects left to scan. Each of you has been scanning four psychics a day, which means you'll be done in about ten weeks. We need to change that. Instead of training, you're going to be using all that free time the Academy has given you to scan 16 students a day. Among the four of you, that process will be done in 17 days."

"16 students?" Matthew asked. "There's no way we'd be able to set up that many sound chambers or sneak into student's rooms."

Beretta tossed Matthew a scanner.

"No need for that. The Awakening has issued us these." Beretta slammed her scanner against the wall and clicked the button. "Simply find the room of the student you need to scan, and the device will detect the brain waves up to 10 meters." Beretta tossed the other scanner to Derek. "Do I make myself clear?"

Derek and Matthew stood side by side, clenching their fists in anger.

"Oh, and if we finish scanning all the students on your list and it turns out that this was all a sham, you're both dead. The Awakening has no use for traitors. If you find the psychic, you'll win back your jobs. If you don't, the Boss has no use for you."

Beretta walked towards the entrance into the Academy and opened the door.

"Hold on!" Derek said. "Why are you going inside?"

Beretta flipped her hair to the side.

"Haven't you heard? I'm the Academy's newest transfer student. I just couldn't *stand* being away from my brothers for so long."

Derek eyed his sister with a harsh glance.

"I wish I could say it's good to see you."

Beretta's brow lowered. She looked like Dad.

"I don't."

She slammed the door, leaving her two brothers in the rain.

A House in a High Rise

It was another beautiful day in the Leonardo Estate. The sun shined in the canopy of a bright blue sky. A professional harp player strummed a tune in the living room as Darius stood on his balcony, eyeing the city of Dain from high above. The buildings of this great city cascaded on the horizon like little mountains or tiny hills—endless spires of magnificent architecture. He wore a pair of high-end sandals, elaborate white robes, and stood smiling with a cup of espresso in his hand. From that height, all the air traffic became nothing but a faint distant echo. Darius smiled as he saw his wife reclining in one of the chairs while she listened to a podcast on her headphones. Kairo was somewhere upstairs studying for placement exams.

"If there's a God up there I better thank him. What a wonderful life I live."

Moments later, one of the servants stumbled onto the balcony in a hurry.

"There's been a disturbance, sir."

"Disturbance?" Darius turned around. "Of what kind?"

"There was a man wandering around in the courtyard. We've detained him and were planning on calling the arbitrators, but…he says his name is Dakari Minathi."

The servant led Darius Leonardo inside.

Dakari Minathi sat alone at the same dining table he had visited months ago. The same man sat there, but he did not feel like the same man. He felt like he had aged a hundred years. He no longer looked the same either. It was no wonder the security guards didn't recognize him: he looked homeless. An untrimmed beard, hair, and eyes that looked restless. He could hardly sleep these days. The nightmares had worsened with Derek's absence. He sat alone in an empty apartment each day with no one to talk to and nothing to do. Any sense of professionalism he used to have was lost.

In the kitchen, he heard Darius speaking to his wife, their tones growing anxious. Several security guards remained in the room, skeptically eyeing Dakari. Eventually, the conversation in the kitchen stopped. Darius entered the room and sighed.

"You're not an easy man to find, Mr. Minathi."

"I'm not a free man either, sir."

"I'm well aware of that." Darius took his seat across from him regardless. "There's a bounty on your head worth 10 million recs."

"Then it's a good thing I came to a man who has all the money in the world. And a sense of hospitality bigger than his bank account."

Darius poured them both a glass of water.

"I rarely extend hospitality to criminals." He slid the glass across to Dakari. "But seeing that we've met before, I'm willing to hear you out."

"Thank you," Dakari said. He reached for the glass, then eyed the three security guards standing in the corners of the room. "I'm afraid they'll have to leave."

"That seems a little bold."

"I have no weapons. If you'd like to keep a weapon on you, I won't be offended, but what I have to say is for your ears only."

There was a notable shift in the stance of the security guards. Even Darius too, who reached inside his coat. Dakari flinched as he saw Darius pull out what he thought was a gun, then realized it was a holopad. He relaxed as Darius clicked his e-pen.

"If it's the secrecy of our conversation that you need…"

Darius wrote something onto the empty pad and slid it across the table. *We can communicate like this.*

Dakari looked at Darius and nodded in agreement. Then, after making sure the guards couldn't see the notepad, he erased the last message and wrote a new one, then slid it across the table. Darius' eyes widened with disbelief.

Your son is a psychic.

Darius stared at Dakari with wide eyes.

"You must think I'm a fool to believe this!"

Both men stood up from the table.

"Darius! I can explain!" Their eyes met in a stalemate as the guards reached for their rifles. "I'm trying to help you!" None of them moved. "There's a reason I left the CDAD. I learned something that's going to upend this world. If you have even a remnant of respect for me, I beg you to hear me out."

The guards shook their heads at Darius, but he ignored them. He took his seat.

"Very well," Darius said, sliding the holopad back across the table. "Explain."

Dakari wrote faster than he ever had in his life. When he was finished, he slid the holopad back across the table and waited with bated breath.

"An underground railroad? I never authorized anything like that!"

"Darius. I'd appreciate it if you voice your concerns on the holopad. Please."

Darius sighed, then kept reading. Dakari nervously tapped his finger on the table. Darius finished the memo and stared off into the distance. Each passing second was more proof that Dakari was in over his head. He kept trying to think of a way out of this if Darius ended up disagreeing with his findings. In the end, he saw none. This entire plan hinged on the cooperation of the Republic's wealthiest man. And Dakari had just insulted him with an accusation against his son. Darius responded.

Are you telling me that Lieutenant Banner has been forging my signature to authorize an underground railroad to transport psychics using my cargo ships?

Dakari erased the memo and wrote his answer.

No. I'm telling you that you've been authorizing this yourself. You just don't remember. Kairo is using you to conduct the operation. Every time you sign this document, he erases your memory of the incident entirely.

They continued to exchange the holopad.

That's a bold claim. Do you have any proof?

Dakari replied.

Yes. We have a recording of the meeting in the past. I can send it to your datapad. I would just ask that you wear headphones.

Darius Leonardo left the room and listened to the recordings outside. He kept his back facing the archway and his gaze at the clouds with both headphones in his ears. Dakari waited in silence as the guards remained at their posts. He started to have hope that things might turn around. Then, he heard the distant creak of footsteps coming down the stairs. Step by step they grew louder as a boy with long dreadlocks stopped halfway down the stairwell and made eye contact with Dakari. It was Kairo Leonardo.

"What is this traitor doing in my house?!" He shouted. "Guards! Arrest him!"

"Your father instructed us not to."

"Is my father here?!"

"That's not exactly the point, Kairo."

Kairo approached the guards. He aimed his fingers between their eyes and snapped. Seconds later they collapsed to the ground, completely unconscious.

"Fine." Kairo's eyes glowed bright blue. "I'll do it myself."

"It's too late!" Dakari stood up. "Your father already knows."

"And why would that be a problem? He's figured out before." Kairo aimed his fingers at Dakari and snapped. Nothing happened. "You're an impurity? No wonder Banner wanted you gone."

Darius entered the dining hall. He teared up when he saw his son's glowing eyes.

"Kairo?" He leaned against the wall for support. "It...it can't be..."

"Relax, Dad." Kairo aimed his fingers. "You won't remember a thing."

Snap! Darius fell to the ground like a tumbling statue. Dakari backed against the wall, watching as Darius lay passed out on the floor.

"That bounty on your head," Kairo said, smiling. "How much is it worth?"

Dakari grabbed Darius' body and held it in front of him like a human shield. Kairo aimed his fingers, then did nothing. Dakari smiled.

"You need him alive, don't you?"

"He is my father. I'd rather not see him dead."

"He's nothing more than a husk! What kind of deal did the Awakening give you to do something like this?"

"The same deal Exodus gave me. Freedom to use my abilities."

Dakari raised a brow.

"Exodus? You mean, you work for them too?"

"I don't work for any of them."

"Then who do you work for?"

"Think a little harder. You've worked with some of us before."

Dakari's eyes narrowed, then widened.

"You're with the Gray Eids."

Kairo smiled.

"Neutrality has its perks, my friend."

Dakari looked around at the three silent bodies on the ground. "Is that what this is? How can you call smuggling psychics for the Awakening, neutrality?"

"Because I do it for Exodus too. Why else do you think I'd have to erase my old man's memories if I wasn't making contracts with two separate groups? You know the rule. 50% go to Exodus, 50% go to the Awakening."

"I guess you missed the census," Dakari said.

"Certainly seems that way."

"Don't lie to me. Neutrality doesn't exist. You have to make a choice."

"I did make a choice. If the Awakening and Exodus go unchecked, they'll wreak havoc on this world. People like me help keep that balance. Power corrupts, but if that power is perfectly balanced, if there's a perfect stasis of hatred and spite between one side and the other–then no one ever wins and no one ever loses."

"Not for long."

"What do you mean?"

"The Awakening is a few scans away from finding a stage 4 psychic."

"You're talking about Quan, aren't you?"

Dakari's eyes widened.

"How'd you know?"

"Doesn't matter. If the Awakening gets a hold of one stage 4 psychic, all Exodus has to do is find the other one."

"The other one?"

"You mean Quan hasn't told you? About his brother?"

"What brother?"

"I shouldn't tell you anything that Quan hasn't told you himself."

"I doubt he even knows," Dakari said. "He didn't even know he was a stage 4 psychic until Derek scanned him."

"Maybe he doesn't, but it doesn't matter. I can't get in the way of the Awakening."

"Why not? We don't even want to find the Krymenodon."

"You don't?" Kairo asked. "Then what are you doing here?"

"Trying to buy more time." Dakari gently set Darius back on the floor. "The Awakening is closing in on us. If you know anything about Quan, then you'd know he wants nothing to do with this war. He wants to leave New Earth."

"That's not what my scouts told me. They said you were trying to contact Exodus."

"Because we had no other choice. The Awakening killed my wife. They killed my son. What else was I supposed to do? Where else could I run?" For the first time throughout their entire conversation, Kairo didn't have a response. "We were only trying to contact Exodus because we were running for our lives. Then we heard about the Sojourner. Plans changed."

Kairo looked down at his unconscious father. Through the window, he saw his mother listening to music on her headphones.

"What better way to bring balance than to restrict everyone's access to the Krymenodon?" Dakari asked. "Neither the Awakening nor Exodus will have a chance."

"But you might," Kairo said.

"No. Quan might. But he could care less."

Kairo knelt down by his father, feeling both fingers under his neck.

"My father will be awake soon. As well as the other guards." Kairo looked up. "If what you're saying is true, I can throw a wrench in the Awakening's plans."

"How will we contact you?"

"You won't. I'll contact you." Kairo pointed towards the door. "Get going."

Dakari bowed.

"Thank you, Kairo."

"Don't thank me yet."

With that, Dakari walked away, then paused in the middle of the doorway. He had a promise to keep. "Hold on." Dakari searched his coat and brought out an unfolded piece of paper. "There's something I need to ask you."

"Make it quick."

"Do you know a man named Aidan Marshall?"

"He's a pilot for L-Transport. What's it to you?"

"Nothing." He tucked the note away. "It's his daughter who's asking–Mirabelle."

"Does she know Quan?"

"Yeah."

"Then I'll tell her myself."

"Why can't you just tell me?"

Kairo reluctantly looked away.

"Better me than you."

Dakari nodded.

"Very well. See you around."

Dakari left the premises. Moments later, Kairo's mother stepped inside. She saw several bodies lying on the floor and Kairo kneeling by his father's side. She shrieked.

"What happened?!"

Kairo scratched the back of his head and nervously laughed.

"Sorry, Mom." He snapped his fingers and caught her before she could fall. "It's better you don't know." With minutes left to spare, he carried the bodies upstairs and began to reconstruct their memories.

The Mystery Man

Alexander and Mirabelle waited with Quan in his dorm. In the span of a few days, Alexander had turned their dorm into an electronic hub. Computer screens rested on the desks and dressers. Wires were taped to the ceiling. A printer copied several documents of old files that Alexander had gathered on some of the missing students. As usual, they were ready to debrief. There was just one problem.

"Where's Derek?" Mirabelle asked.

"I don't know," Quan said. "I've been trying to call him all day."

A sobering silence crept over the group. Then, a few minutes later, Derek Hunt stumbled into the room and slammed the door. Everyone else jerked their heads in his direction and stood up. He leaned against the door, out of breath, and said: "We need to talk."

Quan stood up.

"About what?"

"It's my sister. She's at the Academy."

"You have a sister?!" Mirabelle asked. "Is she as much of a scumbag as you and Matthew?"

"Worse. Way worse."

"What?!" Alexander stood up. "Girls are way weaker than boys."

Mirabelle crossed her arms.

"I sure slapped you silly."

"That wasn't fair though. You've had Gerumandian training. I'm a skinny nerd. The Hunt brothers are the best duelers at the Academy! She wouldn't stand a chance."

"Matthew and I are stage 2 psychics," Derek said. "Beretta is a stage 3. She can erase memories and even sense them in proximity to other psychics. Not only that, but she's been on Telaris for the past three years. She has military training and has weaponized her psychic abilities in ways that Matthew and I haven't. You'd be a fool to underestimate her."

"Why'd she get sent back here?" Quan asked.

"We think the Awakening might be catching onto us. They sent Beretta to speed up the operation. With her changes, we'll have scanned every psychic in sixteen days."

"But the tournament is in 20 days!" Quan said.

"Yeah," Derek said. "And if we don't turn in a psychic after these last scans, Matthew and I are dead. We're running out of time."

No one said anything. They all liked to believe that when they put their heads together, failure was as invisible as the enemy. But that didn't mean it wasn't real. Derek, Quan, and Alexander faintly understood the chances of things going awry, but no one understood that better than Mirabelle. She had been in a situation like this before. And it didn't end well. Before she could worry for a second longer her datapad buzzed. She received an incoming call. It was Dakari.

"Hello?"

"A visitor is coming to your room soon. I suggest letting him in."

"Who?"

Dakari hung up as someone knocked on the door. Everyone exchanged a glance, but no one moved. Then Mirabelle walked across the room and opened the door. A dark-skinned boy in a navy-blue dress suit stood outside, his dreadlocks neatly bound behind his head. He was around their age, maybe younger, but spoke with the confidence of a businessman.

"Someone told me you might be in need of some help." He smiled, waiting for someone to respond. No one did. "Am I wrong?"

"That depends," Mirabelle said. "Are you the man Dakari sent?"

"I wouldn't say he sent me. I sent myself."

Mirabelle held the door open, then let him inside. The door shut as everyone in the room watched him with wide eyes. The young man straightened the sides of his dress coat and gazed at the contraptions over the walls.

"Who are you?" Alexander asked.

He spun around and clinked his shoes together with a smile.

"Pardon me, where are my manners?" He extended a hand. "Kairo Leonardo."

Mirabelle's eyes widened as Alexander shook his hand.

"Alexander Bridges."

"Pleasure to meet you. Unfortunately, you're not the one I'm looking for." Kairo spun around and faced Quan. "I'm here for you."

Mirabelle shoved Alexander aside. She skeptically analyzed Kairo as if he was a threat. There was something off about him she couldn't explain.

"Wait a minute. What did you say your last name was again?"

Kairo turned around.

"Leonardo. From L-Transport." His eyes widened. "Wait a minute...you must be Mirabelle Marshall. I know that name."

A red rage rose in Mirabelle. She felt the blood in her fingers boil as her vision turned crimson from just the mention of the Leonardo name. Kairo had his father's face–the same face that had taken her father away from her ten years ago, the same look of casual indifference to her decade of suffering. Her nerves flared as she took a deep breath, then strangled his neck. Everyone shrieked as she backed him into the wall with a thud and squeezed. Kairo gripped her arms and choked as Mirabelle's eyes narrowed on his.

"And why's that? Remind you of anyone?" She tightened her fingers around his neck until his veins started to bulge. "Like my father?!"

"Mirabelle!"

Derek pulled Mirabelle away as Kairo gasped for breath.

"Don't touch me!" She shoved Derek back. "We may be partnering because you're our best shot at getting in the tournament, but in my eyes, you two are the same."

"And what would that be?" Kairo asked, staggering up to his feet. "By the way. That ship you're all after? You have my father to thank for that."

"And what about all the psychics you've given to the Awakening?" Mirabelle asked. "We have your father to thank for that too?"

"No, actually, that was all of my doing. I'm with the Gray Eids. 50% go to the Awakening, 50% go to Exodus. Because you're not here to help either of them, I'm here to help you. Shall we begin?"

"No." Mirabelle crossed her arms. "I demand an explanation." She looked at Quan. "I won't listen to another word this sellout says until he tells me the truth."

Kairo laughed.

"Sellout?" He stared at the ceiling in disbelief. "Oh, the irony. If anyone's the sellout it's your father. We didn't force him to work for us. He did that on his own."

"You're lying."

"I bet you wish I was," Kairo said. "But it's true. No one in our operation can be vulnerable to mind-snares, which means psychics and impurities are the only people who can do the job. Your father is the best at what he does. It meant leaving you and Martha, but after he saw the salary, he accepted our offer without hesitation." Kairo smiled. "He loves what he does."

Mirabelle's expression was not so easily altered.

"I'd like to hear his side of the story first."

"I'm glad you asked," Kairo said. "There's a hovercraft waiting for you down in the courtyard."

"For what?"

"To see your father."

Mirabelle didn't want to believe it because she suspected it was a lie. It was too good to be true. She stood there with her arms crossed, then looked out the window. If there was anyone who could grant her a meeting with her father, it would be the person standing in front of her, the young man with the keys to L-Transport in his hands. And to see his smiling face. Or his frown. It had been ten years. It pained her to think that Kairo probably knew her father better than she did. She knew what the right thing to do was. But how could she refuse?

"You're saying…"

"You could see him tonight," Kairo said. "I give you my word."

Quan and Alexander anxiously waited for Mirabelle's response. She didn't look to them for approval or support. This decision was hers alone.

"I need some time to think," Mirabelle said, stepping towards the door.

"Then think," Kairo said. "But don't think too long. The hovercraft will leave in an hour. You have until then to decide."

Mirabelle opened the door. Quan tried to follow her, but Derek grabbed his arm.

"Let her go." Derek let go of Quan. "She'll come around."

Quan watched Mirabelle close the door. She didn't even turn around with a parting glance. If she had really decided to leave them, she hadn't even said goodbye. Then Kairo resumed his speech.

"Very well. Where was I?"

Alexander put an arm around Kairo's shoulder and smiled.

"If I recall, you were about to hand over the keys to the Sojourner."

Kairo shoved him aside. "I recall no such thing. If you want that ship, you're going to have to earn it the traditional way. I'm just here to buy you time."

"But the tournament starts in 20 days," Derek said. "In 16 days all the suspects on the list will be scanned."

"What happens if you don't find a psychic?" Kairo asked.

"Game over."

"What if you're the one who brings them in?"

"Our reputation is saved. But the Awakening will ship us all to Telaris after that."

"And how are they going to do that? Seeing that they'd be using my ships." Kairo watched with a smile as the eyes of everyone in the room widened with understanding. "If they use state starships, they'll be flagged for traveling in unauthorized territory. L-Transport ships aren't. That kind of bargaining power could probably get you all a few extra days at least. Maybe even enough to let you win the tournament."

Derek stroked his chin and smiled.

"Potentially. But we can't just turn Quan in. That defeats the whole point."

"Who said anything about Quan?" Kairo snapped his fingers and manipulated the particles around him. "You need someone with the brain waves of a stage 4 psychic. Stage 3 psychics like myself are known to be masters in manipulation. It'd be the same principle of a mirage, really, but instead of creating a false projection of the subconscious, we create a false projection of brain waves on the scanner."

Alexander scoffed.

"Oh yeah? And how do you know what those brain waves look like?"

Kairo smiled. He walked over to Derek and extended a hand. With a bit of reluctance, Derek placed his scanner in Kairo's hands, who then walked over to Quan and clicked the light above his brain.

"We have a live model right here," Kairo said. "But putting the real psychic in the hands of the Awakening is a risk we can't afford. So instead, we turn in someone else, and with a little manipulation of their brain waves, we create the psychic the Awakening is looking for."

"We can't just turn in an innocent student," Quan said.

"And you won't be. I'm turning myself in." Everyone in the room was stunned to silence. "I could easily replicate the proper brain waves necessary to forge a scan. That way, they'd take me in, but in doing so, they'd still have to get through me to ship me off to Telaris in one of my own ships."

"You'd do that?" Quan asked.

"I might be utilitarian in some of my ways, but that doesn't mean I'm heartless. It also gives me control in keeping up the act." He sighed. "It is the only way to keep the balance the Gray Eids need in this world. I will do it."

Derek crossed his arms.

"And what happens when they realize you're a fraud?"

"I'll arrange for some of the other Gray Eids to rescue me. No need to concern yourselves with those details."

"I'm not asking about what will happen to you," Derek said. "No offense, but if they realize you're a fraud before the tournament, isn't that game over for me too?"

"That's the best part of the plan. You're not going to find me. Your sister is."

Derek smiled.

"And then when they find out they got the wrong guy–she gets the blame."

"Precisely. But before I enthrall anyone else with the thrilling details of this plan, I need to speak with the stage 4 psychic himself." Kairo gestured to the door. "Quan? Can we speak for a moment?"

They stepped outside the room and walked down the hallway. He didn't feel comfortable leaving Alexander and Derek out of the conversation, but then again, Kairo didn't exactly appear as someone who would take no for an answer.

"You should know that I only agreed to help you on one condition." Kairo pressed the elevator button. "That if you win the tournament: you take the Sojourner and leave."

"Then you have nothing to worry about," Quan said. "I've been wanting to leave for a long time."

"I don't doubt that. But I am worried that Dakari will try to change your mind."

The elevator door chimed. They both stepped inside.

"Not necessarily. This plan works in everyone's best interests."

"For now. But what happens after your grand declaration to the world? None of you are truly prepared for the chaos that will ensue once the Awakening is exposed." Kairo pressed the button for the rooftop. "There will be blood."

"Not on my hands. Anything that happens after the tournament is your domain." The elevator engines hummed as they made their ascent. "Can I ask you something?"

"Shoot."

"If you've sworn an oath of neutrality, why let the Awakening pursue me? Isn't that favoring one side over the other?"

"It would be if you were the only cartographic psychic. But there are two of you."

"Who's the other one?"

"He never told you?"

"I'm not following."

"Come on. Would it really be that hard to guess?"

Quan looked at his white sneakers, his eyes squinting with confusion. They trailed to the black rubber wristband on his left forearm. His eyes widened. He looked at Kairo.

"Jon?"

"Are you really that surprised? You have the mutation yourself."

"I didn't know he had it too–or that he was even a psychic."

"Then your ignorance is a bit more understandable, but still not merited. Jon, like you, was resistant to mind-snares. He noticed that students were going missing and linked the transportation of their disappearances to L-Transport. After that, it was only a matter of time before he found me. He demanded an explanation but quickly lost interest in the details once he realized that he might be the next one to go. I gave him two choices: stay at the Academy and take his chances or leave on a one-way trip to a planet of his choice." Kairo smiled. "I imagine it wouldn't be hard to guess his choice."

"Where did he go?"

"That's classified. But rest assured, he's enjoying himself quite well. And if you're interested, you could be too."

"What do you mean?" Quan asked.

The elevator doors opened, revealing the Academy rooftop. They walked over to the edge of the railing and stared at the golden-hued, sunlit city. The afternoon sun cast a warm orange glow over their skin and Kairo's navy blue coat. They both rested their forearms over the railing and watched the air traffic in the distance.

"What I'm about to tell you is for your ears only," Kairo said, both hands folded together. "I'm giving you an out. You should leave tonight."

Quan's heart skipped a beat.

"What?"

"I may not be able to get you clearance to the Sojourner, but there are plenty of other starships in my father's arsenal that'll do the trick."

"Why didn't you tell me this earlier?"

"Because there were other people around. Plus, you're the stage 4 psychic. I'm offering you the same exit I offered to your brother."

Quan's expression darkened.

"What about the others?"

"They can come too if you want. But they should know that this is a one-way trip."

"And there's one other thing," Quan said. "If we leave tonight, we'll miss the tournament." He paused. "No one will know about the Awakening."

"But you'll be safe. Leaving the day of the tournament will be a long shot. You're going to have arbitrators and the Awakening on your backs the second you win. I'm not saying it'd be impossible, but it'd sure be difficult."

"I promised Dakari five months."

"Is that your decision?"

"It has to be."

"No, it doesn't."

"I gave Dakari my word. I'm not about to break it now."

Kairo shrugged his shoulders.

"Suit yourself. I won't force your hand." Kairo pulled a piece of paper from his pocket and handed it to Quan. "But should you change your mind, there's a rendezvous point where some of my pilots will be posted. Show up anytime and they'll escort you and anyone else you're with to a safe planet until things cool down here."

"And what about you? How do you plan on escaping the CDAD?"

Kairo smiled.

"Leave that to me. You have decisions of your own to make." Kairo pressed the elevator button and stepped inside. "I hope you choose wisely."

With that, the elevator doors closed. Quan looked down at the piece of paper and then caught sight of the wristband on his forearm. He tucked the paper away and silently stood on the rooftop. Thinking. To stay or to leave.

* * *

Mirabelle opened every drawer in her dresser and started flinging clothes onto her bed. She threw open her suitcase and tucked her belongings inside. With each folded article of clothing, her anger intensified. Every memory of her father's smiling face remained, but now it was complicated. *Did he have a choice to stay? And if he did, why would he leave?* She tried to silence her inner voice, but nothing worked. It was the questions that made her zip up her suitcase. Every tear she had ever shed for him seemed misunderstood. With nearly her entire wardrobe packed, she zipped up her suitcase, then stood up.

She paused, then turned around to see that infamous picture of herself and her father on her desk. It seemed too sweet and innocent. A ray of sunshine entered the frame as he gave her a piggyback ride, looking lovingly into her dark auburn eyes. It pained her to think that that same man had delivered innocent children right into the hands of the people that murdered Zane. With each step she took towards the photograph, a tumultuous wave of anger rose in her. It wasn't just this. It felt like everything she had ever known was crumbling. She learned that there was a cost to every dream she had ever dreamt and every person she had ever loved. She loved her father. Then he left her. She loved Zane. Then he died. And now her father's absence was complicated. She couldn't rest until she knew the truth. With every feeling of love and hope, she felt ten times more heartbreak and disappointment. And what would be next? Each day the Awakening grew closer to snuffing them out. With her last step in front of the desk, a haunting realization occurred to her.

We're going to lose.

The mission would fail. Quan and Derek would lose the tournament. Someone would cut the broadcast. Beretta would find Quan. There was too much room for failure. And with Mirabelle's track record, the odds weren't in her favor. She grabbed the photograph of her father and threw it against the wall so hard the glass shattered into a dozen fragments on the floor. That was the last straw. She wasn't just tired of losing. She was tired of playing a game that couldn't be won. With one quick tug, she grabbed her suitcase and opened the door. It slammed shut behind her. She would've kept walking too if someone wasn't standing in the middle of the hallway, blocking the path to the elevator. She stopped dead in her tracks as Alexander, standing smugly with his blue hair, baggy jeans, and oversized white hoodie, slowly started clapping.

"I did it." He stopped a few feet before her. "I won."

"What are you talking about?" Mirabelle asked.

"What am I talking about!? Don't you see? I once told you that you and I are the same. And today you proved it!"

"I still don't know what you're talking about."

"Oh really? Must I point out the suitcase? Your posture? That scowl on your face?" Alexander crossed his arms and smiled. "You're leaving."

"I've exhausted my usefulness."

"No, you haven't. Not until you've flown the Sojourner. We still need you."

"I never wanted to leave! I wanted to find my father."

"But you gave us your word! We're honoring Dakari's agreement. You need to honor yours." Alexander crossed his arms. "This isn't like you."

"Then maybe I'm not who you think I am. And why is that such a bad thing? No one else seems to act like the people they really are."

"Ahh, yes. A shame about your father. But on the bright side, you've learned a valuable lesson early in life. Everyone's a douchebag. Some are just better at hiding it."

"You don't get it."

"I don't? How about I put it this way instead? You're upset that people didn't live up to your expectations."

Mirabelle crossed her arms.

"They were good expectations."

"They were HIGH expectations!" Alexander shouted. "Do you hear yourself right now?! You want everyone to fit into this perfect frame you've created for them! And when things don't fit–you throw the whole thing away! Don't you get it now, Mirabelle? I. WAS. RIGHT!"

Mirabelle tried to slap Alexander, but he caught her arm, then stared into her eyes.

"Sorry, scar girl. But I learned my..."

KICK!

Alexander's eyes nearly bulged out of their sockets. A slow, whale-like groan bellowed out of his mouth after Mirabelle had kicked him in the groin. He collapsed on the ground and started curling into a fetal position.

"...lesson."

Mirabelle grabbed her suitcase.

"Goodbye Alexander."

She started to walk away. Alexander leaned up from the ground and croaked: "Wait." She stopped. Alexander's face was still red, and his limbs were weak, but he managed to sit up against the wall. "Please don't go. We need you."

Mirabelle turned around. He didn't look like the happy, flamboyant, sarcastic nerd he usually was. His eyes were bloodshot red. Mirabelle stood still, then slowly walked over to Alexander and sat by his side. She looked away and kept shaking her head.

"We're going to lose," Mirabelle said.

"Maybe," Alexander said. "But we don't have a lot of options. If there's even the slightest chance of us leaving, I want to take it."

"Isn't that what I'm doing?"

"But then what about us?"

Mirabelle was silent. Then she slumped her shoulders and sighed.

"I know." She kept shaking her head. "I'm just confused. What if Kairo is right?"

"Does it really matter?"

Mirabelle looked into Alexander's eyes.

"Yes. It does."

Alexander looked at his datapad. She had ten minutes left to decide.

"Can I tell you a story?"

Mirabelle's ears perked up.

"A story?"

"Yeah," Alexander said. "It might help."

Mirabelle sat up and scooted closer.

Alexander looked down at the carpet. "I lost my little sister when I was eight," he said. "I didn't think that AOL people could get illnesses, but apparently some AOL babies are born with compromised immune systems if the drug isn't inherited properly." He paused. "She was one of those babies.

"I sat by my mother's bedside at the hospital every night as Mom held Lily in her arms. She was so tiny, pink, fat, and warm. She didn't cry like other babies and her eyes rarely opened. That's when we knew something was wrong. But the doctors diagnosed her too late." Alexander closed his eyes. "She died a week later.

"There aren't many cemeteries anymore, and because my parents couldn't afford to have her buried in one, my father insisted on burying her himself. They argued about it for weeks. Dad wanted her buried in the front yard, but Mom didn't want her buried at all. She said it would be too painful for her to see her headstone out there every day. But one morning, when she walked down the stairs, she stopped. She looked out the window and saw a headstone facing the street. Dad had buried her in the middle of the night.

"Each morning Mom saw Lily's grave from the stairwell, and each morning I could hear her pause. Dad never paused. He had settled with his grief by burying his daughter himself, but Mom never moved on. They divorced a month later."

Mirabelle looked down at the carpet too.

"I'm sorry for your loss," she said. "But I don't know how that helps me."

"Then think about it this way," Alexander said. "Did it matter why my Dad buried Lily? I believe he buried her there because he genuinely loved her, but Mom believed he buried her there to make her feel guilty. He saw it as a gesture of honor. She saw it as a reminder of a day she wanted to forget. If Mom knew his reasons before the divorce, maybe things would've changed. But they didn't. What's done is done." Alexander looked at Mirabelle. "Your father's been gone ten years. Who cares why he left?"

Mirabelle looked down at her datapad. She still had five minutes left to decide.

"Don't you wish you knew why your father buried Lily?"

Alexander reached into his pocket and pulled out a joint. "No," he said. "Because that doesn't change the fact that she died. And it doesn't change the fact that Mom and Dad got divorced." Mirabelle was too dumbfounded to even respond, then grew even more surprised when Alexander offered her a joint. "You wanna smoke?"

"I don't smoke."

"Have you tried?"

"No. And I won't start today either."

Alexander shrugged.

"Suit yourself."

Mirabelle sheepishly looked over at Alexander. She saw the seconds ticking as her opportunity to see her father ticked away with it. *This may be my only chance*, she thought. She didn't know what to make of Alexander's story. Part of her longed to see Father again. She wasn't like Alexander. She wanted to know the reasons because no two people did the same thing for the same purpose. But if she left now, she would break her word. And that pained her more than anything. It didn't matter what decision she made. She was losing either way. She looked back at the joint Alexander had offered. It was 5:00 p.m. Her ride was leaving.

"Ask me again in a week. Maybe I'll change my mind."

Alexander looked at her with indifference, then smiled. He started laughing in a few short bursts which quickly changed into an uncontrollable chuckle. That made Mirabelle smile. Then she laughed too. They laughed in the hallway by themselves. That was it. She was staying. Win or lose. Hell or highwater, Mirabelle was determined to see this through. She never once questioned whether she made the right choice. The choice was made. It was one she had to live with, nonetheless.

* * *

Alexander entered their dorm room. Quan stood in front of his desk, his arms crossed. "I heard Mirabelle's staying," he said. "What did you tell her?"

Alexander closed the door and said: "Why does it matter?"

The blue-haired tech wizard paused. He noticed that Quan was standing near his computer, then watched in horror as Quan stepped to the side and revealed something on the screen. It was a poem. "Home Burial" by an earth poet named Robert Frost. A poem about a man and woman who bury their child in the yard and argue about their grief. Quan's eyes were red with anger.

"She told me she never knew you had a sister. She told me to check in on you–to make sure you were alright." He showed the text to Alexander. "Why did you lie to her?"

Alexander stared at Quan's datapad with shock. Then, as his eyes met Quan's, his gaze turned to indifference. His brows were flat, and his stiffened body relaxed.

"Because it helped."

Quan's brow narrowed.

"If she finds out this will come back to haunt you."

"Which is why she will never know." Alexander closed the browser on his computer. "And why you will never tell her."

"Oh yeah? What's stopping me from doing that?"

Alexander raised the joint to his lips, then exhaled.

"Our ride off this planet."

Quan didn't move. Alexander sat back in his chair and typed away like nothing had ever happened.

Preliminary Preparations

One week later, Beretta stood outside beneath the overhang outside the Academy. She smiled with the satisfaction of knowing she had this gang of delinquents by the reins. Derek, Matthew, and Bruce waited in the alleyway with their scanners in their hands. Then Donny burst through the door and joined them, hunched over and out of breath. Beretta's smile faded.

"You're late," she said. "Send me the data."

Donny nodded, typed into his datapad, then slouched against the wall and let gravity bring him to the ground. "I can't keep doing this."

"If you slept during the day you wouldn't be tired."

"But we have to train for the tournament," Donny said.

"Relax," Bruce said. "We have two days left. You can sleep when this is over."

Donny already had his eyes closed. Bruce shook him and brought him up to his feet as Beretta finished analyzing all the data.

"Nothing. You're all free to go. We'll meet again tomorrow."

Donny and Bruce were the first to leave. Derek and Matthew waited for the others to go. When they were gone, Matthew leaned closer to Derek and whispered in case they were being watched.

"You better not have been lying to me," Matthew said.

"I wasn't," Derek said. "We were waiting for the last day. That's all."

"It will have to be before they scan you-know-who."

"It will. Don't worry."

"Can you at least tell me who it is?" Matthew asked.

"No. I've already swapped his name on Beretta's list. It's important that Beretta finds him. Sit tight and everything will work out. I promise."

"It better." Matthew walked away. "I trust you know what awaits us if it doesn't." He slammed the door, leaving Derek alone in the rain to hope that Kairo came through on his promises.

* * *

Alexander scrambled from computer screen to computer screen. Photographs and holopads of information were spread out on the floor as Mirabelle categorized their discoveries. Several wires from the largest screen were connected to a triangular device on Quan's desk to prevent them from being tracked. Alexander was having more success in uncovering the files of missing students than anyone could've predicted—at least, anyone except himself.

"Whoever erased these files clearly wasn't expecting anyone to go looking for them," Alexander said. He bit his pencil after jotting down a code to bypass the next security log.

"Why do you say that?" Mirabelle sorted printed documents of the recovered files.

"Because they stored these files in the same place they keep records of graduates and transfer students. They're not even completely erased." Alexander paused. "It's almost as if they used the memory wipes only on two types of people: those who knew the student directly and those who controlled that student's files. Literally, any could find Alan Jones's profile if they wanted to. But because no one remembers him, no one goes looking for him."

"Why not just erase the file entirely?"

"I'm not sure." Alexander pulled up a file. "You recognize this student?"

Mirabelle leaned closer and stared at the girl with blonde hair and blue eyes.

"That's Beretta!" Then Mirabelle paused. "She's…she's so young."

"Yeah. After she killed Roy Andersen she was transferred here, but she

319

only lasted a year before she got shipped off to Telaris. Changed her last name to Keys back then too. The point is that she's back, and it was easy because they had all her old files saved on this system." He paused. "I think we may have some idea what might be happening on Telaris besides military training." He turned around. "I think they're indoctrinating them too. And then they become mindless, obedient puppets for the Awakening. A perfect army of psychic super soldiers."

Mirabelle backed away from the screen.

"Then even if we found people like Alan, they might not ever be the same." None of them said anything. Then Mirabelle broke the silence. "Were you able to dig up any of the audio files of Zane's…"

"Yeah," Alexander said. "I have it right here. Do you want me to play it?" He turned around and saw Mirabelle shaking her head. Alexander raised a brow. Then his confusion slowly formed into understanding. "I see. I guess not."

* * *

Quan and Derek sparred, but this time, Derek made a mistake. He overextended himself, allowing Quan to twist his blade and knock it out of Derek's hands. Before the blonde brute could move, Quan had the edge of his blade an inch away from his neck. Derek smiled as sweat droplets dripped from his sandy blonde hair.

"Excellent work. You're ready."

Quan lowered his defenses and fell on the mat from exhaustion.

"But we sparred ten times. I only beat you once."

Derek set his weapon against the rack.

"We're not fighting to see who wins. We're fighting to make you better."

Quan stood up and handed the blade to Derek.

"I don't get it."

"Then let me be candid. You haven't been training here long enough to win all your battles, but you're good enough with a blade to make them last longer. There's not a single student at this Academy that could best me in the ring. Each time we step on that platform we'll face another team of two. Stay alive as long as you can, and I'll finish off your opponent when I'm done with mine."

"Kind of a lame role," Quan said.

"We all play our part. You should feel honored to be fighting at all."

"What about Matthew? You worried about him?"

"No. We fought once and it ended in a draw, but because he's too prideful to have a partner, we'll be able to make short work of him." Derek looked around the training room. "This is the last time we'll be here for a while. You all packed?"

"Yeah. Crazy how three weeks can go by so fast. I'm not sure I'm ready."

"You're as ready as you need to be. Remember what we've practiced, keep a cool head, and always stay by my side. Do those things and we won't have any trouble advancing to the Final Four."

Quan looked down at his wristband. *Never. Give. Up.* Then another thought crossed his mind. "Beretta's going to find Kairo any moment now."

Derek nodded.

"I know. Let's hope this works. If it doesn't, we may not even have a fighting chance."

* * *

Later that night, Beretta Hunt found the stage 4 psychic. She stood outside the suspect's room as her eyes widened with excitement upon receiving the report. Because there were two students inside, all she had to do now was sneak in quietly and confirm which student was the one. She snuck inside in her green uniform and saw two students sleeping peacefully in their separate beds. With the swipe of her hand, she held the scanner out in front of the first student. The light flashed green, then the data transferred back to her datapad. Non-psychic. She crept over to the next bed and looked down at the student. She paused. She waited. Then she left the room and quietly shut the door.

* * *

Derek felt a vibration from his datapad.

It was a text from Beretta.

Room 451, Section B, Floor 29.

He snuggled back under the covers. Another text.

NOW.

Derek sat up and eyed his uniform hanging over his chair by his desk. He looked back at his datapad and sighed. "You better know what you're doing, Kairo." Seconds later he changed back into his uniform, grabbed a stun blaster, and slid his scanner in his utility belt. He left without looking back.

* * *

Beretta stood outside the suspect's door in the middle of the residential hallway. She looked worried.

"What's going on?" Derek asked. Beretta just kept shaking her head with her fist clenched. Derek's brow narrowed as he stormed towards his sister. "What did you–"

"Shh! Be quiet," Beretta hissed. "You can't tell anyone."

Derek's heartbeat raced. Beretta, who had been clenching her fist this whole time, revealed what was inside. It was her scanner. And it was shattered.

"I accidentally stepped on it."

Derek was speechless. He watched as she apologetically looked into her older brother's eyes. For the first time in her entire life, she looked afraid.

"I know I've been pushing you all too hard. I got nervous and it broke." She lowered her head. "I'm sorry. But I need you to scan them for me."

"Scan who?"

"Both the students inside. It dropped before I had a chance to even scan them."

Derek's eyes widened. A horrible, nauseous feeling crept in his chest

322

as he pulled out his scanner and set it against the wall. He knew exactly what kind of data would register the second he clicked the button. He tried to think of a way out of this. He had no idea if Beretta was telling the truth. But it didn't matter. If he didn't do the scan, she would grow suspicious. He already made the mistake of coming here in the first place. There was no going back. With a trembling hand, he swallowed a lump in his throat and clicked the button. It flashed green. A second later, after the data registered on his datapad, the scan was complete. They had found a stage 4 psychic.

* * *

Later that night, Derek got a private call from Chief Kalak.

"I never thought I'd be saying this," Kalak said. "But congratulations. Who knew that the son of Mr. Leonardo himself would be the psychic we were searching for? He was hiding right under our noses this whole time."

Matthew, Donny, Bruce, and Beretta all watched Derek beneath the overhang.

"Thank you, sir," Derek said. "I was just doing my job."

"And you did it well. I'm pleased to inform you that the psychic has been safely delivered back to the CDAD and will be interrogated immediately. Expect a call from the Boss sometime next week. We'll be making the trip to Telaris soon and we'll need everyone on standby. In the meantime, good luck in the tournament."

"You're letting me join?"

"I don't see why not? After all, effective today your services at the Academy are obsolete. We will be taking matters with the stage 4 psychic into our own hands from here on out. We'll be in touch. Stay safe out there."

"You too, sir."

The minute he hung up, they celebrated outside and cheered. Bruce and Donny couldn't stop fantasizing about their new sleep schedules. Matthew was glad to see that his chance at fighting in the tournament was still alive.

And Beretta…no one knew the reason behind her smile. But she smiled too. In the end, they all went their separate ways. Later that night, Derek laid his eyes to rest, then opened them. They had bought themselves time. *But how much time?* He thought. How much longer until Kalak saw Kairo for who he was? Until their cover was blown? As he closed his eyes to sleep, he couldn't stop seeing the image of Beretta's shattered scanner. And then her smile. He hoped Kairo knew what he was doing. They didn't need forever. Just a few extra days.

A Hospitable Hotel

It was November 7th. A Thursday. A day of nerves and expectations. The weekend of the Gerumandian Dueling Tournament was one day away. Quan, Alexander, Mirabelle, and Derek rolled their suitcases down the marble hallways of the Academy and out towards the courtyard. They walked past rows of reporters. Cameras flashed from everywhere. Most of them kept their eyes forward as their private shuttle opened its doors. But Alexander relished his short-lived celebrity treatment.

"Thank you! Thank you! You're all too kind!"

"Alexander!" Mirabelle shouted.

He put both hands on his hips and looked to the skies with a smile.

"Take all the pictures you want! It'll last longer!"

Some reporters laughed. Others grew frustrated that he was blocking the shot.

"Who the heck is this guy?"

"Get out of the way!"

Mirabelle grabbed Alexander's arm and yanked him inside the shuttle. It was the most luxurious shuttle Quan, Alexander, and Mirabelle had ever seen. The interior was slick black with neon lights, filled with canisters of ice with fresh drinks, leather seats, and tinted glass windows revealing the afternoon sunset and the distant skyrises. Alexander reclined on the seats with both hands behind his back.

"Oh yeah. I could get used to this."

An automaton stored their luggage in an overhead compartment, then faced them.

"Is there anything I could get you all for the ride to Central Dain?"

Alexander sat up with a huge grin. Within minutes, the automaton had brought him three tubs of ice cream, a couple of cans of soda, and several boxes of snap-candy. He had devoured half of the food by the time the thrusters beneath the shuttle hummed to life and shot them up towards the sky. Quan kept his eyes out the back window, watching the Academy from above. The towering multi-layered campus reflected the golden sunlight off its many windows. He nudged Mirabelle.

"We stood there almost half a year ago."

"Has it been that long?" She asked.

"Time flies when you're making progress."

She turned away. The light from the windows cast a dim shadow on her faded red scar across her nose. Her expression darkened.

"I wish it felt like progress. I feel like a tortoise on a treadmill."

Quan smiled.

"Is the treadmill on or off?"

She laughed, and that was that. They both turned away and sat in silence. Quan felt the weight of the folded piece of paper in his pocket. The rendezvous point from Kairo. He said nothing of it and didn't plan on saying anything. He had promised Dakari five months. And now he had only two more days left.

Derek also looked out the window at the Academy. He had spent six long years there. Never in all his time would he have imagined leaving it for good. He felt relieved to leave a place that had too many foul memories.

"You guys nervous?" Quan asked.

"Nervous?" Alexander shoved another scoop of ice cream in his mouth. "You'll be fine. Derek's gonna carry you to the Final Four." He took another bite. "No offense."

Derek pensively stared off into the distance, his green eyes lost in the city lights. He wore a pine green leather jacket with gold buttons. An ouroboros hung on his breast, glimmering with the fading light from the windows. "That is no reason to be careless. Good things rarely come from wishful thinking."

Mirabelle snatched the last tub of ice cream away from Alexander. "You've had enough."

"Oh, come on, I'm not even fighting!"

"Are you five? What kind of 16-year-old eats ice cream like this?"

"A fun one." He displayed his wallet. "And one who's actually 18."

"You and I both know that's not true."

Alexander snatched the tub back.

"It is to the bartender." He took another bite. "And it is to me."

A projector in the middle of the shuttle prevented Mirabelle from responding. It flashed to life as fanfare music blasted from the speakers. The symbol of the Republic twinkled in the right corner of the screen and showed a man standing in front of Cypher Stadium. He wore silver-plated armor with red lines crossing his chest. The plates on his armor overlapped like reptilian scales. There were tiny power cores on each strap and a dagger strapped to his chest. It was almost identical to the suits the duelers wore—minus the sash on his right shoulder with dozens of medals.

"Good afternoon and congratulations to all combatants in the 32nd Gerumandian Dueling Tournament. I'm Eradicator Lee Arakawa with the 4th platoon. In addition to greeting you this afternoon, I have been instructed to provide a brief overview of this weekend's events. By now you should all be en route to the Warrior's Hospice, a five-star hotel across from Cypher Stadium. Competitors and their supporting team will be staying there overnight or until the Final Four Duel on Sunday. Each room will have an appointed arbitrator to escort you to the arena the following morning to get your exoskeleton suits before the tournament.

"There are several rules all combatants must follow before the tournament begins. I will mention the most pertinent of those rules here. Weapons or battle stimulants from outside the arena are prohibited and will result in immediate disqualification. Students who arrive late to the shuttle will be disqualified. No exceptions. Arbitrators will also conduct searches before each match to ensure that no competitor is in violation of these standards. If you have any questions about these rules or any other formalities, please ask the tournament assistants in the lobby at the

Warrior's Hospice. We are excited to witness another momentous occasion in our Republic's history as students showcase their skills in the biggest event of the year. Good luck, Gerumandians. Eradicator Arakawa signing off."

The shuttle made its descent on the landing zone near the elaborate hotel. Directly across from it was Cypher Stadium: the largest stadium in the Republic. Titan-sized statues of war veterans and Waions were engraved on the surrounding stone walls. A retractable dome covered the top of the stadium where fireworks and confetti would erupt for the newly crowned champion. Quan got chills thinking that such a ceremony could be played for him.

They landed outside the hotel, then grabbed their luggage and followed crowds of other competitors inside. They checked in at the front desk, confirmed their exoskeleton suit sizes, and then took the elevator to their four-bedroom suite on the 30th floor. Quan, Mirabelle, and Alexander dropped their bags in awe the moment the arbitrator opened the door to their room.

Their "room" was the size of a two-story house. It was the most luxurious suite any of them had ever stayed in. It had an expansive living room with four doorways that went to other bedrooms, a kitchen, a fireplace, an entertainment projector, and treadmills by the porch overlooking the stadium. Derek walked to one of the doors and claimed his room without taking notice. He started unbuttoning the gold buttons on his leather jacket, revealing his diamond wristwatch. By the time he got back, the arbitrator was gone, but no one else had moved. He raised a brow.

"Uh, it's ok guys," Derek said. "You can come in."

They immediately rushed in to claim their rooms.

* * *

Banner slammed the door as Kalak sat in the interrogation room. Kairo sat motionless on the other side of the table in his tattered gray robes. His black dreadlocks hung down the sides of his smooth brown skin. He refused to make eye contact with Kalak on the other side. Banner found a cozy spot on the wall and leaned against it with his arms crossed.

"Where's your daddy, now?" Banner asked. "He gonna save you?"

Kalak leaned forward across the table wearing his navy blue buttoned-up uniform.

"What were you doing at the Gerumandian Academy?" Kalak asked.

The heir to L-Transport kept his gaze averted. He didn't respond.

"Still hasn't said anything?" Banner asked.

"Nothing. He's been like this for days. But don't worry. We can find a way to make him break. They always do."

"Break?" Kairo asked. "Oh please, not torture. My father wouldn't want that." Kalak and Banner were silent. "It's been three days. He must be worried sick. Don't I have a phone call or something?"

"You're a psychic," Kalak said. "You don't have rights."

"Right. What about bargaining power?"

Kalak smiled.

"Do tell."

"I have the ships you need to get to Telaris."

"We can find other ways to get you off the planet."

"Using whose starships? The Republic Military? Exodus will follow them and snuff out that little base of yours within minutes. That is, assuming I don't call Dad."

Kalak crossed his arms.

"What do you want?"

Kairo smiled and looked away. "Let me think it over. I'll get back to you in a few days."

The Chief's breath became hot air. He stormed out of the room and slammed the door.

* * *

It was a quiet night at the Warrior's Hospice. Quan sat in a chair on the balcony and gazed at the stadium on the other side of the street. It was dark except for the lamp posts shining on empty spaces in the parking lot. They would be filled tomorrow. That meant the stadium would be filled too. 250,000 people and millions more at home. Their eyes watching him. Someone opened the balcony door and let it close. It was Derek. He took the seat next to him. They stared at the towering stadium and the dazzling city behind it.

"You should sleep."

"I can't," Quan said. "I keep thinking of Matthew."

"We won't face him tomorrow. He's in the opposite bracket."

"We'll have to face him eventually."

"Stop thinking of tomorrow's battles when you're still fighting today's."

"Easier said than done."

"Of course, but you're still going to have to do it."

Quan looked up at the night sky, clouded with a faint gray haze.

"It's so strange to think that Jon's up there somewhere. Away from all this." Quan smiled. "I wonder what would've happened if we were both accepted into the Academy the same year. I'd probably be with him right now. We never would've fought. We'd be friends on a planet far off somewhere, blissfully unaware that two groups of invisible enemies wanted us." Quan sighed. "Every trouble that followed that day could have been avoided."

"I've thought similar things," Derek said. "About my own life. But also, about other people's lives. Like Dakari's."

"What do you mean?"

Derek's expression diminished. The shame on his face was hidden in darkness.

"We were talking one day in our apartment. We talked a lot of days. Every day. But some days he showed me a window into his soul. There was a point in his grief where he almost turned to madness. He was laughing like a madman one day. Then he would stop. Then he would laugh again." Derek paused. "I'll never forget the way he looked at me. There were tears in his eyes. He looked at me and he said: 'A dead wife. A dead son. And all of it could've been avoided if we had just taken that damn drug.'"

They were both silent.

"He laughed even more after that. Until he didn't. Then he looked at me with a serious look on his face. He asked me why I wasn't laughing. I told him I didn't find that funny at all. Then he looked almost angry. He said: 'It is to me.'" Derek shook his head. "He got better after that, but I've never seen a man get that close to madness. Then again, I've never seen a man suffer so much in such a short amount of time." Derek looked out at the city. "He forgave me, but I still feel guilty for what I've done. He can forgive me all he wants, but the things I've done have scarred his life forever. It's hard to feel like you could ever be a good man after doing terrible things like that."

Quan leaned forward in his seat and looked at Derek.

"You're the only reason we're at this tournament."

"And?"

"That's a good thing you've done."

"It won't matter unless we win."

"No. It won't." Quan stood up. "So let's win."

Gallant Gerumandians

Quan learned several things as he waited in the lobby of the Warrior's Hospice.

The first: no one is as prepared for the spotlight as they say they are. Until your shoes have touched the crimson red carpet, your eyes blinded by the flashing, flickering, camera lights, the shouting reporters drowning your own thoughts with never-ending questions, you know nothing of what you've longed for. And when you have it, you're terrified. Quan did not feel like a person as he stood in the lobby of the Warrior's Hospice, looking out on the carpet to the limousine. He felt like a god, the praise of the people causing his brain to flatline with ecstasy. And terror. Because the same people that sang your praises would be spitting your curses in the morning news if you failed.

The second: many other people could have, and quite frankly should have, been in your shoes. Quan knew that he was good, but his fight with Matthew showed that he was far from great, and far less great than other students at the Academy that could have very well been Derek's partner. But he was the one standing here, not them. He had to make the most of it. It was like what Mirabelle had said. He didn't have to be the best every day. Just the best today. For a match. For a minute. And maybe, when he was one swing away from victory, only a second. The greatest duelers weren't the ones great all the time. They were great at the right time.

The third: you're never ready. No one is. But someone's gotta make the long walk.

Might as well be me, Quan thought.

Thousands of cars and hovercrafts filled the lots outside Cypher Stadium. Spectators across New Earth tuned in to the show. Reporters from every media outlet scrambled to the end of the railings like animals. In pairs of two, each competitor walked across the walkway to the private limousine that escorted them to the stadium.

"You ready?" Derek asked.

They stood inside the lobby of the Warrior's Hospice with arbitrators by their sides. Quan could feel the sweat inside his silver exoskeleton suit. It was skintight with extra padding around the joints and sensitive areas. He checked to make sure his energy shield was functioning. It was. Quan turned around and looked at Alexander. He gave a thumbs up. Then he looked at Mirabelle. She smiled.

"Yeah," Quan said. "Let's do this."

Back on the projectors, the camera drones panned out and zoomed in on the walkway extending out from the Warrior's Hospice hotel.

"Ladies and Gentlemen, introducing our competitors with a collective total of 170 bids: Quan Son Jerry and Derek Hunt!"

Quan stepped outside the lobby and into a world of flashing lights. Spectators who had VIP passes raised signs and shouted Derek's name. No one knew who Quan was, so no one cheered for him like they cheered for Derek, but that didn't matter. They were partners. A chill ran down Quan's spine as he walked down the carpet. Adrenaline coursed in his veins. His heart pounded like a drum. He had never felt more alive. He stepped inside the limousine and prepared himself for the first day of the tournament.

"And now for our final competitor of the evening. He's the son of the legendary wartime General Carter Hunt, the youngest student to ever achieve the ranking of Juggernaut at the Gerumandian Academy, and the first competitor to join a tournament on his own. With a total of 250 bids: Matthew Hunt!"

An uproar from reporters and fans alike emerged on a scale that no one had ever seen, but Matthew Hunt remained unphased. He walked down the red carpet with his crisp blonde hair swiped back, his green eyes possessed with hunger. Even though he walked alone, his presence took up more space than any other team. To him, the world went silent in its noise. He heard only the sound of his own breath. He saw only the title of the immaculate soldier being engraved in his own name. He walked with the confidence of someone who had already won, because in Matthew's mind, he already had. He shut the limousine door by himself. He was ready.

While the competitors made their way to the stadium in their limousines, Mirabelle and Alexander sat on the couch in their luxurious hotel room. Alexander ordered several ice chests of drinks, a buffet of shrimp, roasted lamb, mashed potatoes, pepperoni pizza, and more food than he could ever eat in a single day. With the tournament having just begun, Alexander raised his glass of cider.

"To us," he said. "Because we're awesome."

Mirabelle paused. Then they clinked their glasses together.

"Derek is going to kill you if he finds out."

"Well, then, we just won't tell him, now will we?"

"That's gonna be hard to do, considering that you put all this on his tab."

A long receipt hung over the arm of the couch. Alexander nervously laughed and tucked it away in the fold of the cushion. "Worry about that later. Wouldn't want to miss the game."

Several commentators appeared on the screen in a booth inside the stadium, the same booth that Alexander planned on raiding tomorrow. Behind both men, a dozen platforms hovered above the pit of water in the center of the stadium.

"Good morning everyone! My name is Chuck Haven."

"I'm Haider Anobai."

"And you're watching the 32nd Annual Gerumandian Dueling Tournament."

Quan and Derek emerged from a dark tunnel and stepped into the light of the stadium. They stood on the outer stone walkway surrounding the hovering platforms. Quan nearly froze in the procession as he saw the cheering crowd of 250,000 people, a crowd of colors, banners, signs, and lights. Then he kept walking forward.

The commentators proceeded to describe the rules of the game as several competitors walked along the sidelines around the stadium. There were 68 dueling teams total split up in a single-elimination bracket. Opponents were inversely matched based on the number of bids they had received from instructors. Each match lasted until one team could knock the other two competitors off the hovering platform and into the pit of water below. There were six rounds leading up to the Final Four, where the last four teams faced off in a battle royale on a larger platform in the center of the stage. That match would take place tomorrow, but by the end of the day, four teams would remain. Because Derek and Matthew were in separate brackets, the chances of them facing off in the Final Four were extremely high. That is if they both made it that far.

"Six rounds," Derek said. They sat on a bench on the stone sidelines on the ground level. The crowd cheered above and around them. "Win those rounds and we move on."

They saw Matthew Hunt on the other side of the stadium. Several trainers double-checked his equipment as he stretched out on the walkway. Quan looked around the stadium with wide eyes. Fans cheered in the stands. Their shouts echoed in the massive enclosure as the overhead speakers blared pregame music. A jumbotron displayed statistics of today's duelers and matches above them as more competitors strapped on their equipment on the walkway. An arbitrator approached them.

"You'll be fighting your first round on platform B in five minutes."

"Got it," Derek said.

They both paused and took in the liveliness of the crowd one last time.

"I've been wanting to fight in this tournament my entire life." Quan looked down at his wristband in his hands. "I was supposed to join with Jon. I know we haven't known each other very long, but if it means anything, you're not a bad second choice."

Derek smiled.

"Never thought I'd be fighting with a Pit Dog, but as far as newbies go, you ain't half bad." Derek stood up and strapped his helmet over his head. "We should head over." He watched as the walkways extended from the sidelines to the platform. "It's starting."

Quan looked down at his wristband one last time, then dropped it in his duffel bag. He strapped on his helmet and joined Derek by the walkway. He took a step forward as the dark waves churned beneath him. He looked up and kept walking forward.

* * *

There were plenty of competitors to be feared that day–but not as much as Matthew. Each elimination was worthy of a highlight reel, but there were some notable moments. A girl charged at Matthew from behind while he fought one opponent, then he dodged her swing and slashed her in the back, colliding her into her partner and sending them flying off the edge. Drones circling the arena displayed the recently eliminated team. A voice boomed from the loudspeakers across the stadium.

"And Matthew Hunt dominates the first match with two knockdowns in thirty seconds! I don't believe it!"

"Should we really be surprised? Matthew's been training for this tournament his entire life on what we call–the road to the immaculate soldier: the tournament's most esteemed title to the dueler with the most knockdowns and victor of the Final Four."

Another match started. Two duelers charged Matthew. He blocked both their swings with the same blade, kicked one, then punched the other across the helmet. He kicked one off the edge, then swept the legs of his partner, dragged him by the collar and tossed him into the waves with a thundering crash. Another boom erupted in the arena: "Matthew Hunt. Four knockdowns."

And then the next match. Matthew Hunt spun in between two competitors, using both sides of his blade to simultaneously block both their attacks. He kicked one in the gut and slammed his blade into the chest of his partner. Matthew ducked as the combatant charged but was flipped over to the ground. Matthew ripped his e-blade from his hand, used it to catch the other opponents' blade in an X shape, crisscrossed his blades against his chest, and then knocked both opponents into the water. Another boom:

"Matthew Hunt. Six knockdowns."

In another match, Matthew sidestepped and vaulted over the swings of both duelers. He stretched his body back as one dueler charged forward. Matthew grabbed his blade from his hand, twisted his arm, then used him as a human shield to block the other opponent's blows. Matthew threw him off the edge, then swung both blades around his body like helicopter blades. The last dueler backed away, then charged. That was a mistake. Matthew pinned his blade to the ground by jutting both blades down in an X shape, then kicked him in the chest. Matthew chopped him up with five swings and finished him off with a blow to the chest, sending him flying off the edge.

Matthew outstretched his arms and faced the crowd with both blades in his hand. "Give me a challenge!" He stared into the camera drone. "Give me Derek Hunt!"

There was nothing quite like Matthew's dominant fighting style. But Derek Hunt was a close second. Quan used a double-bladed katana but held it in the center like a spear to keep the opponents back. Derek dodged both their attacks, parried the last strike, then struck both opponents in the chest, disabling their shields. He finished with a roundhouse kick, sending them both falling into the water. They won in 40 seconds.

"Wow," Quan said. "Guess you don't need me."

"The first round's always the easiest."

The buzzer sounded. Their second match began.

Derek rolled away and led the combatant in his direction. Quan dodged the other opponent and backed away towards the edge, blocking each attack. Derek and the other combatant lost their blades and ended up getting tangled together, each trying to put each other in a chokehold. Quan defended the blow as his attacker lunged behind him and tried to disable Quan's shields. Quan backed away towards the center of the platform. He held his blade out, then flinched as the dueler started pressing him toward the edge. He kept his footwork steady and deflected each blow.

Derek struggled to pin the attacker to the ground not far from where Quan was fighting. He punched the competitor across the face, stunning him, then sprung up and lunged for his blade. He fell to the ground as the competitor grabbed his leg and jerked him to the ground. Derek turned around and slashed across the competitor's face mask, creating a large enough eruption to knock him off the edge.

"Derek!"

Quan staggered back towards the edge. Derek ran and slashed the combatant in the back before he could make his final strike. Quan watched the boy fall off the platform with a splash. A boom erupted. "Derek Hunt. Four knockdowns."

Quan put both hands on his knees.

"These guys are too fast."

Derek gripped Quan by the straps of his suit. "Snap out of it! We have four rounds left! Keep fighting!"

The buzzer sounded. The next match began.

Derek and Quan walked towards the center of the platform with their e-blades in a defensive posture. Their opponents encircled them in the center and surrounded them like patient vultures. Quan carefully moved at the same pace as Derek as they waited to strike. They had prepared for a scenario like this hundreds of times. Quan thought back to his miserable failure at Silverside and his lack of contribution last match. He would not let it happen again.

"Now!" Derek shouted.

They both charged. Quan swung and caught his opponent off balance as their weapons sparked in a flurry of grinding steel. Derek eased around his opponent and moved as fluid as water. He side-stepped then slashed across his visor, the blade slicing and crunching as he then swung for his opponent's pressure points. Several spots of his opponent's energy shield glowed bright red as Derek knocked him off the platform with a finishing stroke. Quan backed away from his attacker, parried each blow, then lunged forward and struck him in the shoulder, then across his chest twice. The combatant froze, allowing Quan to walk past him and slam him in the back, knocking him off the edge. A boom echoed in the arena.

"Derek Hunt. Five knockdowns."

"Quan Son Jerry. One knockdown."

Derek raised both hands in the air.

"There we go, buddy! You're on the board!"

They high-fived each other as a bridge extended out from the walkway of the stadium to the platform. They walked back and removed their helmets as other competitors moved into the arena. They both took a swig of water, then looked at each other. Derek raised three fingers and smiled.

"Three more to go."

A boom echoed in the arena.

"Matthew Hunt. Eight knockdowns."

A fire was lit in Derek's eyes.

"And only two more for him." He stood up and grabbed his e-blade. "Let's go work on a few moves."

Quan put his towel over his shoulders.

"But we just finished!"

"It'll be good to keep moving. Come on."

It didn't matter if they were in the ring or out of it–Derek kept the same mentality. They practiced several fighting forms on the sidelines and stretched to keep themselves in top shape. And then when they entered the ring, even though the competition got better, it was as if Derek was getting better each round. He had a veracity that no one could match, a speed no one could keep up with, and strength that every student in the arena could hope to rival. Except maybe for his brother. Matthew and Derek stole the show. And when they won their last round of the day, Quan could barely stand as the arbitrators raised the arms of the members of the last four teams. Derek and Matthew stood tall. They stood like their lives depended on it. In a way, they did. But it was official. Quan and Derek were advancing to the Final Four. They were moving on.

Problems at the Party Sphere

Several hours later, Derek and Quan made it back to the Warrior's Hospice. There were many things they had to do before they could return to the hotel. They showered, returned their armor, then attended a press conference in downtown Dain. They were fitted in crisp dress suits and were given a private escort to the R-Sports Headquarters where they were interviewed by sports commentators. Quan let Derek do most of the talking. He wasn't exactly in the mood. Of course, he didn't show that on camera, and it certainly didn't stop Alexander from throwing a party the second they stepped in the back into their hotel room. There were balloons, confetti, and streamers hanging from the ceiling. Alexander blew a party horn and stood on top of the kitchen counter. Funk music played from the speakers in the background.

"Surprise!!"

Derek shut the door.

"But we already knew you were here." He looked at the balloons. "It's a boy?"

"I had no part in this," Mirabelle said. "I told him this was a stupid idea."

"They were all out of normal balloons," Alexander said. "But still. Not a bad setup, right?" Derek walked past Alexander and paused the music. "Hey! What's going on?!"

"We didn't win anything so there's nothing to celebrate." Derek started to undo his tie then froze when he saw the mountains of dishes stacked on top of the cart in the living room. He walked over to the couch and grabbed the receipt that Alexander had not-so-discreetly hidden in the couch. "587 recs!! How much food did you eat?!"

Alexander's face went pale.

"Too much."

"I'm not a walking bank."

"No, but your Dad is."

Derek crumpled the receipt in his hand. "The point is that we don't celebrate until we win! Don't any of you understand this?"

No one said anything.

"We have to win the Final Four, and it's not like we have an easy lineup." Derek double tapped his datapad and showed a list of the contestants. "We still have to face the Cobra Twins, Alisha Armstrong and Maxwell Draymond, and to no one's surprise, Matthew." Derek pulled his tie out of his collar and folded it over the couch. "Now if you'll excuse me, I'm going to take an ice bath." He retreated into his room and shut the door behind him.

Mirabelle and Alexander looked over at Quan.

"What's up with that guy, am I right?" Alexander said. "Come on. You, my friend, need to unwind, kick your feet up, watch a show."

Quan walked away from Alexander and went silently towards his room. "Not now." He shut the door behind him.

Mirabelle walked back out to the balcony and shut the door behind her. Alexander stood silently in the living room with the party horn in his hand. A streamer fell from the ceiling. He started to clean up and tuck the decorations away. A few minutes later, Alexander barged into their room. Quan threw a piece of paper in the drawer by the bed and slammed it shut. Alexander paused, raising a brow.

"Everything alright?"

Quan froze at the edge of the bed, his back turned away from Alexander.

"Yeah." He looked up at the window. "Just fine."

Alexander looked at the drawer, then slowly left the room.

* * *

That next day on Saturday morning, someone knocked on the door. Derek left his room in gym shorts and a white tee as Quan stepped outside in jeans and a plain maroon t-shirt. Alexander wore the same old baggy pants and a white hoodie. Mirabelle wore a yellow leather jacket and jeans. None of them were exactly in a talking mood. Derek opened the door as everyone else crowded around him. No one could believe their eyes.

"Good afternoon," Officer Mocroft said. "I heard you two advanced to the final four. Congratulations." He pulled out an envelope from his coat. "I wish I could say I was here to chat, but I was sent here to deliver invitations."

Derek grabbed the envelope and tore it open.

"What is this?"

"Every year there's a party before the Final Four in a club called the 'Party Sphere.' All competitors enrolled in the tournament are invited. Each year there's a pretty good turnout. It's especially common for the Final Four teams to attend as well."

"A party?" Alexander asked. "But you're an officer."

"Who says officers can't have a good time? Squad supports are invited too. It starts at 5:00 p.m and goes until 8:00. If you're interested, a private shuttle will arrive at 4:30. It leaves at 4:35. Don't be late. If you don't plan on attending, simply say the word and I'll remove you from the list."

Derek snatched the tickets away from Alexander.

"Sorry, but we're not interested. We have other things to do."

"Matthew will be there. It'd be a shame for only one of the Hunt brothers to show up. I'm sure people are expecting you." Mocroft shoved the tickets away. "Keep them. If you change your mind you can always contact my agent on the business card inside. I hope to see you there."

Without another word, Officer Mocroft walked down the elaborate hallway of the Warrior's Hospice. Alexander stuck his head out of the room and waved goodbye one last time, then ducked back inside as Derek slammed the door. Quan, Alexander, and Mirabelle waited for his response as he clenched the tickets in his hand.

"We're going to that party," Derek said. Alexander leaped in excitement, then stood up straight as Derek turned around and threw the tickets on the counter. "But we're not staying for long."

* * *

Back in the CDAD, Kairo Leonardo lay bloody and bruised on the floor, gasping for breath. He tilted his head towards the dominating lights of the interrogation room and struggled to move in the straitjacket. Banner knelt over him and gripped him by the collar, staring into his eyes with a menacing smile.

"They say that Leonardos bleed gold!" He punched Kairo across the face another time, his knuckles crunching into his bulbous tomato-colored skin. "How disappointing." He threw Kairo on the ground, who thudded against the wall. "How long did you honestly think this little bluff would last?"

Kairo sat motionless on the floor. A trickle of red blood dripped down his chin. "I don't understand…they say psychics are resistant…"

"Maybe to mind-snares. But did you really think the Boss wouldn't be able to see through those fake brain waves of yours?" Banner scowled. "Gimme a break, kid."

Kalak faced the wall and was fuming with anger. Banner turned around and wiped the excess blood on his hand with a towel.

"What do you want us to do? We could put another bounty on his head."

"What good will that do?" Kalak asked. "Derek has a datapad. If he sees he's a national fugitive on the news he'll just run away. If we send in too many arbitrators someone will warn him." He typed something into his datapad. "Derek Hunt has proven his rebellious nature to the Awakening twice now. He clearly knows the stage 4 psychic and is hiding him or her from us. We need to take a more tactical approach."

* * *

In his penthouse at Cypher Tower, Carter Hunt reclined in a leather chair by the fire and received a call. There were portraits of himself on the walls, mounted heads of Waions, rifles, and blades decorating the scene. And of course, engraved above the fireplace, the Hunt family crest: a snake with its tail in its mouth. The Ouroboros. Beretta Hunt meditated on a floor mat as a gentle breeze snuck into their living room from the back porch. Carter's voice was grating and harsh, but he spoke softly as the fire cast shadows on his face, hiding the darkness in his eyes. He hung up and swirled his glass of gin.

"Beretta?"

Beretta's blue eyes opened.

"Yes, father?"

A grin crept onto Carter's rough leathery face.

"Derek is in need of some discipline."

Beretta smiled, then stood up from the mat.

"Would you like me to take care of it?"

"That would be lovely."

Minutes later, Beretta Hunt changed into her graphene fiber combat suit, strapped on her military boots, slung two e-blades over her back, and slid a pistol by her side.

"Do not hold back," Carter said. "If he refuses to speak, let him be silenced."

Beretta bowed.

"I will. Goodbye, father."

She left without another word. Carter Hunt took a sip of gin and smiled.

* * *

A few hours later, Alexander, Quan, Derek, and Mirabelle were dressed for the party. Derek and Quan wore the same tuxedos they had worn to the press conferences yesterday. With a few minutes of ironing, they were ready to go. Alexander bought a white suit with a black tie from a tailor downtown. And Mirabelle wore a dazzling blue cashmere dress with ebony heels. She had applied some makeup to cover up her acne and hide

344

the faded scar across her nose. The slight curls of her luscious auburn hair sat delicately on her slender shoulders, and her eye shadow gently matched her brown eyes. Quan thought about complimenting her but was embarrassed to say anything. So he didn't.

Meanwhile, as everyone else finished getting ready, Alexander crept around to the dresser Quan had stored something in the night before. He kept looking back over his shoulder to make sure no one was watching. When he was sure he was alone, he opened the dresser and laid eyes on the note inside. He unfolded it and started reading the text.

In the other room, Mirabelle straightened the end of Quan's tie and took a step back. They stood so close that Quan could see the tiny details in her diamond earrings and smell the jasmine–rose scent of perfume. She stood there for a moment with her head tilted to the side.

"You look nice," she said, averting eye contact.

Quan smiled.

"Thanks." He cleared his throat. "You too."

Derek came out of his room in his suit. Alexander came out of his room too. He looked angry. Quan's expression darkened. Their eyes met for a second and not a second longer. There was a harsh glance of spite in Alexander's silver gaze. He walked with clenched fists and stormed towards the door. Quan didn't think much of it. But at the same time, that image remained engraved in his mind.

"Shuttle's leaving in five," Derek said. "Let's go."

Alexander followed him without a word. Then Quan and Mirabelle followed too. After a short limo ride, they walked into the center of the club. There was interior red lighting, distant conversations, the clinking of drinks by the bar, and the sight of teenagers on the dance floor. Some instructors and officers mingled in the upper-level suites. The name of the club was fitting. It was shaped like a sphere. In the center was the dance floor, on the outer rings were bars, booths, and private lounge rooms that could be accessed by the outer stairwell. There was nothing but good vibes. That was until Derek walked away.

"Where you going?!" Alexander asked.

"To find Matthew. I'll be back soon."

They stood motionless as they watched him disappear up the stairwell.

"His loss," Alexander said. "Let's get a booth."

They walked across the changing colors of the dance floor, then scooted on both sides of the violet booth and sat around a glass table illuminated by white lights from underneath. Within a few minutes, they had three glasses of iced water.

"You're joking, right?" Alexander asked.

"We're not here to get wasted," Quan said. "And we're underage."

"Screw that. We have fake IDs."

Alexander walked towards the bar. Mirabelle shook her head and sighed.

"I don't know why we came here."

"Like we have anything better to do," Quan said.

"Are you kidding me? We could double-check the slideshow. We could make a backup recording in case they cut the live stream. We could make sure Dakari knows where to pick us up tomorrow after the tournament. There are literally a million better things we could be doing."

An opportunity for Quan to respond was stolen by the approach of a young, drunk dueler. He was around their age and stopped by their table with a few of his buddies. He bit his lip and leaned in over the table, eyeing Mirabelle closely.

"And they told me I had to travel overseas to study a broad!" Each of his friends laughed as he leaned in closer to Mirabelle. "Name's Dave. What can I–" He paused as if a moment of sobriety broke through his drunken haze. "Ah forget it." He looked at Quan. "Not very attractive for your sidepiece."

Quan stood up. "What'd you say?!"

"Wait. I take it back. She's *perfect* for a dueler like you."

"And what's that supposed to mean?"

"It means you suck." Dave and his friends laughed. "You really proved that with the best dueler carrying you on his back, anything's possible!" They kept laughing as Quan tightened his fists. "Nah, but for real boys. I was kicking his ass until Derek saved him. If this guy were with anyone else, he wouldn't have made it past the first round."

Mirabelle grabbed Quan before he could throw a punch. They howled with laughter and started backing away.

"Even his girl fights his battles! This guy's a joke!"

Dave and his buddies kept hitting each other and making jokes as they made their way back to the bar. Quan's brow furrowed as he looked at Mirabelle.

"What are you doing?!"

"Saving your chance to fight tomorrow."

"While making me look like the biggest idiot in the Party Sphere."

"Dave already beat you to that one."

They both paused. Mirabelle saw a shadow of Quan's old self in his eyes, the same gaze of condescension on anyone who wasn't himself. It was the self he was before Matthew showed him that he was the better fighter. That day Quan had come to terms with this. But now his restlessness had returned. He walked away without a word. Mirabelle groaned.

"Ugh! Quan! Hold on!"

She followed him as he shoved people out of his way and stormed up the stairs.

Rooftop Ruminations

The rooftop balcony was the only part of the building that departed from the Party Sphere's circular shape, jutting out around the circumference of the structure to provide an overlook of downtown Dain. Mirabelle joined Quan behind the railing and looked up to the stars but couldn't see them. Instead, she saw big buildings with hovercrafts buzzing in air traffic lanes. And above all of that, a cloudy, faint, yellow haze. *There was no such thing as a city of stars*, Mirabelle thought. *You got the city lights or the night sky. But you could never have both.* She didn't know why that was the first thing that came to her mind when she gazed out the overlook with Quan. But it was.

"Why do you think it is that we always end up talking on rooftops?" She asked.

They both looked over the edge. It was only a 100-foot drop from the top of the sphere, but beyond that, the lower city was at least 1000 feet below them.

"I don't know," Quan said. "Maybe cause there's a better view." He paused. "And sometimes it's just nice to get away."

"You wanna talk about it?"

"What would I want to talk about?"

"You seemed upset."

"Upset? Did you hear what they said about you?!"

Mirabelle's expression changed. She couldn't imagine that Quan had done those things out of concern for her. In some ways it was flattering. In other ways, it felt weird. She didn't want anyone's pity. But she did like having friends.

"I appreciate the gesture, Quan, but I don't need you to fight my own battles."

"But you weren't going to do anything."

"No. I wasn't."

"Why?"

She paused. Her fingers gripped the railing.

"My father always told me that part of growing up is knowing what battles deserve a fight and which ones deserve your silence." She looked at Quan. "I never fight with fools. That's not the first time I've been told things like that. You get used to it after a while. Then you develop thick skin, and then one day you stop caring."

They stood in silence.

"I guess that makes sense. Sorry."

"You don't have to apologize. You did nothing wrong."

Quan's smiled waned.

"But Dave was right. I made a fool of myself."

"Relax. You're at a club. No one is going to remember that."

"I was talking about the tournament."

"You're being too hard on yourself. At the end of the day is it really going to matter who had more knockdowns if we still win? Sometimes it's better to be in the fight, even if the fight isn't as glamorous as you thought it would be. It never is."

"You really believe that?"

Mirabelle's eyes were dark and distant.

"Some days I do. Some days I don't." Another stretch of silence passed between them. A server gave them some glasses, to which they quickly thanked him and took a sip of cider. Students came and went from the rooftop, but they stayed. They looked up into the sky. "I can't wait to leave."

Quan looked over at her and smiled.

"Yeah. Me too."

* * *

Back in the Party Sphere, Derek and Matthew sat at a table with no drinks. They sat motionless across from one another as the music reverberated in the background.

"We need to talk," Matthew said.

Derek smiled. "Worried you're gonna lose tomorrow?"

"No. You have bigger problems to worry about. They're onto you."

"Wait, did I hear that right? Did you really just show that you care about my wellbeing?"

"Not exactly. If they learn what you did, it's only a matter of time before they learn that I was involved." He leaned across the table as Quan and Mirabelle walked back into the club. "What are you gonna do when I turn Quan in tomorrow?"

Derek smiled.

"He's not sticking around once we win."

"Bold of you to assume you even have a chance." Matthew stood up. "I've kept him a secret for months, but tomorrow his time runs out." He paused. "I trust you know what's going to happen to you when the Awakening finds out you're a traitor."

Derek stood up too.

"And I hope you bring your A-game tomorrow. You're going to need it."

With those words, Derek walked away and joined Alexander in the booth. Matthew stood with both fists clenched, then left the Party Sphere without a word.

* * *

Later that night, Alexander gathered everyone in the living room. Their eyes were wide with anticipation. It was almost 10:00 p.m. Alexander reached into the pouch in his hoodie and pulled out a piece of paper. He threw it on the desk and crossed his arms.

"Someone lied to us."

Silence. Quan leaned forward and tried to grab the paper, but Derek grabbed it first. He unfolded it while Mirabelle read it too. Quan looked

350

away. He had been wondering why Alexander was acting so strange at the Party Sphere. Apparently now they were about to find out why.

"Care to explain yourself, Quan?" Alexander asked. "Or should I explain for you?"

Derek and Mirabelle looked at Quan.

"What is this?" Derek asked.

"It's an out," Alexander said. "A way off New Earth without any need for a tournament." He looked at Quan. "How long have you known about this?"

"It doesn't matter."

"Really? Cause I think it does."

"I made a deal with Dakari. Five months."

"We only made that deal with Dakari because we thought the tournament was our only chance of leaving! This changes things. Besides, I've given him plenty of information."

"But you haven't relayed the broadcast," Mirabelle said. "That was part of the arrangement. He's counting on you."

"You don't have a voice here. I'm talking with Quan right now."

"*Excuse me?*" Mirabelle stood up. "I've been working on that simulation for months so I could fly the Sojourner and you tell me that I don't have a say in this?!"

"Not anymore. We don't need you."

"Alexander!" Quan shouted. "What's going on with you, man!?"

"I'm being *realistic.*"

"You're being an asshole," Mirabelle said. "Wasn't this your plan anyway?"

"It was. But back then the Sojourner was our only way off New Earth, and it was a flimsy plan to begin with. This route guarantees that we make it off Dain alive."

Derek sighed.

"He's right." Derek looked at Quan. "Matthew knows about you. I wouldn't be surprised if he's already arranged a plan for your capture tomorrow. We'll be lucky if we live long enough to board the Sojourner and escape with our lives."

Mirabelle shook her head.

"Unbelievable. And here I thought you changed."

"I have changed!" Derek shouted. "We can bring Dakari with us."

"He won't leave," Mirabelle said. "Not until Zane gets justice."

"Why don't we ask him?"

An old wave of anger rose in Mirabelle again.

"You're a coward."

Derek's eyes widened.

"A coward?"

"Yes. A coward. The only person you're loyal to is yourself."

"How *dare* you?!" Derek shouted.

"Am I wrong?!" Mirabelle shouted. "Wouldn't Zane still be alive if only you had the courage to say something and not watch Matthew shoot a blaster in his face!?"

Derek's eyes welled with tears.

"I've told you a million times! That was *not* my doing! Do you think I asked to be a psychic? Do you think I wanted to join the Awakening?! Unlike you, I didn't have the *nobility* of watching the people I love die! I had two choices! My life or his!"

"Then you chose wrong."

Derek's face fumed red with anger.

"You have no idea what you're talking about. I left everything I had to join this cause! I could've bagged Quan up the night I scanned him, but I gave him a fighting chance. And here you are criticizing me from an ivory tower complaining about how I haven't done enough. Do you think I wanted Zane to die? I did everything I could to avert that case, but Matthew wouldn't budge! I come from a family of psychos and the one time I do something good you have the nerve to tell me it's not enough!"

"Because you haven't finished the job! Just finish it and get out of my life!"

No one moved. Mirabelle's face grew red. She hated that she had spoken what she had felt for months. He was the living reminder of Zane's death, the one who could've changed it all. She meant every word she said, but regretted saying it, nonetheless.

"I'm going for a walk," Derek said.

He stormed towards the door as Mirabelle lowered her head. He reached for the door handle, then turned around. "If she isn't gone by the time we get back, I'm withdrawing from the tournament. Then maybe you all could fight your own battles for once." He slammed the door, leaving them all in a stupefied silence.

Alexander unfolded the piece of paper.

"As I was saying…"

* * *

Derek walked the hallways of the Warrior's Hospice by himself. He kept both hands in his suit pockets. His head was arched low, and his eyes were an amalgam of grief, anger, and guilt. He hated Mirabelle. He was sure of it. Gerumandians were taught how to respond to tragedy in healthy ways, like true soldiers. You could never let it break you, or else you would break yourself, and then others. Mirabelle had let her tragedy flow freely, wrecking her life and everyone else's. It was the invincible argument, the scaffold where reason went to die. *It doesn't matter what I do*, Derek thought. *I could kill Matthew, the Awakening, and bring back every missing student–she'd still drag me to the gallows.* That was the price you paid for forgiveness. If the wrongdoer hated you, they could wield your wrongdoings against you like a club for the rest of your days. And what could you even say in response?

He continued to walk the endless beige carpeted hallways, beneath dim lights, and through narrow passageways. They seemed to stretch on forever. And there was one thing that contributed to their mysteriousness: they were empty. With only four teams left, most students and their trainers had been sent back home. In a way, Derek was walking through a hotel of ghosts. There wasn't a single soul on the 30th floor. That's when he heard the chime. The elevator opened. He figured Mirabelle followed him.

"You better be here to apologize," Derek said.

Then he turned around. A girl had followed him. A girl in a combat suit with a brown shawl, crystal blue eyes, and a sandy blonde ponytail.

"Why would I ever apologize to you?" Beretta asked.

Derek tensed.

"You shouldn't be here."

"I can go where I want. The Boss wants to see you."

"It can wait."

"I'm afraid not."

Beretta examined her nails and sighed when Derek didn't move.

"Very well. Scarred it is."

Beretta drew a silenced blaster from her side and fired. A bright red beam flew in Derek's direction and into a portal in his palm. He created another portal in his right hand and shot it back in her direction. It flew over Beretta's head and incinerated the plaster in the wall. Derek's eyes widened.

"It's not set to stun!?"

Beretta whipped the pistol around and fired again. Derek flowed the blast back again. She dropped the pistol and redirected the blast back in Derek's direction, catching them in a loop of recycling blaster fire.

"Who do you think I am?!" She shouted.

Beretta retracted the red beam into a portal, ending the cycle of blaster fire flow between them. She ran towards Derek and flung several throwing knives out of a tear in her palm. Derek absorbed the knives in a tear as Beretta charged, then leaped into the air and punched several flames through tears in her hands by cocking her fists. Derek crossed both arms in an X and manipulated the matter around him to form an energy shield, which turned from gold to red with each incoming fire blast. It broke as Beretta landed into the shield with a kick and knocked Derek onto the ground.

Derek used the momentum of his fall to spring back up, then snapped his fingers and used a tear to grab an e-blade the second Beretta swung down towards his chest. Their blades clashed in a fury of steel. They swung overhead, spun around each other, then swung back. Beretta yelled with rage and swept underneath Derek's feet as he leaped into the air and kicked her in the chest with both feet, knocking her back down the hallway. He hit the ground hard, then sprung back up on his feet and readied his blade.

"You're better than I thought." Beretta dropped her blade. She held out both fists instead. "But not good enough." She contorted her fingers like she had arthritis. Several spiraling portals emerged in both hands as she planted one foot forward and punched in his direction. A claw-shaped grappling hook launched towards Derek but went between his legs.

"You missed!"

Beretta smiled, then contorted her arm back. Using the same portal she used to launch the hook, she used retraction to pull it back. Derek jumped as the grappling hook retracted under his feet and went back into Beretta's portal. He created another metal shield in front of himself as Beretta fired the grappling hook in his direction. He grunted and flew back into the wall as the hook tore through the shield and scraped his shirt. It missed his skin by inches. He got back up as Beretta retracted the grappling hook, taking the shield along with it. Derek pulled a blaster from his tear and fired at the chain connecting the hook. It shattered and fell across the floor, giving Derek just enough time to fire, but not enough time to dodge the next grappling hook that flew out the next portal. He felt something clamp into his leg and groaned in pain. The blaster fell from his hand. He looked down.

The claws of the grappling hook had clamped into his flesh.

Derek reached for the blaster to fire at the chain, but it was too late. Beretta retracted the grappling hook, tearing a chunk of flesh out of Derek's skin. Blood splattered on the beige carpet like a popped water balloon. He howled in pain, losing all balance as Beretta fired another hook into his left leg, then quickly retracted and ripped out another layer of Derek's skin. The skin on his shins peeled off like drywall and sprayed blood on the walls. He hammered both fists together as a last resort. An energy shield covered every square inch of the hallway between them. Derek used the time to grab his blaster as Beretta fired two more grappling hooks at the same time to puncture the energy shield. Derek shot Beretta in the shoulder. She staggered into the wall and collapsed on the ground. Derek hit the ground with a thud.

He typed into his datapad until a boot crushed the screen. He looked up from the splintered glass and saw Beretta towering over him. Derek tried to grab her leg but was kicked across the face. Beretta snatched his blaster away from him.

"I'm sorry to be the one to tell you this, but Dad lied." She flicked the charge on the blaster and aimed its silver barrel between Derek's eyes. "I was always the favorite."

A blaster fired. Beretta froze, her pupil's dilating, her hands dropping the pistol. She fell face forward on the ground, revealing Matthew at the other end of the hallway. Derek gasped in the corner as he watched his brother approach him.

"You..." Derek gasped for breath. "You killed her!?"

"Don't worry." Matthew aimed the blaster at Derek. "It's set to stun."

Matthew fired. Derek fell over and the world went black.

* * *

"You think he's coming back?" Alexander asked.

They had been waiting in the living room for two hours. Their collective shock had turned to dread. Mirabelle sat on the couch with her head held low.

"I don't know," Quan said. "He hasn't answered any of my texts. I couldn't find him in the hotel either. I'm guessing he went for a walk in the city."

Alexander lost all his joviality. He sat in one of the chairs perfectly still, his hands pensively folded together. His eyes, distant, dark, and angry.

"If we don't have Derek tomorrow we're screwed." Alexander picked up the piece of paper with the rendezvous point. "We need to think a lot more seriously about this."

"We promised Dakari five months," Quan said. "I won't break my word."

"You already have. When we left Silverside, you promised me that when the first opportunity to leave New Earth made itself available, we'd take it."

"And I'm keeping that promise. The Sojourner was our first opportunity."

"But now there's a better one."

"What difference does one day make?"

"All the difference if we die!"

Their eyes met in a tense stalemate.

"This isn't over yet," Quan said.

"You can't win alone," Alexander said.

"What if he doesn't have to win?" Mirabelle asked.

Quan and Alexander turned around.

"What do you mean?" Alexander asked. "He has to win."

"Not necessarily. What if Quan records his speech in a video?"

"And how is that going to help?" Alexander asked.

"Simple. You made a video with pictures of missing students, audio of Matthew's confession, and Zane's death. You're a smart guy. Why don't you just record a video of Quan giving the speech tonight and relay it over the evidence? If he wins, he gives the speech live. If he loses we just use the recording."

"So you're telling me it never mattered whether I win or lose?" Quan asked.

"Oh yes it does," Alexander said. "You going to air that footage yourself?"

"Of course not," Quan said. "You are."

"Not anymore."

Quan and Mirabelle fell silent. They didn't have the strength to speak. They stared at Alexander, at the kid whose silver eyes had normally looked so fondly upon everyone else, whose brow now arched in a flat scowl. It was as if they were looking at a stranger.

"You can't be serious," Mirabelle said.

"I am. We leave tonight."

"But why?" Quan asked. "We could still upload the footage and leave once the tournament is over! Worst case scenario, if I lose, we forget the Sojourner and go to the rendezvous point after we've fulfilled our promise to Dakari."

"That's not the worst-case scenario. You're missing the part where the Awakening discovers who you are at the same time Exodus does. You're missing the part where the arbitrators connect the dots and arrest you. What makes you think you'll have enough time to just fly away after you publicly confess that you're a psychic?"

"We'll move fast."

"No. This was a stupid plan to begin with."

"Then why'd you agree to be a part of it?"

"Because it was our only plan! And I want to leave!" Alexander looked at Mirabelle. "Tell him what you told me a few weeks ago."

Mirabelle crossed her arms.

"I don't know what you're talking about."

"Sure, you do. You said it right before I stopped you from leaving us."

"I wasn't really going to leave."

"No? You don't remember telling me how slim our chances were of winning the tournament? And how even if we did win, we'd have to outrun Exodus, the Awakening, and not to mention the arbitrators that will hunt Quan down the instant he confesses he's a psychic."

"The whole point was that Exodus might help."

"They won't," Alexander said. "They'll see Quan as nothing more than a tool."

"Then we'll cut the part of the speech where he confesses he's a psychic."

"Ok great. Then I'm sure the reporters won't have any follow-up questions after we reveal the Republic's biggest conspiracy of the century. I'm sure they'll thank us for the information and send us on our way."

"What is your point?!" Quan shouted.

"My point is that regardless of whether we win the tournament, we still lose!"

Another stumbling block, another seemingly insurmountable challenge. Quan felt the gravity of their situation more clearly as he stood in silence and thought of a way out of this. Then, like a lovely dream, he saw the answer before him, as bright as day.

"There still might be another way," Quan said.

"Do tell."

"Forget the Sojourner, forget the rendezvous point. Dakari said there's one way that psychics have been transported for years without anyone noticing: the underground railroad."

"But 50% go to Exodus, 50% go to the Awakening. How is that a good plan?!"

"Because Kairo Leonardo controls the railroad."

"Who's currently trapped in the detention center."

"But his father isn't," Mirabelle said.

Quan smiled.

"Exactly. I'm sure he's worried sick about his son. Dakari has earned Mr. Leonardo's trust. He can arrange a plan to rescue Kairo using one of the cargo ships."

"How does that help us?" Alexander asked.

"Because he won't just be rescuing Kairo. He'll be rescuing me too."

"What?!"

"Stick with me! I fight in the tournament tomorrow. Maybe I win, maybe I lose. Either way, you air the footage. Then, after the fight, Amelia can be the arbitrator to arrest me and take me back to the CDAD, where I'll soon be transported to the detention centers. Then, before an Awakening vessel can even think of shipping me to Telaris, Dakari and Mr. Leonardo use the underground tunnels to escort us to safety."

"Then why do you still have to fight in the tournament?"

"We need to honor Dakari's agreement and upload the footage."

"Why can't Dakari and Mr. Leonardo just rescue you from the stadium?"

"Because Mr. Leonardo isn't going to agree to help if there isn't anything in it for him. Plus, it's the least we could do for Kairo for buying us time."

That was it. The dead-end. Quan knew it. Alexander knew it. The backup plan, albeit riskier than any of them could have imagined, was formed. It was all in Alexander's hands now, who turned away and shook his head.

"You're a good guy, Quan. I commend you for that. But I can't agree to something like this, not when there's a free ride off New Earth waiting for us tonight. That's the only way."

"I just told you another way!"

"And I just said it won't work. Don't you see? Derek didn't leave to clear his head. He knows our odds so he's taking better chances. We should too."

"You're despicable," Mirabelle said.

"No. Just honest."

"Really?" Quan asked. "Like when you told Mirabelle about your dead sister?"

Mirabelle's eyes widened.

"What?"

"Go on," Quan said. "Tell her. Tell her it was all a lie."

Alexander looked into Mirabelle's eyes. He took several calculated steps and stopped inches before her. He paused, then slightly smiled. "It was all a lie. And you bought every word." Mirabelle's expression crumbled from confusion to disgust. Alexander walked towards Quan, who looked even more shocked too. "I've made up my mind. I gathered the evidence and can still send the footage to Dakari, but I'm not waiting here to die. I've fulfilled my end of the bargain." He poked Quan in the chest. "You fulfill yours."

Quan stood straight and tall.

"I have a better bargain to keep."

Alexander sighed. He couldn't understand. He did not see other people in the room. He saw only fools. There was no other "I" but himself. The others were only "its." He didn't see Quan and Mirabelle, he saw a black-haired, pale, annoying male standing next to an olive-skinned, dressed-up, stuck-up female. To Alexander, they were two-legged walking clumps of flesh driven by dead virtues. And because they no longer served his interest, they served no purpose to him.

"Then I guess we'll be going our separate ways." He grabbed the paper with the rendezvous point and walked towards the door. "I'm sorry things had to end this way."

Quan watched as his best friend gazed his way one last time.

"I wish you were telling the truth."

With that, Alexander closed the door, leaving Quan and Mirabelle alone. None of them could even move. They both just blankly stared at the floor, stunned by Alexander's horrible moment of betrayal. Every act of Alexander's previous kindness was now stained with his true intentions. He was revealed to be nothing but a selfish bastard.

"That's it I guess," Mirabelle said, collapsing on the couch. "It's over."

Quan looked down at his wristband again, the same one he shared with his brother, the same one that said: *Never. Give. Up.*

"If I win, I could still give the speech live. My testimony might be enough."

"You don't know that."

"I don't. But it's worth a shot."

"Assuming you get that far."

"You don't think I can win?"

Mirabelle paused, her gaze drifting away as if deciding whether she wanted to tell Quan what he wanted to hear or what she knew to be true.

"I mean. Do you?"

"I have to. If I don't then who will?"

Mirabelle typed into her datapad.

"I'll call Amelia."

"And I'll call Dakari," Quan said. "Let's hope he's still on good terms with Darius. There's still one more favor we need from the Leonardo family."

* * *

"What seems to be the problem, Corporal?"

The bald arbitrator stood on the other side of Kalak's desk, one hand on his head.

"I'm not sure. I'm just not feeling well."

"Some of the others said they caught you sleeping at your desk," Kalak said. "Is that true?"

"I can't really remember. It would explain the headache, perhaps."

Kalak stood up.

"It will not happen again. Understood?"

"Yes, sir."

"Good. Send in Lieutenant Banner on your way out."

"Of course, sir."

The bald man left the room as Banner entered and shut the door. Kalak sat back in his chair and buried his face in his palm. Banner stood in his grey buttoned-up coat, both hands by his side.

"That's the sixth man today," Kalak said. "Not to mention the dozens of others over the past few days." Kalak spun his chair towards the window and faced the other officers below, working in their cubicles. The scaffold stood in the center of the room.

"Perhaps you're working them too hard," Banner said.

"These are Central Dain arbitrators. They're not lazy."

"Men and women have their limits, sir."

Kalak slowly spun to face Banner, who quickly saw he was not amused. "Any news from Beretta?"

"None."

"And what about Kairo?"

"Nothing. He's been meditating in his cell for days. He won't talk."

Kalak stroked the black and gray hairs of his beard.

"Then it's a waiting game now. Check back with Beretta in the morning. If she doesn't answer..." Kalak stood up from his desk. "We'll find Derek ourselves."

* * *

In their living room at the Warrior's Hospice, Quan sat in the center of the couch in a white suit and tie. He straightened his coat. A faint orange hue from the dying fireplace reflected off his skin. A tiny curl of his black hair hung down his forehead. He sat still as Mirabelle set up the tripod and steadied the camera in his direction.

"What did Dakari say?" Quan asked.

Mirabelle adjusted the aperture, then slightly lowered the video recorder.

"It's not like he had much of a choice," she said.

"So, he agreed?"

"Of course, he agreed. But he does have his reservations."

"Such as?"

Mirabelle raised a brow.

"Do I really need to spell that out for you?"

"Yes."

Mirabelle sighed.

"It's been weeks since Dakari last spoke with Mr. Leonardo."

"So?"

"He's changed. Kairo had to erase some of his memories after their last meeting. That means he's not even sure if Darius will remember him. Tomorrow Dakari might be nothing more than a total stranger in his eyes." Mirabelle paused. "And this time, he'll be an enemy of the state."

"Then let's hope Kairo didn't erase too many memories."

Mirabelle nodded, then stepped back from the tripod.

"Ok, it's good to go." She looked at Quan. "I still don't see the point in doing this."

"It's a backup plan."

"But none of us know how to upload it."

"No, but Alexander does."

Mirabelle quelled her laughter.

"You have too much faith in him. He's not coming back."

"It's still worth a shot, isn't it? If I text him the recording of the video, he could attach it to the file he has and overlay that stream over the broadcast."

"That's assuming he comes back. You're basing this plan on a whole lot of what-ifs."

Quan's expression darkened.

"This whole plan is. But it's the best chance we got in case I lose." Quan rolled his white sleeves and hid the wristband on his arm. He sat up straight and closed his eyes. He took a deep breath, then stared directly into the lens of the camera. "I'm ready."

Mirabelle pressed the record button, then watched in silence as Quan gave his speech.

* * *

An hour later, Alexander received a text as he rode the midnight metro. He looked down at his datapad, then shut it off when he saw it was from the black-haired psychic boy. He was dead to Alexander, no matter how much his memories wanted to tell him otherwise. He gazed down at the rendezvous paper and smiled. He would be arriving at the location soon. That made him smile even more. With that thought, he rested his head against the back of his chair and closed his eyes. He was ready to leave.

* * *

Dakari stared at the ceiling, lying in bed, alone. The fan in the corner of the bedroom gently rotated 90 degrees, stopped, rotated 90 degrees, stopped, and continued in the mindless procession of machines. *A meeting with Darius?* He thought. *Marching into the CDAD? Into the heart of Kalak's lair?* It was a suicide mission. A sham. A white light from the projector in the old apartment blinked, then darkened, only to blink and darken again. Dakari rolled over in bed, the sound of shifting sheets strangely noisy to him. He sighed. He didn't want to make any sounds, but sometimes he had to move. He didn't want to move anymore. He wanted to sleep. And sometimes to sleep he had to move. But that made noise. And the gyre spun on. Hopelessly spinning. Derek was gone. Alexander was gone. A hopelessly spinning fan. Desta was gone. Zane was gone. They all passed in the shadow. And if Dakari stepped foot in the CDAD, he would be too.

Dakari rubbed his eyes and wiped his damp tears on the pillow. He sniffled, then rolled around again as the rotating fan blew a stream of recycled oxygen in his direction. The saltwater tears felt especially cold in the breeze, then warm and stale as the fan spun away. *They snuffed out Kairo,* he thought. Beretta was coming for Derek. And Mr. Leonardo would not remember him. Zane and Desta would get no justice. They would die and remain forgotten like all the other impurities. *And I will too.* He clenched the sheets, then weakened his grip. There was a pistol on the bedstand. He rested his hand on it as the breeze blew over his eyes. That felt good. He kept his hand there as the breeze blew away. He closed his eyes. He patted the pistol, then grabbed it, sat up from the bed, and pressed the end of the barrel into the center of his forehead. He took a deep breath and felt the circular barrel, cold and hollow, aimed at his gyre-spinning brain. It wouldn't shut off. It never shut off. He inched towards the trigger, then patted it with the tip of his index finger. Then he rested it there on the trigger. He exerted the slightest amount of force, feeling the springs ever so slightly recoil, not enough to fire, but enough to tempt him. He stopped, relinquished the force, then gently pressed down again. One more time. He stopped, breathed, then pressed down again as the nerves in his feet and legs tingled and felt like they were being pricked by a million tiny pine needles. He closed his eyes and tested the limits of the trigger's sensitivity one more time. He exerted a fraction more force than before. Then...he set the pistol back on the bedstand. He snuggled beneath the covers and closed his eyes as the fan blew again. He stopped moving. He looked at the ceiling no longer. Five long months of lonely nights and quiet tears and staring contests with blaster barrels in the dark hours of the morning had come to an end. He slept with the hopes that against all odds, justice would be served–one way or another.

Justice in Jeopardy

It was November 10th. The day of the Final Four. Dakari Minathi woke up and looked out the same window of his apartment with weary eyes. He took a quick shower and shaved for the first time in months. It was strange to see that man in the mirror again. Each clump of hair he removed from his scalp and face was another layer of madness he stripped away from himself. He saw himself as the proud Deputy he used to be. He gazed at his wife's wedding ring tied around his neck and his son's dog tags. The sight of them made him smile.

"Today the world will know your names."

Dakari stepped out of the bathroom and opened the closet. He stared at his old uniform inside. He hadn't worn it since the day he became a public enemy, but today, for some strange reason, he felt an urge to wear the navy blue CDAD coat proudly on his shoulders, to wear his badge with pride. He ceremoniously swung it over his back and fit his arms through the sleeves. Though he held his head high with the prospects of justice, his eyes were dark with knowing the task that lay ahead of them. With Derek missing and Alexander gone, their chances of winning the tournament, exposing the Awakening, and escaping with their lives were slim. But Dakari had never backed down in the face of insurmountable odds, and he certainly wouldn't start today. With that in mind, he left his apartment and walked to a taxi shuttle by the end of the curb. He sat in the backseat and shut the door.

"Where to, sir?"

He typed the private address of the Leonardo household into the console, then closed his eyes as the shuttle ascended into the skies.

* * *

Kalak sat in his office with both hands running through his gray head. He sprung up from his desk the second Banner entered the room.

"Any word?" Kalak asked.

Banner shut the door.

"Nothing," Banner said. "She's gone off the grid, sir."

"Then what are you doing here?! Get out there and find her yourself!"

"But where do I go?"

"Where do you think?" Kalak said. "The Warrior's Hospice."

* * *

Back at the hotel, Beretta Hunt lay tied down to a bed with a rag over her mouth. Each hour, Bruce and Donny crept inside the room to give her another dose of lizolai, sending her right back to a sleepy, drugged, and useless state.

"Don't give her more than 5mg an hour," Matthew said. "It could be fatal. We need her alive."

They did the same thing to Derek, although he was stored in one of the other rooms. Matthew stood in the living room of his suite at the Warrior's Hospice in his dress suit and watched as Bruce and Donny dragged his younger brother's half-conscious body into the living room. There were two massive, bloodstained bandages wrapped around his legs. His green eyes, normally bright with life, were hazy and half-closed.

"Set him down there."

They threw Derek on the couch. He coughed and struggled to keep his eyes open. Bruce and Donny straightened his back and extended his feet out on the coffee table. Matthew turned on the projector. A pregame interview took place with several commentators as they prepared the arena for the match. Derek's eyes widened.

"That's right," Matthew said, watching as Bruce and Donny tightened the cuffs behind his back. "Today's the day. I'm going to wipe that Pit Dog off the face of the map and turn him into the Awakening. Father will welcome me back with open arms, and you'll have the best seat in the house to witness it all." Matthew started to walk away. "Enjoy this time while you still can. I'm afraid you don't have much time left."

Bruce raised the needle of lizolai and injected it into Derek's neck. A cooling and numbing sensation washed over him as the world started to spin. He passed in and out of consciousness as the world carried on.

* * *

"And you're sure Amelia is going to be there?" Quan asked. He paced around the hotel lobby in his dress suit with blue and white stripes. Arbitrators, spectators, and other squad supports crowded around the room as different limousine escorts arrived to take the last four teams to Cypher Stadium.

"Yes," she said. "I double-checked this morning."

"And Dakari?"

"He's on his way to the Leonardo Estate as we speak."

Quan looked out the entrance of the hotel and saw the sprawling red carpet.

"What do you think happened to Derek?"

Mirabelle looked at the carpet too. Reporters waited with cameras as the first two competitors walked towards their limo. Lights flashed. Fans waved. It was starting.

"I'm not sure," she said.

"You think he ran away?" Quan asked.

"Derek's a lot of things. But he's no coward."

"Maybe you were wrong about him."

A gut-wrenching feeling churned in Mirabelle's stomach. Derek was the last person she wanted to think about. It was easier to flag him as a traitor and be done with it, but for some reason, Mirabelle didn't believe that. She also didn't believe that he ran away to save his own skin. She wished she could believe that. Part of her wished more than anything in the world that he would just be the scumbag he used to be so she could drive this gut-wrenching feeling away. But she couldn't. She remembered the look in Derek's eyes, his tears, his apology. It made her sick. Something had happened to him. Her gut never lied, and this time her instincts were screaming. *Something happened to him*, she thought. *And I refused to go looking.*

Another team stepped onto the red carpet. Then something distracted Mirabelle's gaze. An arbitrator patrol car parked outside the Warrior's Hospice. A stout man with faded blonde hair stepped through crowds of reporters and entered the lobby. He double-tapped his datapad and spoke angrily with someone else on a call. Mirabelle watched the Lieutenant come within several feet of her before walking towards Matthew. He gripped Matthew by the shoulder, yanked him away from the crowd, and started shouting at him mere minutes before he was supposed to walk out on the red carpet.

"Where is she?!" The arbitrator shouted. "Where's Beretta!?"

"I don't know!" Matthew shouted.

The rest of their conversation became inaudible, but Mirabelle couldn't look away. Eventually, Matthew ignored the Lieutenant and walked away, leaving the man furious.

"I will find her!" He shouted. "And then you're next!"

The Lieutenant stormed away, his shouts drowned in the commotion of the lobby. Then Matthew's eyes met Mirabelle's. That was the first time they had made eye contact in months. She felt terrified, then angry–angrier than she had ever been. They each held that stare for a moment across the room from one another. Matthew, who normally appeared stone-cold, ruthless, and fearless, almost seemed embarrassed. He quickly looked away from her, but it was too late. She knew what that look meant. And it haunted her to think that she might be wrong, that Derek's apology might have been genuine, and that he was paying for his betrayal in some hotel room. She looked at Quan, who double-checked his dress suit, oblivious to the implication of Matthew's gaze. If she said nothing, this would all blow over. But she had been down that road of silence before. It didn't lead anywhere–or at least, anywhere good.

"I think Matthew did something to Derek," Mirabelle said.

Quan froze.

"What?!"

"Think about it? Who else would've had a greater incentive to capture him?! Don't you see! He's trying to get you out of the fight!"

"You don't know that!"

"I saw his eyes!" Mirabelle said. "I know!"

"Team 3!" An arbitrator said, walking up to them. "Time to go!"

"Can you wait a few more minutes?" Quan said. "My partner is running late."

"Nope! If you're not on that carpet in 30 seconds, the limo's leaving without you."

The arbitrator clicked his datapad and started the timer.

"Then I guess it won't matter, will it?" Quan said. "It's too late for him to join."

"But not too late to save him."

Quan's blue eyes widened, he looked at the carpet, then back at her.

"If you don't come with me to the tournament, we'll have no way of getting you from the Warrior's Hospice. You'll have to get to the CDAD yourself."

"I know that."

"And what if you're wrong?! What if he's not here and you're throwing everything away because you have some hunch that Derek was captured!?"

Mirabelle's eyes narrowed.

"Don't play that game with me."

The arbitrator clicked his datapad.

"20 seconds!"

Mirabelle took a step closer to Quan.

"Derek gave everything he had to help us get this far." Mirabelle turned to the side, her hair hiding half her angry face. Then she looked back up at him. "If there's a chance of saving him I have to take it."

Quan took a deep breath and nodded in understanding. A strange mixture of conflicted feelings rose within him, feelings he could not explain.

"Then I guess this is goodbye," he said.

Their eyes were enveloped in each other's gaze.

"For now," she said. "But there will be another time."

"You should be happy. You were always trying to get rid of me."

"It's hard to hate you when you're not being an asshole."

"I'll try to take that as a compliment."

Mirabelle wrapped her arms around Quan, who wrapped his arms around her. They closed their eyes and held each other tight for what very well could have been the last time. They stayed there until the arbitrator buzzed his datapad.

"Time's up! It's showtime."

They pulled away from each other. Mirabelle backed away as Quan straightened his suit and looked at her. He saw something in her that the standards of the world could not account for–standards that could not see the beauty in the scar. He felt guilty for the way he had thought about her months ago. He felt foolish. *How could I have been so wrong about her?* He thought. She had made him better than he ever thought he could be. And he had not deserved any of it. He couldn't make sense of it, and the more he thought about it, the more he wanted to hold her and thank her. But he couldn't do those things. He had a match to finish.

"Very well," Quan said, then looked forward. "Send me out."

With a heavy heart, Quan stepped back across the red carpet with no one by his side. He heard gasps from the crowd and shouts from reporters as Derek was nowhere to be seen. Then he stepped inside the limousine and shut the door himself. And as Mirabelle watched from inside, she pinched herself to quell her tears. Something told her that she wouldn't be seeing him for a long, long time. She hoped she was wrong.

* * *

The shuttle flew over the Leonardo estate.

"Set us down there," Dakari said.

"But that's private property! I don't have authorization!"

Dakari clicked his blaster and aimed it at the driver's head.

"Land there or I'll do it myself."

The taxi driver activated the landing thrusters without another word. Dakari tossed the man a pouch of recs and left the shuttle, which immediately took off the second Dakari closed the door. He walked down the landing pad as several armed servants stormed out of the courtyard, aiming their blasters at Dakari.

"Mr. Leonardo was not expecting visitors! Identify yourself."

Dakari did, and almost in the same manner as his last visit, Dakari was removed of his weapons, escorted inside, and sitting at the dining table. Dakari sat there alone, tapping his hairy finger on the mahogany wood. He stared at the glimmering chandelier, then heard the crescendo of slow, descending footsteps down the stairs. He looked up and saw Darius Leonardo walking towards the table. Dakari's expression faltered. It was like he was looking at a different man.

Darius' white robes were ragged. There were purple bags under his eyes, stubble on his dark face, and remnants of tears in his bloodshot eyes. Dakari was familiar with that kind of countenance. It was the countenance of a man who missed his son. Their eyes never left each other as Darius took his seat, folded his hands together, and stared into the depths of Dakari's soul with an arching scowl.

"My men tell me we've met before," Darius said, looking him up and down. "I don't recognize you."

"I'll cut to the chase," Dakari said. "I know where your son is."

Darius' eyes widened. He looked happily surprised, filled with hope, precisely as Dakari had expected. But then his eyes narrowed. His hope turned to anger.

"Where?"

"He's being held hostage at the CDAD. He was brought in on accusations of psychic abilities."

Darius smiled, then started to laugh. A few of his servants exchanged a glance as Darius slammed his hand on the table and looked back at his servants for approval.

"My son! A psychic?!" He turned back to Dakari and frowned with a coiled fist. The laughter was gone. "You're out of your mind!"

"I speak the truth. And I'm only here because I need your help to save him."

"Save him? Why do you care about saving my son?"

"Why wouldn't I?"

"Like I said. I don't know you." Darius unveiled his datapad beneath his sleeve. "But my datapad does. And it tells me you're a wanted man." Darius smiled as horror dawned on Dakari's face. "A clever plan, I'll give you that. You kidnap the son of the richest man in the world, blame the CDAD, then hold him for ransom? You might've fooled any other man, but you won't fool me. You don't become the richest man in the world without being a tad bit clever too."

"Have I asked you for money?" Dakari asked.

"No, but you will ask for something." Mr. Leonardo paused. "Am I wrong?"

Dakari lowered his eyes.

"No. I need someone rescued from the detention center too."

"Then you have asked me for something."

"Please. Hear me out. Don't you remember me? We met half a year ago. You authorized the use of L-Transport cargo ships for an underground railroad, the same railroad we can use to rescue your son if we hurry."

Darius's expression was as immovable as stone.

"I'm not a fool. I would've remembered signing something like that."

Dakari leaned back in his seat. He didn't know whether to feel despondent or angry. He clenched his fist at the thought of Kairo. *Why?!* He thought. *Why did you erase so many of his memories?!* And then those feelings turned to despair. The only reason Darius had heard him out last time was because Darius knew who he was. But now he was sitting across the table as a stranger, and not only that, but a wanted stranger, whose head could be bought and traded for a hefty price.

"There's a bounty on your head worth 10 million recs. Give me one reason why I shouldn't turn you in?"

"You don't need the money."

"Money? No. But heroism? Public praise? No one gets tired of that."

Dakari felt some invisible force snatch his breath away. Each tick of the clock on the back of the Leonardo wall pushed him another inch to a place his mind did not want to go, and yet was forced to reconcile with, nonetheless. He saw the window of opportunity dimming, its drapes darkening his hopes on a safe return. Or any return at all.

"Mr. Leonardo, if there's *anything* I can do to earn your trust, please say the word. We're running out of time."

Darius stood up.

"Then you can stop wasting mine."

"How am I wasting your time! I just told you where your son is?! Don't you remember me?!" Their eyes met. Mr. Leonardo's dark brown eyes showed no hint of recollection. They only saw the traitor the media framed Dakari to be, not the man whom Darius had shared his home with many months ago.

"I don't extend hospitality to criminals," Darius said. "And I won't start today."

But you did, Dakari thought. *You did to me.* But Kairo had stripped this man's memories clean. Back then he had done it for extra precautions in case Mr. Leonardo gave Dakari's location away on accident, but now Dakari realized that Kairo had gone too far. And the price for it had yet to be paid.

"Then explain something to me," Dakari said. "Why would I, a wanted man, tell you to take me to the CDAD if my intentions weren't only to rescue your son and save my friend?!"

"Because you're using me to bail out your friend."

Dakari's anger erupted like a roaring volcano.

"DARIUS! For the love of Dain! Listen to me! I am on your side!"

Several servants entered the room. One was carrying handcuffs.

"Then prove it. I'll escort you to the CDAD. If my son is there, I will pay

374

for both your bonds myself."

"I'm an enemy of the state. They won't offer prison bonds for traitors."

"They will if I want them too." Darius grabbed the handcuffs from his servant and handed them to Dakari. "What do you choose?"

"If we use the underground railroad system, we can save your son and my friend without anyone knowing. If the Chief sees me, he will have me executed."

"Like I said, if you're telling the truth and I see my son, that won't happen."

"You may not have a say in it."

"I'm the wealthiest man in the Republic. I have a say in everything."

Dakari remembered using Mr. Leonardo as a body shield against his own son. *What did your wealth do for you then?* Dakari thought. Nothing. And it wouldn't do him any better against a department of psychics. But time was running out. The match would be starting soon. And if Dakari couldn't make it to the CDAD in time, he would be the one breaking promises, not Quan. With one last breath of freedom, Dakari clicked the handcuffs over his wrists. He looked up at Darius with a heavy gaze, who met his expression with a sly smile.

Happy Hunting

On billions of screens across the Republic, citizens tuned into the Final Four as Chuck Haven and Haider Anobai appeared beneath the red and blue infographic of R-Sports.

"Welcome back, folks," Chuck said. "For those just tuning in, there's been a bit of a strange occurrence today. The renowned dueler, Derek Hunt, has been disqualified from the Final Four after failing to show up to the escort on time."

They showed footage of reporters pestering Quan as he entered a tunnel into the stadium. He kept his gaze forward, ignoring all of them. Several arbitrators escorted him away.

"That's right, Chuck. No official statement from Quan either about the reason behind Derek's disappearance or where he might be. All we know is that he's still planning on fighting regardless. Though we can't help but imagine there might've been some altercation between them."

"No doubt. And while Derek's whereabouts are unknown, one thing's for sure: if you're planning on making some recs today, you might want to withdraw your bets on the Jerry boy. Some predictors have placed Quan's chances of winning as low as 2%."

"2%?"

"Stranger things have happened."

Chuck laughed.

"I guess you're right, but still. This will certainly be one for the history books. Reporting to you live, I'm Chuck Haven with R-Sports."

* * *

With Cypher Stadium packed with 250,000 people, the shouts of the crowd rumbled in the locker room. Echoes of pregame music rumbled the walls and reverberated in Quan's chest. He stood before the mirror in his silver exoskeleton suit. An arbitrator double-checked the pads around his joints and tested his energy shield. With that last checkup, the arbitrator gave a thumbs up.

"Looks good. Be on standby for the walkout in five minutes."

"Got it. Thanks."

Quan took a seat on one of the benches and held his hands over his head. *This is it,* he thought. *This is the day I have to be the best.* In many ways, it felt like only yesterday that Mirabelle had told him those words, but they didn't seem to bring him any comfort. Part of the pressure had previously been alleviated with Derek fighting by his side and then even more compounded when Mirabelle said they didn't even need to win. But now Derek was gone. And Alexander was too. That meant winning was a necessity. And even worse: he had to do it alone. As he sat with his hands clenching his curly black hair, he heard the careful footsteps of a familiar figure enter the room.

"Funny," Officer Mocroft said. "You were sitting the same way before your last match at Silverside."

Quan looked up and smiled. It was good to see a familiar face.

"You really go out of your way to make yourself relevant in my life, don't you?"

"I certainly try." He sat by Quan's side. They shared the silence for a few moments as the echoes of a roaring crowd raged outside. "Something on your mind?"

"Something? More like everything."

"You don't have to be vague around me. I know you better than most people."

Quan wished that were true. At that moment he wished Mocroft knew everything. He even thought about telling him. But he had come this far.

Mocroft was loyal, but even Quan wasn't sure what loyalty would mean to him if he learned that he was a psychic. But still. Quan would be lying if he said it wasn't good to talk with him.

"You ever had to fight a battle you were certain you were going to lose?"

Mocroft's eyes darkened, then pensively looked at the floor.

"Do you know about the Battle of Cypher Docks?"

"Yeah. What about it?"

"I fought in that battle."

Quan's jaw dropped.

"What?! But that was almost forty years ago."

"The AOL drug has a way of keeping us young," Mocroft said. "There are lots of moments we remember from the War for New Earth, like Colonel Winchester's raid on the Waion satellites, Ledarius Xing's assault of the city we now call Dain, and most notably, Carter Hunt's attack on the AA guns that secured our victory. These battles made our Republic look strong. Not many lives were lost. But Cypher was not one of those battles. We didn't take the port city until the war was won, and even then, the remaining Waions refused to submit to the yoke of slavery. They died among the thousands of other human bodies scattered on that shore. I was lucky to escape with my life."

"But you came out the other side. You won."

"It never seemed that way. You never really know what you signed up for until your boots touch the beach, until you hear the battle cry of a ten-foot Waion, until you see your comrades bite the blaster fire. Some men stood their ground. Some ran for the boats. Some died before they could even see their enemy. And the lucky ones, depending on how you look at it, we saw it all happen and lived another day. The scary thing is that I don't see any good reason why I lived. A Waion's rifle doesn't discriminate. It fires at anything that moves and anything it sees. I guess I moved at the right places at the right times."

"And then you decided to teach high school dueling?"

Mocroft smiled.

"Why not?"

"I don't know. It just seems elementary after fighting in a war."

"Civilian life often seems that way. But life goes on, does it not? And if there are no wars to fight, we must do our duty back home."

"But why high school? You could've gone straight to the Gerumandian Academy."

"I could have. But I didn't."

"Why?"

"Because people are not always what they seem." Mocroft stood up. "A word of advice: every battle is uncertain, the ones you think you'll lose, and the ones you think you've already won. But you might as well fight to win because your enemy is too. And often an overconfident enemy is forgetful of his faults and weaknesses."

A dark expression brought Quan's face low.

"Not Matthew."

"Perhaps. But then again, no one knows until the fight begins. If it means anything, I'll be rooting for you."

Quan's spirits rose. He stood up too.

"I thought you were Matthew's trainer?"

"And not yours too?"

"Not officially."

"Titles are silly things. It was official to me." Mocroft smiled. "Good luck."

They shook hands, then they walked their separate ways.

It was time.

* * *

"Ladies and Gentlemen, what a wild ride this had been! What started as a team of duos has now transformed into our second one-man squad of the tournament. From the Northwest tunnel, the only Pit Dog to ever advance to the Final Four, give it up for Quan Son Jerry!"

Waves of people cheered and shouted his name. Quan took that first step out of the tunnel alone. The lights darkened in the arena as music blared from the speakers. Quan saw himself walking alone on the jumbotron. Without Derek, he felt the eyes of the world turn on him. They welcomed him with thundering and overwhelming applause.

He strode around the walkway and stopped by the edge of the stadium. A massive sandstone platform hovered above the pit of water. He didn't look down. He already knew what awaited him if he failed. He closed his eyes and silenced the noise of the roaring crowd. His pulse pounded to the beat of the music. At that moment he felt in absolute control of every nerve in his body. He felt completely alive. The announcers brought out two more teams which left only one more. Every spotlight in the darkened stadium turned towards the southwest corner as the world awaited the man of the hour. With one step, Matthew Hunt stepped into the spotlight, the lights shining on his sandy blonde hair and his helmet in his hand. He walked to the sound of the most thunderous cheer of all. No one else walked with him because he didn't need anyone else. He had come here for the immaculate soldier. And he wasn't leaving without it.

* * *

"That should be you right now!? Right buddy?!"

Bruce and Donny sat on both sides of Derek on the couch. There were bruises all over Derek's body. He sat cuffed with both hands behind his back, his eyes bloodshot red from a night of no sleep. A half-empty needle of lizolai sat on the coffee table next to open pizza boxes and empty beer cans. They had been giving Derek an hourly douse of lizolai all night to keep him buzzed and half asleep. He could barely keep his eyes on the screen for more than two seconds. Matthew had given them strict orders to keep Derek's hourly dose low to keep him alive. That warning, however, was forgotten after they each finished their tenth beer. Donny hiccupped and rolled over onto Derek's lap.

"Matthew's gonna kill us if he finds out we were drinking."

Bruce laughed as he watched Matthew walk across the walkway on the projector.

"Then he won't find out!"

Bruce and Donny howled with laughter. They meant to elbow each other but ended up elbowing Derek instead, who fell in and out of consciousness. Then he saw Bruce lean towards the coffee table and grab the needle. Derek's eyes widened as the last active brain cells in his body screamed with alertness.

"Don't…" He muttered under his breath. He felt like he was seeing the world through a pinhole as everything started to spin. "Too much…"

"Uh oh! You know what time it is, Derek?"

"Time to take your medicine!" Donny shouted. "Doctor's orders!"

They stopped as a loud thud came from the door. Donny staggered up from the couch and fell on the floor. He pushed himself back up and leaned against the wall. "Maybe Matthew came back because he forgot something!" He opened the door. "Who are you?"

A stout, angry arbitrator gripped Donny by the collar.

"Who am I?!" He slapped the boy across the face. "Are you awake?"

Donny's eyes glazed over the arbitrator and then faded back to the ground.

"Yeah, man. I feel fine."

Bruce's eyes widened. He stood up as his senses alerted.

"I never sleep!"

"Thank you." The arbitrator let go of Donny. "My name is Lieutenant Banner. I've come for…" Banner paused, his eyes drawn to the sleepy figure on the couch. Too tired to move, but not too tired enough to recognize his old interrogator. Banner maniacally smiled and walked towards him. "Well, if it isn't the Republic's most honest man. Or I guess you're not really a man, are you? You're a boy. And certainly not an honest one."

Derek wheezed and shifted his posture. His bloodshot eyes met Banner's.

"I don't know what you're talking about."

Banner smiled the wildest smile the world had ever seen.

"Still trying to play that game, are you?" He waved towards the door. "The rest of you are dismissed."

Derek squirmed back into the couch as Banner approached. The footsteps of Donny and Bruce echoed until they fell silent with the closing door. Banner took a seat on the coffee table while the projector showed Matthew and Quan walking onto the platform to begin the tournament. *Just a little longer*, Derek thought. If he could keep Quan a secret until the match was over, they could air the footage. He had to stay silent for maybe ten minutes. He took a deep breath and readied himself, then flinched as he watched Banner pull a switchblade out from his utility belt.

"I've never been a fan of torture," Banner said, picking his nails with the tip of the blade. "I think it's rather disgusting." His eyes looked at Derek's. "But you know what I find even more repulsive?" Banner flipped the knife so that the soft end rested against Derek's bandaged knees. He felt a flash of hot pain as the handle of the blade pressed into his legs. "A two-faced, swindling, lying *bastard*!"

Banner punched the bloody leg. Derek's eyes widened, his back arched, and he screamed as every fiery nerve stung like tiny needles seeping into his skin. He closed his eyes and clenched his fist as Banner pounded his fist against Derek's leg and pressed it there.

"Ahh, you know, don't you? You know *exactly* who the psychic is and where he is. If you thought that hurt…" Banner let go and flicked the blade between his fingers. "Wait til I show you what this thing can do."

Derek's eyes welled with tears. He saw the countdown of the match on the screen. 90 seconds. And that was until the match started. And Banner was growing as impatient as ever.

"Nothing?" He asked. "No matter. We have time."

Banner wrapped his hairy fingers around Derek's bloody bandaged leg and squeezed. The world grew red as Derek howled and pleaded and cried and punched the side of the couch and gritted his teeth and prayed the pain would stop while Banner squeezed harder and harder until Derek thought his leg would pop and—

Someone barged through the door. Banner let go and stood up.

"I said no interruptions!"

He froze. There was a tazer aimed between his eyes. On the smart end of the weapon stood an auburn-haired girl with eyes that harbored anger.

A faded red scar ran across her face. Derek nearly cried at the sight of her. And before Banner had the chance to say a word, Mirabelle fired. Banner's body jolted as his hand limped for his blaster, then jittered out of control. He collapsed on the ground as the two probes caused bright purple orbs on Banner's forehead. He lay motionless on the ground, twitching in frantic fits. Mirabelle dropped the tazer and stole Banner's blaster and stun baton, then ran to Derek's side. She set the weapons on the couch and gasped when she saw his wounds.

"Your leg!" She knelt by his side. "What happened?"

"Beretta happened."

"Where is she now?"

A thud came from the bedroom door. Derek and Mirabelle paused.

"There," Derek said, turning pale. "It appears the lizolai has worn off."

The Final Four

Cypher Stadium swelled with the sound of cheers. The crowd became a toneless choir of rising excitement, growing louder and louder as the six competitors lined up evenly spaced across the hovering sandstone platform. Matthew stood on the opposite side of the giant slab with both hands by his side. Quan gripped the center of his spear, the leather of his gloves creaking with the squeeze of his fist. He eyed Matthew through the visor of his helmet. The silver scales of their exoskeleton suits glittered beneath the stadium lights.

60 seconds. Matthew heard nothing but silence. He eyed the VIP suite where his father was sitting, barely able to see his figure standing behind the glass. He couldn't see his face, but he figured it was that same perpetual scowl. It was never anything else. *It won't stay that way for long*, Matthew thought. *I will win the title and my father will welcome me with open arms.*

30 seconds. An adrenaline rush overwhelmed the stage 4 psychic. He saw waving banners, signs, and flags. The noise reached such a crescendo that he couldn't tell whether the sounds were the bass from the pregame speakers or the thundering beat of his fluttering heart. He thought about all the years that led to this moment, all the nights he spent dreaming of standing on this stage and how that dream had changed. Instead of joining with Jon, he had joined with Derek. Maybe now Derek was watching him. He stood alone but didn't feel alone. That made all the difference in the world. Enough to give him confidence that he could win. Now that Alexander was gone, he had to. *Alexander*, he thought. *I wonder. Where is that bastard?*

10 seconds. Quan gripped the handle of his blade as the Cobra Twins made their blades dance in their spinning hands. Alisha Armstrong and Maxwell Draymond shouted something inside their helmets. Matthew stood still and proud, his ebony katana outstretched away from his body. He didn't move. He waited.

A buzzer blared inside the stadium.

The match began, immediately separating into two separate fights. Three fighters encroached Matthew on the southern end of the sandstone slab while one of the Cobra Twins advanced towards Quan. A song of steel rose in the air from behind Quan's approaching combatant as Matthew switched into a defensive stance and parried the onslaught of swiping swords, repelling them back by twirling his sword like a helicopter blade. The rules of the game were simple: don't get knocked off the platform. Instead of being disabled, however, their shields retained kinetic energy with each hit, increasing the chances of causing a massive eruption from an attack and sending them flying off the edge.

Cobra swung at Quan with two battle axes in a single motion, to which Silverside's pride and glory recoiled back, and then lunged close with the shaft of his spear. The previously excited combatant backpedaled, deflecting Quan's thrusts with clangs of his battle axes batting away the poking spear. Cobra broke the pace of his deflections and jabbed fast and low, piercing Quan's left calf. The slight scrape sparked Quan's knee with a faint red glow, forcing him to change into a defensive stance. He swung again, but Quan quickly parried his attack and thrust the tip of the blade into Cobra's stomach, engendering a loud gasp from the crowd as it replayed on the jumbotron. That forced him to move back as Quan took the offensive. Cobra stepped to the left, bringing Quan's momentum to one area, then struck both axes on Quan's side with one sweeping powerful strike. Quan jolted from the shock and jumped back. Then a thought occurred to Quan.

If he couldn't beat him with strength, maybe he could win with balance.

Cobra lunged forward as Quan realized he was being pushed towards the edge. Matthew had already kicked Draymond off the edge but appeared to be taking numerous hits on the glowing spots of his armor. Quan continued to back away and deflect Cobra's attacks, ever mindful of the looming drop-off behind him. Then he dashed to the side and swiped at Cobra's knees with a quick lunge, changing positions and forcing Cobra towards the edge instead. However, before Quan could press him back any further, Cobra caught the end of Quan's blade in the hook of one of his battle axes and pinned it onto the floor.

Quan yanked his blade from the ground and swung at Cobra's helmet. He got a good hit on his visor, causing Cobra to stagger back, then lunge forward. Quan blocked his attack, then felt the other ax sweep him by his legs. He hit the ground with a thud, rolled over to dodge the next attack, then jumped back up on his feet. Their blades met again at a standstill. Quan gritted his teeth, then yelled and shoved Cobra back in a fit of anger. He side-stepped, using Cobra's forward momentum to grab him by the arm and spin him in the opposite direction. It worked. Cobra went rolling across the ground in Matthew's direction with only enough time to stand up and block Matthew's attack. Having finished off the other three combatants, Matthew kneed Cobra in the gut, then threw him towards the edge of the platform. Cobra skidded across the ground and reached for his e-blade, but it was too late. Matthew swung at Cobra's chest like a baseball bat, and since Quan had knocked his shields enough, an eruption burst between them and sent him flying off the edge.

Quan stopped when he realized that his fight with Cobra was over. Before he even had a chance to intervene, Matthew had eliminated him. That left just the two of them. Quan couldn't believe it. Matthew had finished four opponents. There were red glows all over his silver-scaled armor. Adrenaline coursed in Quan's veins as he stared at the menacing Hunt brother who awaited him. The crowd cheered as the last two fighters took offensive stances and readied their weapons.

"End of the road, pal," Matthew shouted. They faced each other as they walked in a circle, carefully studying each other's footwork, and preparing to strike.

"It's not over yet," Quan said. "And judging by your armor it looks like you've taken quite a few hits." Bright red pressure points scattered across Matthew's armor-like polka dots.

"I guess that's how you like to do things, isn't it? Let me do the hard work taking on five opponents to soak up the damage so you can make the last knockdown."

"All is fair in love and war."

Matthew paused. If he was smiling before, he wasn't smiling now.

"No, it's not. There's nothing fair about this world. You should know that."

"I do. We just differ in how we respond to that unfairness. You really think getting that title is gonna make your dad love you any more than he does now?!"

Matthew gripped his blade tighter as they continued their circle.

"Watch it, Quan. You're out of line."

"Because you know I'm right?"

"Because you're wasting time. I know about your speech. A shame you won't even get the chance to give it."

"Why don't you give it instead?" Quan asked.

"Me?" Matthew scoffed. "Go against my own people!"

"It wouldn't be the first time. Plus, you've kept me hidden for this long. Your brother switched sides. Why haven't you?"

Matthew's heart skipped a beat. He stood motionless as the crowd became more hostile and impatient. They stood there like statues for several moments. Matthew's eyes looked up to the VIP suite where his father stood behind the glass. He looked at Quan, then at his father, then at the e-blade in his hand. A singular chant from the crowd grew louder and louder. It started as a small echo, then became a thundering collective battle cry. It was the sound of his own name. It was music to his ears. Matthew gripped his e-blade as Quan stood back in a defensive stance.

"*Matthew Hunt! Matthew Hunt! Matthew Hunt!*"

He smiled.

"Sorry Quan. We're not exactly headed down the same road. Kind of funny how the last person I'll finish off is a Pit Dog!"

"Pit Dog? I'm Silverside's pride and glory, remember?" Quan smiled. "And you won't steal my thunder. Not today."

They charged. Their last battle was underway.

* * *

Beretta slammed against the bedroom door again, the hinges creaking and shaking with each thundering blow.

"You have to go," Derek said.

"I'm not leaving you," Mirabelle said.

"Beretta isn't like Matthew and me. She'll kill you."

"Not if I can help it."

"She's a psychic!"

"But she's weak."

"Beretta's never weak."

"You said it yourself. She's been hit with a stun rifle and nearly overdosed on lizolai." Mirabelle's auburn eyes darkened. "I've had Gerumandian training too. I can take her."

The bedroom door thudded. Its wooden edges creaked and clattered. It sounded like some terrible beast was pounding its body against it, waiting to burst through and kill anyone in its sight. Derek grabbed the blaster. Mirabelle grabbed the stun baton.

"I'm firing the first chance I get."

"And I'll finish her off if you miss."

Derek smiled.

"I don't miss."

The door banged again. Mirabelle clicked the baton.

"We'll find out."

With one thunderous gust of wind the door broke off the hinges and flew across the room. It shattered against the kitchen counter and splintered into dozens of wooden pieces. An angry, blonde, bandaged girl stepped out of the room with two tears in each hand. The sight of her stunned them both. Even in shambles, she resembled a fierce, stunning warrior who offended everyone with her beauty and cruelty. Her sky-blue eyes glowed as she smiled.

"So." Beretta flipped her hair to the side. "Who wants to die first?"

Derek fired. Beretta flowed the bright red blaster beam back in his direction, missing his head by an inch as he ducked on the floor. Mirabelle used this time to rush forward and smacked Beretta in the knee. She staggered back as the impurity swung again, but Carter's daughter blocked the attack with a katana she drew from a tear. Mirabelle pressed Beretta against the wall as their weapons remained fixed against each other, the lightning shocks from the arbitrator rod flickering against Beretta's black blade. They held that position as Beretta started to tilt the edge of her katana slowly towards Mirabelle's cheek. Beretta smiled as she realized she was winning, and Derek's expression faltered when he realized he couldn't fire at Beretta from his angle on the floor.

"Look at you!" Beretta said, her crystal smile widening with each inch the blade moved closer to Mirabelle. "Bet you wish you would've taken that drug!"

Mirabelle gripped the baton tighter and swung up, breaking the standstill in their fight. Derek fired, but Beretta absorbed the blast into a portal in one hand and deflected Mirabelle's swings with the other. Then Beretta punched Mirabelle in the gut and shoved her into the bedroom, out of Derek's firing range.

"No!" He shouted, firing at the wall.

Beretta dodged the blast by following Mirabelle inside. Beretta's eyes maniacally gazed into Mirabelle's soul. She swung her sword, missing Mirabelle in the chest and striking bedside pillows instead. Fluffs of cotton and feathers exploded in the air as Mirabelle parried Beretta's attacks with the stun baton. Then Mirabelle backed into the glass balcony door. Beretta swung. Mirabelle dodged. The glass shattered, the momentum of Beretta's force sending her staggering to the overlook. Mirabelle followed her as the wind rattled their auburn and blonde hair. Beretta rested one hand on the edge of the railing, then yelled and swung at Mirabelle. She deflected the blow, then fixed the baton against Beretta's blade as she backed her onto the edge of the balcony. There was a seven hundred-foot drop below them. As they eyed each other with their weapons once again fixed and inching back and forth towards their faces, the wind howled.

Beretta kicked Mirabelle in the shin. She staggered back and leaned away as Beretta swung, her blade slicing the side of Mirabelle's shoulder. Blood pooled where the blade pressed into her skin, causing Mirabelle to stagger back against the wall. With a quick motion, Beretta withdrew her blade and slashed down again, this time meeting the baton between their faces. Mirabelle kept the baton steady as a red pain seared in her shoulder, then used every ounce of strength to slam her bloody shoulder into Beretta's side while her body was overextended. Beretta fell back against the balcony railing, surprised Mirabelle had attempted a maneuver. She could see the weariness in her eyes, how she slouched her shoulders against the railing. *Just a little longer*, Mirabelle thought.

"That was close," Beretta said. "But not close enough."

Mirabelle staggered forward and swung, but Beretta blocked it. Their weapons pressed against each other once again. Mirabelle gritted her teeth and tried to push the blade to Beretta's shoulder, but she pushed back, inching the stun baton to her face.

"You think you can beat me!?" Beretta said, laughing as the wind ruffled her sun-kissed hair. With each word she spoke, Beretta pushed the electrifying stun baton towards Mirabelle's face by the force of her katana. "I'm a Hunt." An inch closer. "I don't lose." Another inch. Mirabelle could almost see the electric shocks stinging her pupils. "And I would certainly never lose to an ugly…" Another inch. "No good." Half an inch. "Impurity." The end of the baton zapped Mirabelle's shoulder. *"BITCH!"*

A red rage rose in Mirabelle. With one moment of insurmountable strength, she thrust Beretta's blade aside and whiplashed the baton across her face with a wide, vicious swing, slashing her across the nose. Something cracked as Beretta's body fell like a statue against the balcony, her body jittering in fits and shakes. Blood trickled from a gash across her face. Mirabelle stood over her with her wind fluttering and her shoulder bleeding, thinking that she very well could have killed Beretta with that swing. And she didn't care.

Footsteps echoed in the bedroom. She turned around and saw a blaster aimed between her eyes. It was Lieutenant Banner. "You want to live?" He clicked the blaster. "Drop the baton."

That was it. The guttural feeling had come full circle. With the release of her hand, the baton rattled on the ground, signaling her end. Her intuition about this mission had been correct. She had beat Beretta. But in the end, she had failed.

Ballad of the Brawlers

The bright beams of Cypher Stadium's spotlights cast long shadows of Quan and Matthew, who now advanced towards each other in their silver-scaled exoskeleton suits. Spectators stood in the receding rows of benches yelling and yammering with shouts and cheers. Carter's golden child held his black katana with an outstretched hand, then brought down his first downward swing, catching Quan's quick thrust as he parried the sword away, creating a safe distance between the two of them. Matthew's armor was spotted with so many dots that one well-placed hit might be enough to send him catapulting off the edge. Because of that, the highest ranking Academy student maintained a defensive stance as they circled each other in the center of the sandstone platform, eagerly awaiting each other's next move.

Quan jabbed with the smart end of his spear, but Matthew thrust it aside with a quick swing and lunged forward, to which the stage 4 psychic recoiled back and spun the other end of his spear up to smack the end of the incoming blade. Steel screeched against steel as they both pulled back again and resumed their attentive footsteps. With the cheers of the crowd swelling his heart with pride, the Jerry boy jabbed again. To his surprise, Matthew caught the spear with his free hand and hacked at Quan's head, to which he ducked and yanked the javelin out of the blonde-haired brute's grasp. They resumed their walk, noticing the reflection of each other in their black visors.

"Sometimes I wonder," Matthew said. "In a different life, you may have joined us."

The seasoned Gerumandian met the shaft of Quan's spear at the base of his swing, then clashed in three successive jabs from the left, right, and center.

"I'd never join you!" Quan shouted. He lowered his grip on the spear and swept at Matthew's leg in broad swings, forcing him to backpedal away. The end of the slashing spear scraped the sandstone platform like a weed whacker chopping the floor. The trick put Matthew on the defensive until he caught onto Quan's rhythm and parried the spear away with a swift swing. The stage 4 psychic clung tightly to the spear but spun in the momentum of the deflection, leaving his back exposed for just a moment. A blade scraped down the back of Quan's exoskeleton. A sharp sting flared up to the underdog's spine, causing him to face the blonde-haired brute and resume an offensive posture as he did his best to deflect a torrent of incoming slashes. Steel sang in the space between them, their blades sliding and clashing and clanging with perilous speed.

Cheers from wide-eyed spectators rose and fell with each blow, leaving both combatants puzzled as to who the mob wanted to win. The mysterious underdog? Or Carter's golden child? Their battle soon reached a period of stagnation, where Quan would jab, Matthew would deflect and strike, only to miss as the stage 4 psychic lunged back to make a swing of his own, only to meet the chrome black edge of Matthew's blade.

"What's the point in fighting for a losing cause!?" Matthew shouted, parrying Quan's blade.

"I already told you! I don't want anything to do with your gang!" Quan shouted, sending the spear at the blonde-haired brute's chest. "And definitely nothing to do with you!"

Matthew deflected the blow, backstepped, and smiled.

"Then why don't you do something about it?! Finish the job!"

The stage 4 psychic charged with every ounce of anger bursting from his soul. Their duel underwent a metamorphosis. Quan lunged from several angles, slashing his blade against Matthew's and rotating the edges of his weapon like helicopter blades, an old trick he used in duels that allowed both tips of the double-bladed sword to slash against Matthew from both sides. The seasoned Gerumandian parried these blocks, of course. He fought with every ounce of strength in his body, and as he did, Officer Mocroft watched from the sidelines with a smile. The crowd raised their voices in a cheer as Quan started to press Matthew towards the edge of the platform. Matthew staggered back and nearly lost his balance, giving Quan the chance for a killing stroke, which he then took advantage of and jabbed towards Matthew's chest. But he underestimated Matthew's balance and watched as he dodged his attack, pulling his momentum right. It was his first mistake in their entire duel.

And his last.

He knew it too as Matthew swung towards Quan's chest and smacked the edge of his blade across his armor, the boom erupting between them as the stage 4 psychic flew back in the air and lost his footing. His spear flew from his hand as he fell off the edge of the platform. He met Matthew's gaze as his body arched in the air and gravity brought him towards the pit of water below. Time slowed down. He saw the hands of thousands of fair-weathered fans cheer their champion on as Matthew stared him down from the top of the platform. Mocroft watched in shock. In that slow fall, Quan saw the overhead lights of the stadium brighten and block his vision of his own descent. A great weight clutched his chest–the weight of letting the people he loved down. And in that slow fall, the sound of the crowd drowned out the sound of his body plummeting beneath the water.

There was nothing but a splash.

He closed his eyes as the darkness of the water surrounded him.

He had lost.

* * *

Back in the Warrior's Hospice, Banner threw Mirabelle on the couch next to Derek. They laid there in silence, out of breath and out of wits as the final four came to an end on the projector. Banner cuffed them both and called in for backup. Every breath of Derek's grew shakier than the last. Mirabelle leaned into his chest, shutting her eyes to drive away tears as the announcers revealed the victor. She couldn't believe it. Matthew Hunt had won. It was too terrible to believe. Her heart shattered into a million pieces as she grew nauseous from the blood loss from her shoulder. She tried to unsee it, but their loss was as clear as day. On the screen, Matthew removed his helmet, raised his arms in the air, and smiled on the platform like all was right with the world again.

"We...we lost." Her lips quivered as she struggled to say the words, then looked into Derek's eyes. "And Alexander's gone."

Horror dawned in Derek's bloodshot eyes.

"What? I thought–"

"He left us. He took the other way out."

Derek let out a deep, shaky breath. The glow was fading in his eyes.

"Then this is how it ends, huh?"

Their eyes met. In the wake of their suffocating failure, they felt like they were the only two people in the world. None of them could bear to think of Dakari's reaction. A hot acidic feeling churned in Mirabelle's stomach. Desta would get no justice. Zane would get no justice. Like all the rest, they would become forgotten names–souvenirs of a better age. Mirabelle clenched Derek's coat and buried her face in his chest, failing to quell a river of tears. She closed her eyes and tried to pretend this world didn't exist.

"I was wrong about you," she said.

Derek's bloodshot eyes barely opened to see her face.

"So was I."

* * *

Alexander sat in the stands of Cypher Stadium-paralyzed with jealousy. Golden lights shined on Matthew as he basked in a rainfall of confetti and praise. Trainers and coaches rushed onto the bridges connecting to the sandstone platform and celebrated their newly crowned champion. L-Transport had denied Alexander's ticket to the rendezvous point. Without Quan, they told him, there was no point in flying. And so, Alexander went to the only place he figured he could go–back to Quan. Throughout their fight he had clung so desperately to the chance that his old friend might win that the reality of him losing was almost too much to bear. The cheers of spectators went silent in his ears as he fell back in his seat and lowered his head. He could still see the ripples in the water where Quan had submerged. Several arbitrators escorted him back to the sideline, where he sat hunched over, his face buried in his hands. Alexander looked to the jumbotron and saw Matthew smiling as the world shouted his name. Confetti continued to fall like glimmering snow. And fireworks erupted outside. He stood up and clenched the USB device in his hand with the footage.

"Fine. If we're going to hell. Then you're coming with us."

Alexander shoved his way through the crowd and eyed the broadcast booth high up in the stadium. He pulled back his sleeve and saw the grappling hook he had purchased months ago, the same one Quan had told him was a waste of a purchase. Maybe that was true back then. It certainly wasn't true now. He aimed his datapad at the top of the booth and fired.

In the broadcast room, the announcers discussed the victory.

"And that's it! Matthew Hunt has officially won the 32nd Republic Dueling Tournament! He's the first student to win the Final Four and receive the title of the immaculate soldier with a total of 31 knockdowns! History has been made!"

Several cameramen flinched as a grappling hook punctured the window. Seconds later, a kid in an oversize hoodie with teal hair came crashing through, breaking the glass as he rolled across the ground, then pulled a blaster from his hoodie.

"You leave! You live. You stay! You die."

No one protested. They ran–too preoccupied with their salaries to risk losing their lives. Alexander enjoyed watching them run like cowards. With the sounds of thunderous applause and bass booming music, Alexander ran to the control panel and yanked one of the USBs out of its port from the main panel, replacing it with his.

Alexander uploaded the file and shut off the music and the lights. A deafening silence took its place, which was then followed by an angry uproar. He heard the backup security guards racing up the steps as the video started to play on the jumbotron and across entertainment projectors worldwide. He dropped his blaster and put his hands in the air, waiting for the inevitable. A blonde-haired arbitrator entered the room with her blaster aimed at Alexander.

"Alexander?" She asked.

He froze with his hands up.

"Should I know you?"

She holstered her weapon.

"I'm Amelia Lancaster. I was told you left."

"I'm a man of many surprises."

Amelia smiled.

"Hardly a man. But if that's the broadcast, then we need to leave. I've already got Quan ready to go in an arbitrator car. If you stay here, they'll arrest you."

"Guess I'm getting arrested either way," Alexander said. "Where we going?"

"The CDAD."

Alexander looked out the booth as the footage began.

"Alright. Lead the way."

* * *

In the back of a high-speed ambulance, Beretta lay flat on a stretcher with several bandages wrapped around her nose. Mirabelle and Derek lay side by side with IV tubes in their arms, watching the broadcast on her datapad, barely conscious enough to see Quan sitting before the camera in a video he had recorded the night before. Several Awakening troops in black suits with A's on their chests sat against the wall. Each of them listened as Quan gave his speech to billions of people across the world.

"If you're hearing this message, it means I've lost the tournament, but my message would be the same if I won: I'm asking the world to wake up. A war is being fought beneath our eyes. We cannot see it. But it is there. Every day, psychics like myself, Matthew, and Derek, psychics that you welcomed and embraced with open arms, struggle to live in a world where we are treated as monsters when the world finds out who we really are. We hide our abilities to stay sane, but some have chosen to use these abilities for ill ends. An underground cult called the Awakening has been kidnapping psychics for years. Their choice is simple: conform to the Awakening code and live. Resist and spend eternity in a cell."

A photo montage of every missing student flashed on the screen.

"These students are some of the few that have been taken in recent years. You don't remember them because the Awakening has erased them from your memory with mind-snares. For some of you, this may have been the best friend you never knew existed, the son or daughter you forgot you had." A picture of Zane Minathi flashed on the screen. "Impurities who are resistant to mind-snares suffer far worse fates. If you recognize this kid from a few months ago, you are wrong about one thing: his death was not a suicide. It was a homicide." A picture of Matthew Hunt appeared on the screen. "And the man you crowned champion was his murderer."

Matthew Hunt stood on the platform surrounded by a silent crowd. He held the trophy with tears in his eyes as he watched his father's gaze drift from the jumbotron to his own son. With one long stare, Carter straightened his collar and walked away. Audio of Matthew's confession aired as they showed the face of Zane Minathi. Derek had bugged Zane and Mirabelle's rooms to spy on them, and in turn, had captured Matthew's allegiance to the Awakening. The evidence against him was damning.

Dakari's ears perked up in the back of the hovercraft as Mr. Leonardo flew them to the CDAD. He closed his eyes and smiled.

"We are not asking for retribution. We are asking for help. We want the Awakening to lay down their weapons and seek a new world with humans and psychics alike. If Exodus is out there, we need your help." The world watched as the last shot of footage cut to Quan. "I am the psychic you've been searching for." He looked up at the camera. "I am the cartographer. And I'm here to stay."

The broadcast ended and the lights in the stadium turned on.

In the back of Amelia's patrol car, Quan looked at Alexander.

"You came back."

Alexander's eyes darkened.

"I did."

"Why?"

The patrol car turned right and drove past the CDAD, their final destination.

"Because I couldn't let him win," Alexander said.

"We're not out of this yet." Amelia threw two hoodies in the back. "Put these on."

Alexander lifted his jacket.

"Don't you think this will look a little suspicious?"

"Suspicion I can live with. Suspicion buys us time." Amelia opened the door. "It's a long walk to the main elevator, but once you're down, Dakari should be there to pick you up. You ready?"

Quan and Alexander exchanged a glance.

"Yeah," Quan said. "Let's do this."

They stepped out of the patrol car and began the long walk up the stone steps of the CDAD.

* * *

In the main room of the CDAD, where the cubicles and scaffold could be seen from the upper glass walkways and briefing rooms, Darius Leonardo stood proud with Dakari Minathi in handcuffs. The old Deputy rarely made eye contact with his ex-officers. Some of them gazed at him with disgust. Others with questions in their eyes. And then there was Chief Kalak, who stood behind the silver scaffold with a handcuffed Kairo Leonardo. Kalak's eyes were bright with satisfaction, his smile—wide with relief.

"Mr. Leonardo, your son—as promised," Kalak said. "We believed we had evidence of his psychic abilities, but further scans proved otherwise. I am deeply sorry for the misunderstanding."

"Misunderstanding?!" Darius shouted. "He was locked in a cell! He was beaten!"

Kairo's face was full of bruises. Some healed. Some still ripe.

"Again, you'll have to forgive me, Mr. Leonardo. Kairo underwent the standard procedure for interrogating psychics. It was only after the interrogation that we realized we were wrong."

"And you call yourselves professionals! I could have you all fired for this!"

The Chief smiled in a way that disagreed.

"You may be a rich man, but even rich men are not above the law. You will hand over Mr. Minathi, and in exchange, we will give you the ten million rec reward as well as your son. That seems like a fair trade."

"It's no trade. Just the right thing to do."

Several armored arbitrators approached Dakari and grabbed him by the shoulders. They forced him up the steps of the steel scaffold, then returned by Kalak's side. Every arbitrator in the department could see him standing there, both hands cuffed in front of him, his eyes dark with anger, but not despair. He stood tall, his back straight, his shoulders hunched up. Dakari met Kalak's intimidating gaze with a harsh stare of his own. And beneath his boots, Dakari felt the cold metal of the electric scaffold. He had seen many psychics, traitors, and criminals electrocuted where he stood. And now he himself stood on death's doorstep.

"What about my son?" Mr. Leonardo asked.

A door opened. Amelia Lancaster walked down the main corridor with two hooded figures. They did not escape Kalak's gaze.

"Deputy Lancaster! You've arrived just in time to witness Dakari's execution!"

Amelia stopped, as did Quan and Alexander. They turned towards the center of the room, where a crowd of armored and unarmored arbitrators stood gazing at the long-lost traitor himself. And in looking, Quan and Alexander revealed their guilty faces before Chief Kalak as his eyes widened with even more glee. Quan's heart dropped the second he saw Dakari. His stomach churned with sickness. His brain flatlined with horror until only one thought remained. *Maybe Alexander was right*, he thought. *Maybe we were fools to think that this could've ended any differently.*

"What is this!?" Kalak shouted. "It's the *cartographer* himself! The renowned stage 4 psychic!" Kalak stepped towards him as several arbitrators followed him, then looked at Amelia. "You've done well, Amelia. We'll take him from here."

What do we do? Quan thought. A million thoughts raced in his mind as the white armored soldiers approached him. He didn't look at Amelia. If he did, it would blow her cover, and Kalak did not seem like a man who forgave traitors. Quan made eye contact with Dakari again, who stood on the scaffold looking at him. He nodded approvingly, to which Quan nodded back. He stayed silent. He let the arbitrators approach him. Amelia did too.

"I was just doing my duty, sir," Amelia said, swallowing a lump in her throat. "I was going to take them to the detention center."

"No need," Kalak said. "These men can take it from here. Besides…" Kalak looked back at Dakari. "If you left now, you'd miss the show."

The arbitrators grabbed Quan and Alexander by the shoulders and led them down the corridor. *No*, Quan thought. *There has to be another way! Something! Anything!* Nothing came to mind. The arbitrators led him down the white corridor at a fast pace. The steel doors of the main elevator grew larger with each step, then appeared like titans as the arbitrators slid their IDs and opened the doors. With a creak, they opened. Both arbitrators pushed them inside. Their metal footsteps echoed as the arbitrators joined them and pressed the buttons to go to the lower floors. Then the doors started to close, enough time not for parting words, but for one last glance.

Dakari Minathi, bald, clean shaven, and weary with unfulfilled justice, the man who had spared him from the detention centers, who had lost so much and yet had still found room in his heart for Quan, looked at him at that moment as if he was saying goodbye to his own son. His stoic expression was challenged by his tear-brimmed brown eyes, and then challenged even more with his subtle smile that seemed to say: "There was no other way." No. Not that. "We gave it our best." No. What else? And then Quan's heart rested as their eye contact broke with the closing doors. That last look said one thing: "We have played our part and we played it well. I wish you the best." The doors closed. The main engines of the elevator roared, and the lights dimmed. They made their descent into the belly of the CDAD where psychics went to die. Or disappear. *At this point*, Quan thought, *what difference does it make?*

* * *

Matthew Hunt, after storming through crowds of questioning reporters and fans, arrived at the VIP suite. They had asked him a million questions. Are the allegations true? Are you a psychic? Who is Zane Minathi? Did you kill him? How does it feel to earn the immaculate student? He did not give them a single answer. He was too occupied with seeing the man he had done this for, and with the hounds of reporters and even a few curious arbitrators at his heels, he escaped their presence and found himself standing outside the door of his father's VIP suite in a silent hallway, ready to face him with the golden trophy in his hand. He took a deep breath, closed his eyes, then opened the door.

"Father! I did it! I won!"

The door closed behind him.

There was no one there. Matthew gripped the trophy and saw a note on the desk. *A note? A note!* Matthew thought. *That's good enough! Of course! Father is a busy man! He wouldn't have time to meet with me in person but at least he gave me his words.* That was all Matthew ever wanted–until he started to read the words that Carter had left him. With the note in his hand and the trophy in the other, Matthew's eyes scanned the paper, then brimmed with tears. It said a simple, foreboding message:

"You should've turned Quan in the day you scanned him."

-The Boss

Matthew's eyes widened in a stupendous revelation. The note fell from his hand like a feather. *The Boss? Carter Hunt? Father!* A million memories overcame him as he shook his head and idly paced around the room. His heart rate increased. Sweat dripped from his brow. He started to mutter things under his breath as nausea overcame him. Then the anger came. He gripped the trophy and walked to the window. With seven heavy pounds he repeatedly smashed the trophy against the glass. A large crack splintered the window as the golden trophy fell with a thud on the ground. In the haze, Matthew stormed out of the VIP suite and dashed down a set of mostly vacant stairs. He left the stadium and stepped into the sunlight, fleeing from crowds of people and meandering into the busy parking lots. He waved his arms in the air like a madman as cars drove past him. Then one stopped. It was a taxi. He swung open the back door, sat inside, and slammed the door shut as the noise of the crowds faded to a dull silence.

"Where are we going today?" The driver asked.

Matthew, jittering and shaking, his blonde hair streaking down his face, clutched the back of the leather seat.

"Get me as far away from here as possible! NOW!"

The taxi driver floored the pedal and swerved down the main lanes outside Cypher Stadium. Matthew sunk into the back of the car and closed his eyes. He pretended that this was all a bad dream. He pretended that when he opened his eyes again, he would finally wake up. But he didn't. The taxi drove on. And his mind drove into madness with it. Back in the VIP suite, the note lay on the ground next to a cracked trophy by the window. It became nothing more than a souvenir of a sour dream, and a remnant of all that had gone wrong.

The Honest Pay the Hefty Price

On the main floor of the CDAD, Dakari Minathi stood on the scaffold. Kalak stood before him with Amelia Lancaster by his side. Every arbitrator had gathered in that room for Mr. Minathi's execution. They waited in a sobering silence as Mr. Leonardo berated Kalak for not giving him his son back, but Kalak did not even give Darius something as respectable as a glance. He just kept looking at Dakari, perfectly happy, perfectly at peace.

"I do not want him executed!" Darius shouted. "Understand!?"

"What you want does not matter," Kalak said. "The law does not discriminate with what you want. It only condemns what has been done. This is a guilty man."

Darius Leonardo paused. He looked at Dakari, then back at Kairo. Suddenly his promise to Mr. Minathi seemed so distant in the face of his son.

"Very well. Then at least give me back my son."

"In time, Mr. Leonardo. In time. But first, we have the main event."

"The main event!? I don't care about the main event! I want my–"

An arbitrator tazed Darius in the back, sending him convulsing on the ground in his white robes. Kalak smiled and nodded at the arbitrator who did the deed.

"I thought he'd never shut up."

Kairo's eyes widened in shock. Some of the arbitrators laughed. Others stood silent in confusion and murmured their concerns to their neighbors in whispers. The Chief grew less concerned by the minute. He knew they would all forget. *They always forget*, Kalak told himself. *It's too easy*. He was going to enjoy this moment. He had earned it. And now the moment had come. With the eyes of every arbitrator on Dakari, Kalak stepped beneath the scaffold and faced the man condemned to die.

"Dakari Minathi, by the law of the Republic and the creed of the Central Dain Arbitrator Department, you are hereby convicted of treason and sentenced to death."

Dakari returned Kalak's confident gaze with his own.

"Treason? A traitor?" Dakari asked. "Who have I betrayed?"

"You released a psychic against the will of the CDAD."

"Yes. I did." Dakari watched as the eyes of the arbitrators gazed with questions, the same ones that had plagued him when he was still employed under the banner and not condemned by it. They wanted answers. He would provide them. "But if that is a crime then you should be standing on the scaffold with me!"

Kalak tensed. He had not expected Dakari to die easily, but he had not expected this.

"Are you accusing me of your crimes?"

The spotlight in the entire department shifted on Dakari. Half the men and women who had served with him stood in sheer silence as their old comrade stood like a giant on the raised platform of cold steel. He looked fearless. He looked proud. He looked like the Dakari Minathi they knew and loved, not the traitor that Kalak framed him to be. Then there were the other half of the officers. They shared Kalak's spiteful gaze, relishing his position on the platform. They longed to see him die.

"No," Dakari said. "Accusing you of treason would not be fitting for a man who was never on our side!" There were several gasps among the crowd, and then roars of laughter. "You laugh at me? Why? Have I said something funny? Have I given you reason to laugh? Or do impurities always die under the laughter of a foolish crowd?" Dakari paused. There was nothing but silence. "Where's your laughter now? Are you afraid you might be wrong? That maybe there's a reason no one lets you into the detention centers? That I might know why you can't remember the name of every psychic you've ever caught?"

Dakari smiled.

"Yes. You have felt the friction. I know because I felt it too, but I peered behind the curtain and paid the price!" A pause. "Honest men always pay the hefty price. And yet, even if I showed you the truth what would change? You've seen it all before. Your memories lie in Kalak's hands!" Dakari looked at the Chief, whose smile was slowly waning by the minute. "And you. You're one of those cowards that believes the law is never broken if the crime is never seen." Dakari paused, his lips tightening with anger, then releasing the truth that he had harbored inside himself for what felt like decades. "But I saw the crime.

"They say an accidental explosion killed my wife. I saw the crime. They saw suicide for my son. I saw the crime. And every psychic taken below–they say they've disappeared. But I know what I've seen. If the law means anything to any of you–if your minds have forgotten but your hearts still remember the crimes Kalak has committed, then let the law do its work and bring this lying scoundrel to his knees! I have worn this badge with honor. I wore it for them. And this man has disgraced it like a groveling dog! He is no Chief! He is a coward! The only thing I'm guilty of is not killing this man while I still had the chance! Of that I confess! Of that I am guilty! Cut me down if you wish but remember this! Kalak may have erased your memories, but he can never erase your hearts!"

Some of the arbitrators' eyes swelled with emotion and pride. They stiffened and stood straight. Others scowled at him. Others were silent and looked away. And Kalak stood with that same terrible smile. He was the sole man in that room who gave him a slow, crescendo of solitary applause, then stopped.

"A wonderful speech," Kalak said, then looked at the other arbitrators. "And a true one too. Dakari speaks no lies. The Awakening has overtaken this department right under your noses. You have all become puppets in a grand play, to which I have heartily enjoyed tugging at your strings." They were too stunned to respond. "Like I said. A wonderful speech." Kalak raised his fingers, then made eye contact with Dakari. "And yet–a shame that no one will remember it."

Dakari's eyes widened. As did Amelia's.

Kalak snapped his fingers.

One by one, several arbitrators started falling to their knees, going limp by their sides. They fell to the ground with a lifeless thud as others watched in horror. Dakari's moment of triumph and truth turned out to be nothing more than a forgotten sham. An indescribable wave of despair washed over him as he saw men and women he knew close their eyes with the impending doom of the mind snare.

And yet, after about four arbitrators fell, the falling stopped. The majority of them stood up unscathed, unforgotten. They looked at each other as the Chief snapped his fingers again. Nothing. A gradual horror dawned upon Kalak's face as Kairo's smile widened. The Chief's heart dropped as he gripped Mr. Leonardo's son by both shoulders.

"What on New Earth have you done?!"

But before Kairo could even respond, Kalak's eyes darkened with understanding. There was no need to tell him. Kalak remembered everything: the tired arbitrators, the men and women falling asleep at their desks, and the strange headaches. Kairo smiled.

"You don't need to leave your cell to give mirages to the people upstairs."

Dakari's hope returned as Kalak's eyes met his.

Kairo had gotten the message.

And yet the Chief's anger festered.

"Fine. You want to take my allies?" Kalak aimed his blaster at Dakari. "I'll take yours."

"NO!" Amelia shouted, shoving Kalak's arm away.

Kalak fired and hit a cubicle, causing several arbitrators to draw their rifles, half of them unsure who they were even fighting for. Amelia drew her baton and whacked Kairo's handcuffs down the center to set him free. Then with her other arm, Amelia drew her blaster. Dakari raised his cuffs before his chest. She fired, causing them to break and fall down at Dakari's shoes, setting him free. Kalak backhanded Amelia across the face.

"Traitor!"

He fired. Blood burst out the back of Amelia's skull as her body fell

407

lifeless onto the ground. Dakari's legs started to shake.

"NO!" Dakari yelled. The Chief aimed the blaster at him next, but before he could fire, a gust of wind shot out from a portal in Kairo's hand, sending Dakari rolling over the ground and out of Kalak's range of fire. A bloodbath ensued in the main room as arbitrators instinctively took sides and began to retreat around cubicles for cover. Some came to Dakari's rescue and shielded him behind a set of desks as others aimed for his head. There were shouts and screams and cries as red laser blasts flew over office spaces, destroying computers, sending volleys of paper into the air, and splatters of blood on the floor.

Dakari grabbed a blaster from the floor and leaned behind a desk. He sat next to an arbitrator who had taken his side. They both raised their heads behind cover and analyzed the scene. The main offices turned into a shootout between those who had taken Dakari's side and those who had taken Kalak's. Dozens of dead bodies sprawled across the ground. Kalak's eyes glowed red as he shot a volley of flames out of two tears in his hands. Kairo used a tear to shoot the flames back, but Kalak drew a blade in one hand and slashed at the young Leonardo's knees. He screamed and fell to the ground as blood shot out his legs. Then Kalak twirled a pistol out from his fingers and shot another arbitrator in the head who was aiming in his direction. Dakari fired and hit Kalak in the shoulder. The Chief staggered back in shock as Dakari fired again, but this time, Kalak reversed the blast in his direction with a portal in his hand. Dakari ducked as Kalak held his shoulder and fled towards the stairs.

"Corporal!" Dakari shouted. "Hold the line! I'm going after Kalak!"

"Understood, sir! Good luck!"

Dakari sprinted around the cubicles as blasters fired in his direction, missing him by inches. He suppressively fired in their direction and then ran past Amelia and Kairo's bodies. Then a hot beam punctured his side. He winced in pain and hobbled to the stairway before another blast could hit him, then paused once he was behind cover. He leaned against the wall and pressed his hand against his side. Blood stained his fingers. His hip was scorched flesh with char and blood. Dakari gritted his teeth in pain, then saw blood on the stairs. A newfound confidence gave him the strength to make the climb. Kalak had lingered long enough. It was time for him to die.

* * *

Kalak scrambled into his office and locked the door. He limped to his desk with his hand pressed against his bloody breast. His hands shook as the world started to go blurry. He crouched behind his desk and aimed his gun at the door. Then he made a call on his datapad, his bloody fingers staining the screen.

"Are you awake?" Banner asked.

"I never sleep!" Kalak shouted. "Where are you!?"

"About a block away. What's up?"

"I need backup! It's a bloody mess in here!"

"I was told I'm needed down below instead."

"What?!"

"The cartographic psychic is of top priority. Losing you isn't."

Kalak's eyes widened with fear. His heart rate increased as he heard screams outside his office, then the silence of Banner hanging up on him. He froze, unable to hold his pistol with two hands. He looked at the door, then flinched as several red beams burst through the wooden door. The Chief closed his eyes and fired back but never got off anything more than a shot. A beam knocked his blaster out of his burnt stump of a hand. He screamed as the Deputy that had been sentenced to die kicked down the door. Dakari wheezed, his side a red mess, then clicked the blaster and aimed it at Kalak, who gazed into the spiraling black barrel like a cowering child.

"How does it feel to stare death in the eye?" Dakari asked. Kalak backed up against the glass window, too weak to move. "How do you think it felt for Desta? Or Zane?" Dakari stepped closer.

"You seem to have forgotten," Kalak said, smiling. "I'm an immortal man."

"You don't look immortal."

409

"Neither do you."

"I'm a man, same as you," Dakari said.

Kalak looked at the portrait of themselves from the Gerumandian Academy on the wall, then back at Dakari. His eyes darkened.

"No," the Chief said. "That's where you're wrong. I AM NO MAN!"

"No man can cheat death!"

"I AM NO MAN!"

Dakari smiled.

"You are today."

Bang.

A beautiful red beam tore a hole through Kalak's forehead and shattered the glass behind him. The force of the blast blew his body out the window and into the main room of the CDAD, where dozens of other dead arbitrators lay scattered around the room. Shards of glass fell with him, his head arched back, his eyes up towards the ceiling. Dakari stood tall in the office watching the Chief fall until he splattered on the marble floor with a dull splash. The immortal man was no more. The deed was done. Justice reigned. Then Dakari felt the pain in his hip return. He staggered back to the desk and fell to the ground.

* * *

In a dark tunnel, half a mile beneath the ensuing bloodbath, Quan and Alexander waited in silence with two arbitrators towering over them. None of them had said a word since they were down here. After leaving the hallway they had traveled through several narrow white passageways and then through a secret wall entrance leading to the infamous underground railroad. It was completely black. And quiet. They waited for what seemed like hours until they heard the distant echo of a shuttle engine and saw its faint light rounding the curve of the tunnel.

"That's your ride," the arbitrator said. "The Awakening escort has arrived."

Quan swallowed a lump in his throat as the shuttle emerged into view. Its

410

bright lights blinded his sight, blocking the figures inside the cockpit as it came to a stop several yards in front of them. One arbitrator left Quan and Alexander and stepped onto the platform. The doors opened, then a blaster fired. The arbitrator dropped to the ground, dead. Quan and Alexander's jaws dropped in shock as the last arbitrator left their side, raised his rifle, then stepped forward.

"What's the meaning of this!?" He asked. "Are you awake?!"

The last arbitrator crept forward with his rifle aimed at the shuttle. Then a bright blue beam flew through his head, sending him staggering to the ground. Quan and Alexander waited with bated breath as a tall figure emerged from the tunnel, too far in the shadows to be seen clearly. Then he walked towards them. Alexander and Quan couldn't believe their eyes.

"You called to Exodus for aid," Officer Mocroft said. "And Exodus answers."

Without a word, at merely the relief of seeing a familiar, friendly face, Quan and Alexander followed Mocroft inside the shuttle and retreated inside its welcoming doors.

✳ ✳ ✳

Almost no one survived the bloodbath in the CDAD. With no real way to distinguish friend from foe, arbitrators killed each other without hesitation. And now their bodies were scattered across the main floor, with seemingly only the scaffold remaining unstained with blood. Lieutenant Banner stepped over the bodies. He stopped when he heard the sound of shaky breathing. It was Kairo Leonardo, lying next to the recently deceased Amelia Lancaster. Banner gripped Kairo by the collar.

"What. Happened?!"

Kairo's eyelids flickered, barely able to open. He held his bleeding leg.

"They all turned on each other. It all happened so fast."

"I'm not talking about up here." Banner's grip tightened. "We've lost contact with our men in the underground railroad."

"I don't see how that's my problem."

"Our troops were sent there to recover Quan! What happened!?"

Kairo smiled.

"I guess Exodus beat you there first." Banner threw Kairo on the ground, causing him to cough and rollover on the ground. Banner drew his blaster. "Wait!"

"Why should I wait? You're running out of time—and usefulness."

"I can get you the other one."

"Octavian won't help us."

"Not him," Kairo said. "His son."

"Quan is Octavian's son."

"His *other* son...Jon."

Banner lowered the blaster, his mind racing with decisions. After a brief moment of thought, the Lieutenant knelt beside Kairo and tapped his datapad. "Alright then. Where is he?"

* * *

In the cockpit of the underground shuttle, Mocroft stood behind the pilot with his hands folded behind his back. Several men in dark blue armored suits stood inside the cabin with a silver letter *E* stitched to their chests. Quan and Alexander stood by his side, hammering him with questions.

"Not now," Mocroft said. "We have more important matters to attend to first. Like getting you to safety."

"I understand," Quan said. "But I have to know."

"Know what?"

"Why didn't you save me earlier? If you knew."

"What makes you think I knew before today?"

"You've been keeping a close eye on me ever since middle school. There's no way you could tell me with a straight face that this was all a coincidence."

The officer's expression darkened.

"Your mother forbid you from getting involved unless it was by your own volition."

Quan's heart rose.

"You mean–"

"Yes. Not your adopted mother. Your birth Mom."

"Where is she now?"

A silence swept over the shuttle again.

"It's best we don't talk specifics now. There's a lot we need to catch you up on. We were one psychic in debt to the Awakening. By capturing you that makes two. They're not going to be happy about this, especially now that we have you."

"What are you saying?" Quan asked.

Mocroft took a deep breath, then let out a long-awaited sigh.

"Whether we like it or not, today the war begins."

* * *

Halfway through Banner and Kairo's conversation, Dakari Minathi fell down the stairs and onto the main floor. Banner stood up, then relaxed when he saw the dying arbitrator struggle to get up on his feet. A dark red gash stained the side of Dakari's coat. He couldn't even hold onto his blaster anymore. And then when he saw Amelia's dead body, a flood of tears came to his eyes. It was an unceremonious end to one of the most honorable arbitrators he ever knew. He lay there as Banner slowly walked over to him, then stopped.

"Well, well...if it isn't Mr. Minathi himself," Banner said. "You don't die, do you?" Dakari couldn't answer. He just laid there. "Nothing? Very well then. You'll die in silence."

"There will be no such thing."

A towering man emerged from the front of the CDAD in his Brigadier General coat. Banner immediately stood up straight as Carter Hunt and a golden-armored soldier approached him.

"But sir!" Banner shouted. "This man is our enemy!"

"He's also dying," Carter said.

They looked down at him. Dakari laid on the floor of the CDAD with his hand pressed against his side. He leaned against the foot of the stairwell as his breaths became faint and indistinct. It was strange to come face to face with the father of the man who killed his son. Each medal on Carter's coat was worth millions of recs. He gazed at Dakari with a furrowing scowl, his sharp jaw tensed, his blonde hair slicked back. And his eyes were green. But the most noticeable thing about him was the Hunt family crest on his breast. An Ouroboros. A snake with its own tail caught in its mouth. That same symbol was engraved in the center of the golden arbitrator's armor. *A Hunt mercenary*, Dakari thought. The golden-green hues were almost hypnotizing. Carter looked at Banner.

"I was told that Quan got away," Carter said. "Why weren't you there?"

"We learned that Kairo wasn't a stage 4 psychic."

"So you went to the Warrior's Hospice?"

"We knew Derek was there. He knew who the psychic was."

"And if he lied to you not once, but twice, what makes you think he'd tell you the truth the third time? We needed you underground."

"There is some good news though."

"Oh? You got Quan back?"

"Uh...no. But we know where his brother is."

"Do you have the location?"

"Yes."

"Send it to me."

Banner typed the location into his datapad. Carter's datapad buzzed.

"You've done well, Banner." Carter pulled a blaster. "Send Kalak my regards."

Bang. Banner's body fell to the ground with a thud. Carter strolled towards Dakari and wiped the end of the barrel.

"You going to kill me too?" Dakari asked.

Carter threw the rag aside and then slipped the pistol back into his holster.

"Lars? Get this man to his feet. Be gentle."

Dakari's eyes widened. Lars, the golden armored arbitrator, paused, then stepped over the bodies and gently gripped Dakari by the shoulders. He helped him back on his two feet and slung his arm around his shoulder to keep him steady. Dakari kept waiting to feel a switchblade ram him in the gut or a blaster beam pulverize his head. But nothing happened.

"I...I don't understand."

"We may be enemies, but I'm no barbarian. You can't do anything to hurt us any longer and we have everything we need. It's certainly too late to take you to a hospital, but I will give you the luxury of choosing where you wish to die."

"Wouldn't it be easier to just finish me off here?"

"Is that what you want?"

Dakari paused, gazing at the mess of bodies around him.

"No. But I don't believe you'd give me that."

"It depends on what you want." Carter stepped closer. Their eyes met on the same level now. "Don't look so surprised. Fate has pitted us against each other, but death brings us together. It's only fitting that we show a bit of the civilization we promise each other in times of peace." Carter paused. "Even knights used to sheath their swords on Sundays."

Dakari's expression darkened. A strange, amorphous, hollow feeling strangled him. He started to feel more like a fading spirit and less like a man of flesh and blood.

"Do you have a car?" He asked.

"I do."

"Then I know where I want to go."

* * *

A man in a gray suit drove Mr. Leonardo and his son home. Kairo sat in the back seat with bandages around his legs. He looked out the window and watched the city. Several arbitrator hovercrafts raced towards the scene at the CDAD. *There will be hell to pay*, Kairo thought. *The world will never be the same.*

Darius opened his eyes. He felt the bandage on his forehead.

"What happened?"

Kairo kept looking out the window.

415

"You wouldn't believe me if I told you."

They drove on through the city, away from the madness.

* * *

Carter rested his hand on the steering wheel as the black sports car rounded the hill of the outer city cemetery. It was a warm, orange afternoon. A few clouds caressed the sun as its beams shined on the hillsides where the wind blew the grass and the city of Dain and all its problems stood so far out in the distance. Dakari sat in the back, looking out the window with a smile as the car came to a stop.

"Do you need help getting out?"

"No. This is fine." Dakari let out a sigh and closed his eyes. It was time. He felt a strange sort of lightness as the pain subsided. He was getting close now. "Can I ask you something?" Silence. "About Derek and Mirabelle. What will happen to them?"

"They're on their way to Telaris as we speak."

Dakari looked out at the sky, at the thousands of blinking starships soaring in the stratosphere. He liked to think that he was seeing the starship they were sitting in. That because death was stripping him of formal goodbyes, his long-missed gaze was enough.

"What will happen to them?"

"Whatever needs to happen to them to serve our cause."

"And what cause is that?"

Carter paused.

"A new Republic. A new age. A day where psychics reign not in the shadows but in the sunlight. And then, when the world reveals how indebted they are to us, they will fall down on their knees and worship us for the gods we really are."

Dakari looked at Carter.

"With all due respect, sir. I hope you lose."

Carter smiled.

"Farewell, Mr. Minathi."

416

With that last word, Dakari opened the door, stepped onto the sidewalk, and shut the door behind him. He smelled the sweet autumn breeze of the countryside and watched the changing leaves blow in the wind. He forgot the pain in his side as he stepped across the grass towards the two headstones. He had bid farewell to them months ago. Now he approached them again. But this meeting held no sadness. And it was no farewell. It was like the homecoming he never had. He limped all the way to the two Minathi headstones and got down on his knees. He gazed upon the stones of "Zane and Desta" Minathi with tears in his eyes and a smile on his face. Desta. Zane. The power of their names alone brought warmth to his fluttering heart. To think that he had spoken those names not to stones but to people months ago. To smiling faces. To a woman he used to dance with. To a son he used to look proudly upon with a smile. He pressed one hand above the grass Desta was buried in and another on the grass that Zane lay in. He closed his eyes. He could almost hear them whispering to him to be done with it, to join them in the Heavens. God seemed to be waiting for him in the grave.

Dakari crawled forward, then lay down directly between their headstones. He faced the diamond blue and reddening sky. A few leaves flew over his head as he imagined sitting next to his family. And then he didn't have to imagine. He could hear them again. *Their voices! Their sweet voices*, he thought. With their presence close to him, Dakari felt part of his spirit and soul leave him. His eyelids started to close, darkening the sky. And then they grew heavier as if he was lying down for one last sleep, but one with no nightmares. He closed his eyes at last. But there was no darkness. There was something else. Something better. In his last thoughts with closed eyes, he smiled. *I am coming home. I am coming home. Today is over. But tomorrow will last forever. I am coming home.*

Epilogue

Carter Hunt rode the elevator below the CDAD, but he did not stop at the detention center. There was a deeper abyss, a deeper prison that no one else knew of but himself. It was not half a mile, but a mile underground. And instead of containing a labyrinth of corridors and prisons, it had one hallway. And one cell. When the doors opened Carter Hunt straightened his collar and took the first step down the long white hallway. At the end of it was the infamous door he had walked to only once before. But desperate times called for desperate measures, bringing him to the door once again.

Carter pressed his palm against the scanner outside the cell. His heart raced and then his eyes glowed. A cell that could only be opened by psychics. Then the three green lights raced along the sides of the door. It was opened with white steam hissing beneath Carter's boots as he saw a sitting figure behind the mist. The man who sat on the stone was not a man to be reckoned with. In that chamber Carter bowed before the great evil he had awakened. He knelt with his head held low, preparing himself to tell the truth.

"Forgive me for awakening your slumber," Carter said. "But there was no other way." Vrin sat still, shrouded in the mist. "The world has woken up. We have found the cartographer."

Vrin's yellow eyes shined through the mist.

He woke up too.

About the Author

Joshua Kapusinski grew up in San Diego, California, where he developed an interest in science fiction stories from a very early age. He wrote comic books for his friends in elementary school and started his first novel, *The Awakening*, in 8th grade. He graduated from the Cambridge School in 2019 and is currently studying English at Grove City College.

You can connect with me on:
- https://www.joshuakapusinski.com
- https://www.instagram.com/joshuakapusinski

Made in the USA
Las Vegas, NV
06 July 2022

51160048R00246